Equipped to Go
to an Unreached People

A Cross-Cultural Manual for Prospective Missionaries

I0561575

Vision: What the Bible says about the unreached peoples.
Organizational techniques: useful to the missionary as administrator.
Cultural orientation: forming missionary attitudes.
Mission strategy: for planting strong churches that will multiply within an unreached people group.

by Don Marchant, M.A.

© 2004   Don Marchant / "Equipped to Go" Ministries / Box 877 / Lake Forest, CA 92609 / USA
Phone or fax: 949-457-1024
etgmins@cs.com

Dedication

This manual is dedicated to Jesus, who has given us so much, so freely, we can only join him in this wondrous venture to tell the world.

Secondly, this manual is dedicated to my lovely wife, Noreen. Her gentleness and wonderful support have been so essential. Her meaningful additions have always been incorporated into the text. They have benefited me personally, and will help future readers.

Noreen has taught these principles with me, to students in Africa, Asia, Latin America, and the USA. Her partnership in this has been a cause of glory to the Lord, and of immeasurable satisfaction and comfort to me.

Equipped to Go
to an Unreached People Group

Contents

Before we get started...

This book is based on this premise: *You can plant strong churches that will multiply among an unreached people.*

How do we know this premise is true in your case? First, we presume you know the Bible and are of average abilities. Second, the strategy we present is not impossible or overly complicated. It is based on Bible principles and is logical. Its components have been used successfully.

We believe we have given you a sound strategy that is workable. Some of these basic principles will serve you well in any mission circumstance.

We assume, in this book, you are going to an unreached people group to evangelize, and that you will make your own decisions regarding how you will minister. If, however, your mission is not as described, and/or if your supervisors will decide how you will work, you will nevertheless benefit by knowing the principles involved in mission. These are best studied as parts of a viable strategy for planting churches, a whole scenario, detailed as much as seems necessary, so you can understand the reason for each component. We believe we have given you such a strategy.

Keep in mind, we aim here to prepare you to *plant strong churches that will multiply among an unreached people.* If you master the concepts presented in this book you will have more mission preparation than many successful missionaries who went to the field before you.

We do not imply this book is all the preparation you will need.

We have prayed for your perseverance and your success, for God's glory, for his kingdom, and for your own personal satisfaction and joy. Pray much yourself. The more you read here, the more you will understand why.

We have used the term "unreached" in our title. The "unreached" people groups have yet to hear the gospel. A generation ago those people groups, or more simply "peoples," were called "hidden peoples." The Church in general failed to see them. Perhaps you yourself are unaware of the 10,000 people groups who have no gospel penetration, or so little that the few believers among each of them cannot or will not spread the gospel effectively to the entire people.

These 10,000 peoples comprise 33% of the world's population. There are enough energized churches in the world to evangelize all these peoples in a few years, if the "unreached" peoples become "targeted" peoples, at whom each local church has aimed fervent prayer and strategic action.

Since you are reading this book, you must have some interest in the unreached. Ask God to give you a burden for these, the most needy ethnic groups on earth, comprising the most needy individuals. Each person is indescribably important to the Lord. Jesus has commissioned us, the Church, to bring them the good news. Allow the Holy Spirit to anoint you for moments of impassioned prayer that they might be reached.

He will show you his heart is wondrously burdened for them. Your desire to be involved in their deliverance from the bondage of evil and ignorance will sustain you as you work through this study.

May the Lord open the eyes of your heart. May he fill you with his love for people. May he cause his joy in this venture to grow within you. May this crowd out every self-inspired thought that will attempt to present itself to you as more important than his plan for you, whatever that may entail.

Blessings to you as you begin to become equipped to go in his name to an unreached people group. They have been waiting 2000 years to hear what you will be anointed to tell them.

Introduction

This is a manual for cross-cultural missionaries who will bring the gospel to an unreached people and plant strong churches that will multiply. We began gathering these ideas in 1983.

Our purpose then and now is twofold: first, that believers might understand God's heart for the unreached; second, that those who will go to the unreached with the gospel will have a simple explanation of the best ideas missionaries and missiologists have been discussing for the completing of the task of world evangelization.

Giving credit to authors whose ideas we have used is a problem for us. We began to gather material many years ago, combining their ideas with each other and with our own, and putting the results into simplest English for use overseas. We have tried to simplify the material, to be understood by those for whom English is a second language. We cannot easily identify sources for specific ideas, especially since most of what is expressed here is a mixture of thoughts from multiple sources, including conversations.

Where we have quoted, we have given the source.

We in America have given much materially to evangelize beyond our borders. We have less enthusiasm for getting *personally* involved. Few churches pray for the unreached peoples during regular services. Few sermons are preached to motivate believers toward mission service. Pastors are surely aware of the importance of the Great Commission. Perhaps they avoid preaching about career missionary service because we in the pews are "turned off" by it.

There is a prevailing mindset about mission work that "knows" only the best educated believers are qualified to do it. Yet, some of the most productive missionaries, including at least one who has led a people movement, have had minimal training, or none at all!

Only a small percentage of our missionaries go to people groups who need them most. Many are unaware of the 10,000 ethnic groups that have no significant gospel penetration. They find themselves among people groups who have had the gospel for generations.

Pastors are great men of God. God is entrusting them with heavy responsibilities. We admire these men and women of God who labor for the kingdom.

Many pastors, in our opinion, would benefit the kingdom by emphasizing more the importance of reaching people groups who have not been touched by the gospel. Praying with passion for those who cannot do anything to help us in return is a maturing experience. It parallels the young new father's spiritual growth, who, holding his first newborn child determines in his innermost heart that he will give his life for this little one who can nothing for himself or others.

Pastors want their churches to grow spiritually and numerically. When they teach on the Lord's prayer they exhort their flocks to pray that God's kingdom might come more efficaciously in their own believing hearts. They miss wonderful opportunities to connect *Hallowed be thy name, thy kingdom come,* with the Great Commission.

Of course, there are wonderful exceptions.

Within the developing countries, on the other hand, joy and hope, love and maturity are more visibly related to the Great Commission. It is there that we have found willing hearts to enter into the will of God for the unpenetrated nations, that they might hear the good news, and that God might be glorified as entire people groups come to him.

As you study these pages we heartily recommend you subscribe to "Global Prayer Digest, noted at the end of the bibliography, and pray regularly for the various unreached peoples described there, one for each day. Short prayers are good! Intercessors will want to take longer. Desire, compassion, love are important ingredients. Jesus is interested in giving us what we truly desire.

> *If you abide in Me, and My words abide in you, you will ask what you desire, and it shall be done for you* (Jn. 15:7 NKJ).

Section 1

To Be a Missionary You Must Have God's Vision

The call to the unreached is clearly written in Matthew 28:18-20.

All authority in heaven and on earth has been given to me. Therefore go and make disciples of all nations, baptizing them in the name of the Father and of the Son and of the Holy Spirit, and teaching them to obey everything I have commanded you.

"And surely I am with you always, to the very end of the age."

Chapter 1

God's Vision for the Nations

God's Wonderful Plan

God had a wonderful plan for us when he created us. A plan that would bring him glory, and would bring us the greatest terrestrial and eternal joy!

All holy God, to whom alone greatness belongs, created us with free will. We chose to disobey him. God then initiated an alternative plan that theologians agree is more filled with wonder, more astounding in every way. God set everything right again by sending his own Son, Jesus, to die for all our sin, totally satisfying God's justice, and giving us the way of faith to restore our relationship with God.

God did this because he loves us. His desire is that each of us, through love, might freely choose to turn from his sin, and receive through faith the gift of eternal life, which Jesus has earned for him on the cross.

Every future missionary needs a thorough immersion in God's teaching on grace.[1] Until we understand this concept, we are in danger of reproducing legalistic believers, thus robbing them of much kingdom joy.

After 2000 Years

God wondrously fulfilled this plan to save us, 2000 years ago. Jesus gave his life on the cross. When he had arisen from the dead to demonstrate that all he said and did was real, Jesus commanded the Church to take the good news of salvation to all the peoples of the earth.

But the Church worldwide has been making some mistakes. God's part was perfect of course. But ours has not been perfect.

---

[1] An excellent book on this subject is, *Grace Works*, by Dudley Hall. See the bibliography.

First, from the beginning we have misunderstood how important it is that the peoples of the earth hear the good news. Many believers feel that a God who is so good and so perfect would not condemn to hell people who have never heard the gospel. Romans chapter one has the answer to this. They who have no one to tell them, have no excuse. Creation itself is a language God has used to write the truth about himself for all to see.

So, even without a missionary, the peoples can know God. But in their blindness and selfishness, they ignore the message all creation is meant to tell them.

Second, in our English Bibles, the word "nations" seen in Matthew 28:19 has been misunderstood. "Nations," almost every time in the New Testament, comes from the Greek word "ethne" and means "ethnic group" or "people group" or "culture group." It does not mean "country" such as India or The United States.

Third, the Church in general does not give proper importance to the great Commission, the command of Jesus to make disciples of all people groups. The Church, over the centuries, has given the true meaning of the Great Commission only secondary importance.

Our number one priority as the Church is surely to worship God. Worship of God, for his glory is first, not mission. The purpose of mission is that the nations might worship God, bringing him glory. Worship will continue throughout eternity. Mission will not. Mission exists because there are people groups who do not yet worship God. Worship is not happening among the 10,000 unreached peoples of the earth! The Church is commissioned to correct that situation.[2]

The Church tends to look inward, and to strive to perfect itself. Only by obeying God can we better ourselves spiritually. The Church must obey the Great Commission if she is to be whole.

Because of our failure to take the Great Commission seriously enough, countless souls are lost. This is an eternal tragedy. It will continue until we, the Church, realize our responsibility and take action.

---

[2] John Piper, <u>Let the Nations Be Glad</u>, p. 11.

Unreached Nations

An unreached nation is a people group among whom there are no Christians, or so few that the gospel is not spreading faster than the population is expanding. We, the Church, must send missionaries to such a group, to introduce the gospel. Neighborhood evangelism will not help a non-believing member of an unreached people, for he has no Christian neighbor to tell him about Jesus.

An unreached nation, or people group, presents the Church with a big challenge. We call this challenge, a culture barrier. Each people group, or ethnic group, considers all other people groups foreign, and not to be trusted. Each people group resists ideas that come from another people group because such ideas are foreign and therefore not needed by them. Each people group believes its own culture is the best, and that ideas from other cultures are inferior.

Missionaries learn how to overcome this culture barrier, as we shall see.

The Heart of God for the Peoples of the Earth

We must understand the heart of God for the lost. If God is calling you to go "to the nations," or to pray for the unreached peoples, make this chapter a meditation project. Search out every scripture mentioned here. Read prayerfully a few each day. Let each verse be a subject of intimate conversation with the Lord. He will reveal to you things otherwise hidden in these verses. Let him show you which verses to memorize, that you might recall them as you go about your days.

In this way, you will understand the heart of God for these neglected peoples. You will see what God sees. You will begin to feel what God feels. You will then pray the prayers the Spirit of God places in your spirit to pray. And you will pray with the desire, the energy, that can only come from him.

Have you ever found yourself in a state of anguish, not knowing if your little child is safe? This concern was built into your character by him who created you in his own image. Your heavenly Father is like that.

Nevertheless, the Father sent Jesus to die in your place. In permitting his own Son to be in such a vulnerable position, the Father revealed his heart for you. In sending the Church, his own children, to bring the gospel to the unreached peoples, our Father revealed that he has that same love for them!

But further meditation on his Word will reveal to your innermost being much more of what God feels for the peoples yet unevangelized.

We need to see the situation of the unreached peoples as God sees it. We need to feel what God feels for the billions who belong to these people groups. We need to understand how God views the many who are still lost, hidden behind culture barriers that make it almost impossible for them to know the truth without missionaries.

Almost impossible? Well, yes. God can reveal himself to unbelievers without a missionary. But this is not God's method of doing it. He has chosen to depend on you and me. Why? He decided to give man rulership over the earth (Gen. 1:26). This places the unreached within our sphere of responsibility.

God Told Abraham About the Unreached

We tend to think the Great Commission begins in the book of Matthew. It begins in Genesis, the book of beginnings!

In Genesis 12:3 we read that God told Abraham, "All peoples on earth will be blessed through you." What is that blessing? That blessing is **the** blessing. That blessing is Jesus, who descended from Abraham. That blessing is salvation, the most magnificent of all gifts, the pearl of great price!

God repeats this message twice for Abraham's hearing, then again to Isaac, and again to Jacob. God has caused this same message to appear five times in Genesis alone so that we would understand its importance. Look at these repetitions in Genesis18:18, in 22:18, in 26:4, and in 28:14. What we see here is the heart of our Father, repeating over and over his desire, his dream for the nations.

16

Many Scriptures Remind Us of the Unreached Peoples

As you read your Bible, mark in the margin, using some simple symbol, verses that refer to the nations, the unreached ethnic groups. You will be amazed at the number of them.

God has heavily sprinkled throughout the pages of the Bible reminders of his heart for all the peoples. In some of these verses the key word is "Gentiles." Expressions such as "all the earth" also occur. Look in your concordance, using these words as well as "peoples," and "nations."

Of course, many of the verses listed in your concordance do not tell us of God's desire that the peoples be reached. Some are warnings to the people groups. Some tell of God's wrath toward them because of their idolatry. But many do reveal God's heart for ethnic groups that do not know of him.

In the Old Testament, God Often Spoke of the Unreached Peoples

The Book of Psalms alone has dozens of references to the unreached. Psalm 67 begins, *May God be gracious to us and bless us... **that your ways may be known on earth, your salvation among all nations.*** The Spirit of God speaks to us clearly in this verse of the Father's concern that every people on earth know God's ways! This is why God is so gracious to us!

In this same Psalm, verses 3 and 4, The Holy Spirit reveals a most marvelous truth about our relationship with God. Praising God and being joyful are marvelously connected. This is a most uplifting concept. God has built into our nature not only a capacity for giving God glory, but a response of gladness when we glorify him! The nations who do not yet know him need that gladness which we so readily enjoy. Glorifying God releases something in man that causes him to know more profoundly who God is, and to experience a freedom in God that allows the worshiper to see things in perspective, to revel in who he is in Jesus.

As believers, we wonder how anyone can be fully human who does not know God. Glorifying him is fulfilling to us. We find our identity in him. Can we be satisfied knowing there are entire people groups who are encapsulated within cultural "walls" that prevent their hearing the good news with understanding?

When the newly liberated people of Israel fell into worshiping the golden calf, God declared his wrath to Moses and said he would destroy the people. *But Moses sought the favor of the Lord his God. "O Lord," he said, "why should your anger burn against your people, whom you brought out of Egypt with great power and a mighty hand? Why should the Egyptians say, 'It was with evil intent that he brought them out, to kill them in the mountains and to wipe them off the face of the earth'?"*

God relented. God is here speaking to us about his high priority on the salvation of the unreached peoples of the earth.

When the people rebelled against God, refusing to take possession of Canaan because they feared the Canaanites, God again told Moses he would destroy them. *Moses said to the Lord, "Then the Egyptians will hear about it! ...The nations who have heard this report about you will say, 'The Lord was not able to bring these people into the land he promised them on oath...'"* (Nu. 14:13-16).

Again, God is telling us, he desires that the peoples of earth know him.

David, even as a boy, was well aware that all the peoples of the earth should know about the one and only, true and living God. David appeared before Goliath, alone and without armor. He had his shepherd's staff, five stones and a sling. Goliath stood with all his hulk, covered in armor, with his shield bearer in front of him, and his enormous sword at his side.

> Goliath *said to David, "Am I a dog, that you come at me with sticks?" And the Philistine cursed David by his gods. "Come here," he said, "and I'll give your flesh to the birds of the air and the beasts of the field!"*
>
> *David said to the Philistine, "You come against me with sword and spear and javelin, but I come against you in the name of the Lord Almighty, the God of the armies of Israel, whom you have defied. This day the Lord will hand you over to me, and I'll strike you down and cut off your head. Today I will give the carcasses of the Philistine army to the birds of the air and the beasts of the earth,*

and the whole world will know that there is a God in Israel. (1 Sam. 17:43-46)

The whole world needed to know precisely what David announced they would know. The Holy Spirit put these words into David's mind and heart, not only so that those present would hear them, but that we would realize their importance. God cared even then for the unreached, and he has not changed.

In Psalm 96:10 we are commanded to tell the peoples of the earth, *The Lord reigns*! In this one psalm we see seven references to the unreached peoples.

Psalm 97 has a few distinct examples of how God is mindful of the unreached ethnic groups. *The Lord reigns, let the earth be glad; let the distant shores rejoice*!

Psalms 98, and 117 are especially dedicated to the peoples. They show how the Holy Spirit moved upon psalmists to sing to the Lord moving words that either plead for the unreached, or exalt the Lord who will bring the nations to himself for his glory, and for their enrichment and fulfillment.

Striking portions appear in twenty-two of the Psalms. In some Psalms there are several references.

Solomon, under the inspiration of the Holy Spirit, called the attention of Israel, and of us now, to the unreached peoples as he prayed during the dedication of the temple he had just completed. Later Solomon was to drift away from the worship of the true God, but on this solemn occasion he prayed, *"As for the foreigner who does not belong to your people Israel... when he comes and prays toward this temple, then hear from heaven, your dwelling place, and do whatever the foreigner asks of you, so that all the peoples of the earth may know your name and fear you..."* (2 Chr. 6:32, 33).

Isaiah spoke about the unreached ethnic groups of the earth. In 26:17, 18 he laments that the Hebrew nation had failed to bring eternal life to the Gentiles, the people groups who did not know God. So we see, God intended that his chosen people would bring salvation to the unreached peoples before Jesus was born, but they did not.

In 40:3-5 Isaiah foretold the ministry of John the Baptist, who would prepare the way for the Messiah, proclaiming that all mankind would see it together!

In Chapter 51 Isaiah announces to Zion, joy and gladness with thanksgiving will be heard in her. And in verses 4 and 5 he proclaims, speaking for the Lord, *"My justice will become a light to the nations... my arm will bring justice to the nations. The islands will look to me and wait in hope for my arm."* God wanted the unreached peoples to know him.

In 56:6, 7 he scolds the people of Israel for not keeping the court of the Gentiles, an outer part of the temple, as a place of prayer for all nations. Jesus later quoted Isaiah's words (Mk. 11:17) as he drove the money changers out of the court of the Gentiles.

It is clear then, from this selection of texts from the Old Testament, that God desires the peoples of the earth for himself. God's plan is that all nations will have a relationship with him, through Jesus Christ.

The Old Testament has other references to the nations.

The New Testament

The New Testament has many such references also. God's first words to Abraham in which God foretold that all the peoples of earth would be blessed through him, that touching dream of God himself about the unreached, is found near the beginning of the Book of Acts (3:25). Peter spoke those words to help the people understand why a crippled beggar was now walking and leaping and praising God. Peter said, in effect, "Jesus was sent to you first, to bless you."

The Holy Spirit used Peter to underline that verse from Genesis so all would know God's heart for the ethnic groups who did not yet know him. He is underlining it now for you, as you read these words. He wants all of us, in every age, to know God's heart.

He used Paul that way. In writing to the Galatians (3:8) Paul noted, *The Scripture foresaw that God would justify the Gentiles by faith, and announced the gospel in advance to Abraham: "All nations will be blessed through you."*

Jesus was fully aware that his work of redemption would benefit, not only the members of his own Hebrew race, but *"whoever believes in him"* (Jn. 3:16).

Jesus' love was clearly toward the nations. He knew the crowd would reject him. He told his disciples the mysteries of the kingdom were not for the crowd, but for them, the twelve.

For this reason, Jesus found time to spend with the twelve, apart from the crowd. To be free to do this, Jesus sometimes told a person he had just healed, *"Don't tell anyone."* He was guarding the time he could spend with the twelve, preparing them to turn the world upside down, to impact every ethnic group on earth with the good news of salvation.

The Roman Centurion

Jesus took time to point out for his disciples the faith of the Roman centurion (Mt. 8:5-12). Why? Surely because he wanted to help the twelve realize that faith, and grace, were not restricted to the people of Israel. He was preparing their minds and hearts to take the gospel to the nations, the peoples.

The Canaanite Woman

On another occasion, a Canaanite woman cried out to Jesus, *"Lord, Son of David, have mercy on me! My daughter is suffering terribly from demon possession"* (Mt. 15:21-28).

Jesus did not answer her.

This was not at all like Jesus! Why did he not show compassion, as he always did, even for Samaritans and for the Roman centurion?

He humbled this woman even more when he said, *"I was sent only to the lost sheep of Israel."*

The woman was not discouraged. She came and knelt before him and said, *"Lord, help me!"*

We are amazed at Jesus' reply! *"It is not right to take the children's bread and toss it to their dogs."*

Now Jesus has brought this woman to the point where she clearly tells her hearers, and tells us who read her words today, that she really trusts Jesus and his power to heal her daughter.

In humility she accepted what Jesus said to her, but insisted on the healing for her little girl saying, *"Yes, Lord, but even the dogs eat the crumbs that fall from their masters' table."*

Thus Jesus gave his disciples another example of faith outside Israel. This is another illustration of his concern for those outside the covenant. Jesus was reflecting the same compassion his Father expressed as he said to Abraham, over and over, *"All peoples on earth will be blessed through you."*

The Samaritans

In Luke 9:51-55, we see another example of the concern of Jesus for the Gentile nations. The Samaritans did not welcome Jesus into their village. The disciples wanted to call down fire from heaven to destroy them!

But Jesus reflected the heart of his Father for the Samaritans, a people isolated from the full revelation of God. Jesus neither punished them nor spoke out to denounce them. Instead he directed his company to another village, probably another Samaritan village.

Jesus won many Samaritans to himself through the woman he met at the well, and then through his own personal ministry to them. After the ascension, the Holy Spirit directed even more ministry to the Samaritans. He used Philip the deacon to work signs and wonders, and later, Peter and John to introduce them to the fullness of his life in the believer.

The Greeks Wanted to See Jesus

Some Greeks were going up to Jerusalem to worship. Andrew and Philip told Jesus. The Lord clearly indicates to us that this was a special time for him. *The hour has come for the Son of Man to be glorified* (Jn. 12:23).

Then Jesus prayed about his coming sufferings and death. *Now my heart is troubled, and what shall I say? "Father, save me from this hour?" No, it was for this very reason I came to this hour. Father, glorify your name!*

Instead of avoiding suffering and death by crucifixion, Jesus thought of those Greeks, and of all the other peoples as he said, *I, when I am lifted up from the earth, will draw all men to myself.*

Why did Jesus reflect on that fact at this time of great emotion in his life? Surely this was for our benefit. He wanted us to know his heart, his desire for the nations. He delighted in the fact that his death, his being lifted up on the cross, would cause **all** men to come to him.

Jesus wanted, as his Father wanted, all people groups to be saved.

After the Resurrection

After the death of Jesus, two of his disciples were walking to Emmaus (Luke 24:13-47). They were speaking to each other of the things that had happened. They were very discouraged because they thought Jesus was out of their lives forever. They had hoped he was the one who would redeem Israel. But now that he was crucified they had lost that hope.

Jesus had a purpose in this meeting. They were hurting. He wanted to comfort them. He questioned them. He wanted them to state why they thought he had come to earth. *We had hoped that he was the one who was going to redeem Israel* (v. 21).

These two disciples were right. Jesus was the Redeemer of Israel. But he was much more! He was the Redeemer of the world! That same day he would correct their limited understanding of his ministry on earth.

That happened in the upper room, right after these two disciples joined the eleven and the others. The astonished two told the brethren what had happened on the road to Emmaus. Then Jesus suddenly appeared there in the upper room. He gave them a most important and impressive explanation of the scriptures saying, *This is what is written* (v.45). He wonderfully and concisely summed up the ancient writings into two brief messages. First, *the Christ will suffer and rise from the dead on the third day.* And second, *repentance and forgiveness of sins will be preached in his name to all nations...* (v. 46, 47).

We can take great personal comfort in the fact that Jesus was not satisfied to allow two of his disciples to go on to Emmaus and miss this revelation of his purpose. They were not among the inner circle, the eleven. But they were his, and he went after them.

There's more. Jesus' two-fold summary of the scriptures is further evidence that the nations are precious to his heart. The two disciples had missed this point. Even the eleven needed this summation so they would be prepared to hear the Great Commission later (Mt. 28:18-20).

Jesus' purpose in both meetings was the correction of this misunderstanding of his mission. It is important that we also realize Jesus did not come only for **us**, or for **our** people, or for **our** ethnic group.

The Great Commission

Two passages of scripture have been used over the centuries to promote personal growth and holiness, though their original intent was to promote the gospel among the pagan peoples.

One of these passages is part of the Lord's prayer. *"Father... hallowed be your name, your kingdom come..."* (Mt. 6:9, 10).

The literal meaning of these phrases is clear. Jesus taught us to pray that the name of the Lord be hallowed by those who do not now hallow the Lord's name. He encouraged us to pray that God's kingdom might come among peoples who do not yet belong to that kingdom.

However, when preachers use these verses they are almost always encouraging the members of the kingdom to hallow the Lord's name more, or more enthusiastically, than they already do. This is a good use of these verses, but it is not delivering the primary message Jesus conveyed in those words!

The second passage is the Great Commission itself, given most clearly in Matthew 28:18-20. In these verses Jesus clearly sends us to people groups that have not yet heard the gospel. But this passage is more frequently used to encourage believers to engage in neighborhood evangelism, among their own people. Again, this is not a bad use of the passage.

But for both of these passages, their true meaning becomes blurred when believers never, or very seldom, hear them preached according to their literal and prime meaning. The result is, believers are not challenged to obey the Lord by praying for the unreached as Jesus challenged us to do in the Lord's prayer. And believers are not challenged to go to the unreached as Jesus challenged us to do in the Great Commission.

Sadly, as the Church, we do not see the unreached peoples as **our** challenge. Some of us do not really believe a loving God would condemn them to hell forever. Others of us are comfortable where we are, doing what we have always done. We are unwilling to change. We don't want to hear preaching that challenges us to do the radical things Jesus commanded us to do!

As for personal growth and holiness, nothing promotes these as much as preaching the pure, untainted Word of God. Is there anything more maturing, more reviving, as boldly obeying the Word because we love Jesus who saved us forever?

Notice the timing Jesus used for announcing his Great Commission, the end of his time on earth. In the Bible, this announcement occurs at the end of the gospels, and at the beginning of the Book of Acts (1:8). This draws extra attention to the importance of the command. The last words of a great man are often quoted as his last legacy to those he leaves behind. The Great Commission is the final message of the Son of God before he returned to heaven to sit at the right hand of his Father.

What exactly did Jesus say in the Great Commission? Beginning in verse 16 we note the disciples went from Jerusalem to Galilee, to a mountain, obeying Jesus' instructions. They had to do something in obedience to the Lord before he would give them this glorious added revelation about the Gentiles, the unreached.

Why a mountain? Why not tell the eleven what he wanted of them right there in Jerusalem at the temple? He could have chosen Calvary as the venue. Before his death he said he would go ahead of them into Galilee (Mt. 26:32). Then why not meet them by the lakeshore for their convenience? A mountain, and we presume it was atop that mountain, was away from the natural habitat of these fishermen.

In this writer's opinion, Jesus chose a mountain to demonstrate that we don't get much revelation, much inspiration, or answers to many of our questions by sitting around and waiting. God gives us direction as we move.

The classic illustration is the boy on a bicycle that is a little too big. He only needs one bicycle riding experience to learn he cannot steer unless the bicycle is moving. Once it stops, the boy tumbles to one side or the other.

Jesus unveiled a most dynamic plan for the conquest of the hearts of men, worldwide, at that mountain in Galilee. Never was so grand an objective, for so much benefit to man, and perhaps for so much joy and glory for God, expressed so concisely, to so humble a gathering, as on that mountain two thousand years ago.

They worshiped him; but some doubted (v.17). They worshiped him. They knew who he was. This is clear from the Word, especially chapter 17 of John's gospel. What was the subject of their doubts?

Perhaps they doubted themselves. Perhaps they could not figure out how they, of all the people of Israel, came to be chosen by Jesus as his disciples. Before his resurrection it was difficult to imagine. Now, after this astounding show of power, of authority, even sovereignty, perhaps some of them doubted themselves.

Then he spoke. Read his words for yourself (Mt. 28:16-20). They had no reaction recorded in the Word. They must have been totally speechless, blown away by the awesome nature of the task he placed in their hands to accomplish.

They were human, like you and me. You and I know we could never achieve anything of eternal value unless God himself were to work it through us.

He will.

Jesus prophetically announced to his disciples, on his first visit to the upper room after he arose from the tomb, that the unreached peoples would hear the good news (Lk. 24:47). On this occasion Jesus *opened their minds so they could understand the Scriptures* (v. 45). We have already looked into these words. Let us look again.

What does it take to understand the Scriptures? What must we understand so that the Scriptures will make sense to us? Two things. *This is what is written.* First: *The Christ will suffer and rise from the dead on the first day.* Of course that had already just happened, only hours before Jesus spoke these words. Second: *repentance and forgiveness of sins will be preached in his name to all nations...*(v. 46, 47).

Unless we understand that *repentance and forgiveness of sins will be preached in his name to all nations,* we cannot understand the Scriptures.

Luke's introduction to these words of Jesus is interesting and important: *Then he opened their minds so they could understand the Scriptures.* The Holy Spirit is saying here, that every one of the unreached people groups will hear the good news, and this is an important part of God's message to **us**. We therefore need to keep it in our minds and hearts. It will affect our thoughts, our desires, how we evaluate things.

Since Jesus spoke these words right after his resurrection, it must have happened before the Matthew 28 event. If so, the disciples were prepared to hear the words recorded at the end of Matthew.

God is so gentle with us. His commands are radical, but he gives us time to understand them, to count the cost, and to prepare our hearts and minds for the challenges. We might still experience some uncertainties, as the eleven did. Some doubted. But the Lord will help us. The Holy Spirit is the Comforter!

God Used Philip, a Deacon to Show the Way

How wonderful that God used a deacon, Philip, to reach the Samaritans (Ac 8:4-25). In Samaria, among an unreached people, Philip saw the mighty power of God working through him, a humble deacon! There is no evidence that miracles happened in Philip's ministry before he left Jerusalem. But once he crossed that cultural barrier, once he went to a people not his own, once he obeyed the Great Commission, then he saw wonders. God confirmed to the Samaritans that Philip was sent by him, and he confirmed it to Philip as well!

Philip probably reflected on the words of Jesus, ... *I chose you and appointed you to go and bear fruit - fruit that will last. Then the Father will give you whatever you ask in my name* (Jn. 15:16).

These words of Jesus are seen in action in deacon Philip's ministry before anyone else's! The eleven, still in Jerusalem, first felt the reality of the Great Commission when they heard reports from Samaria, reports of what God did through an obedient deacon!

In Philip, the Lord shows us his own heart toward the unreached peoples.

Paul the Missionary

Paul was the last apostle to see Jesus (1 Cor. 15:8). Paul also experienced the promise of Jesus in John 15:16 quoted above. Once again, the eleven were still in Jerusalem when Paul was appointed to go and bear lasting fruit. He went to the Gentiles, the unreached peoples, obeying the call of God to bring the good news further, *to preach the gospel where Christ was not known...* (Rom. 15:20). God richly answered Paul's need for miracles in his ministry.

Perhaps Paul was the one disciple who understood best the heart of God for peoples beyond the revelation of truth. Read the fifteenth chapter of Romans. Notice the insight God had given Paul regarding the importance of the unreached peoples.

He even goes so far as to write that Christ became a servant of the Jews to confirm the promises of God so that the Gentiles may glorify God for his mercy (v. 8, 9)! Jesus became a servant of the Jews that the unreached peoples might receive eternal life and glorify God!

Paul, then, had a clear understanding of the importance of bringing the gospel to the peoples who have not heard. He calls this *the revelation of the mystery hidden for long ages past, but now revealed...* (Rom. 16:25, 26).

Paul writes about this mystery in Romans, in Ephesians, in Colossians and in 1 Timothy. While the Jews in general saw the importance only of their own people, Paul, the former Pharisee, saw clearly God's purpose to win the nations (Rom. 16:25, 26; Eph. 1:9; Col. 1:26, 27; 2:2; 1 Tim. 3:16).

What is the Situation in the World Now?

We have seen that the Spirit of God has given us much scripture to tell us: God does indeed desire all nations. He points our hearts emphatically toward those 10,000 ethnic groups who have yet to know the good news of their salvation.

In Illustration 1 we see how much of the world has been exposed to the gospel, and how much work still remains to be done.

The entire rectangle represents the population of the earth, 6 billion individuals (6,055,000,000).

The top box represents the number of persons who are born-again believers, 600 million (600,000,000). One out of every ten individuals on earth is a genuine believer in Jesus.

Box 2 represents the number of "nominal Christians." These are persons who say they are Christians, but who have never trusted Jesus to give them his gift of eternal life, saving them from hell. Many of these do not understand what it means to "believe" in Jesus.

These persons represented by Box 2 have heard and rejected the gospel. Some have heard many times. They cannot be expected to go to the unreached peoples and make disciples. They are unsaved, and have no power and insufficient understanding to achieve that.

Box 3 represents that portion of the world's population who know they are not Christians. They will tell you they are Muslims, or Hindus, or Buddhists, or atheists, or of some other faith. But their ethnic groups are reached with the gospel. These persons can hear the gospel from their relatives, friends, or neighbors within their own people group. They do not need missionaries.

Illustration
1
The Situation on the Earth

The world population in the year 2000 was 6.055 billion.*

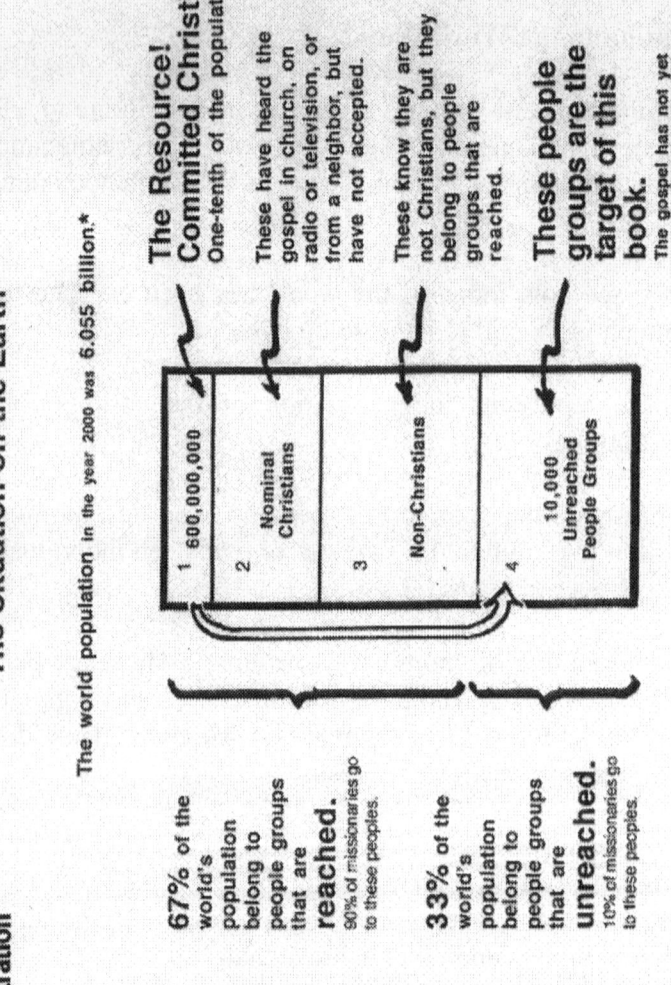

The Resource!
Committed Christians
One-tenth of the population

These have heard the gospel in church, on radio or television, or from a neighbor, but have not accepted.

These know they are not Christians, but they belong to people groups that are reached.

These people groups are the target of this book.
The gospel has not yet penetrated these groups, or not adequately. They need missionaries.

1 600,000,000

2 Nominal Christians

3 Non-Christians

4 10,000 Unreached People Groups

67% of the world's population belong to people groups that are **reached.**
90% of missionaries go to these peoples.

33% of the world's population belong to people groups that are **unreached.**
10% of missionaries go to these peoples.

2 These will be reached through neighborhood evangelism.

3 These will be reached through neighborhood evangelism.

4 These *must* be reached through cross-cultural missionaries, who will come only from box #1 representing committed, Bible believing Christians.

These individuals are not the target of this book. They need the Lord, but they will hear the gospel, or have heard it, even many times. Many of them have rejected the gospel, or are postponing accepting the Lord, which is a form of rejection.

Finally, the largest of the boxes, box 4. The size of this box shows you the portion or percent of the world's population that belong to people groups who have yet to hear the gospel. These comprise 33% of the world's population.

They are the most difficult for us to "see" or understand. It is difficult for us to imagine what it is like to belong to a people who are totally non-Christian. We must force ourselves to consider what this means if we are to understand it.

It means, if this condition continues, each individual will never hear the gospel. No member of the people group has heard the gospel, so no member can explain it to his friends.

Furthermore, there is a special problem that tends to prevent each person from accepting the gospel from a missionary! The missionary will be an "outsider." People tend not to believe outsiders. Foreigners are distrusted generally. We shall see how to overcome this problem.

Illustration
2

Every people group surrounds itself with a
Culture Barrier.

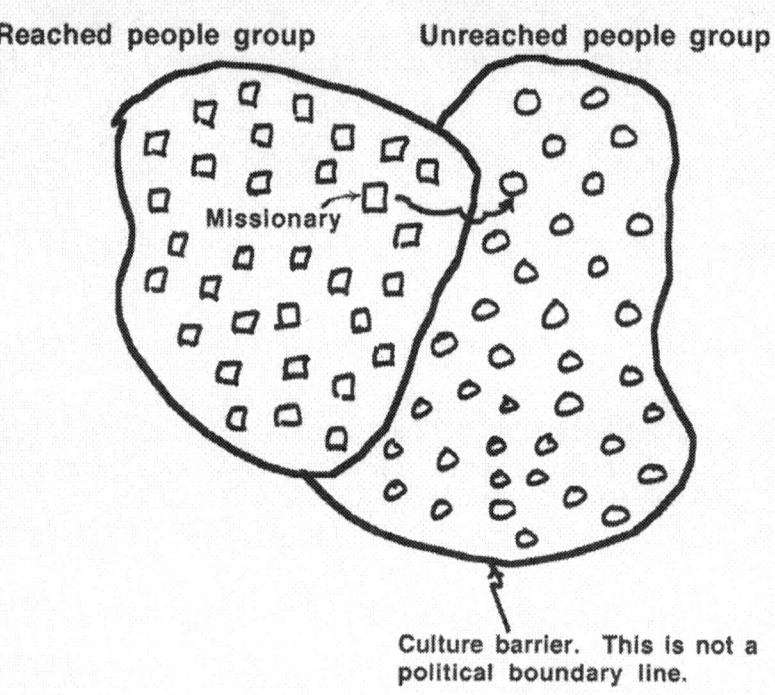

Reached people group   Unreached people group

Missionary

Culture barrier. This is not a
political boundary line.

We illustrate this problem in Illustration 2. Surrounding every people group is what we call a "culture-barrier." In the illustration, this barrier is represented by a solid line. This line is not a political boundary on a map. Political boundaries separate countries such as Mexico and Guatemala, or Thailand and Burma. These boundaries separate political entities we call countries. However, "nations" in the biblical sense means, not countries, but people groups. The Greek word for which our English Bibles have the word "nations" is "ethne." Our word "ethnic" also comes from this Greek word. The translators chose the traditional word "nations" rather than a less poetic sounding phrase such as "ethnic groups" or "people groups."

Most nations or countries have hundreds of ethnic groups. Ethnic groups know they are very separate, each one from the others, because of culture, and often because of language difference.

Missionaries learn how to overcome culture-barriers. These barriers exist in the minds or attitudes of persons who recognize that a certain individual is not a member of their own people group, but is instead a foreigner, and should therefore not be trusted.

Box 4 of Illustration 1 represents 10,000 people groups who have either no Christians or so few that they cannot evangelize their own people without outside help. The population of the group is expanding faster than the gospel is spreading.

We call these 10,000 groups "unreached peoples." Missionaries must go to all 10,000 groups and evangelize. Otherwise the people will continue to die without a knowledge of the Savior, without an opportunity to choose to trust Jesus completely for their salvation.

These 10,000 Unreached Peoples are the Target of This Book

Sadly, only 10% of missionaries go to these 10,000 peoples. That means 90 of every 100 missionaries are working among people groups that already have a significant percent of Christians among them, and many missionaries.

How wonderful that you are reading about the unreached. Surely the Spirit of God will remind you to pray for their salvation. Here's a question that might help you draw the attention of your friends to the necessity of turning our hearts and our minds toward these billions who have no one they can go to for the truth.

Here is that question: Can you complete this verse? *"Be still and know…"* You will probably respond, as most do, *"…that I am God."* To that we reply: You have left out a very important part. *Be still and know that I am God. I will be exalted among the nations, I will be exalted in the earth* (Ps. 46:10).

Most of the verse concerns our Father's heart for the unreached. Yet, most of us only notice the first part, a very wonderful command of God to acknowledge him, but we overlook completely the part about his desire to be known among those who have not heard!

The omission may seem a small thing, but it is indicative of how we have, for generations, even centuries, lost our vision for the unreached peoples.

Read on. We will learn how to penetrate the "culture barrier" of an unreached people and lead them to the Lord, planting strong churches that will multiply among them.

Questions
on
Chapter 1

At the end of each chapter you will find questions about that chapter.

Each question is a numbered sets of four choices lettered A, B, C and D. In cases where only one of the lettered choices is correct, choose that one. In cases where three of the lettered choices are correct, choose the one that is not correct. Your responses must be based on the material in the chapter.

1. God wants everyone saved, but what about those who have not heard the gospel?

    A. They who have no Christian neighbors to communicate the gospel to them will be saved anyway because, as John tells us, *God is love.* Creation itself is a language, which God has used to write the truth about himself for all to see.
    B. They who have no one to tell them about Jesus have no excuse. They must work for their salvation. Creation itself is a language, which God has used.
    C. They who have no one to tell them the message of salvation will be saved by doing their best to please God with the knowledge and understanding they have.
    D. They who have no one to tell them how to be saved have no excuse. Creation itself is a language, which God has used to write the truth about himself for all to see.

2. Usually, when the Bible speaks to us of "nations," we should remember:

    A. it is referring to political entities such as Thailand, Sudan, Mexico.
    B. the translators did not understand the full impact of their error.
    C. the closest meaning for the word "nations" is "ethnic group."
    D. that countries and nations are one and the same.

3. The number one priority of the Church is:

    A. worship, except where mission is involved.
    B. mission, especially mission to the unreached.
    C. nurturing the believers so they will obey God.
    D. worship.

4. Wherever worship does not exist:

    A. the pastor should teach it more thoroughly.
    B. mission is needed.
    C. tithing should be taught more thoroughly.
    D. reverence is lacking.

5. An unreached nation is a people group among whom there are no Christians…

    A. and no literacy.
    B. or no portions of the Bible translated into the local dialect.
    C. or so few that the gospel is not spreading faster than the population is expanding.
    D. or so few that we cannot verify their existence.

6. Each people group resists ideas that <u>come from another people group</u> because such ideas are foreign and therefore not needed by them.

    A. This statement is about "culture barrier."
    B. This sentiment is found only in deprived, or primitive cultures.
    C. This statement would be true if we substitute for the underlined words this expression: <u>are indigenous</u>..
    D. The statement would be true only if we changed the first three words to: Each nomadic people group…

7. In Genesis 12:3 we read that God told Abraham, "All peoples on earth…

    A. will be blessed through you."
    B. will receive truth through you."
    C. will be drawn to me through you."
    D. will reject you."

8. Psalms 67, 96, 98, and 117:

    A. are especially dedicated to the unreached peoples.
    B. emphasize God's wrath for those who reject him.
    C. include moving words that either plead for the unreached,
    D. some verses exalt the Lord who will bring the nations to himself for his glory.

9. Who prayed this prayer? *"As for the foreigner who does not belong to your people Israel… when he comes and prays toward this temple, then hear from heaven, your dwelling place, and do whatever the foreigner asks of you, so that all the peoples of the earth may know your name and fear you…"* (2 Chr. 6:32, 33).

    A. Jeroboam
    B. Nehemia
    C. Solomon
    D. Rehoboam

10. These passages of scripture have been used over the centuries to promote personal growth and holiness, though their primary meaning promotes the gospel among the pagan peoples. Which expression below least fits this description?

    A. *hallowed be thy name*
    B. *thy kingdom come*
    C. *the whole earth is full of his glory.*
    D. *go and make disciples of all nations*

11. *I chose you and appointed you to go and bear fruit - fruit that will last. Then the Father will give you whatever you ask in my name* (Jn. 15:16).

   A. The first disciple recorded to act on these words of Jesus was Peter.
   B. The first disciple recorded to act on these words of Jesus was Philip.
   C. The first disciple recorded to act on these words of Jesus was a deacon.
   D. The first place where this was seen in action was Samaria.

12. Paul refers to *the revelation of the mystery hidden for long ages past, but now revealed.* He is writing here about:

   A. the mystery of the Trinity.
   B. God's infinite power.
   C. why God revealed himself to Abraham and established his name among the Hebrews.
   D. the importance of bringing the gospel to the peoples who have not heard.

13. In Illustration 1, the box (or boxes) that refer(s) to individuals who belong to people groups that are considered reached with the gospel are (is):

   A. Box 1 (at the top).
   B. Boxes 1 and 2.
   C. Boxes 1, 2 and 3.
   D. Box 4.

Chapter 2

We Must Be Serious about Prayer

Pray for the Unreached Peoples

The most powerful thing any one of us can do for people groups with no gospel witness is pray. You are probably called to do more. But you are definitely called to pray. And your prayer is powerful because in prayer you link together the infinite power of God himself with the problem of the unreached peoples.

This is what intercession means. The word "intercession" comes from two Latin words. "Inter" means between. "Cession" means placing. When you intercede, you place yourself between God and the unreached peoples.

Because you are covered by the blood of Jesus, God answers your prayer. Because you are in Christ, your prayer is powerful.

This does not mean you can be satisfied to pray and do nothing else. Not at all! In his Great Commission Jesus does not even mention prayer for the unreached. But he does exhort us to pray the Lord of the harvest that he send laborers. Someone has said we must pray as if everything depended upon God, and work as if everything depended upon us.

Better still, pray knowing that God is infinite and can do a mighty work as you pray. And work knowing that, as you work, God is doing the spiritual work, the effective work, using your efforts but combining them with his own infinite power to bring about eternal results.

Why Doesn't God do the Work Himself?

Why does God wait for me to pray when he has all the power it takes? The reason is found in Genesis 1:26. God gave man charge over the earth, to rule. When God gives us charge of something he does not then push us aside and do the work himself. But he is available if we need help.

39

If we are humble enough to ask for his help, his mighty power is standing by, ready to undertake for us. Our admission that we need him, gives him glory. That's what we were created for!

Thank God he has chosen to use us in this and other ways! He has created us in his image. Therefore we are givers. Intercession is giving. God has arranged for us to participate in his giving. We need to give to experience a full Christian life.

Yes, your prayer is powerful. The most powerful thing you can do! Coupled with obeying the Great Commission, prayer for the unreached is unbeatable!

How Can We Pray for the Unreached People Groups?

Using the words of Jesus is a most powerful means of praying for the unreached. For example, "Father, hallowed be thy name among the 10,000 unreached peoples of the earth. Your kingdom come among them, Lord!"

The number-one ingredient in our prayer should be desire. Jesus said, "Whatever things you desire," these are the things I will do for you. This desire, that the unreached peoples might be saved, is a desire that is totally agreeable to the Spirit of the Lord.

Pray with desire. Tell the Lord your own salvation is precious to you. Tell him how precious. Tell him why it is precious. This will cause you to desire that the lost be saved.

Ask the Lord of the harvest to send laborers into these 10,000 harvest fields. In other words, pray for more missionaries. Pray also for the missionaries who are beginning to labor among some of these unreached peoples. Praying with or about specific bits of information you might have is more satisfying. Perhaps that's because it is more effectual. Perhaps it's more effectual because it helps us pray with more ardent desire.

For specific facts, "Global Prayer Digest" is a great help. We mentioned this earlier. See the note in the bibliography. It is published monthly in English, Spanish, Portuguese, Korean, and soon in Japanese. Each page presents information about one unreached people group to be prayed for, one group for each day of the month.

Take authority over the principalities and powers, the demonic forces that are holding those 10,000 peoples in bondage. Many of these peoples have demon-worship woven into the fabric of their culture. They live in fear of spiritual forces that take the lives of their children if the parents fail to sacrifice to these evil spirits.

Jesus had authority over evil spirits (Lk. 4:33-36). A careful reading of the following scriptures will show you have authority to act in the name of Jesus: Mt. 10:1; Mark 3:15; 6:7; 16:17; Luke 4:36; 9:1; John 15:16; 17:11, 12. Ministering "in the name of Jesus" is not an empty ritual, a sort of formula, on the lips of a believer who understands the meaning of "the name." Because you have a son or daughter relationship with almighty God, you are authorized to minister in his authority.

Use that authority to bind those evil beings and to loose the peoples from that bondage.

Do not pronounce the name of Jesus as if it were itself somehow magically potent. The name of Jesus is powerful because Jesus is who he is, and because you are his own. It is your kinship tie with Jesus that enables you to use his "name," his authority, effectually.

Use the authority of Jesus, the Living Word, as a sword to slash through these demons, causing them to lose their "grip" on the enslaved peoples. What you bind here, is bound in the heavenlies. What you loose here is loosed there (Mt. 16:19; 18:18).

Then ask the Holy Spirit to move among those oppressed peoples. Ask him to penetrate their darkness with the light of Jesus. Ask him to soften the hearts of the people, that they might perceive his presence, and know his character by looking at his creation (Rom. 1:19, 20; Ps. 19:1-6).

If you examine Psalms 96:7-9; 98:4-6; 100; 117; 148:7, 11, 12 you will find that you can speak to these peoples, commanding them to worship the living God! So, speak to them! Command them to look up at the stars and know there is a God who loves them. Let the Holy Spirit show you what to say to them.

What effect will that have? The Holy Spirit had the psalmist sing commands to "all nations." Surely this is a model for us. Let God do with your scriptural intercessions whatever his wills.

In all you do regarding intercession, remember this: worship is an important part! In worship, we are in awe of God. In worship, God is active in speaking to us, and in changing us, making us more like his Son. As we worship, God ministers to the situation we're interceding about.

Why is Prayer so Important?

If you're too busy to pray, you're too busy! Make time to pray for the unreached. As you pray for them, God will give you wisdom about how to minister to them. You will discover that some of your most "creative" ideas for ministry will come to you as you worship and intercede.

If God is calling you to become a missionary to an unreached people, surely he will move you to pray for the unreached peoples, or perhaps for the specific unreached ethnic group he is sending you to evangelize.

Prayer, especially worship, puts you in a better frame of mind, enabling you to get more done. Spending time with him who is the source of all wisdom will help you make wise, time-saving decisions!

Pastor, You are the Key!

If the Church around the world is to become what Jesus intended we should be, a house of prayer for all nations, it will be because you, Pastor, and thousands like you, have responded to what God is saying. You are the one the church members will follow. Your preaching and your example are crucial.

You are reading this book! You have a heart for the unreached. Therefore it is not likely you are one who needs to read this little segment.

Pastor, can your people be mature Christians without being involved in the Great Commission? Praying for those most in need, those who will not repay them, promotes growth.

Commitment to the Great Commission is like tithing. People fear it until they experience it. Then growth takes place. Christian life without tithing is a crippled walk. Can a believer walk in full joy without participating in the Great Commission?

When pastors in general become convinced of the importance of reaching these peoples with the gospel, they will pray. They will lead their people in prayer. They will preach about career missionary service. Some will take up the missionary challenge.

The unreached will be reached.

Intercessors, Here is Your Challenge!

Reaching the 10,000 unreached peoples is not a high priority for the local church just now. This is my opinion after ministering in 20 countries.

We all must bear the blame for this, I who am older, perhaps more than you if you are younger.

Our hope for change is based upon:

1. The Holy Spirit. He will motivate pastors to preach the Great Commission.
2. The Word of God. After the nations are reached, then the end will come (Mt. 24:14). John saw people from every ethnic group standing before the throne, worshiping (Rev. 7:9).
3. The pastors of the Church worldwide. Their people will listen to them. Let us pray for pastors. *The heart of the king is in the hand of the Lord* (Pr. 21:1).

Pastors are the apple of God's eye. Their hearts are most tender toward the Lord. They bear heavy burdens in their efforts to bring their people to maturity in Jesus.

We who pray, often fail to realize our power with God. Pray!

Now is the Day of Salvation!

For 2000 years the Church has taken less than a clear-eyed view of these facts. For 2000 years we have stressed personal growth and holiness, and of course this is important. But we stress holiness seeing no connection between it and the Great Commission!

Many pastors have actually said, "My people are not ready for the Great Commission. They must learn to walk in righteousness first." These pastors say, "Jesus sent us first to Jerusalem, and then to the uttermost parts of the earth." A careful reading of Acts 1:8 reveals this is not what the Word says. Examine Acts 1:8:

But you will receive power when the Holy Spirit comes on you; and you will be my witnesses in Jerusalem, and in all Judea and Samaria, and to the ends of the earth.

The regions are not given a priority order. There is no mention of "first" or "second" or "last of all"!

In Luke 24:47 Jesus does say the spreading of the good news will begin in Jerusalem. He does not command that it begin there. It will of course begin there because of the events that had already taken place just outside its walls, and because the Spirit was soon to fill the disciples in that city. There is no reason to believe that Jesus wants us to work among our own people until more of them accept him, or until the believers become more mature.

Acts 1:8 supports our point impressively: Jesus has in his heart and mind the salvation of the unreached peoples as a high priority. For us, our relationship with Jesus, worshiping Jesus, is higher. If we were to draw up a priority list based on scriptural values we could build an excellent case for deciding the Great Commission is next.

Was Philip out of order in going so soon to Samaria? Surely not! We admire his boldness in following the Holy Spirit. He was not one of the twelve, yet he was the first to obey the Great Commission!

If we believe this is God's scale of values, we need to be ready to share this revelation with others. Otherwise, the Church will make the same mistake in the future we have been making over the past two thousand years.

We cannot force anyone to change his views or his priorities, but our prayer is powerful. We can do what the Lord shows us to do to tell others what we understand from the Word. Only the Holy Spirit can change hearts. We must listen to those who disagree. We must not condemn anyone who is obeying what he believes is God's direction for him. We must be patient, and let God do his work among us.

Adopt a People Group!

You can adopt one of the unreached peoples of the earth. It means you will pray especially for that group. You might also find out which missionaries are working among that group so you can pray for them. Perhaps you will give to help support the work of one of those missionaries. God might even send you to help them!

To adopt a people group, write to Adopt-a-People, P.O. Box 17490, Colorado Springs, CO, 80935 USA. They will help you choose a group for whom no one is praying.

Worship Energizes Mission. The Goal of Mission is Worship.

We must not overlook the impact and importance of worship in our daily lives as believers. Neither can we afford to overlook worship as a vital force in our cross-cultural ministries. In worship we receive energy to carry out mission.

We see this in Isaiah 6:1-8. Isaiah saw the Lord. God's majesty filled the temple. Isaiah saw the angels worshiping, crying *Holy, holy, holy is the Lord Almighty; the whole earth is full of his glory.*

The place shook and was filled with smoke. Isaiah was in awe in the presence of God. This happens to us in moments of profound worship. He cried, expressing his own unworthiness, and the unworthiness of mankind, and yet... he was beholding the King of Kings!

An angel purified his lips, saying, *Your guilt is taken away and your sin atoned for.*

Then it happened! Isaiah heard the heart-beat of God Almighty! He heard it in words that penetrated his servant-heart. He heard, *Whom shall I send? And who will go for us?* Isaiah responded immediately, *Here am I. Send me!*

He could have said, "Let me see if I can find someone who feels called to go." Of course, he never considered that. He wanted to be the one. God knew how Isaiah would respond. He knew Isaiah's heart.

In our most delightful times of worship, God will send us. He will also enlighten us in ways we did not anticipate. During worship we seem to grow wonderfully. We find it difficult to behave. We want to cry out as Isaiah did. We want to lift our hands and dance as David did. In private it's great to be free to do both. Some restrictions apply in some churches, of course.

We are called to participate in the glory of God, to contribute to his glory, to promote it where it is not happening, and even to enjoy it with God as God determines to let us experience it with him. This is all part of what it means to be created in the image of God. It is the nature of God to seek his own glory. He is committed to what is the highest good, which is his own glory. He is committed to what is best for us, which is again, his glory. When we are really whole, we know that the most delightful thing for us to do is to glorify him and to help others to do the same.

It is our nature to seek his glory. We are most fulfilled while we are worshiping him. He is most glorified in us when we are most delighted in him.[3]

All of this is vital to mission. A certain executive of a large mission organization once asked, "Why are believers so taken with worship? They need to get busy about mission!"

This man was exasperated about the lack of vision among many believers. But we must not make the mistake of even appearing to downgrade worship. Only as they worship are people likely to desire that the nations receive life and fall on their faces in worship of God whom we so adore.

---

[3] John Piper, Let the Nations Be Glad, p.26.

In worship, the Holy Spirit speaks to us as he did to the church at Antioch (Ac 13:2,3). *While they were worshiping the Lord and fasting, the Holy Spirit said, "Set apart for me Barnabas and Saul for the work to which I have called them." So after they had fasted and prayed, they placed their hands on them and sent them off.*

Worship gives energy to mission. The goal of mission is to incorporate into Christ the unreached peoples that they might worship.[4]

Fasting deserves a book on its own, and there are many written. Fasting opens us up to receive revelation from the Lord. We see more clearly into kingdom matters when we fast.

Fasting does not qualify us, or make us worthy of God's gifts. It should never be entered into for the purpose of deserving anything, or paying God back for anything. Fasting seems best understood by those who fast in order to draw closer to the Lord, to behold him with more clarity.

Your Prayer Time is a Vital Part of Your Life, and Your Ministry

Paul Yonnghi Cho once found himself so overloaded with work that he took extra hours in prayer. Why? He explained that it was the only solution to an impossible situation. He recognized his need for divine help!

Years ago someone estimated that the average pastor in a certain country prayed only five minutes each day! This shows clearly a lack of confidence in God or an overconfidence in self! If we neglect prayer, our motives soon become self-promoting, and our decisions will be based on corrupt motives.

If you think you cannot pray because you cannot sustain, more than a few minutes, your concentration on the Lord, perhaps this listing (below) will help you.

---

[4] Read about this in John Piper's excellent book.

Eighteen Things You Can Do in Your Prayer Time

If you cannot seem to pray, try some of these suggestions.

1. A good way to begin is to tell the Lord you are setting aside this time just to please him (Ps. 19:14). Try to mean it! Actually, we pray because we cannot live without God. We need him. Admit this to him, but tell him you desire to spend this time pleasing him. You do please God. *The Lord delights in those who fear him, who put their hope in his unfailing love.* (Ps. 147:11). Ask him what he wants you to do in this part of your prayer time. Then, believe your next thought is from him, if it agrees with the Word.

2. Pray through the Lord's prayer (Mt. 6:9-13). Use these verses as a guide. Put the ideas into your own words. The first three expressions are actually commands. For example, "Hallowed be thy name." When we pray this, we are commanding that the name of the Lord be honored, even by those who are not aware of his existence!

3. Pray other portions of the Bible. Use verses such as Isaiah 6:3; Rev. 5:8-14..

4. Take other parts of scripture and change the words slightly so that they become your own words directed toward God. For example, use Isaiah 12:2, *Surely God is my salvation.* Pray this back to God by saying directly to him, "O God, you are most certainly my salvation, my only salvation. For I am so weak I cannot even begin to save myself. Only by your cleansing blood, Jesus, could I ever have been saved. Thank you for giving me your own righteousness."

5. Ask the Lord to send forth laborers into the harvest fields, the unreached peoples.

6. Take authority over demons that are holding the unreached in bondage. Bind evil powers that are hindering the Church, or you, or your loved ones.

7. Speak directly to the nations, as in Psalms 96:7-9; 98:4-6; 100:1-5; 117.

8. Confess your weakness in prayer to the Lord. Rejoice that in your weakness, God's strength is manifest (2 Cor. 12:10).

9. Rejoice in the Lord. Tell God one reason why you are rejoicing in him. Dance before him as David did. When you are totally

alone, you can do this with great freedom. God is watching and rejoicing over you with singing! (See Zep. 3:17.)

10. Thank God for just one or two things. Do this with all the enthusiasm of a servant who has been given a rich treasure by the king, and who has just this one opportunity to tell the king how delighted he is with his gift. Psalm 50:23: *He who sacrifices thank offerings honors me, and he prepares the way so that I may show him the salvation of God.*

Some translations use the word "praise" instead of "thank," indicating that the Hebrew word must incorporate both ideas. So we're looking at the importance of praiseful thanksgiving, or thankful praise.

Notice how important it is that we be grateful and praisers of the Lord, as a **lifestyle**. By our praise, by our thanks, we make a path so that God can rescue us! Don't wait until you know you need rescuing. You always need him! Remember, we're talking here about a lifestyle!

Thank him occasionally for something fundamental like salvation itself! Most of us see only a small fraction of what God is doing for us. We need to thank him for things we notice, and ask him to show us more of these blessings.

Don't make the sophisticate's mistake of calculating, "Oh well, I suppose the reason why that pain left my shoulder is that whatever was causing it was temporary." Remember whose in charge! God doesn't take his eyes off you. He's responsible for everything being here on earth, including earth, and everything else. Give him credit for caring for you. That's what he does.

11. Praise God for his works, and for his wonderful qualities, such as faithfulness. Have one or two specific reasons. Tell him what they are and why they are great. Go into detail with this. I believe God is pleased with our enthusiasm about him.

12. Make a joyful noise to the Lord! If others are nearby, you might prefer to "shout" in a whisper. God will hear very clearly, and so will you. We do well to use our bodies in this way. We are not bodies. We are spirit-beings. But we have bodies. We should use them to glorify the Lord. David danced before the Lord! Why not?

13. Proclaim God's reign. Use a verse like Psalm 86:9.

14. Write down ideas God gives you. God will give you ideas totally unrelated to what you are doing as you pray and celebrate the Lord. Have pen and paper handy.
15. Make your requests known to God and thank him for the answers before you see them (Phil. 4:6, 7).
16. Read God's Word. Talk to him about what you are reading. Thank him or praise him for what he said or did. Obey his Word.
17. Pray in the Spirit. Paul wrote, *I will pray with the Spirit* (1 Cor. 14:15).
18. Worship God for who he is. We discuss this below.
19. God wants to speak to you. Some say God is always communicating with us, but we miss most of it because we seldom listen. Listen! Write down what he tells you. Date these messages. Respond to everything the Lord speaks to your heart. Put that in writing, too. Look up the scriptures that support what you have received from him, demonstrating that what you received in this way agrees with his written Word. If it's from him, of course, it will agree.

Prophecy, one of the nine gifts of the Holy Spirit, is a message from God, which one receives into his mind to be given to another. The purposes are, edification, exhortation and comfort (1 Cor. 14:3). You can also receive words for yourself. Expect this to happen. We all need God's edification, exhortation and comfort.

If you have a timer of some kind, you might try using it to time your prayer time. Then you won't be thinking of all the things you need to do after prayer. You will feel relieved of the concern that you must keep your eye on the clock. Your attitude can be one of total freedom, relaxing in the arms of Jesus.

Once I found myself burdened about prayer. There were several things I felt troubled about and wanted to be sure to talk to the Lord about. Suddenly I realized, it's not I who make things happen in the spiritual realm. It's Jesus! And he already knows about them. I felt I was looking into his face, climbing up on his lap, and just letting him assure me, with his arms around me, that he was taking care of my burdens.

Don't feel you must use all of these 18 ideas. Let the Holy Spirit show you what to do. But be free to try as many as you want. Jesus has set you free! Determine to please God! He delights in hearing you.

How Do We Worship?

You need worship every day for peace, love, joy, and mental health!

Begin by surrendering yourself completely again to the Lord, giving yourself to him without reserving anything for yourself. Do this to the best of your ability. Admit to God your shortcomings, and tell him how sincerely you want to be totally his.

Surrender is not the same as worship. We surrender for our own well-being, like a prisoner of war. You can surrender to an enemy who has a weapon aimed at you, but you would not be worshiping. Surrender is all about us.

Worship is all about God. When you realize to some extent who God is, worship *almost* automatically follows.

The worshiper acknowledges things about the nature or character of God that cause the worshiper to be in awe, or profound admiration of God. The Book of 1 Chronicles 29:10-13 gives us an example of worship. Use these verses as a guide occasionally.

How incredibly full of wonder God is! It's true that when we worship, we do ourselves a favor. But let's not be satisfied with that as a motive. God deserves our undivided hearts.

This kind of communication with God brings us into a close fellowship with him. We "see into" the reality of the spiritual realm. We are overwhelmed with a sense of God's greatness. We sense the awesomeness of God, his infinite power, his goodness, his majesty, his glory. We come to a "place" of wonder, understanding a little of his richness, his splendor. We realize in a deep and satisfying way, our own sonship with him, that we are his possession, that he is our God, the center of our lives.

Something glorious happens to us when we worship. Read "Glory," by Ruth Heflin. Worship is something we do. Glory is something we can experience to some degree, as we worship.

In the wonder of his presence you will probably intercede for the unreached peoples. This is because you understand the emptiness in their hearts. You will desire to give to them from the glorious fulfillment you experience in God, the depth of understanding and satisfaction he gives you. In the kingdom you are secure. You have all you really need for eternity. You can safely reach out to others. The unreached peoples need someone like you to pray and to go. They need many someones.

We are changed most as we worship the Lord, delighting in him

Be Honest with God as You Pray

Read Numbers 11:11-25. Notice how honest and open Moses was in speaking to God. Moses seems angry! But this is not likely. Moses was the meekest of men. But he was certainly troubled, and he told God plainly how difficult things had become.

Read Exodus 33:12-23 to see how God responded to Moses at a time when Moses was deeply dissatisfied and needed God's special help. He was most considerate of Moses' feelings of discouragement and frustration, and he took steps to change the situation for Moses.

Those who call on the Lord are the ones he saves (Rom. 10:13). Don't hesitate to be honest in your prayer time.

The Lord is near to all who call on him, to all who call upon him in truth (See Ps. 145:17-20).

Don't become angry with God. This is impatience. Trust God to work in all things *for the good of those who love him, who have been called according to his purpose* (Rom. 8:28). If you really believe that, you will be patient with what God is doing. Ask him to help you, but don't get angry as if God were unjust, uninformed, or acting unwisely! *Now I, Nebuchadnezzar, praise and exalt and glorify the King of heaven, because everything he does is right and all his ways are just. And those who walk in pride he is able to humble* (Dan. 4:37). Nebuchadnezzar, a pagan ruler, had been influenced in his beliefs by Daniel and chastened by the Lord himself (v. 28-36).

But be honest with God. He will treat you, as he treated Moses, with love and concern.

Are You Convinced About Mission?

The unreached peoples cannot be saved without the gospel. Otherwise Jesus would not have made the Great Commission the finale of his life's work, and the substance of his final summation of the sacred scriptures (Lk. 24:46,47).

He would not have sent us at all if the unreached could be saved by their own good will or good works. Our testimony would only hurt them if their ignorance could save them.

What then should our lives be about? Second only to worshiping God, to relating to Jesus, our Savior and our God, we need to be about our Father's business. Ministering to our spouses and children, yes, but then to those most in need of the most relevant necessity, the most real security, the most genuine requirement for everlasting well-being... eternal life, life in Jesus.

Is God sending you? Get ready. When your spouse senses the same call to the unreached people groups it will be time to take big, bold steps.

For now, pray... and study onward.

Questions
on
Chapter 2

1. Speaking of helping the unreached:

   A. The most powerful thing I can do for people groups with no gospel witness is become a missionary.
   B. When I intercede, I place myself between God and the unreached peoples.
   C. Because I am in Christ, my prayer is powerful
   D. In his Great Commission Jesus does not even mention prayer for the unreached

2. Which of these statements is not true?

   A. God gave man charge over the earth, to rule.
   B. We should carry on without crying out to God for help.
   C. Our admission that we need God's help, gives him glory.
   D. Coupled with obeying the Great Commission, prayer for the unreached is unbeatable!

3. To pray in faith effectively we need:

   A. to be relaxed.
   B. desire.
   C. to live without sin.
   D. to choose the good.

4. In prayer…

   A. the name of Jesus on your lips is powerful because Jesus is who he is, and because you are his own. .
   B. what you bind here on earth is bound in the heavenlies. What you loose here is loosed there.
   C. it is your kinship tie with Jesus that enables you to use his "name," his authority, effectually.

D. use the name of Jesus and, as they say, "hope for the best."

5. Can we speak to the unreached peoples?

   A. In several Psalms The Holy Spirit shows us we can speak to the unreached peoples about worshiping God.
   B. In several Psalms The Holy Spirit shows us we can command the "nations" to worship the one true God.
   C. In several Psalms The Holy Spirit shows us we can preach to the unreached peoples.
   D. We can not scripturally speak to the unreached peoples without going to them.

6. About prayer…

   A. In worship, God changes us, making us more like Jesus
   B. In worship, God speaks to us.
   C. Intercession should not be mixed with worship.
   D. As we worship, God ministers to the situation we're interceding about.

7. The segment especially intended for pastors is essentially saying…

   A. pastors should regard the Great Commission as an essential part of the Christian walk for all believers.
   B. the Church would be mature if all believers would tithe and send missionaries.
   C. pastors should preach about the Great Commission.
   D. pastors are the ones believers follow.

8. In the segment directed especially toward intercessors, the author is essentially saying…

   A. We need intercessors who understand the Great Commission, so they will pray more for the unreached peoples and for more missionaries to go to those people groups who have no gospel.

B. pastors should encourage intercession in their churches, that the unreached peoples might be reached..

C. Intercessors are needed to pray for pastors, that they might understand more clearly the importance of the Great Commission, and lead their people into a more active role in it.

D. All of the above.

9. Which of these is not one of the author's views.

A. Worship connects us with God in ways that glorify him and benefit us. We are given glimpses into the heavenlies.

B. We must be about our Father's business. We need to worship God, relate to our Savior, and minister to our spouses and children. Then we need to minister to those most in need of salvation, the ultimate security, eternal life.

C. Nurturing the body of Christ should not be a high priority for pastors.

D. It's true that when we worship, we do ourselves a favor. But let's not be satisfied with that as a motive. God deserves our undivided hearts.

10. Concerning the unreached...

A. Jesus did not need to send us. The unreached can be saved by their own good will or good works.

B The unreached peoples can be saved without the gospel.

C. The unreached peoples cannot be saved without the gospel. Otherwise Jesus would not have made the Great Commission the finale of his life's work, and the substance of his final summation of the sacred scriptures (Lk. 24:45-47).

D. Without any knowledge of the gospel, ignorance alone will save them.

Section 2

Administrative Skills You Will Need

The Skeptic: Should a man of God be involved in a subject like "administrative skills"?

The Wise Man: Only if he realizes how unimportant that subject is to his life, and to his success as a minister. Administrative skills are low in importance compared to the great importance of his relationship to God, and his relationship to his family, and his relationship to other people.

Chapter 3

Why Study Administration?

Planning is Not "Unspiritual"

Some spiritual leaders object to any sort of preparation for doing the work of the kingdom. They quote verses like Psalm 81:10, "Open your mouth and I will fill it."

They object to planning or preparing to minister. They point out how wonderfully God filled the mouth of Peter when he responded to the Sanhedrin's threatening interrogation saying, *"We must obey God rather than men"* (Ac 5:29). We see a holy boldness in his words as he speaks of Jesus to this angry and powerful council.

"Why," say those who despise planning, "should we prepare in our own flesh for a sermon, as if our efforts could add anything to what God wants to say through us?"

But look at the circumstances of Acts 5. The apostles had been taken by the soldiers who found them preaching and teaching in the temple, having miraculously escaped from prison during the night. Peter did not know he would be preaching to the Sanhedrin that day. He did not prepare what he would say.

Peter was, however, prepared. God had made his heart and mind ready. Perhaps Peter had prepared himself through prayer while he awaited his deliverance there in prison.

Preparing one's heart before preaching is certainly as important, and even more important, than preparing a message. God can give us a message in an instant when we need it, and our hearts are right before him.

Acts 5 does teach us much. There is no question, God wants us to lean on him, to trust him, to acknowledge him in all our ways, and to recognize his hand in all that happens. There is a genuine danger that we might become so impressed with our own abilities to minister and to plan logically how to motivate people, that we will forget who is actually doing the spiritual work, attaining for his own glory the spiritual effects that result from our feeble efforts.

However, Jesus spent three years preparing the twelve. God has given us the Word with which to prepare ourselves and to prepare how we will minister. Our Creator has given us intellects. What better use have we of our intellects than to prepare well for ministry? God trusts us to do our part, using what he has given us.

Some Verses in "Proverbs" Concern Planning

Proverbs 15:22 says, *Plans fail for lack of counsel, but with many advisers they succeed.* This verse speaks mainly of seeking counsel. But it clearly favors planning.

Proverbs 16:9 tells us, *In his heart a man plans his course, but the Lord determines his steps.* Proverbs 19:21. *Many are the plans in a man's heart, but it is the Lord's purpose that prevails.*

These verses do not tell us to live without plans. They simply remind us, our plans are not sovereign. God is sovereign. We do well to bring God into our planning by asking him to give us his plans. His ways are better than our ways. If our plans are in conflict with his, he will make adjustments.

Proverbs 16:25: *There is a way that seems right to a man, but in the end it leads to death.* This verse warns us that we cannot be saved by simply doing good and avoiding evil. Such a plan of salvation seems right to men, but it leads to the second death, eternal damnation. We can only be saved by trusting in the saving work of Jesus on the cross.

This verse does not refer to planning in the general sense, but to devising our own scheme for saving ourselves from eternal ruin.

Proverbs 20:24. *A man's steps are directed by the Lord. How then can anyone understand his own way?* The apparent meaning of this verse is this: No one can understand the path he is walking, because God is directing us as we take steps.

Here again, we are not told to avoid planning. Each of us has discovered that things happen to us, as we walk with the Lord, things that we cannot fit intelligently into the general direction we believe we are taking. Only God knows fully what is happening. He directs our steps, even when we cannot see what that step should be. But just as God has made plans for our salvation, and just as he has spelled out his plans for man in the Bible, so we should determine what it is God is leading us to do for his glory. We his children should also plan. With his guidance we should plan how we can best cooperate with him to achieve his plan for man.

If we ask him, he will show us how we can best co-labor with him for the salvation of an unreached people. This goal is worth careful and prayerful planning.

Proverbs 20:18: *Make plans by seeking advice; if you wage war, obtain guidance.* Here we are told how to make plans. It is clearly implied that making plans is good or wise.

Proverbs 18:9 teaches us we need to be industrious. *One who is slack in his work is brother to one who destroys.* If you recognize planning as a good and virtuous activity, then you must admit lack of planning is a form of slackness. It is akin to destruction!

Proverbs speaks directly about study, or research, a basic part of planning. *The heart of the discerning acquires knowledge; the ears of the wise seek it out* (18:15).

It is not good to have zeal without knowledge, nor to be hasty and miss the way (19:2).

Determination Helps us Succeed

And from the days of John the Baptist until now the kingdom of heaven suffers violence, and violent men take it by force (Mt. 11:12). Jesus is encouraging us here to be determined. Determination and planning go hand in hand. Planning is evidence of determination.

Should a Missionary Study Administration?

Yes!   The missionary should enter into the glorious enterprise of evangelism by preparing to do it well. Worldlings are eager to make plans in their efforts to gain money.   They have proved planning is effective. Let us be just as eager to plan, as we join the Lord to make disciples.

We study administration to learn how to make plans, and to learn how to use well the resources of time and money God will give us, and how to delegate responsibilities to people whom he will eventually assign to help us

Questions
on
Chapter 3

1. Here's what we learn from meditating on Acts 5:

    A. Peter did not prepare what he would say to the Sanhedrin, but God had made his heart and mind ready.
    B. Perhaps Peter had prepared himself through prayer while he awaited his deliverance there in prison.
    C. Preparing one's heart before preaching is certainly as important, and even more important, than preparing a message. God can give us a message in an instant when we need it, and our hearts are right before him.
    D. Preparing a message is an act of distrust of the Holy Spirit, who is able to fill our mouths with his words and our hearts with his desires and our minds with his thoughts.

2. Proverbs 16:9. *In his heart a man plans his course, but the Lord determines his steps.* Proverbs 19:21. *Many are the plans in a man's heart, but it is the Lord's purpose that prevails.* These verses teach us:

    A. It is unscriptural to make plans.
    B. God is sovereign. If our plans conflict with his, he will make adjustments.
    C. Our plans are not sovereign.
    D. We do well to bring God into our planning by asking him to give us his plans.

Chapter 4

Priorities for Your Life

Priorities Based on the Word of God

Priorities are important ideas or responsibilities. Some priorities are higher, or more important, than others. Let us consider the three most important responsibilities of the Christian.

Our Highest Priority, Our Relationship with God

Even unsaved persons will admit their highest priority, their greatest need, is to be properly related to God. They realize God has something against them. They often sense they are enemies of God. They try to do good, hoping to earn their salvation. Of course, we know they cannot be saved by works, but only by grace received through faith.

Some unsaved persons even realize they need to surrender fully to God. They generally realize they need God, or easily come to realize this when taught. Even for them, he is their first or highest priority.

As a Christian you already have a relationship with God. Every believer has received this relationship as a gift, through believing in Jesus and what he did on the cross. For the Christian, developing that relationship is the highest priority. When he believed, his desire to do good greatly increased.

The Christian worships God. He reads and studies the Bible. He prays. He fellowships with other believers. He obeys God. He knows he is God's friend, God's child. He wants to enjoy continuous fellowship with God. He is led by the Holy Spirit.

The Christian is not perfect. He sins less often and less grievously than he used to. He repents quickly confessing to the Lord, who is then faithful to forgive him, and to cleanse him from all unrighteousness (1Jn. 1:9).

The believer's good works will be rewarded in heaven. However, no one can attain heaven as a result of his own good works. Only the work of Jesus on the cross can pay for our sin and merit heaven for us.

The unsaved person yearns for self-esteem. He finds it difficult to like himself. The believer finds his self-esteem in God, especially in worship. There is no peace, no joy, no self-satisfaction as deep and meaningful as that found in worshiping the Lord.

Our relationship with God is our first or highest priority as Christians, or even as humans. We cannot be fully human, enjoying all God intended for us when he created Adam, without worshiping the living God. We cannot worship God without a loving relationship with him. We cannot have that relationship without repenting of sin and accepting the gift of eternal life which Jesus earned for us on the cross.

Jesus was asked which commandment is the greatest. *"The most important one,"* he answered, *"is this: 'Hear, O Israel, the Lord our God, the Lord is one. Love the Lord your God with all your heart and with all your soul and with all your mind and with all your strength'"* (Mk. 12:29-31).

Our Second Highest Priority is Our Relationship with Our Family

Paul told Timothy he must not appoint a leader who does not manage his family well.

1 Tim. 3:2-5. *Now the overseer must be above reproach, the husband of but one wife, temperate, self-controlled, respectable...not violent but gentle, not quarrelsome, not a lover of money. He must manage his own family well and see that his children obey him with proper respect. (If anyone does not know how to manage his own family, how can he take care of God's church?)*

Clearly, our relationship with our families is a higher priority than our ministries! The highest family relationship and the greatest challenge for us concerning this priority is our relationship with our wives. Thank God, for he has graciously made this relationship simple. He has not made it easy, but it is not complicated.

Husbands, love your wives, just as Christ loved the church and gave himself up for her to make her holy, cleansing her by the washing with water through the word, and to present her to himself as a radiant church, without stain or wrinkle or any other blemish, but holy and blameless. In this same way, husbands ought to love their wives as their own bodies (Eph. 5:20-28).

Husband, if you meditate on these verses, you will see exactly how to treat your wife. This will cause her to know beyond all doubt that you truly love her. A loved wife is a contented wife, and one who is easily "managed."

God created men and women with similar emotional and intellectual abilities and responses. However men tend to be more influenced by logic or reason. Women tend to be more sensitive to emotional influences. Men cannot as readily integrate logical and emotional aspects of a problem. Women cannot as readily separate the two. Men are less sensitive to the spiritual realm. Women more readily receive revelation from the Lord. Men must learn to share their feelings with their wives. Wives value feelings highly and share them more readily. A man will be offended by harsh criticism, but will recover quickly. His wife has a different emotional structure and will suffer more deeply and longer.

By nature, the husband initiates and the wife responds. Yet both can and should do both.

The husband needs to work at his relationship with his wife. He is the head. The responsibility is his, more than his wife's. The wife naturally responds to the treatment she receives from her husband. Both have free will, but each has a different emotional and intellectual response to the same stimulus.

A wife wants to be cared for, nurtured, loved. She is artistic. She is perceptive. She is intelligent. She finds contentment in a loving submission to a loving husband who appreciates her, one who honors and respects her.

Husbands should encourage their wives to be artistic. They should help them choose avenues of development that will cause them to be more fulfilled and more able to minister.

A man should encourage his wife to use her talents. He should free her to use her gifts. He should relieve her of tasks so she can investigate, minister in new ways, follow the Lord's leading.

The husband who will do these things will have a joyful, loving wife. That will be her natural response. *He who loves his wife, loves himself* (Eph. 5:28).

Husbands make a tragic mistake when they demand that their wives submit to them. First of all, a wife's submission is between her and the Lord. God does not ask the husband to make his wife submit. Secondly, both are commanded to submit to one another in Ephesians 5:21, before wives are told about submission in the next verse.

From Ephesians chapter 5 we can see God intends for a woman who is in ministry, not only to be in submission to her husband, but to love her husband and to consider her second priority to be, not her ministry, but her relationship with her husband and her children.

Because of her emotional structure, submission is very difficult for a wife who doubts her husband's love. She naturally responds to his carelessness with coldness and resentment. Yet she is sinning when she does, for God commands us to give of ourselves, unconditionally (Eph. 5:21, 22, 25, 33).

God uses our relationships to form us, more than any other element of our lives. He uses the spousal relationship more than any other.

If you are single, God wants you also to be in right relationship with your family, your parents and your siblings. Seek the counsel of your pastor if you are unsure of how to relate to these loved ones, and to others among your extended family. Rules of conduct vary from culture to culture, but all must honor their parents. Tradition can show us how to do that.

Even the married leader has responsibilities toward his or her parents and parental family. But God's instruction to leave one's family and to cleave to one's spouse must be understood as vitally important, and followed with love, gentleness and firmness.

This Problem Can Ruin Your Marriage

We speak now to the husband, either missionary or other minister. However, what we say here will apply considerably to the wife who is in ministry, also.

Missionary husband, if you have come to believe your ministry is as important as your relationship with your wife, take counsel before you go any further. This writer can virtually promise you, your mistake will take a heavy toll, especially on your wife and children, but also on you.

Your ministry might not be affected so much. God can use one weak minister as well as another, and all of us are weak. A successful ministry does not indicate that your family is in God's order.

If your family is out of order, others learning from you will produce the same sad results. Just as many children grow to repeat the sins of their parents, so many spiritual children repeat the sins of their spiritual leaders. You and they will perpetuate this disorder through the children and the children's children. Along this branching trail, many wives will suffer deep emotional and psychological scars, and some will find solace in the sinful embrace of another man who at least seems to honor them for the treasure hidden within them.

Take counsel first of all from the Holy Spirit. See what he will say to you as you meditate, with open heart and mind, on the verses we have referred to above. Pray over Ephesians 5:19-33.

God First, Spouse Second, Ministry Third

Does this subtitle above make sense to you? Or do you believe that, because your wife loves the Lord, she must be content with a husband whom God "requires" to love her less than a businessman must love his wife. A businessman or a common laborer must love his wife more than he loves his work. But must you, because of the sanctity of your call, love your work as much as, or more than, your wife? You cannot find that in the Bible!

God loves you. He wants your heart. He can do very nicely with less of your service. He loves the Church and gave himself for her. He commands you to see the parallel between this and your love for your wife. He never has said to you, "Love your ministry as I love the Church." That comparison is reserved for your wife. Love her as Christ loves the Church (Eph 5:25).

What has been happening is this. You have become infatuated with the ministry God has given you. You desire the uplift, the excitement God has placed in ministry for anyone who will receive his inspiration and pour it out freely on hungry souls. Perhaps you are unaware of the selfishness in your own heart.

It is a terrible thing when a man of God is seduced into thinking God wants him to abandon the deep emotional needs of his wife and children. He who disregards even just the physical needs of his family has denied the faith and is worse than an infidel (1 Tim. 5:8)!

But God never intended that you receive your self-esteem from your work. That comes from him, as you worship him and obey him. Obey him in what he tells you about loving your spouse and your children. You will see the difference in them, and in you, and yes, even in your ministry.

Your Third Priority is Your Ministry

It is possible for a man to miss God's truth badly concerning loving his wife, and yet minister to others wonderfully, with the unction of the Holy Spirit. But no disobedient minister has a right to expect that. Peter clearly warns us even our prayers will be hindered (1 Pet. 3:7).

Your ministry will flourish all the more, if you're ministering from a position of strength because your house is built upon the solid Rock. With love, peace and joy reigning at home, you will be free to concentrate on the issues of ministry with an untroubled mind... and heart!

Your ministry is important. Being your third priority does not mean you can neglect it. It is not acceptable for a missionary to be consistently so absorbed with chores at home that he has only shreds of time to give to his ministry. In consultation with his wife and perhaps with his children, he needs to explore how this problem can be resolved. It probably grew out of the difficult time of arriving at his mission field, and the stress of first adjustments. But it must not continue beyond what is needful.

The missionary is called to lay down his life for his new-found friends (Jn. 15:13) in the culture of his adoption. We deal with this in our section on strategy. The missionary is called to make disciples of individuals of an ethnic group for whom churches do not exist (Mt. 28:18-20).

You are being trained for front-line participation in the greatest enterprise on the face of the earth! Give it your best. Pray sincerely, because everything depends upon God's anointing. Work diligently because God has entrusted to you this wonderful task.

Questions
on
Chapter 4

1. Some fundamentals:

    A. Our good works will be rewarded in heaven
    B. no one can attain heaven as a result of his own good works.
    C. Worship is an exception and merits heaven for the worshiper.
    D. Only the work of Jesus on the cross can pay for our sin and merit heaven for us.

2. Concerning our highest priority:

    A. Our relationship with God is our first or highest priority as Christians, or even as humans.
    B. Worship of false gods entitles the worshiper to God's mercy.
    C. We cannot have a relationship with God without repenting of sin and accepting the gift of eternal life which Jesus earned for us on the cross.
    D. We cannot be fully human, enjoying all God intended for us when he created Adam, without worshiping the living God.

3. Our second priority:

    A. A man or woman with a God ordained pastoral ministry must consider that ministry his second priority once his congregation becomes large.
    B. A man or woman with a God ordained prophetic ministry must consider that ministry his second priority if his prophetic activities take most of his time.
    C. A man or woman with a God ordained apostolic ministry must consider that ministry his second priority.
    D. A man or woman must consider his or her spouse (and children) his second priority.

4.   In Ephesians 5 we learn:

    A.   Husbands are to love their wives, even though their wives do wrong things.

    B.   Husbands are to demand that their wives eliminate wrong-doing from their lives.

    C.   Since wives value most the time their husbands spend with them, husbands must spend adequate time with their wives.

    D.   If a wife is discontent, her husband should take time out from his ministry to learn from the Lord, both directly and through his wife, what he needs to do to change things.

5.   About husbands…

    A.   Husbands are required to love their wives more than their jobs unless they are in "full-time ministry."

    B.   God has different rules for husbands in ministry.

    C.   Husbands are commanded to love their ministries as Christ loved the Church.

    D.   Husbands are commanded to love only their wives as Christ loved the Church.

6.   With love, peace and joy reigning at home, you will be free to concentrate on the issues of ministry with an untroubled mind… and heart!

    A.   It is not acceptable for a missionary to be consistently so absorbed with chores at home that he has only shreds of time to give to his ministry

    B.   Your ministry is only your third priority, so it's not very important.

    C.   The missionary is called to lay down his life for his new-found friends (Jn. 15:13) in the culture of his adoption.

    D.   Pray sincerely about your ministry because everything depends upon God's anointing.

Chapter 5

God Has Been Preparing You

What has He Been Preparing You for?

Are you uncertain of your calling? Are you unsure of what God has planned for you to do?

Man's steps are directed by the Lord (Pr. 20:24). Ask the Holy Spirit to help you look back and see how the Lord has been directing you. He has been preparing you for your ministry. He will use, for his glory and for your success in ministry, everything in your past.

Many have looked into their past and felt a confirming touch of the Lord regarding their future. Perhaps you would benefit by such a review.

Before you look back, read James 1:5-8. Then ask God for the wisdom spoken of there in his Word, and believe as James exhorts us to believe.

Elements in your past that you might prayerfully examine should include these. Perhaps you should make notes under these headings as part of your examination.

1. **Your birth and upbringing.** You are to a great extent a combination of the qualities God has built into your parents. You learned things from your parents. Is there anything about your parents, or in the way they raised you, that shows you what God has been preparing you for?
2. **Your education and training.** Do these indicate what sort of ministry God has been preparing you for? You are studying how to be a successful missionary. Has God led you to this study? Does your participation in this training seem to be a reason for believing God wants you to be a missionary? List what your education has been, and what you feel God might be showing you through this.
3. **Your supernatural and natural gifts** can be clues that help you decide what God has been preparing you for. Paul wrote

to Timothy, *Do not neglect your gift, which was given you through a prophetic message when the body of elders laid their hands on you* (1 Tim. 4:14). List the gifts of the Holy Spirit (1 Cor. 12:8-11) in which God has used you.

Include other gifts mentioned in Romans 12:6-8, Ephesians 4:11 and 1 Peter 4:10, 11. Of all these ministry gifts, has God been using you in any? Has he been in some way pointing you toward any of them?

Mechanical abilities, writing and musical skills, are examples of natural gifts. They are special talents for which you might have some natural or acquired facility. If you realize God has gifted you in any of these ways, write that down under natural gifts.

4. **Your experience.** God will use everything in your past. List the experiences that come to mind as influences in your life that God might use. In 1 Samuel 17:34-54 we read that, when young David killed a lion and a bear he was being prepared by God to trust the Lord to give him victory against Goliath. Those experiences prepared David to volunteer to defeat the giant.

David had no experience with the heavy armor King Saul offered him, so David decided to use only his sling. He knew from experience how to use that. God uses our experience from the past to direct our steps in the present.

5. **Your interests.** These are things you like to do, or might like if you tried them. Taken together they might point to ways in which you might serve God now or in the future, ways that you believe would be interesting or challenging and exciting. Write down what these are. Then see if two or more of them do point to any particular sort of service for the Lord. Write that down.
6. **Closely related to interests are desires.** Do you have a desire to serve the Lord in some particular way?

Many believers make the mistake of believing their desires are totally selfish, and are not a reflection of what God wants for their lives. This can be true in some cases, but not always. A person called to the mission field, for example, might think himself not mature spiritually, and therefore unworthy of such a calling. No one is worthy of any form of

78

spiritual ministry. No one is worthy of being the Lord's hands extended toward those in need.

The gifts of the Holy Spirit are not for those who have deserved or earned them. No one can meet that standard. All fall short! But gifts are given. They are free. They are not merited by spiritual maturity. They are simply received, the way a child receives a gift.

Maturity itself is not a gift. Maturity is earned. We learn patience, for example, by practicing patience in trying circumstances. The fruit of the Spirit (Gal. 5:22, 23) in a believer shows him or her to be mature. Love, joy, peace and patience are developed as we obey the Lord.

Is there a type of Christian ministry you often find yourself dreaming about? Do you think you would love to be used by the Lord in that way? This is quite possibly the very thing God has implanted in your heart to lean toward. Your desires can be a very revealing bit of evidence of what God is preparing you for!

Your desires are not a certain or absolute sign of what God is doing. But he does say, *Delight yourself in the Lord and he will give you the desires of your heart* (Ps. 37:4). Write down those desires.

7. **Things or people?** Each of us is either more comfortable working with things, or with people. Which are you? Do you prefer working with things, or with people? Or are the two about equal for you?

If you prefer working with people, this indicates you are more naturally inclined toward ministry that involves direct contact with people. Perhaps you are to be involved in one of the five ministries in Ephesians 4:11.

If you prefer working with things, you are more inclined toward positions in which other people are not involved, or not so directly. Such a person might be an effective researcher or an expert accountant in a church or a mission agency. As a person who works with things, you will be important to any organization, large or small. Your work is a valid ministry.

A believer caring for the children of missionaries gives physical and spiritual nurture to those children. Such a person needs to be people oriented more than things oriented.

Let us say a man named Sam takes a position, a job, with a Christian organization, because he knows God has called him to this work. He is a believer, and wants to glorify God through his employment. He is paid every week.

His work is not preaching or teaching or evangelizing. He works with a broom and a scrubbing brush. Is Sam ministering when he goes about his daily chores?

If you ask Sam what he is doing you might find out how well Sam understands he is ministering. If Sam says, "I'm scrubbing this floor" then you have some reason to believe he doesn't realize the full impact of his work.

If Sam responds, "I'm helping reach the Muslims in Iraq with the gospel," you will know Sam is aware he is in fact ministering to the Muslims. He understands that his work is not "people oriented," but it is helping his organization fulfill its mission to bring Jesus to the Muslims. The simple fact is, the organization cannot function for long without Sam's role.

Ministry is often a matter of being called, and of having a ministry attitude. Is this not why Paul refers to a ministry of serving (Rom. 12:7)?

Whether you are oriented more toward people or things, God can of course call you to minister to people. However, if you do prefer to work with things, and God is calling you to minister to people, ask him to show you how you can be more effective in communicating with people. Ask him to give you more joy in working with people.

Then, take advantage of every opportunity to interact with people. Work with God in this way, to build up your confidence in the Lord's ability to help you become more people oriented.

And in the church God has appointed first of all apostles, second prophets, third teachers, then workers of miracles, also those having gifts of healing, those able to help others, those with gifts of administration, and those speaking in different kinds of tongues (1 Cor. 12:28).

Questions
on
Chapter 5

1. *Man's steps are directed by the Lord* (Pr. 20:24)

   A. When you ask God for wisdom, don't assume you have it. Wait until God shows you that you have it.
   B. Ask the Holy Spirit to help you look back and see how the Lord has been directing you.
   C. God has been preparing you for your ministry. He will use, for his glory and for your success in ministry, everything in your past.
   D. Ask God for the wisdom spoken of in James 1:5-8, and believe as James exhorts us to believe.

2. About the decision to become a missionary...

   A. Many believers have desires for ministry that seem to them to be totally selfish, and not a reflection of what God wants for their lives. However, these desires may very well be God's way of calling such believers into ministry.
   B. A person called to the mission field might think himself or herself too immature spiritually, and therefore unworthy of such a calling. The fact is, no one is worthy of any form of spiritual ministry.
   C. The gifts of the Holy Spirit are only for those who have deserved or earned them.
   D. The gifts of the Holy Spirit are received the way a child receives a gift.

3. People oriented or things oriented?

   A. If you prefer working with people, this indicates you are more naturally inclined toward ministry that involves direct contact with people. Perhaps you are to be involved in one of the five ministries in Ephesians 4:11

B. If you prefer working with things, you are more inclined toward positions in which other people are not involved, or not so directly. Such a person might be an effective researcher or an expert accountant in a church or a mission agency.

C. A believer caring for the children of missionaries gives physical and spiritual nurture to those children. Such a person needs to be people oriented more than things oriented.

D. If you are people oriented you will fall behind in your work. You will spend too much time with people.

Chapter 6

Four Steps Toward Managing Your Time

Should You Manage Your Time?

At this time in your life you may feel no need to manage your time. If you are required to follow a time schedule designed by someone else, your time is being managed for you. Don't discard the ideas you find in this chapter. You will probably need at least some of them later on.

If you make decisions for yourself about how you will use all or part of your time, this chapter will help you use time much more efficiently. Someone described it as "not working harder, but smarter."

Some disciples of the Lord say, "I have lived many years of my life without these ideas. I don't want to change now."

This can be a mistake. Why not be more "business-like" about time? What do you have to lose? You might gain a whole new understanding of how to be effective in your work for God!

As you try these ideas you will see ways to make them work better for you by changing them either slightly or greatly. Don't hesitate to change them so they serve you better.

If you try a particular idea, and after seeing what it can do for you, you decide not to use it at all, don't discard it forever. Keep notes about it, or keep your copy of this book. You will want to try some ideas again later, when your ministry becomes more complex.

Goals

A goal is anything you want to accomplish. Without goals we don't get much done. As soon as you decide there is a particular thing you want to accomplish, either to enlarge the kingdom or to improve your ability to minister, you will feel a desire to accomplish that goal.

In studying about goals, you should keep in mind that at some time, perhaps not now but in the future, God is going to send you helpers to make you more effective in your ministry. Try to keep this in mind as you work through the remainder of this book.

A goal, to be most useful to you and your team, must have three qualities.

1. A goal must be written.

If today the Lord gives you a wonderful idea in your prayer time, write it down. You will probably not remember it two days from now. We forget many ideas we receive, in a few hours!

If you realize right now that there is something you want to accomplish, either this week or in the distant future, write it down now. Write it in a good place where you can always find it easily. Arrange now to store such ideas in an orderly way, so you can find any one of them later as needed.

A goal must be committed to writing.

2. A goal must be clear.

In any team sport, every member of the team knows what the goal is. Every member of your ministry team should be just as well-informed about your team's goal or goals. You and your team must write your goals in words that make the goal clear to every member. Questions from the team usually mean the goal needs more clarity.

If a stranger walks into your office and reads your goals, he should know exactly what you are trying to accomplish.

3. A goal must be measurable.

The most difficult quality of a well-written goal is this one. Your team should always know how close they are to completing the task, to achieving the goal. This can usually be done by using numbers and a target date within the goal.

For example, this is **not** a measurable goal: We will evangelize the Motos people group.

This **is** a measurable goal: We will lead 200 Motos to the Lord by February 31. At any time, as we continue working to achieve this goal, we can determine how much remains to be accomplished, and how much time we have in which to accomplish it.

Here is a poorly written personal goal: I will learn to speak Spanish.

Here is one way that goal can be made clearer and measurable: I will score 80% or higher in every chapter test, and finish the "Say It in Spanish" beginners textbook by August 1.

Rewrite These Goals Making Each One Clear and Measurable

If you decide any of these is already clear and measurable, write "OK."

1. From now on, we will try to keep bits of paper off the sanctuary floor.
2. I want to improve my typing speed.
3. We will buy new carpeting and install it in the sanctuary by April 15.
4. Grades 7 through 9 will learn about missions in Sunday School during October.
5. We will spend time Sunday morning learning about one unreached people group and praying for them to be reached.

Take time now to rewrite each goal that needs improvement. Then compare your answers with what follows here. Do not read the following until you have written your answers.

****

Now compare your answers with these. Your answers might be different, and still be correct, even better than the ones below.

1. During September we, the deacons in charge, will take turns appealing to the congregation on Wednesday nights, asking

them to pick up scraps of litter they see on the floor as they leave the church after each service.

2. I will get my typing speed up to 35 words per minute by July 4.
3. OK. [This goal is clear and measurable as it is. More decisions are required. Team members must be delegated tasks so this goal can be achieved. We deal with delegation later.]
4. Each teacher of grades 7 through 9 will submit for committee approval, both a list of mission topics he or she will teach during October, and a written test on which the class will achieve an average of 80% or higher.

[If this goal requires planning, it is better to incorporate that fact: "The following committee of three will devise a plan by which..."]

5. Albert will appoint an elder each week during January and February to take five minutes on Sunday morning to tell the congregation about one unreached people, and to lead the flock in prayer for that people group.

Get Help with Making Plans

Have you been wondering whether you should be doing something different? Have you been considering steps toward becoming a missionary? Are there any goals you have been thinking about achieving?

Pray about the thoughts you have been pondering. Ask God to show you his plans, his goals for your life, or perhaps just for this year.

Once you have reason to believe God wants you to "lean" in a particular direction or goal, you need to take some sort of action. You need to take steps toward achieving what God has shown you. Always keep in mind: God might clarify what he wants, or he might redirect you at any time. If he does, praise him and follow his leading. What looks to us like a change in God's direction might actually be evidence of a mistake we had made in discerning the leading of the Lord. In any case, the Lord is glorified and pleased with us when are hearts are genuinely focused on him, and on following him.

For major decisions, it is wise to seek counsel. Pr.15:22: *Plans fail for lack of counsel, but with many advisers they succeed.* Pr.12:15: *The way of a fool seems right to him, but a wise man listens to advice.* Pr.19:20: *Listen to advice and accept instruction, and in the end you will be wise.* Pr.20:5: *The purposes of a man's heart are deep waters, but a man of understanding draws them out.* Pr.20:18: *Make plans by seeking advice; if you wage war, obtain guidance.*

Here are Four Steps that will Help You Manage Your Time.

1. Plan what goals you will work on during the next many months, and decide during which week or weeks you will spend some time working on each of your goals. Illustration 3 shows you a form you can use to do this. We explain more, later.
2. Plan how you will spend your time for the coming week. Illustration 4 shows you a form for this purpose. We explain more, later.
3. Plan how you will spend your time tomorrow. Your weekly plan, using a form like the one in Illustration 4, shows you how you thought you would be spending each day. But after working through your plan for any one day, you will realize you want to change your plan for the next day. See Illustrations 5 and 6 for forms you might use to re-plan one day. More about this later.
4. Use the "Block Plan" for deciding what you will do during a "block" of time you discover you have not planned for. For example, if you normally attend a class for three hours on Saturdays, and the class is canceled, you have three hours during which you can achieve some things you hadn't planned doing. The "Block Plan" will help you organize to accomplish the greatest results during such a "block" of time.

Illustration
3

Calendar Chart

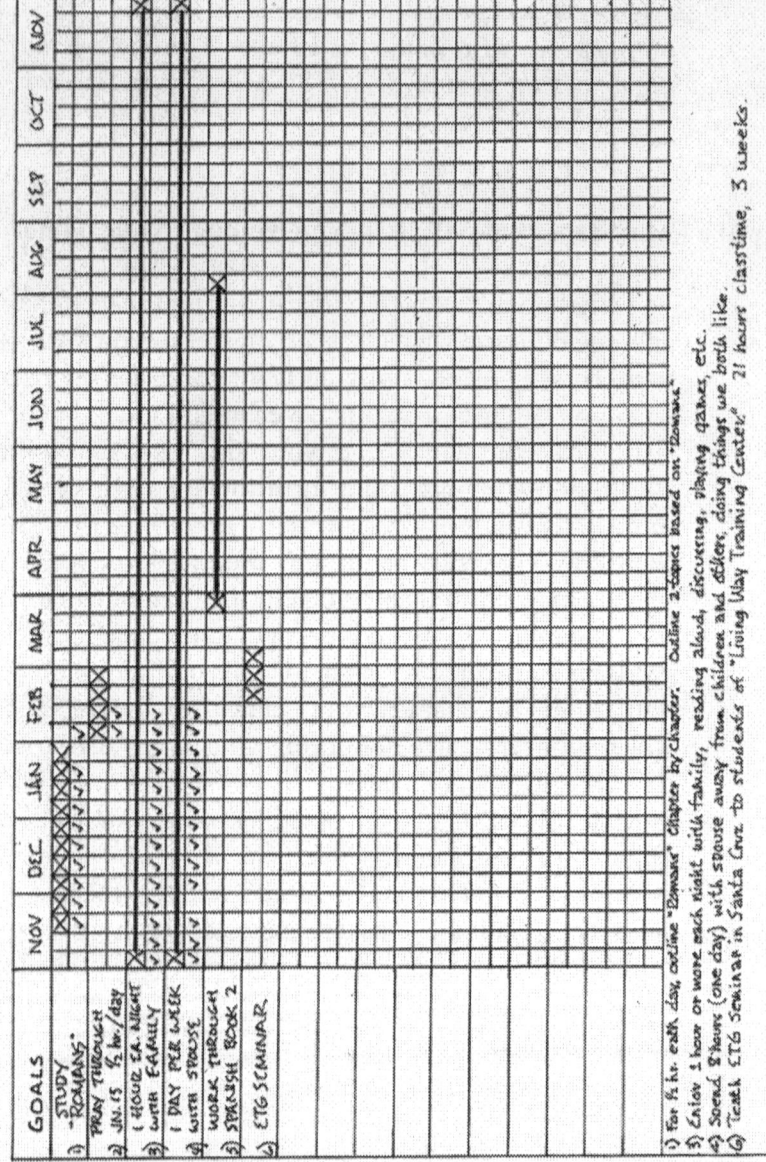

GOALS	NOV	DEC	JAN	FEB	MAR	APR	MAY	JUN	JUL	AUG	SEP	OCT	NOV
1) STUDY "ROMANS"	⊠⊠	✓✓✓✓	⊠⊠✓										
2) PRAY THROUGH JAN.15 ½ hr./day	⊠	✓✓✓✓	✓✓	⊠⊠									
3) 1 HOUR EA. NIGHT WITH FAMILY	⊠	✓✓✓✓✓	✓✓✓✓✓										
4) 1 DAY PER WEEK WITH SPOUSE	⊠	✓✓✓✓✓	✓✓✓✓✓										
5) WORK THROUGH SPANISH BOOK 2	✓✓	✓✓		⊠⊠	⊠								
6) ETG SEMINAR						⊠			⊠				

1) For ½ hr. each day, outline "Romans" chapter by chapter. Outline 2 topics based on "Romans."
3) Enjoy 1 hour or more each night with family; reading aloud, discussing, playing games, etc.
4) Spend 8 hours (one day) with spouse away from children and others, doing things we both like.
6) Teach ETG Seminar in Santa Cruz to students of "Living Way Training Center." 21 hours classtime, 3 weeks.

88

Illustration
4

Weekly Plan

Week of: Feb. 21

	SUN	MON	TUE	WED	THUR	FRI	SAT
6:00							
6:30		B I	B L E	S T U	D Y		
7:00	PRAY	THROUGH	JOHN	CHAPTER	15		
7:30							
8:00							
8:30			PREPARE	FOR	SEMINAR		
9:00		ETG	SEMINAR				
9:30							
10:00	C						
10:30	H						
11:00	U		WITH JOSEPH				
11:30	R		REGARD'S EVANGEL'M				
12:00	C						
12:30	H						
1:00							
1:30		ANSWER CORRES-			ANSWER		
2:00		POND'CE			CORRESP.		
2:30							
3:00	TEACH			VISIT RONGO		COUNSEL	
3:30	LEADERS					RAUL & STELLA	
4:00		MEET					
4:30		WITH					
5:00		HELPERS					
5:30		PLAN	FOR	TOMORROW		PLAN FOR NEXT WEEK	
6:00							
6:30							

You will be far busier than it appears from this plan. Unexpected things will happen. You need to be free enough to be flexible.

Before planning for next week, glance at your Calendar Chart to see what tasks (if any) you planned to begin during next week. Plan on Friday to begin these tasks at specific times during next week, even if you can only find time to think about how you will go about achieving them.

Illustration
5

Daily Plan

Date: *Feb.* 23

6:30	*Bible study.*
7:00	*Pray through John* 15.
7:30	
8:00	
8:30	*Prepare for seminar.*
9:00	*Seminar.*
9:30	
10:00	
10:30	
11:00	*Joseph / evangelism.*
11:30	
12:00	
12:30	
1:00	
1:30	*With Alice re: new responsibilities.*
2:00	
2:30	
3:00	*Phone Occidental re: coverage for helpers.* 555-0021.
3:30	
4:00	*Interview Bill and Susan Kalou for admission to mission course.*
4:30	
5:00	
5:30	*Review goals. Revise plan for tomorrow.*
6:00	
6:30	
7:00	
7:30	*Family time. Discuss our plan for Saturday. Pray / Bible.*
8:00	
8:30	
9:00	
9:30	
10:00	

Notes:

Illustration
6

Daily Plan

Date: *Feb.* 23

Time from / to:		
6:30	7:00	Bible study.
7:00	7:30	Pray through John 15.
8:30	9:00	Prepare for seminar.
9:00	10:30	Seminar.
11:00	11:30	Joseph / evangelism.
1:30	2:30	With Alice re: new responsibilities
3:00		Phone Occidental re: coverage for helpers. 555-0021.
4:00	5:30	Interview Bill and Susan Kalou for admiss to miss course.
5:30	6:00	Review goals. Revise plan for tomorrow.
7:30	9:30	Family time. Discuss our plan for Sat. Pray / Bible.

Notes

The "Block Plan"

You will probably find this plan the most helpful in your present circumstances, unless your day is complicated with many activities.

You might need to put aside for years what you will learn about the other aspects of planning, but you will surely use this "Block Plan."

Here are the simple steps for using the "Block Plan."

1. Make a list of the things you want to get done during the time available.
2. Prioritize this list. That is, place a numeral "1" in front of the task on your list you should do first. It might be first because it is most urgent, or most important. Or perhaps it is the most difficult or the least interesting, and you know how good it will feel to get it done!
3. Rewrite the list in priority order. In other words, write your number-one task first. Then your number-two task under that. Continue in this way with all the tasks. Draw a little box to the left of each task. This box draws your attention to the fact that this is something waiting for you to do.
4. Now get started on your number-one task. When it is finished, place a check mark in its box and begin task number two. Try to finish all the tasks in the available time.

Advantages of Using the "Block Plan"

After spending a few minutes creating your prioritized list, you will feel highly motivated to try to accomplish all the tasks on your list. For this reason alone, you will get more done!

When you begin working, you know exactly what you want to do first. Without a plan, you will often discover, after working for some time, there is a task which you have overlooked, and which must be done right away. Then you will have to turn to this other task with the unsettling feeling that you have not finished anything yet. You will feel disorganized and you will be less productive.

When you finish task number one, and place that check mark in the small box to the left of that task, even this small action causes you to feel good about your achievement! At the end of the available time, you will see a list of boxes checked off. This becomes a record of what you did that day. If you use this plan as your regular daily plan, it will be wise to use a book and date each day's list of goals. Records kept on loose bits of paper are not easy to access weeks later.

Some well-organized and productive workers use the "Block Plan" as their one and only planning method. Each evening they create a "Block Plan" that shows them how they will work tomorrow. This is not adequate for major decision makers, but might be sufficient for those who assist them.

It is always better to plan the evening before, what you will do the following day. Ask God to guide you. Planning your day as the day begins is unwise. Early morning emergencies arise and you will find yourself working all day, or even for some days, with no plan. You won't realize it for some time, but working this way causes problems for you, and others working with you. Your time is out of control. Some of your responsibilities are being neglected! You're not getting as much done.

The "Calendar Chart" is for Long-Range Planning.

The Calendar Chart, Illustration 3, allows you to list many goals down the left column, and to indicate during which weeks over the next many months you plan to work on each goal. An "X" shows you planned to work on that goal (to the left) during that week (numbered above) of that month (named above).

Each up-and-down column of small boxes represents one week. The Calendar Chart accommodates four weeks for each month. This is not precise but is adequate for long-range planning.

Notice the abbreviated goals in the left column. Notice the two side-by-side X's under the month November. These X's show you planned to study the Book of Romans during the 3rd and 4th weeks of November.

The check marks under the X's show you did study Romans during those third and fourth weeks of November.

Notice you planned to study Romans during every week of December and January. Did you follow this plan perfectly? No. There is no check mark for the last week of January. But you made up for that by studying Romans during the 1st week of February. Notice the check mark that indicates that.

For goal number 3, that long, horizontal, heavy line takes the place of X's. It saves time. Use a long series of X's if you prefer.

Why are there no check marks on the right half of the Chart? Either you were unable to continue with your goals, or those weeks have not arrived yet. If they haven't arrived, what week are we about to begin?

The answer is, the third week of February.

Notice the goals are written out in full at the bottom of the Chart. The expression "I will" is left out of each goal to save time and space.

Are the goals clear without that expression? Are the goals measurable? If these are personal goals for you only, you will probably understand your own abbreviations.

Advantages of Using the Calendar Chart

It relieves stress.

Let's say you have several goals you must achieve within the next so many months, or there will be unhappy consequences. Just the decision to give these goals your maximum effort during the selected weeks, when you will have more time, puts your mind at ease. Now you have good reason to believe you will achieve them.

Without such a chart, you will not know what you should be doing, or by what date you should accomplish anything! You don't know when you should begin working on each goal, in order to have them all reached by the deadline.

Perhaps your only deadlines are those you give yourself. God has put excitement in your heart about certain goals. You would like to achieve them but you lack the enthusiasm to begin. You plot on your Calendar

94

Chart when you will work on each. You choose weeks during which you will be less busy than most weeks. You allow enough weeks to realistically achieve each goal.

Now you have the joy of realizing you might be able to accomplish all these goals within so many months. This relieves the stress caused by the gnawing realization that there are important or helpful or interesting things you could do, but which you are not even starting to do because you haven't taken the first step!

The Chart is a constant reminder. When the time comes to begin working on goal number one, you will have been looking forward to it.

Once these things are assigned to weeks when it is most likely you will have some time to give to them, you become motivated. You work to get other things done so you can work on your goals. What was a vague wish has now become a probability!

The "Weekly Plan"

Blank copies of each of the forms we use in this study can be found at the end of this chapter. Do not write on these. Make enlarged copies which you will keep on file as "originals." Copy these as needed

Copy your "original" Weekly Plan. I will call this copy, "Alpha." On Alpha, fill in the things you must remember to do every day or every week. Alpha is now a sort of picture of your "standard week." Alpha shows you every task you must do every day and every task you must do every week. Do not write anything else on your Alpha.

Make a copy (Beta) of your Alpha every Friday and use it to plan the upcoming week. Now Beta shows you every task you know you will need to accomplish during the coming week. Other tasks will need to be done, but you will only find out what those are as the week goes on. For this reason, it's great to have lots of black spaces on your Beta.

You will often revise your standard week, so you will not need many copies of Alpha.

Beta, then, is your working plan for the coming week. Unexpected things will happen during the week. Some of these unexpected events will make it necessary for you to alter your plans for the remaining days of that week. To revise each of those remaining days, use the Daily Plan form.

Illustration 4 is an example of a completed Weekly Plan, the Beta. Notice that all the long-range goals you decided to work on this week, goals which you see on the Calendar Chart, have time assigned for them on the Weekly Plan. Verify this for yourself, so you will understand the Weekly Plan. Then answer these questions. The answers are given below.

1. What time is set aside for praying through John 15?
2. What time is for preparing to teach the ETG Seminar?
3. How long does the Seminar take on its closing day?
4. When will you revise your Weekly Plan for Wednesday*?
5. When will you plan for next week?

Here are the answers: 1. From 7 until 7:30 every morning.   2. From 8:30 until 9:00, Monday to Friday.   3. One hour.   4. Tuesday at 5:30 p.m., before quitting for the day.   5. Friday at 5:30 p.m.

*In question #4 above, you notice you can not expect to follow the Weekly Plan all week. Unexpected things happen. You will seldom find you can follow the entire plan, day after day without changes. One way to make these changes is to use another form we call the "Daily Plan." See Illustrations 5 and 6. Instead of trying to change the Weekly Plan for Tuesday, through Friday, plan again for Tuesday on Monday afternoon, using the Daily Plan form. Plan again for Wednesday on Tuesday afternoon, and continue in this way for the remainder of the week.

Planning over again for each of these days will be easy and quick, since your Weekly Plan and your Daily Plan for the day will show you most of what needs to be done during this week.

As you complete an activity make a check-mark through it either on your Beta, or on your Daily Plan sheet, so that with a single check-mark you are recording the fact that this activity was completed, and when it was done.

Am I a Failure if I Don't Do All These Things?

Leaders of even medium-size organizations deal with so much variety, they need to draw up a new plan at least each week.

If your work is very repetitive, week after week, you might need to make up only one Weekly Plan, and keep using it over and over for each week. If every day you repeat the same tasks, you might need only one Daily Plan. Eventually you will want to change it, but it will serve you well every day until you have it memorized and never need to look at it.

Don't be discouraged if you find you have failed badly to follow your Calendar Chart. Analyze why this happened. Try again either now or later. Perhaps you have underestimated the number of weeks you should assign to each goal.

As you try different ideas you will discover what works best for you in your situation.

If using any of these ideas helps you achieve even 10% more, it has served you well. It has made you more efficient. If worldlings use these techniques effectively to earn more wealth (and they do!) should we not try using these techniques to advance the kingdom of God?

Remember, if these forms are useless to you at this present stage of your life, keep them in mind for later, when your ministry might become much more demanding and you need to get much done in a short time.

Do You Already Realize You are Not Getting Enough Done?

Here are some ideas that will help. Remember, none of these methods will substitute for a close relationship with the Lord. None of these suggestions will ever be as important as spending time with him.

During worship, God can drop thoughts into your mind that will save you days of frustration and fruitless waste of energy.

The Lord is God. Him only will we serve! He is the center of our lives. Our efforts, however clever, are nothing if we are not walking in love with him.

Some Tasks are Important. Some are Urgent. Some are Both. Some are Neither!

Look at Illustration 7. Some tasks fit into box "A." That is to say, they are high in urgency and high in importance. In other words, they must be done soon, and if they are not done something bad will happen.

Some tasks belong in box "B." That means they are low in urgency but high in importance. In other words, they need not be done soon, but if they are not done something bad will happen.

Some tasks belong in box "C." These tasks must be done soon or it will be too late. But if they were not done at all, nothing very serious would result.

Some tasks fit into box "D." These are tasks that are neither very urgent nor very important. They do not need to be done right away, and if they were not done we could still succeed in our work.

Of course we all respond to "A" tasks. If something is both urgent and important, we focus on that task. Some "A" tasks should probably be delegated to able and responsible helpers.

Illustration

7

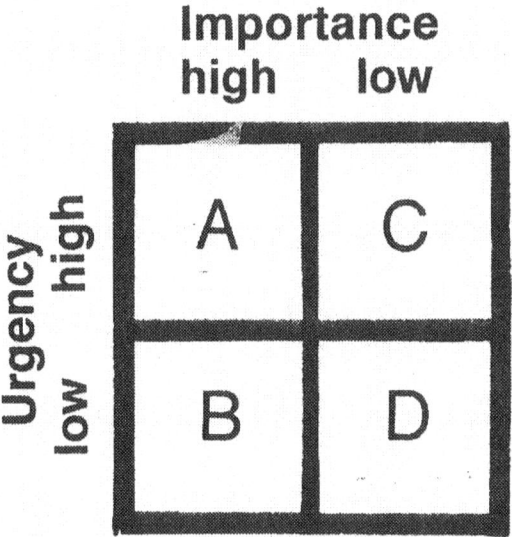

"B" tasks are often the ones leaders neglect. Box "B" includes long-range goals such as doing a study of 1 Corinthians. Bible study, and other self-improvement goals, seem to be the ones we can postpone because they don't need to be completed by the end of the week. But the fact is, these are the tasks only we can do! These are the tasks that will have a deep and lasting effect on our work as servants of the Lord! Examine "B" tasks carefully. Do not procrastinate on important tasks just because they do not seem urgent!

Set aside a portion of your day for these "B" tasks. Spend from 30 minutes to an hour three to five days each week. By the end of a month you will have accomplished much, on a goal that is very important.

Illustration

8

Pareto Principle

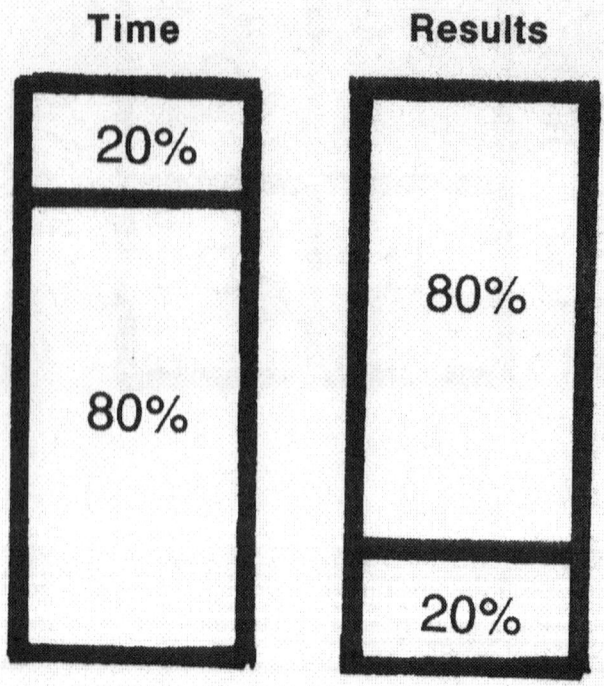

Time   **Results**

20% of your time produces 80% of your results.
80% of your time produces only 20% of your results.

The "Pareto Principle"

An Italian economist named Pareto claimed (Illustration 8) that we use
only 20 percent of our time on the tasks that produce 80 percent of our

results. We spend 80 percent of our time on tasks that produce only 20 percent of our results.

If we could spend less time on the less productive tasks, and more time on the most productive tasks, we would be more effective!

Some of the tasks we spend most time on should be assigned to a helper. This would free us to do more tasks that produce big results.

Perhaps some tasks should be dropped completely.

Ask the Lord what he wants you to do about this. Some of us want to continue tasks that are almost useless, either because in the past they were fruitful, or because we enjoy doing them!

The "Time Log" is for Serious Leaders Who Cannot Get Enough Done

Do you wish there were more hours in a day? Do you wonder where your time goes? See Illustration 9, the Time Log. Here is a form that will show you how you are spending your time. You will almost certainly find you are not spending it the way you think! You will see tasks that take much of your time, but which someone can do for you, releasing you to do the more important tasks.

On the Time Log you record briefly what you are working on, or doing, every fifteen minutes. Keep this up consistently for at least three days. A full week is better.

You need some sort of timer to alert you every fifteen minutes. Record only what you are doing at that very moment. Abbreviate as much as possible.

Illustration
9

Daily Time Log

Date: _____

TIME	A.M. Activity	BILLABLE	PRIORITY	PLANNED ACTIVITY	INTERRUPT.	P.M. Activity	BILLABLE	PRIORITY	PLANNED	INTERRUPT.
6:00										
6:15										
6:30										
6:45										
7:00										
7:15										
7:30										
7:45										
8:00										
8:15										
8:30										
8:45										
9:00										
9:15										
9:30										
9:45										
10:00										
10:15										
10:30										
10:45										
11:00										
11:15										
11:30										
11:45										
12:00										
12:15										
12:30										
12:45										
1:00										
1:15										
1:30										
1:45										
2:00										
2:15										
2:30										
2:45										
3:00										
3:15										
3:30										
3:45										
4:00										
4:15										
4:30										
4:45										
5:00										
5:15										
5:30										
5:45										
NOTES										

At the end of each half-day or day, fill in check-marks in the columns to the right. Use the categories A,B,C,D as shown on Illustration 7 in the column provided for that on the Time Log. Place a check mark in the next column if the activity was not on your plan. If the activity could be described as an interruption by someone else, and if these are too frequent, consider whether you could avoid such interruptions by setting up better procedure for office interaction.

If your work is hindered by these interruptions, perhaps you need to reorganize things a bit to avoid them. Where your office or your desk is located can be crucial. Very busy chief executive officers have someone screen their phone calls and office visitors. If these unplanned events are important, and only you should be handling them, perhaps you have enough qualified or trainable staff to take on some of your tasks, so you have time to handle the unplanned events.

When you finish the three or more Time Log days, add up the amounts of time you spent on things of the greatest importance, your "A" and your "B" activities. You might be surprised to notice you spend only 20% of your time on most important tasks. Add up the amount of time you spent on "C" activities, and the amount spent of "D" activities.

Add up the time for each of the other columns. Give serious thought to whether each activity is something you could delegate. When your Time Log experiment days are concluded, add up the time you would save if someone else had done those tasks you now recognize as possible to delegate.

Now you have the fruit of this experiment. You have analyzed how your time is being spent, based on those Time Log days. Perhaps you can now arrange to spend more of your time on high priority tasks that only you can or should be doing.

Later we will study "delegation." This is the skill of selecting and training persons to do specific tasks, or to shoulder specific responsibilities, under your supervision.

It takes a step of faith to trust a helper, especially if he or she is to be paid. You will perhaps think you do not have enough money. If God leads you to hire someone, he will provide for that. God intends that you bear fruit.

Why Do Many Spiritual Leaders Feel They Accomplish Little?

Are you discouraged because you are not getting your important tasks done? The "Time Log" will surprise you. You are doing things you don't need to do. What are they? You need to know! God **is** giving you enough time to do what he is asking you to do.

"Delegation" is treated in chapter 7. There you will learn how to get more done by trusting your helpers with tasks you should assign to them.

Don't Let Valuable Ideas Slip Through Your Fingers

Perhaps you have discovered some ideas you want to use. Don't lose track of these ideas. Write down enough about them now, or be sure you have marked them in this book clearly, so you won't forget them. As you worship the Lord, he will show you more.

Often our best worship times are those we voluntarily take, pulling our heads out of what we're doing, relaxing in the presence of Jesus, and focusing on him. During these moments he sometimes gives us our most creative ideas about how to improve our ways of doing things.

Chapter 6
Questions

1. About administration:

   A. As you try these ideas you will see ways to make them work better for you by changing them either slightly or greatly.
   B. Don't change or adapt these ideas. They won't work as well if you do.
   C. If you try a particular idea, and after seeing what it can do for you, you decide not to use it, don't discard it forever. Keep notes about it, or keep your copy of this book.
   D. You will want to try some ideas again later, when your ministry becomes more complex.

2. A goal must be:

   A. written.
   B. in clear language.
   C. measurable.
   D. something you know you can accomplish.

3. Which one of the following is the poorest designed goal?

   A. I will teach the congregation on worship on the next four Sunday mornings. The result will be, at least 90% of the people will, on an evaluation form, indicate that they look forward to worshiping the Lord in church more than before. 50% will indicate "much more than before."
   B. We will recarpet the floor of the sanctuary by April 15 using carpet selected by 70% of the church council, and costing no more than $3000.
   C. By June 1, we will build a foot-bridge across the creek, so the people living east of the church don't have to travel all the way round via the old Gaston ferry.

D. By February 15 we will have Roger Nolan teach CPR to 60% of the parents who attend church. We will ask the Red Cross to test the students, and 85% of them will pass.

4. Which one of these is not an action step for getting help with making plans:

A. Pray about the thoughts you have been pondering.
B. Once you have reason to believe God wants you to "lean" in a particular direction or goal, you need to take some sort of action.
C. God might clarify what he wants, or he might redirect you at any time.
D. Seek counsel if the gravity of the matter requires it.

5. Regarding the "Block Plan," the term "block" refers to:

A. the configuration of the form for writing the details of the plan.
B. the time span during which you will achieve certain tasks.
C. the simplicity of the structure of the planning method.
D. the difficulty one must overcome in making the decision to plan.

6. Which of these is not one of the four steps that will help you manage your time?

A. Plan what goals you will work on during the next many months, and decide during which weeks you will spend some time working on each goal.
B. Plan how you will spend your time for the coming week
C. Plan how you will spend your time tomorrow.
D. Use the "Speed-Up Plan" for clearing your desk.

7. Which of these is not one of the steps of the Block Plan?

A. Make a list of the things you want to get done during the time available.
B. Prioritize this list.
C. Organize your work area for better working conditions.

D. Get started on the task you have numbered one.

8   Advantages of the Block Plan:

    A. It works best for more complicated goals.
    B. You will feel highly motivated to try to accomplish all the tasks on your list.
    C. You will achieve more.
    D. When you begin working, you will know exactly what you want to do first

9.   The main advantage of using the Calendar Chart:

    A. Your Block Plan becomes useful.
    B. Fewer friends take too much of your time.
    C. Interruptions take on a special meaning..
    D. It relieves much stress.

10.   About the Weekly Plan:

    A. It's a great idea but it usually has to be changed during the week.
    B. You make changes in your Weekly Plan by using the Daily Plan form.
    C. You are not permitted to photocopy anything from this book.
    D. Your "standard week" means the things you will do every day or week.

11.   About making plans:

    A. Everyone should use all the forms in this book.
    B. If you cannot use any of these forms now, save them. You might need them later..
    C. The Lord is God. We should follow him, and write plans we believe he is giving us.
    D. People of the world use planning so they might become wealthy..

12. Goals that are often neglected are:

    A. long range goals.
    B. goals for next week.
    C. goals for tomorrow.
    D. goals we like to work on.

13. The Pareto Principle...

    A. says we spend 80% of our time on tasks that produce only 20% of the desired results.
    B. says we need to work harder if we want to achieve more than 80% of our potential.
    C. says we spend only 20% of our time on tasks that produce 80% of the desired results.
    D. suggests we should consider whether we spend too much time on relatively unimportant tasks.

14. Using the Time Log:

    A. you will almost certainly find you are not spending time the way you think you are!
    B. you will see tasks that take much of your time, but which someone can do for you,
    C. can result in your getting more of the important things done.
    D. means stopping work every five minutes to write down what you're doing.

The three planning forms on the following pages are provided so you can make copies.

You might want to make enlarged copies.

Calendar Chart

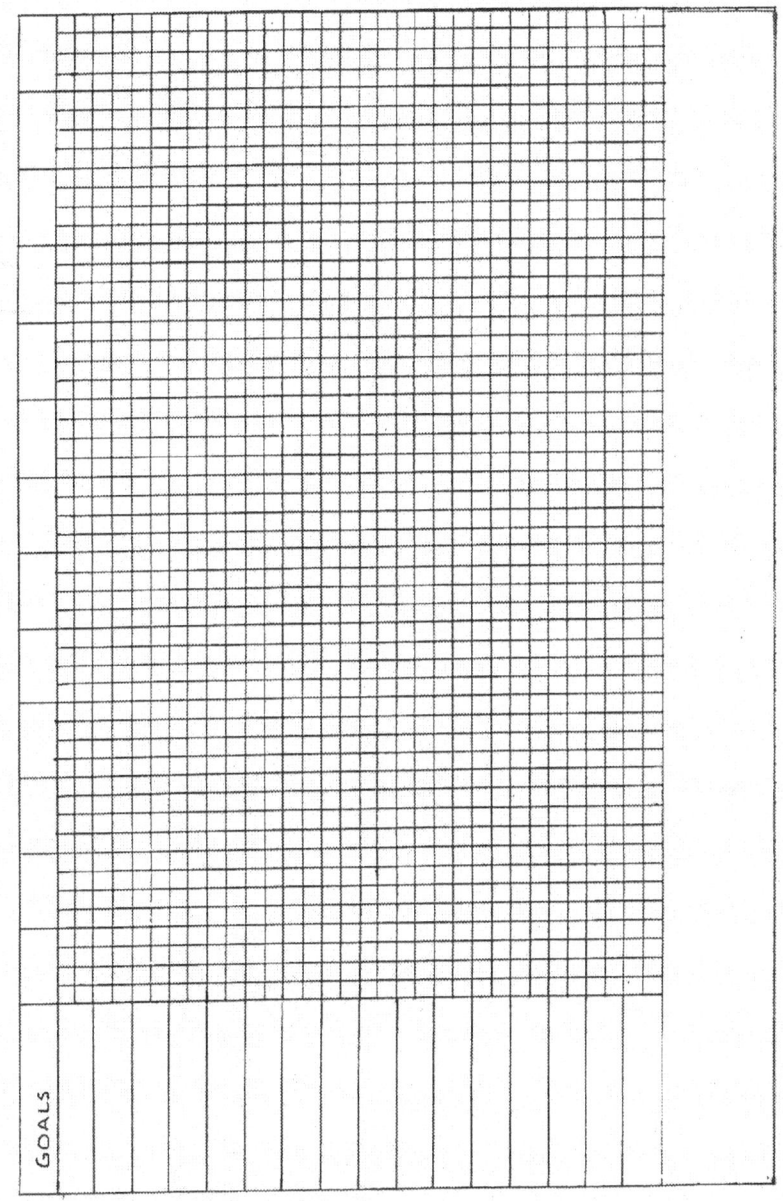

GOALS

Weekly Plan

Week of:

	SUN	MON	TUE	WED	THUR	FRI	SAT
6:00							
6:30							
7:00							
7:30							
8:00							
8:30							
9:00							
9:30							
10:00							
10:30							
11:00							
11:30							
12:00							
12:30							
1:00							
1:30							
2:00							
2:30							
3:00							
3:30							
4:00							
4:30							
5:00							
5:30							
6:00							
6:30							
7:00							
7:30							

Daily Plan

Date:

6:30	
7:00	
7:30	
8:00	
8:30	
9:00	
9:30	
10:00	
10:30	
11:00	
11:30	
12:00	
12:30	
1:00	
1:30	
2:00	
2:30	
3:00	
3:30	
4:00	
4:30	
5:00	
5:30	
6:00	
6:30	
7:00	
7:30	
8:00	
8:30	
9:00	
9:30	
10:00	

Notes:

Chapter 7

How to Plan a Simple Project

For the "Seven-Point Plan" we use the "Control Form"

We could have titled this chapter, "How to Plan for an Event," or "to Achieve a Goal." Or "to Carry out a Project." In other words, the "project" mentioned in our title could be the achieving of anything.

To plan a project that is not too complicated, you might use what we call the "Seven-Point Plan." See Illustration 10, the "Control Form." This form helps you, the leader, to control the progress of the work planned on the form.

Use this plan for a project or goal that does not involve many steps or objectives. You and your team of helpers will decide what tasks must be done or what steps must be taken along the path of achieving the goal.

The project could be building a bridge, or giving a fundraising banquet, or staging a missions weekend at church. Or the goal might be to raise $5000 for a missions project, or to give a missions training seminar, or to build an addition onto the church.

If the goal requires many steps or objectives, we recommend another kind of plan. We'll discuss that later.

The Parts of the "Control Form"

To study the "Seven-Point Plan" we will look at the parts of the "Control Form," Illustration 10.

Notice the goal is written in the column to the left. We studied in the previous chapter that a goal must be written, in clear language, and it must be measurable. You will only fit one or two words beside each other because the column is narrow. Of course, you can rotate the form 90 degrees clockwise and write the goal sidewise if the goal is long.

Illustration
10

Control Form

Goal	Objectives	Steps toward achieving the goal	Target date	Person responsible	Authority 1,2,3	Cost	Date achieved

The next space on the form is the very large space. Here you number and write the steps that must be taken, or the tasks that must be performed, so that the goal can be achieved. These tasks are themselves goals, or sub-goals, leading us to the main goal which we have written in the goal column to the left.

Write the steps in the order of their starting dates (chronological order).

These objectives, or steps, then must be written in clear language, and they must be measurable.

To the right of each objective we write the target date, which is the date by which that objective must be achieved. If circumstances permit, an objective can be completed before the target date. This is ideal. We should aim at finishing each step before the deadline, or target date. Finishing after the deadline might cause serious problems.

This is true because usually several persons, or team members, are working on the objectives. Often, one objective cannot be completed until another objective is achieved.

To the right of the Target Date on the Control Form we write the name of the person who agrees to be responsible for the achievement of that objective. He might not be the person who will actually do the work, but he will see that the objective is finished on time.

The next column is for that person's "level of authority." At times you might assign a helper a task and tell him he is to accomplish it without reporting back to you or the team. We refer to this as "authority level one." Reserve this level for simple, non-crucial tasks, and for helpers in whom you have great confidence. Level one should rarely be used.

Level two requires the person responsible to do the task and then report to you or the team how he accomplished it, and any details the team should know about. This level is most often used.

Level three means the person responsible is not to do the task at all. He is to research how he would accomplish the task, and report back to the team. Perhaps he will decide what expert should be hired to do the work, and what the cost will be.

When he reports back with this information, you might decide to have him follow-up and see that the task is achieved on schedule, or you might have someone else do the same research and report back. You might do the task yourself because of its importance, now that you have the benefit of that helper's research.

The investigator, or research person, may not be the orderly person who can best manage the job through to a timely conclusion.

The last column on the Control Form is titled "Cost." This is the amount of money you or the team agrees is the most that should be spent for this task. Encourage the persons responsible for the tasks to spend less than this estimate if possible. No helper has permission to spend more than the amount you write in that column unless he has your approval.

Some tasks require no cost.

The "finish date" in the last column is the actual date when the objective was completed. This column motivates the person responsible to finish before the target date.

The Advantages of the "Control Form"

The Control Form you will use for your team should be much larger than the one shown in Illustration 10. It should be displayed, with all the information filled in, where the entire team will see it during the meetings you will hold perhaps every week or two as the project proceeds. You might indicate by a circle around the step number, or by a check mark, that an objective has been accomplished, or you might be satisfied to let the finish date show this fact.

The form shows you, and the team, at a glance, what is supposed to be happening at any given moment, who is making sure each task is being done, who are the persons who must report back so the team can discuss what should be done, and when these reports are due. It also reminds the team members that they can spend only the stated amount.

The form summarizes some basic principles about administration. While studying (above) the various parts of the form, you have been learning those principles. But the form itself may not satisfy your needs because of the nature of your goal. Knowing the basic principles, you and your team can perhaps devise a better form for your specific project.

The "Card Plan" is for Planning a Project Involving Many Tasks

You may prefer to use the Card Plan even for uncomplicated projects or goals. The Card Plan is far superior to the "Seven-Point Plan" if your goal involves objectives that interrelate with each other in ways that impact on how they will be achieved.

You will need cards or sheets of paper, about 8 inches by 11 inches. Sheets of paper which are commonly used in offices or schools are inexpensive. Each of these cards or sheets of paper will show one objective, or step toward achieving the goal. One of these cards will show the goal itself.

You will need large marking pens, or some cheap paint and small brushes, used for making temporary signs.

Look now at Illustration 11. The boxes represent the cards, or pieces of paper described above. In box "G" we show how each card is to be divided. Draw lines on all your cards to make each card look like card "G," except for the letter "G." The height of the three small boxes on each card should be about one-and-a-half inches.

You will need a blank wall, or a large area on a wall, or a large chalkboard for displaying these objectives.

You will need your team. You and they must be willing to spend hours planning to achieve this goal.

How to Create a "Card Plan"

Announce your first meeting well in advance, so your team members can arrange to be present. Of course, you will pray at the beginning of every meeting, during every meeting whenever there is need, and at the end. During this first meeting, you might need to teach about goals from the previous chapter in this book. Then explain to the team what is on your heart, what God has prompted you to achieve. Explain that you need them to help you with this plan.

If the team is enthusiastic about the idea you believe God has given you, proceed to plan with their help. If they fail to see the importance, or if they are not at least somewhat enthused, you might get them to express their doubts or concerns. We will deal with principles of leadership in another chapter.

With the help of the team, write the goal on the chalkboard so all can see it. Work on the wording so the language of the goal expresses clearly what you want to achieve. When the goal is both clear and measurable, copy it onto one of the large pieces of paper, using the large marking pen. Someone gifted for clear, large lettering should be chosen for this. If larger paper is needed, make that decision now, and rewrite the goal on larger paper so all can read the goal from where they sit during these meetings.

Wording the goal properly might be all you can do in this first meeting. In fact, it might be too much to expect. It might be enough to teach your team about goals, if they are not familiar with planning, and to describe for them what you believe God has encouraged you to achieve.

Illustration
11   The Card Method

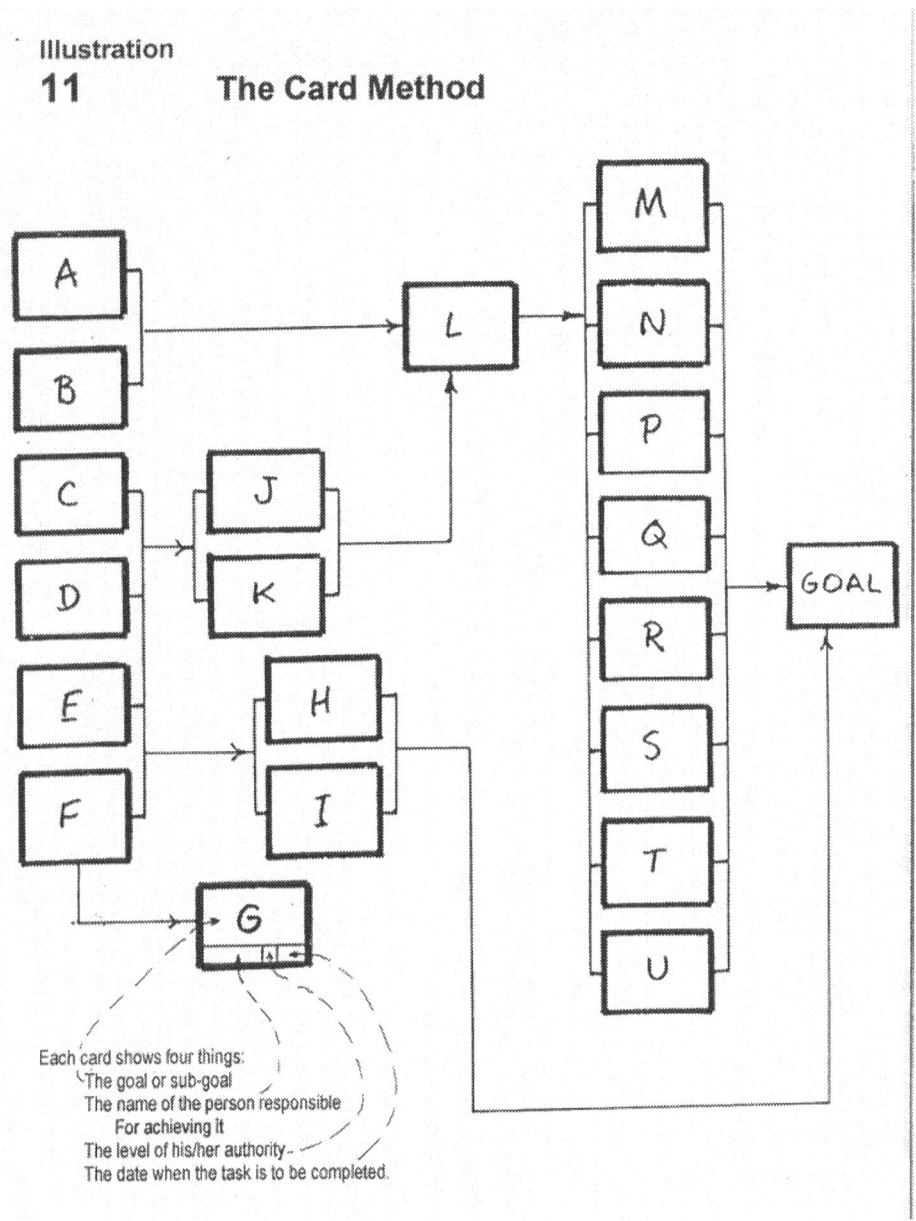

Each card shows four things:
The goal or sub-goal
The name of the person responsible
For achieving it
The level of his/her authority
The date when the task is to be completed.

Setting the goal, expressing it in clear terms, and making the goal measurable, is the foundation of success. Be sure your helpers understand the goal. Answer their questions. You might need to ask them to explain the goal, so you are sure they understand. Then discuss the value of the goal so that all appreciate it and understand its importance.

Determine whether the members are highly motivated to achieve the goal. You might ask the team how many of them believe you should work together to achieve this goal.

If there is a lack of enthusiasm for the goal, ask all to pray and ask the Lord whether you should be working at this goal. Have them report back about this.

You yourself should ask the Lord how you should proceed about this. Be sure to listen patiently and respectfully to your team members when they report back after praying.

If you are going ahead with the planning, your team must now help you think up the objectives, the steps, which must be taken in order to achieve the goal. Objectives are like smaller goals within the main goal. Each objective, like the goal itself, must be written, must be in clear language, and must be measurable.

Place the paper or card on which is written the main goal to the far right of the area of wall you will use to display your Card Plan. Illustration 11 shows this. Some Card Plans take more up-and-down (vertical) space. Others take more side-to-side (horizontal) space.

How to "Brainstorm"

The Spanish word for "brainstorming" is "a rain of ideas." The "rain" must not be interrupted by comments or questions.

You, the leader, will ask your team, "What ideas comes to your mind as a step or task that should be done as we work to achieve this goal?" At this point, the ideas may not be clear or measurable objectives.

When a team member says, loud enough to be heard by all, what came to his mind, that idea must immediately be written where all may see it. A chalkboard is good for this, or huge pieces of wrapping paper taped to the wall, and a wide-tip marker, will be excellent. Have at least two persons write the ideas as they come. There should be no waiting for the writers to finish. If the brainstorming must wait for the writers, ask another writer to help.

It might work better if each giver of an idea writes his own idea anywhere on the chalkboard, and then sits down to give other ideas as he thinks of them. Experiment until you get the brainstorming session to work smoothly, without interruptions.

Some ideas will be discarded later. For now, accept all of them without discussion or clarification. Evaluating at this time will discourage others from giving their ideas. Evaluating will take everyone's mind off the question or problem.

Some ideas will be impossible. That's fine. A ridiculous idea might inspire a more practical idea in someone else. Encourage all ideas, however foolish they might seem.

With a large team, you might require each person with an idea to stand, and to give his idea in the order of standing. But impose only the rules that help the process to move on quickly.

A large team could be divided into two groups if you have another room. But train the team to brainstorm well while they are all together.

When the team has no more ideas the brainstorming is over.

After "Brainstorming," what's next?

Now have the team decide which of the ideas written before them expresses the first task that needs to be done. You can easily change the order later, so don't spend much time on this decision. Then place the numeral "1" next to that idea. Move on this way through all the ideas, discarding any that seem unnecessary.

Often, two or more tasks can be accomplished at the same time because one does not depend on the completion of the other. Give these tasks the same numeral. They will be arranged in a special way later. Remember, errors can be corrected later. There is time here for some discussion, but don't let disagreements over minor decisions take too much time. Solutions to difficulties will often be automatic as the team sees the bigger picture take shape.

When this is finished, take the idea for task number one. Rephrase this idea so it is a clear and measurable objective. Have someone copy this objective on one of those large white cards or pieces of paper shown in Illustration 11. The copier should then erase that idea and objective from the chalkboard.

Remind the team they must not write in the boxes at the bottom of the cards.

Do the same for idea number two.

If your team is too large to move quickly through this task, you might divide into groups for the rewriting of the objectives. Have at least three persons in each group. Assign objectives by their number to each group. Assign all but the last three or four objectives to one or another of the groups. The remaining objectives you can assign, one-by-one, to groups that finish sooner than the others.

How to Arrange the Cards in Proper Order

You have already placed the goal-card to the far right of the wall, or the area where you will assemble your Card Plan.

Now select the step or objective, which should be achieved last, before the goal is achieved. Place this objective-card or task-card to the left of the goal-card. Leave a small space, the width of three fingers, between cards.

Continue in this manner with all the task-cards. Some tasks came from ideas that appear on the chalkboard with the same numeral. You recall, these tasks can be done independently of each other. They can be worked on at the same time. Place these cards in a column, one directly above or beneath the other.

In Illustration 11, tasks M through U can all be started at the same time. Also A through F can all be done at the same time. However, A through F must be done before M through U can be done.

Look again at Illustration 11. The arrows show something about the necessary order of events. Some tasks must be completed before other tasks can be started. The task the arrow points to, cannot be started until the task or tasks at the left end of the arrow have been finished.

For example, task L cannot be started until both A and B are finished. The bracket connecting A and B tells us that the arrow is speaking to us about both A and B.

Perhaps You Can Now Answer These Questions!

1. What tasks must be accomplished before J and K can be started? Answers are given below.
2. H and I are below J and K, and somewhat to the right. This is to show J and K must be **started** before H and I can begin. But what tasks must be **finished** before H and I can be started?
3. What task or tasks must be finished before G can be started?
4. Now for the most difficult question. How many tasks must be finished before S can be started?
5. Task G is not connected to the goal! What does this mean?

Here are the answers to the above questions.

1. C, D, E, and F.
2. C, D, E, and F. Notice A and B are not connected to J or K.
3. Only F must be finished before G can be started. If we wanted to show that C, D, E, and F were to be finished before G can be started, we would have to move the arrow that connects F with G. That arrow would have to come from the bracket alongside C, D, E, and F, and point to G.
4. The answer is nine. All the tasks except H, I, and G and M through U, must be finished before tasks M through U, including S, can be started.
5. If task G is never completed, the goal can still be achieved.

The Small Boxes at the Bottom of Each Card

In Illustration 11, card "G" explains the use of each of these boxes. Levels of authority are explained above, as part of the "Control Form."

You will not want to draw permanent lines and arrows on a wall. Use sticky tape of a different color from the wall color.

If You Find This "Card Plan" Too Complicated...

It is difficult to learn how to do something complicated just by reading about it. If you and your top helpers work together you can experience how this plan works. If you have a better plan, use your own.

This plan has worked successfully for projects that are very complex and require much management by the person or persons who make the important decisions.

You probably need to try this method of planning to understand all its benefits. Be willing to try something that might be a big help to you over years of use.

Another Kind of Plan - the "Solution Plan"

We will look at this plan in chapter 9, on godly principles for the missionary who is the manager of his own ministry. Much of a missionary's life, if he is penetrating an unreached people group, will be solving problems. There are general principles that are scriptural, or godly, that we will examine.

This is not to say that a missionary who brings the gospel to an unreached people must have a big organization. Jesus deeply changed the world with only twelve men, including Paul.

By looking at these principles we will see that the important one is following Jesus in the temple of our own hearts. He will lead us his way.

The "Checklist"

A checklist is a list of things to be done, or of items to be purchased or dealt with in some way. Each item on the list must be "checked" off by placing a mark in a small box, which should appear in front (to the left) of each of the tasks or items listed.

The checklist is for important procedures that are repeated, such as packing your personal luggage for a journey. A checklist has so many little details you cannot depend upon your memory

Many procedures can be drawn up in the form of a checklist.

Some checklists become more like Control Forms because the user adds items he or she finds helpful, such as:
- the target date when the task should be completed
- the date when the task was actually done
- if others are to be involved, the person who will perform the task.

Checklists can be photocopied before you mark them with check-marks so they can be used again and again. When completed they can be filed so you have a record of what happened.

Checklists have four important advantages:

1. They force us to think through what we will be doing, so the details are all included and are in logical order.
2. They relieve us of the stress, the fear that we might be overlooking an important detail.
3. They save us the time we would otherwise spend doing over again parts of a procedure because we have accidentally omitted an important step
4. The form we used for the checklist becomes a record of what we did.

The "Flow Chart"

A flow chart (Illustration 12) looks like a map because it traces out a path. The items or tasks along the path are each enclosed in a box, a circle or other shape. Each shape or figure can have a specific meaning.

Arrows show the direction of progress. Within some figures you will find the circumstances that will cause you to take one direction or alternative rather than the other.

The flow chart in Illustration 12 is a pathway showing tasks or steps you might want anyone to follow who wants to be on your team of helpers. If you were to use it, you would have to make many changes in it to make it fit your needs.

Flow charts can be photocopied for repeated use. The copy to be used can be marked with the name of the prospective team member, and dates showing when things happened, or other information to make it a more complete record. It can be saved for future reference.

Illustration
12   Candidate for helper.

For illustration purposes only.

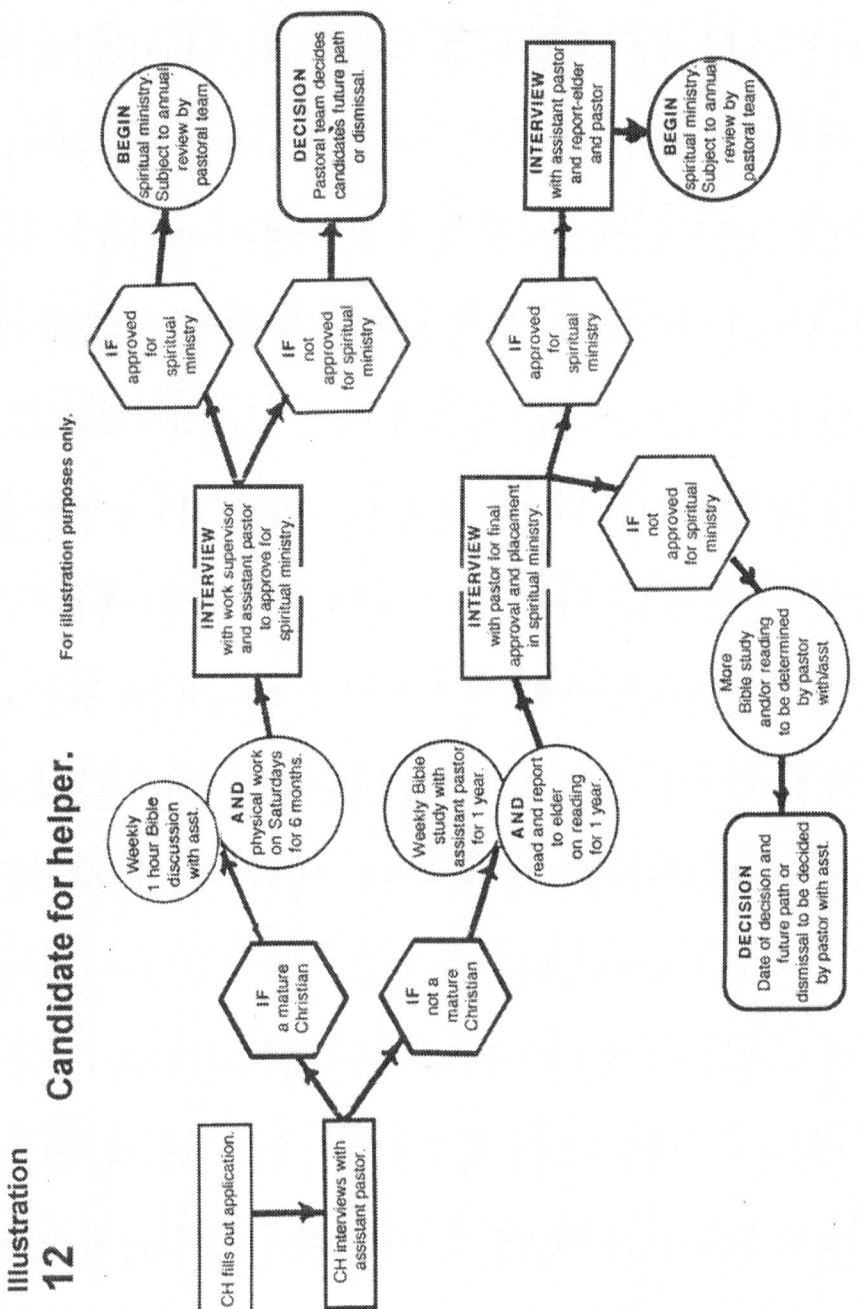

129

Chapter 7
Questions

1. The "Control Form"...

    A. is for planning a project that is not too complicated.
    B. Is helpful when we're using the Seven-Point Plan.
    C. headings are the seven steps of the Seven-Point Plan.
    D. headings are: goal, objectives, target date, cost, person in charge, purpose and authority level.

2. Which of these is not one of the levels of authority?

    A. Accomplish the task any way you see fit. Do not report back to the team.
    B. Don't do the task. Research and tell us how you would go about achieving it.
    C. Do the task the way you think best, and report back to us when you finish.
    D. Research first, and then do the task in the least expensive way. Report back to us when you finish.

3. The "Card Plan"...

    A. is for a simple goal that requires little planning.
    B. is named for the fact that it requires small, pocket-size cards.
    C. should be devised by you and explained later to your team.
    D. involves cards that will each have four items written on it.

4. Each goal, and each objective, must be:

    A. written so that all may see it and keep in mind what they are to achieve.
    B. phrased in clear language so the team cannot misunderstand its meaning.
    C. concise, consisting of twenty words or less.

D. measurable so that team members will know how close they are to achieving the goal.

5. Things to avoid in creating a "Card Plan":

A. The team believing that the plan is not God's plan for them
B. Long discussions without praying.
C. Using cards that can be read only by those sitting close to them.
D. Giving everyone time to explain his ideas.

6. In "brainstorming" …

A. the leader encourages all to give any idea that comes to mind, even if it seems foolish.
B. everyone comes prepared to give well thought-out ideas
C. everyone is free to speak, even while someone else is saying something.
D. every idea is written for all to see, except those that could never succeed.

7. In placing the cards on display…

A. Objectives that depend on each other for completion are placed one under the other.
B. Objectives that depend on each other for completion are connected by arrows that show which must be done first.
C. Objectives that depend on each other for completion are placed on one card.
D. Objectives that depend on each other for completion are placed nearest the goal card.

8. You would be wise to draw up a checklist for …

A. Tasks you need to consider doing before you leave on a long journey.
B. Groceries you should look for in your kitchen to be sure you will not soon need replacements.

C. A chronological list of tasks you will perform monthly as you create a monthly newsletter.

D. Reminding yourself to take your suit to the cleaners on Monday.

9. Some checklists are more useful if we add to each task or item:

A. the name of the person responsible
B. the date when the task or item should be completed
C. the date when the task was completed
D. a statement of the purpose of the checklist.

10. A flow chart…

A. traces out a path
B. has "forks in the road" to show alternative paths
C. can be used in place of the Block Plan
D. might bear the name of a person who is to follow it

Chapter 8

Administrative Concepts Missionaries Need

Keep in mind...

You, as missionary, are not to seek first to be an excellent administrator. Seek first the kingdom of God and his righteousness, and God will work wonderfully in you to enlighten you and energize you. He will work wonderfully in others through you.

Administrative skills are useful. They clear the path of obstacles such as:

- our lack of understanding
- our laziness
- our natural passivity concerning new ideas we wrongly undervalue.
- confusion about our purpose or goals.

Administrative skills cannot replace God's anointing. They must not be pursued as ends in themselves, but only as helpful tools in advancing the kingdom.

What is an Administrator?

Another word for "administrator" is "manager." An administrator is one who manages. "To manage" means to control, to direct, to treat with care.

Managing is done in differing ways in different situations. In some situations it is customary for helpers (subordinates) to be consulted about many things, and to help make some decisions by voting. In other situations, a manager will consult his or her helpers about decisions, but the manager himself makes the decisions. In some other situations, the manager makes decisions like an officer in the army. A military officer usually does not consult his men, or allow them to make decisions except trivial ones.

There is a difference between the directing done by a military officer and the directing done by a manager. The military officer must train his men to wage war. There is no time for discussion in battle. A general is not much affected by the ideas or feelings of his subordinates, though he might seek the advice of officers directly under him. He is obeyed without question.

The manager, however, often gets excellent help from his subordinates. He is concerned with their feelings because he knows they perform better if they are treated with care, and if their ideas are considered, and used where feasible.

When the manager decides what is to be done, he issues orders or commands, but in a different spirit from the military officer. Within limits, the manager is ready to listen to any subordinate who wants to improve things, or even to complain.

The military commander, when he discovers that a subordinate disobeyed orders, will usually simply impose the penalty prescribed in the book of military procedures. The manager will usually call the disobedient subordinate into his office, and ask why he did not obey. He might impose a penalty or give a warning.

In ministry, we always look to Jesus as our model. Jesus was the good shepherd. The shepherd in Israel did not drive his sheep. He knew them each by name and called them to follow him. The shepherd always had in mind the well-being of the sheep. He led them to good pasture and clear water. If one wandered off, the shepherd sought him and rejoiced to find him, perhaps even carrying him on his shoulders back to the safety of the flock.

In business, the motivation for good management is financial gain. If the business is making a good profit, all is well. If the business is going into debt, the owners of the business might sell the business. The workers then might lose their jobs. They are not usually considered a high priority.

In ministry, the motivation is different. In one way or another, every minister is motivated to glorify God and to benefit people. Those who work toward the specific goals of the ministry are usually important to the top executives. One of the objectives of the ministry is to build leadership skills among the workers, so that some can establish their own ministries and thereby multiply the exaltation of the Lord, and increase the spiritual benefits to people in need.

In ministry, those top executives help subordinates develop their leadership skills for another reason: the subordinate's benefit, or personal fulfillment. *Each of you should look not only to your own interests, but to the interests of others* (Phil. 2:4).

Later we will see more how these aspects of leadership are reflected in the Bible. Regardless of your cultural background, you need to base your leadership on Bible principles, not on the traditional norms of your birth culture. Those norms or principles are to be honored or followed when they do not conflict with Bible principles of morality.

Very often the cultural norms neither promote nor violate the Word of God. Often the Word deals with the attitude of heart we bring to the carrying out of traditional norms. For example, the Bible tells masters how to deal with their slaves.

Masters, provide your slaves with what is right and fair, because you know that you also have a Master in heaven (Col. 4:1).

What is "Management?"

"Management" is the art of getting things done through people. This is the simplest definition. Here is a more complete definition.

"Management" is the skill of:

1. Setting goals (with the advice of helpers and overseers).
2. Directing events toward those goals by:
   a) assigning responsibilities (to well chosen people).
   b) monitoring performance (including achievement, use of time, and use of money). This monitoring must not be so controlling that it hinders progress. Managers must not discourage initiative.
3. Controlling conditions. (Conditions are always changing.)

These definitions apply to both the business world, and to ministry. God has created us in such a way that subordinates generally respond better to good management than to poor management. In both business and ministry, we want our leaders to manage us with fairness and mercy or understanding. We want them to be just, but to be gentle, thoughtful and forgiving when we question things, or even fail to obey.

The Organizational Chart

Perhaps the most fundamental way of avoiding confusion about authority is to:

> a) have an organizational chart, and
> b) teach all who are in your organization what it means.

Look at Illustration 13. An organizational chart shows the chain of command within an organization. The persons who report directly to you are shown immediately below you. There are several. They are shown side-by-side.

Each individual on the chart can tell to whom he must report, or from whom he must accept orders, by following the lines that either immediately or indirectly lead upward on the chart. Positions shown higher on the chart are higher in authority and responsibility.

Each person on the chart can see who is appointed to assist him, and to receive orders from him, by noticing what persons are listed below him on the chart.

We deal with being a good follower in a later chapter.

Much conflict can be avoided if everyone understands:

1. he or she gives orders to those positioned directly below him or her on the chart.

On Illustration 13, E gives orders to K and L.

2. he should not give orders to someone below, but who is responsible directly to another manager, without that manager's involvement. E should not give orders to N without involving K.

Illustration 13
Organizational Chart

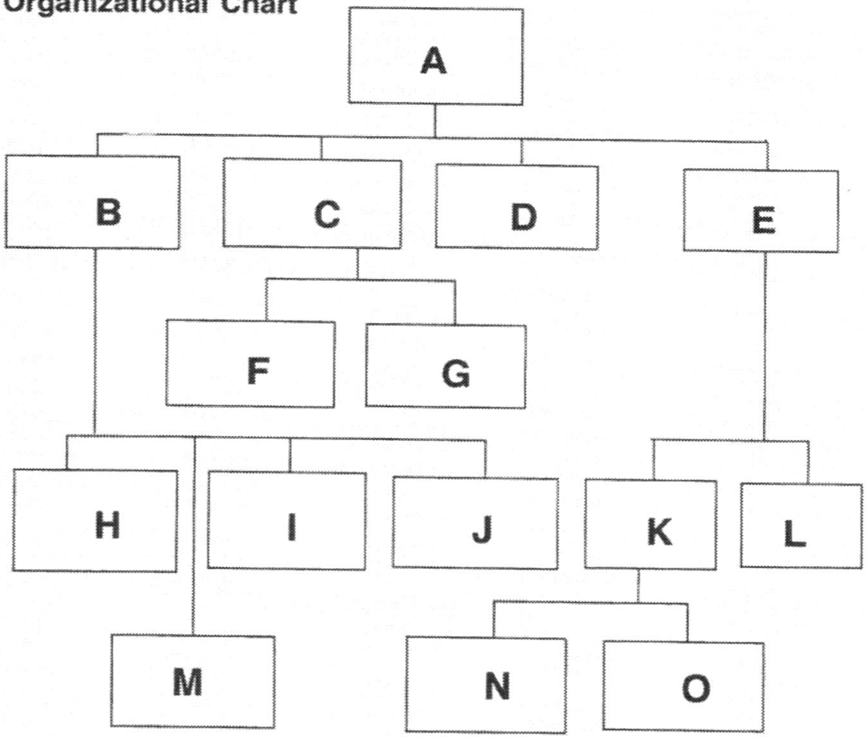

Each letter on the chart represents a person responsible for a management position within the organization.

Questions

1. To whom do the following give orders? B, C, D, L, A.

2. From whom do the following receive orders? E, L, J, M, A.

Answers

1.
B: H, I, J, M.
C: F, G.
D: no one.
L: no one.
A: B, C, D, E.

2.
E: A.
L: E
J: B.
M: B.
A: No one within the organization.

139

3. he must obey orders given by the person immediately next to himself, up the chain of command. N must obey orders given by K.
4. he must also obey orders given by anyone above his supervisor within their chain of command. N must obey orders given by E. Everyone must obey A.
5. he must not accept orders from anyone not upward of himself within the chain of command to which he belongs, without first consulting his supervisor. N must not obey orders from J, or F, or C for examples, without consulting K
6. in most organizations, he has the authority to give orders to anyone down the chain of command he heads, but he does well to have that person's manager give the order. In that way, each person is responsible to only one supervisor.

We deal with conflict in a later chapter.

Leadership

A group of chief executive officers, highest ranking superiors of their companies, met together to analyze a problem. The problem was this. Each of them noticed many of his top managers were leaving the company after a few years. The top leaders asked this question: "How can we cause our best managers to want to stay with us?"

They decided to try increases in salary for each year of service. This succeeded, but only for a few years. Soon key managers began leaving the company, even though their next job offered less pay!

The group of executives met again and again, trying bonuses for excellent performance, time off, special privileges for longer service, and everything they could think of to cause their best managers to stay. All of these things succeeded for a time, but each of them failed eventually.

Finally the executives decided to give their managers more responsibility! This meant giving them more work! More difficult decisions to make!

This plan worked and is still working! People generally want to be challenged. They also want to be free to try their own solutions to problems. The executives found that some of the decisions made by managers were not good decisions. Some "solutions" only added to the problem they were meant to solve.

But even in those cases, the managers were quick to see their failure, and quick to change the procedure until they got the desired result.

Again, this is the result of the way God made man! He made man after his own image. Man is an intelligent being! He delights in using the gifts, the abilities God has given him.

What can you, the future leader, the future missionary, learn from this story? Simply this. Don't insist on making all decisions yourself. Decisions regarding how your organization will achieve its goals should be made, as much as possible, by you with the help of your top leaders or managers.

To the extent that it is possible, give to your best managers or helpers, considerable responsibility for leading some aspect of your ministry. Let's see how this is commanded in the scripture.

Chapter 8
Questions

1. Administrative skills clear the path of obstacles that prevent us from achieving, such as:

    A. lack of understanding
    B. laziness
    C. purposelessness
    D. a tendency to do nothing that might result in failure and embarrass us

2. A manager is:

    A. one who wraps important packages.
    B. an administrator.
    C. someone who controls the way things are done.
    D. one who directs, one who cares for how things are done.

3. A manager...

    A. sets goals.
    B. directs events so the goals are reached.
    C. hires people who measure up to the standards.
    D. controls conditions which change often.

4. A simple definition of management is...

    A. getting behind the cart and pushing with creative ideas.
    B. the art of getting things done through people.
    C. eliminating interruptions and requiring the best of the workers.
    D. harnessing the horse to the cart and driving.

5. The only persons who can give orders to those above them on the organizational chart are:

   A. those in the very highest positions.
   B. those in the very lowest positions.
   C. those whose contract permits it.
   D. no one.

6. An employee must obey…

   A. everyone above him within his chain of command.
   B. only the supervisor immediately above him.
   C. anyone in the organization who has more seniority than he does.
   D. his supervisor and those with more seniority.

Finally the executives decided to give their managers more responsibility! This meant giving them more work! More difficult decisions to make!

This plan worked and is still working! People generally want to be challenged. They also want to be free to try their own solutions to problems. The executives found that some of the decisions made by managers were not good decisions. Some "solutions" only added to the problem they were meant to solve.

But even in those cases, the managers were quick to see their failure, and quick to change the procedure until they got the desired result.

Again, this is the result of the way God made man! He made man after his own image. Man is an intelligent being! He delights in using the gifts, the abilities God has given him.

What can you, the future leader, the future missionary, learn from this story? Simply this. Don't insist on making all decisions yourself. Decisions regarding how your organization will achieve its goals should be made, as much as possible, by you with the help of your top leaders or managers.

To the extent that it is possible, give to your best managers or helpers, considerable responsibility for leading some aspect of your ministry. Let's see how this is commanded in the scripture.

7.	Executives discovered that they could keep their top managers with the company by giving them:

	A. more money.
	B. the best parking spaces.
	C. more responsibility.
	D. titles that carried high prestige.

8.	As a missionary, you will succeed better if you...

	A.	delegate to your top helpers some measure of decision-making authority.
	B.	recognize that your top helpers have leadership abilities given them by God.
	C.	ask your top helpers to help you set goals.
	D.	oversee every detail of what is done by your helpers to prevent mistakes.

Chapter 9

Managing People God's Way

God Teaches us About Managing His People

Philippians 2:1-11 tells us much about leadership.

> *1 "If you have any encouragement from being united with Christ, if any comfort from his love, if any fellowship with the Spirit, if any tenderness and compassion, 2 then make my joy complete by being **like-minded**, having **the same love, being one in spirit and purpose.** 3 Do nothing out of selfish ambition or vain conceit, but in humility consider others better than yourselves. 4 Each of you should look not only to your own interests, but also to the interests of others.*

> *5 "Your attitude should be the same as that of Christ Jesus: 6 Who, being in very nature God, did not consider equality with God something to be grasped, 7 but made himself nothing, taking the very nature of a servant, being made in human likeness. 8 And being found in appearance as a man, he humbled himself and became obedient to death-- even death on a cross! 9 Therefore God exalted him to the highest place and gave him the name that is above every name, 10 that at the name of Jesus every knee should bow, in heaven and on earth and under the earth, 11 and every tongue confess that Jesus Christ is Lord, to the glory of God the Father."*

If you, the future leader, will fashion your own thinking and your desiring after the thinking and the desiring of Jesus, you will be a wonderful influence on your followers, your helpers, to do the same. This will foster in them the "likeminded" quality Paul mentions in verse 2, above. This will unite you with your followers in that "same love, being one in spirit and purpose."

You, need to lead especially in Christ-like motivation, in godly purpose. Guard against, pray against, becoming enrapt in the success-patterns of the world. Do not look upon fundraising as your chief concern. Be bold in offering people participation in your work through giving to the Lord. But never trust in your own craftiness in "getting" people to give. Rather, look to the Lord for both the funds you need and the methods you will use to ask believers to give.

Verse 3 tells you how to deal with your helpers, those the Lord sends to you to help you achieve what he has called you to do. *Do nothing out of selfish ambition or vain conceit, but in humility consider others better than yourselves.*

As the leader in your own ministry you will be tempted to "use" your helpers to enhance your own work, even to the point where you will deprive your helpers of opportunities to grow in their abilities as managers.

For example, you will notice you do not have time to do all that needs to be done. You will assign tasks to your helpers so you yourself will have time to get to the essential things which only you can do. But in this process of assigning tasks, do not forget the growth of your helpers. Instead of assigning them only tasks that are least important, give able helpers charge of some significant aspect of the ministry. This experience will help them grow as leaders themselves.

Do not allow yourself to be so conceited that, in your mind, only you can do those things that are more challenging than the unchallenging or even menial tasks. In humility consider others better than yourself! At some of the more demanding tasks, the more challenging responsibilities, some of your helpers will be more capable than you, once they are a little experienced in those tasks.

In this way you are building them into leadership caliber. This is indeed looking *to the interests of others* (v. 4). It also benefits the kingdom of God.

Verses 5 to 10 speak to the leader who is concerned about his own position, the leader who fears helping his helper to grow. He thinks, "This subordinate will assume more and more influence among my helpers. He will then leave me, form his own ministry, and take with him all my best staff!"

The leader's solution is to hold tightly all the authority God has given him, sharing nothing, and helping no one to become a leader like himself.

Search the scriptures and see if there is any suggestion that you keep your subordinates powerless so they cannot replace you. The opposite is true, as you see in these verses. Model your heart and mind, fashion your leadership style after that of Jesus! If he causes you to be replaced it will only be because he is doing something better in your life.

Let the Lord develop in you such a giving heart that, if one of your helpers becomes so experienced and able, you yourself will encourage him to begin his own ministry, giving him the help he needs to succeed.

This is one way to multiply yourself for the glory of the Lord and the benefit of his kingdom!

In 1 Peter 5:1-6 we read this:

> *To the elders among you, I appeal as a fellow elder, a witness of Christ's sufferings and one who also will share in the glory to be revealed: Be shepherds of God's flock that is under your care, serving as overseers--not because you must, but because you are willing, as God wants you to be; not greedy for money, but eager to serve; not lording it over those entrusted to you, but being examples to the flock. And when the Chief Shepherd appears, you will receive the crown of glory that will never fade away."*

Then Peter instructs in how to be a good follower.

> *Young men, in the same way be submissive to those who are older. All of you, clothe yourselves with humility toward one another, because, "God opposes the proud but gives grace to the humble." Humble yourselves, therefore, under God's mighty hand, that he may lift you up in due time. Cast all your anxiety on him because he cares for you.*

As a follower, never expect a leader to be perfect. That quality is for Jesus alone. Become more like Jesus yourself, and accept the leader God has chosen for you without grumbling. That leader will be imperfect, just as you are imperfect and just as you will be imperfect. Submit to that leader while God has you under his supervision.

A good leader begins by being a good follower. Let your desire be to make your superior a successful person. Be sincerely dedicated in this. This is what you would do if you were working under the visible supervision of Jesus himself!

Notice how Jesus teaches this attitude of heart, in Matthew 20:25-28

> *25 "Jesus called them together and said, 'You know that the rulers of the Gentiles lord it over them, and their high officials exercise authority over them. 26 Not so with you. Instead, whoever wants to become great among you must be your servant, 27 and whoever wants to be first must be your slave-- 28 just as the Son of Man did not come to be served, but to serve, and to give his life as a ransom for many.'"*

Having a servant heart, and serving cheerfully, will teach you what a good follower looks like. You will learn how he thinks. You will feel how his heart reacts to certain situations. You will experience what his temptations are

Being a good follower prepares you to lead. It will help you recognize a good follower among your own helpers.

If you need more scripture to instruct your heart and mind as a follower, study Titus 2:9, 10 and 1 Peter 2:18. Notice that even slaves are not told to resist their masters! How much more should the believer submit to those spiritual leaders God has placed over him!.

Barnabas was Not Concerned About Losing His Position to Paul

As a leader, you will do well to study the heart of Barnabas as he brought Paul to the apostles in Jerusalem (Ac 4:36). He did not try to discourage Paul. He did not tell Paul, "There is no chance for you here in Jerusalem. The church here regards you as an enemy. What you did at the execution of Steven will never be forgotten. What you have been doing to the saints here cannot be wiped out of our memories. Leave town while you can."

Barnabas never said anything like this to Paul, though Barnabas might have hoped he himself would be given a position of power within the ministry in Jerusalem. By elevating Paul, Barnabas might lessen his own chances of promotion.

Nevertheless Barnabas decided to show the leaders Paul's heart for the kingdom. He encouraged Paul and brought him to the apostles. Barnabas told them of Paul's conversion and of his preaching about Jesus in Damascus. The result was, Paul moved among believers freely in Jerusalem.

"Barnabas" was given this name by the apostles. It means "son of consolation." Barnabas was an encourager.

Later, when the leaders sent Barnabas to Antioch to see what was developing there, he of course encouraged the new believers. Then he went to Tarsus to get Paul to come help him with the work in Antioch (Ac 11).

We notice "Barnabas and Saul" are mentioned in Acts, in that order, indicating that Barnabas was the leader. In Acts 13:7 this is still the order of mention. Later it changed to "Paul and Barnabas." Paul gradually became the leader of the two.

There is no evidence that this troubled Barnabas. He accepted what God was doing, promoting Paul over himself. Barnabas undoubtedly rejoiced to be part of the powerful ministry of Paul.

This giving attitude is what you need to cultivate, helping your subordinates to attain experience and confidence in the Lord, helping them rise to leadership. You can do this under the grace and direction of the Holy Spirit. Make the attitude of Jesus (in Philippians 2:5-8, above) your own attitude.

Some of your subordinates will one day have ministries of their own. They might even consult with you in later years. God will have you pray with them and prophesy over them, encouraging them as Barnabas did for many.

What Should You Do with a Lazy or a Self-Centered Helper?

Should you accept selfishness in your subordinates? Or should you dismiss any helper who shows an attitude of self-exaltation, self-gain, self-promotion?

Perhaps the answer is "No" to both questions.

Consider this other way. Do not accept self-centeredness. Meet with such a subordinate. Include another person in whom you have great confidence as a counselor. In a spirit of love, explain to the selfish one what you have observed. Try to avoid interpreting his or her motives, but simply relate what you have seen, the words he spoke, the tones of voice, the gestures. Listen to his explanations.

Explain to him the attitude of Jesus, the attitude you fail to see in his words and actions. Be sure to listen to all he says. Get him to tell you more, but do not let him wander from the topic.

If your own attitude is open, teachable, ready to accept what is reasonable, you can help this brother or sister to change.

If you see no improvement within a few months, you might decide, after prayer and consulting the counselor, to dismiss this person with the understanding he can apply again, after 6 months, for membership on your team if he believes he is changed.

This same method might apply to a lazy helper, one who let's others do all the distasteful tasks. Jesus taught us to wash each other's feet!

Concerning promoting helpers to higher responsibilities, keep in mind what Jesus taught about being a servant (Mt. 20:27). Promote servants.

"Delegation" is the Skill of the Successful Leader

"Delegation" is the skill of selecting and training persons to do specific tasks, or to shoulder specific responsibilities, under your supervision. Such persons thereby free you from those tasks so you can do crucial things that will make your ministry more fruitful for the kingdom.

We have seen, giving responsibility to helpers causes them to grow in leadership ability. What should you keep in mind as you delegate?

1. **Be willing to delegate.** Otherwise your ministry will be limited in growth. We studied this earlier.
2. **Be selective.** Give to a helper responsibilities which he will be able to handle successfully after making some errors. Every helper will be able to handle some level of decision-making. Expect much from each one, but not too much.
3. **Every helper will make mistakes**, especially at the beginning. Be patient. Spend time training him or her. This will pay off later, because you will be freer to handle bigger responsibilities, which God intends you to bear.
4. **Never delegate tasks or responsibilities without assigning report-back dates.** These are dates when your helper should meet with you to discuss progress. If you do not require reporting, you are "dumping" jobs on people who may not be able or willing to do well. Their failures are then your fault. You have set them up to fail. They need your guidance. They need to know they are doing well, or they need to know what to do to improve.
5. **Don't give any helper responsibilities without a "job description,"** a written list of tasks you are assigning him or her to achieve. Give the helper a copy of his "job description." Go over each phrase in this document so you will know your helper understands what he is expected to accomplish. Ask him to sign and date your copy. Keep this document. Review it with your helper periodically until you know he understands it completely. Make needed changes as time passes. Ask if your helper thinks he can achieve what you're asking. Ask if he would like anything changed. Don't lessen his work until you know it's a good idea. Be ready to increase his responsibilities when he is able to handle more. You might have to give to someone else tasks which this helper no longer has time for. With more challenging responsibilities, he may not be able to handle the less challenging ones.
6. **If your helper is failing, do not blame him immediately.** It is probably your fault for not training him well, or for giving him more than he can manage. Your attitude should be: "I want to help you succeed." It should not be: "We must meet because you are not a good person, or not a good worker." Assigning

blame is not usually important to success. Analyzing why the failure occurred and revising procedures to enable success **are** important. If a helper refuses to acknowledge his mistake, when he has made one, you will want to talk to him about this. Admitting one's mistake is being truthful. Deception shows immaturity.

7. **Part of good delegation is the holding of meetings** of your staff of helpers every week or two. In this way, everyone becomes familiar with everyone else's responsibilities. You can pray with and encourage each other. You can motivate your team. You can make announcements to keep all informed of what is happening. If there is a project in progress, all can see the status of the project by looking at the large, displayed control form described in chapter 7 of this section. Daily meetings can be times of high motivation for your workers. However, they can later become counterproductive. They can lose their inspiration. Consult your team. Follow the Lord. If you decide to meet every day with your team, review the decision with the Lord every month or so.

How to Keep Meetings Short and Meaningful

1. Create an agenda of topics to be dealt with during the meeting. Distribute copies of the agenda, a full day before, to all who must attend the meeting. Anyone who is to give a formal report should be given more advance notice.

2. Appoint a secretary who will take notes on all decisions that are made during the meeting, and all topics that come up, including the names of team members involved.

3. If someone brings up a topic that deserves time but is not urgent, after you have heard enough, explain to the team that we will discuss this further in a future meeting. If necessary, delegate to someone the task of doing research on this topic. Some topics will require a special meeting of their own.

4. If you only need to meet with a few helpers for a particular project, do not bring that project before the entire staff. Arrange a special meeting with the persons concerned.

5. If it will help, have each helper bring his plan for the week (or two) so all will know what the others are going to be doing. This is necessary if some of the staff must interact to achieve a

particular goal. A copy of each one's plan should be given to each person present. Everyone should use the same form for that plan.

6. Use the chalkboard freely to illustrate things. This increases attention and understanding. It also impressively helps everyone remember what you said. If you expect helpers to take notes on a subject, your use of the chalk will give them time to keep up with you. It might be better to have a secretary take those notes and distribute copies after the meeting.

7. Avoid embarrassing a helper during these meetings. These should be times of fellowship and prayerful encouragement, rather than correction. Circumstances might cause you to use a particular session to call someone to task, but this should be very exceptional.

Conflict, an Opportunity for Growth

If you find, as a leader, that one or more of your team are against you in some way, do not be discouraged. This can be for you a wonderful opportunity for drawing closer to them, a time for you to bond with them, and for them to bond with you and with each other. It can be for them, a wonderful time to know and understand you and your vision better. If you manage conflict properly, the result will be, your ministry will be stronger than ever.

This is a threat to the enemy. Satan is plotting your destruction. Those feelings you have that are critical of team members, especially the bitterness that is growing in your heart as you think about the problem you are having with certain of your helpers, are all part of Satan's design to bring you and your ministry crashing down around you.

For Satan to succeed, you need only follow the dictates of your fallen nature. If you nurture those thoughts and feelings, you are aiding the enemy. He will not reward you, except with more misery.

If you act in anger with your team, or some of the members, you are following along the path Satan has been preparing for your feet.

But what about those wonderful results that **can** happen? What about the bonding, the understanding, the drawing of the team together?

For these things to happen, you, the leader, must act wisely according to the Word of God. You must not allow yourself to react unwisely according to your corrupt nature.

In James 1:2-4 we see we should count trials as joy! Testing will bring us to a deeper walk with the Lord, to maturity. God has a plan. He wants to use conflict in your life to mold you into a more exact image of Jesus.

If you will read again Philippians 2:1-15, you will see how Jesus wants you to deal with the situation. Conditions of the heart and mind are so important if we are to become more like him (Col. 3:1-4)!

Action Steps to Take to Resolve Conflict

1. Confront, without bitterness, the person you feel is most responsible for the conflict. To confront means "to face." You need not be hostile when you confront.

   Do not approach the person in a warlike manner. Rather, let your confrontation be bold in its honesty, brave in its openness, but peaceful in its tone of voice and in its choice of words.

2. Most conflicts happen because the conflicting persons misunderstand each other. Each needs to do a very difficult thing. Each needs to listen to the other.

Listening does **not** mean accepting unscriptural positions. Listening **does** mean not interrupting until the speaker finishes. This is difficult!

Sometimes we allow the other to speak and we think that in itself means we are listening. It means we might be listening. We might also be plotting our next barrage of words aimed at defeating our opponent. That is not listening.

The purpose in genuine listening is to understand the point of view of the speaker, and to know what he or she is feeling.

Instead of interrupting, write down a few words that will remind you of what you want to ask the speaker. Spend as little time as possible writing.

There will be time for your questions later. Some questions will be answered as the speaker continues uninterrupted.

Look at the speaker as you listen. This is a courtesy. If you seem to be doing something else you are offending. You are sending the wrong message!

Listening well helps you obey Paul's exhortation to *look not only to your own interests, but also to the interests of others.* (Phil. 2:4).

Both men and women have a problem with confrontation. We all prefer to ignore our problems, hoping they will go away. But a problem with a subordinate does not usually go away. If ignored, it more often grows.

Confrontation does take courage. Avoiding it opens doors to rebellion, discontent on both sides, and distrust, all weapons and devices of the devil.

Do not begin to confront while either of you is in the midst of a heated flow of angry words. Ask your opponent to talk with you at a specific time and place, an hour or two later. Give a precise time for this meeting. Be punctual, but don't be upset if the other person comes late.

For your first meeting, meet with only one opponent. We use the word "opponent," not to connote "adversary," but only to refer to the person, your team member, who is dissatisfied. If meeting with only one seems unsatisfactory to either party, after you both try it, you might each have a counselor or friend attend a second meeting with you. Your aim is to allow this one staff member the opportunity to express himself fully, without hindrance from a more vocal member who might interrupt him too much.

You will take the anger out of this meeting by making it less adversarial. Be willing to listen. You have much to gain by understanding what your opponent is thinking and feeling.

Refrain from certain inflammatory expressions such as:
>"You always..."
>"You never..."
>"Your attitude is bad..."

"I cannot tolerate..." Sometimes this expression might be necessary in later meetings, but never early. This is a learning time. Let your opponent teach you about himself and his intentions.

Don't allow yourself to become angered or frustrated by crafty devices such as arriving late at the meeting. By keeping you waiting, your opponent might be trying to assert his own importance. He might also have been unavoidably delayed.

Let no "clever" maneuver put you off your course. Instead, open your heart to the Lord. Realize your significance comes from him and is something you feel each day when you worship him from your heart. In love, but without any sense of "I am holier than you are," direct the meeting toward the issue. Do this sincerely.

Remember, do not interrupt. Your goal is not to win an argument, but to understand the other person's point of view and feelings.

When your opponent realizes he or she has your full attention, and that you only ask questions because you want to understand his or her position in this situation, he or she will usually relax and try to give you genuine answers.

When we seek to win rather than to understand, we use hostile words. Our adversary wants to find the best words to fight back. Neither of us is seeking truth or godliness. Each wants to score the crushing blow with the most convincing, and often hurtful, words.

At the end of the conflict, both sides must feel satisfied. Since you are the leader it is up to you to manage this. If either your opponent or you are dissatisfied the conflict is not over. It is only taking a short recess.

Five Ways to Handle Conflict

1. **AVOID IT.** If the matter is trivial, this might be the best way. Otherwise, this is the wrong way to handle conflict. Wounds that are ignored can easily fester and become serious infections requiring strong medicine.

2. **LET YOUR OPPONENT HAVE HIS WAY.** This might be the best way if your opponent has a reasonable request or demand, and if the matter is not important. Otherwise, this too is not the way to handle conflict.

3. **WORK WITH YOUR OPPONENT** to come to a solution that will satisfy you and him or her. This is the method we have been describing above. The key to your success in using this loving and wise method is "listening." God gave each of us two ears and only one mouth. Let this fact remind you to listen more than you speak.

   Be ready for a good experience when the meeting with your opponent begins. Expect to learn more about your helper/opponent. Expect to learn more about the conflict itself. We learn a great deal from others when we are willing to listen.

   We assume here that the disagreement is a significant one. Trivial matters should not be scorned or treated as if they were totally unimportant. Let the Holy Spirit show you how to handle minor problems in love.

4. **COMPROMISE.** This means you agree to surrender some of the benefits you hoped to gain in this conflict, and your opponent does the same. Never surrender on moral issues, or on principles God wants you to insist upon.

Compromise is usually part of #3, above.

5. **MAKE A DECISION YOURSELF**, without the agreement of your opponent or opponents. This is the only righteous way to end the conflict if your opponent is demanding something that is clearly against the will of God, and he will not accept correction, will not change his demand.

   If this seems the only solution, postpone announcing it until a later meeting. This allows you time for prayer, consultation, further thought, and even an unscheduled attempt to convince your opponent. He or she might come to you with a satisfactory suggestion.

If you have not already done so, take time to teach from the Word the Bible principles upon which your decision is based. Be willing to answer questions. Remember to listen to objections, and to respond in love. Your teaching might open eyes and result in your opponent accepting your decision spiritually, intellectually and emotionally. Your opponent or opponents might even help you formulate your decision, thus contributing to the solution of the conflict in a good attitude.

What Causes a Settlement to Endure?

Two conditions make a settlement last for a long time. First, if each party in the disagreement openly negotiates with the other, admitting what he or she wants, giving the reasons, and listening to the others, the resulting settlement will likely be enduring. Otherwise he is just dropping out of the process, feeling he cannot change anything because his opponent is too forceful. He surrenders now, but will be angry later.

Second, each party must get something important in the settlement, something he needs in order to believe the settlement is a good one. Otherwise, neither party will enjoy the renewing of the bond of friendship and mutual respect that every conflict can bring about. The entire team might miss out on the benefits of this good result.

Two Ways of Preventing Conflict

1. Prepare the hearts and minds of your team by teaching them to discuss problems openly. Hold training sessions for the purpose of discussing feelings about certain aspects of the ministry. Divide a large team into sub-groups so all may speak without spending so much time. Then, in a total-team meeting, one from each group should summarize what was said in his group.
2. When circumstances indicate there is a misunderstanding or disappointment, hold a meeting to discuss the situation. Do not wait until the disappointment has turned to bad feelings or even rebellion.

Conflict on the Mission Field

There are studies that show conflict among missionaries is the number-one problem on the mission field. This should not be! But fallen human nature, and the influence of the evil one, make it a factor in mission life for many.

Missionaries are often determined, strong-willed people. The Great Commission is an overwhelming challenge! It appeals to determined, strong-willed individuals. These can find themselves trusting too much in their own natural strength, rather than in the power of the Holy Spirit.

When two such persons are involved in the same project, they sometimes disagree, and cannot resolve the conflict. Be ready for this! Be ready to use method #3, working with your opponent to come up with a solution If you can confront your opponent and discuss your problem, listening to him even when he is not willing to listen much himself, you will come to know your fellow-missionary far more deeply, and understand the problem far more clearly. The acceptance and forgiveness required to resolve the conflict will bond the two of you together. It will make you more like the Lord, and more fruitful in his kingdom.

This ability to resolve conflict will help you in your relationships with persons of your adopted culture. Christlike qualities in you will draw people, opening doors for you to share the gospel.

Conflict is Not Always Bad

Remember, conflict, if managed well, results in bringing the conflicting parties closer together. God honors harmony. He looks for unity.

> *How good and pleasant it is when brothers live together in unity!*
> (Ps. 133:1)
>
> *I in them and you in me. May they be brought to complete unity to let the world know that you sent me and have loved them even as you have loved me* (Jn. 17:23).

Chapter 9
Questions

1. Philippians 2:1-11 encourages us to:

    A. consider the interests of others as well as our own interests.
    B. forgive those who have betrayed us.
    C. use employees to make our ministries more productive.
    D replace loyal workers when they show weakness.

2. When a leader gives significant responsibility to a helper he is:

    A. giving that helper an opportunity to grow into leadership.
    B. benefiting the kingdom of God.
    C. multiplying himself, getting some important tasks done through others.
    D. making a mistake that will damage the work of the Lord.

3. As a follower:

    A. never expect a leader to be perfect.
    B. Become more like Jesus, and accept the leader God has chosen for you without grumbling
    C. secretly take over as much authority as you can so you will gain experience.
    D. submit to your leader while God has you under his supervision.

4. As a follower:

    A. be a good one, as part of your preparation for leadership.
    B. hide your skills from your leader if possible.
    C. make your superior a successful person.
    D. do not expect your leader to be perfect.

5. Barnabas:

   A. was suspicious of Paul, believing Paul wanted to replace Barnabas among the leaders in Jerusalem.
   B. was not concerned about losing his position to Paul.
   C. decided to hide from the leaders Paul's heart for the kingdom.
   D. tried to convince Paul to leave Jerusalem because the leaders distrusted Paul.

6. Barnabas:

   A. means "son of consolation."
   B. was given this name by the apostles.
   C. made Paul the prominent apostle he eventually became.
   D. brought Paul to Antioch to help in the ministry there.

7. What should you do with a lazy or a self-centered helper?

   A. Accept his attitude. Pray for him.
   B. If he is skilled, accept his attitude of self-exaltation, self-gain, self-promotion.
   C. Separate from him before the others begin to imitate him.
   D. Explain to him how Jesus behaved. Give him a chance to change. Dismiss him as a last resort.

8. "The skill of the successful leader" is:

   A. knowing when to quit.
   B. understanding mathematics applied to management.
   C. delegation.
   D. intelligent listening.

9. Guidelines for leaders dealing with assistants:

   A. Be selective about whom to trust with significant responsibilities.
   B. Don't give second chances to a man who has made a notable mistake.

C. Job descriptions take too much time and are often too limiting.

D. Try to do things yourself rather than trust a subordinate.

10. To keep meetings short and meaningful…

A. Prepare an agenda.

B. have a secretary take notes on decisions.

C. Avoid using a chalkboard. It takes too much time.

D. Avoid embarrassing a helper during the meeting.

11. If some of your team seem to be against you:

A. this can be an opportunity for growth in understanding and bonding.

B. if you act wisely your ministry will be stronger than ever.

C. Satan will put upsetting thoughts in your head and unkind feelings in your heart.

D. Harmony is vital. Dismiss anyone who speaks against you.

12. To resolve conflict:

A. Confront whoever opposes you.

B. The ideas is to eliminate all opposition and preserve your ministry.

C. Be bravely open, but peaceful in your tone and your words.

D. Be boldly honest.

13. To be a good listener…

A. Concentrate on what you will say next.

B. Accept your opponent's ideas, even if they are wrong.

C. Be sure the conclusion satisfies your opponent as well as yourself.

D. It's important that you win each argument.

14. When your opponent is speaking…

   A. write down a few words that will remind you of what you want
      to ask the speaker.
   B. Look down, to avoid eye contact with the speaker.
   C. Look at the speaker as you listen.
   D. Ask questions but without interrupting the speaker.

15. Avoid conflict altogether…

   A. if the matter is trivial, and no one is upset or unfairly treated.
   B. if the matter is too complicated and you can see it will time to
      manage.
   C. if the matter will embarrass you or someone on your team.
   D. if only one or two persons are affected.

16. Let your opponent have his way…

   A. never.
   B. if he has too many staff members on his side in the conflict.
   C. if his request is reasonable and the matter is trivial.
   D. if you are busy.

17. Make the decision, settle the conflict, yourself…

   A. if you're fed up with the problem.
   B. if there seems no other quick and easy solution.
   C. if you have to.
   D. if your opponent is demanding something that is clearly against
      the will of God, and he will not accept correction, will not
      change his demand.

Chapter 10

Managing Finances

Keep Accurate Records

There must be accurate records that show how much money your ministry has received each month and each year, the date when the money was received, and where the money came from. Records must also show how much money was spent, for what purpose, and the date of each expenditure.

Someone who is gifted in mathematics and is meticulous about accuracy and completeness should be assigned the job of "keeping accounts" or "bookkeeping."

If this person is not trained in bookkeeping, you will need to have him or her take some instruction from an accountant, or from someone who understands bookkeeping. This expert will need to know what your needs are, so he can design a system of keeping numeric records to show how much revenue came to the organization, and how the money was spent. Receipts for all expenditures must be kept in an orderly way so that any receipt can be found without much trouble.

If the government, or some organization, requires monthly or annual reports from you, your bookkeeper will need some training so he can fill out the forms for this purpose. Such forms might constitute the framework for your bookkeeping system, so that in following your accounting procedures you are at the same time filling out the reporting forms.

Whether anyone else needs financial records or not, you need them. You need to know that all money is handled with complete honesty. Set up a system with your bookkeeper that both he and you can point to and say, "This proves we have used God's money properly." An expert can show you how to establish such a system.

Should your ministry tithe? We say, "Yes!" Seek God about this, and about where the tithe should be sent. Should it be sent each month to the same organization or organizations? Should those organizations be ones that do the same sort of ministry yours does? Ask the Lord.

In your culture, is it easy to borrow money? Lenders charge interest, an extra fee for the use of their money. In some parts of the world borrowing is a great temptation.

A good general policy is this: I will not borrow money, either for myself or for the ministry. Versions of the Bible have differing translations for Romans 13:8. *Owe no man any thing...* Five versions (KJV, NKJ, NAS, RSV and the paraphrase TLB) have this wording for this verse. The other version reads: *Let no debt remain outstanding...* (NIV).

God is able to supply your needs. Assume you do not yet need what you do not yet have money to pay for. Wait until you have the funds before beginning a work that costs money you do not yet have. Otherwise you can easily get into debt that will take months or years to repay. In our opinion, Romans 13:8 (above) is clear enough on this point.

Some will argue: God is not commanding us to absolutely refuse to borrow no matter what the circumstances, but only to repay our debts quickly. They point to the New International Version (above) as the clearer translation of this verse.

If you are now in debt, pay it off. Do not let the debt remain outstanding (unpaid). The wicked borrows and does not repay, But the righteous shows mercy and gives (Ps. 37:21).

We believe the Lord wants us debt-free. Otherwise we are bound to our lender. We are not totally free to follow the Lord wherever he leads us. *The rich rule over the poor, and the borrower is servant to the lender* (Pr. 22:7).

Does God Want You to Save Money?

In the house of the wise are stores of choice food and oil, but a foolish man devours all he has (Pr. 21:20).

Do not store up for yourselves treasures on earth, where moth and rust destroy, and where thieves break in and steal (Mt. 6:19).

Jesus answered, "If you want to be perfect, go, sell your possessions and give to the poor, and you will have treasure in heaven. Then come, follow me" (Mt. 19:21).

Seek the Lord about whether you should save for expenses you may face later. Proverbs, above, tells us not to squander what we have. In Matthew 6:19 quoted here, Jesus is telling us we should not be attached to wealth as to a treasure - what we value highly - and that our treasure should be spiritual riches in heaven. In Matthew 19:21, above, Jesus is speaking to a rich young man for whom riches are too important.

If anyone does not provide for his relatives, and especially for his immediate family, he has denied the faith and is worse than an unbeliever (1Tim. 5:8).

Does Jesus want you to be devoid of savings here on earth? There may be a time in your life when the Lord will say to you, "Yes!" This might be because he is training you to depend upon him, and not on earthly goods. At another time in your life he might say, "No! I want to teach you to take care of your loved ones. Put ten percent of your income away for your children's education."

The question is, "What is God saying to you now?" If you are married, your spouse and you should be in harmony about the answer. When you are in harmony about what God is saying, you can obey with joyful confidence in him.

What About a Budget?

If you are

1. **tithing**, and
2. **careful** about spending, and you are
3. **saving** what God wants you to save, and you are
4. **never totally without money**...

169

perhaps you don't need a budget. If at any time you find that one of these four factors is missing in your economy, you need a budget to fit in the missing factor.

A budget is a plan for spending expected income. It can help you avoid being without money and going into debt. It prevents you from overspending on some items.

If you find you sometimes have no money and cannot buy food, you need to do one of these two things. 1) spend less, or 2) budget the money you receive.

Perhaps you can spend less by living in a smaller place, or by doing without some things that are expensive, and which you don't really need.

Rich or poor, we all find we cannot afford everything we want. We are blessed because God supplies all we need. Undisciplined spenders cannot resist buying things they later realize they cannot afford. A budget will protect them from such mistakes, if they are faithful to their budget.

Budgeting your money means you will limit your spending for each item you need or want. A budget is a plan showing how your income will be used and how much you will save during each pay period.

Being a believer, your first item on your budget list of expenses will be "tithe" because God says this portion is his.

Can a Lack of Funds Prevent You From Ministering?

Some say they cannot do the will of God because they don't have the funds. The fact is, God provides all we need to do his will. If we have no funds it might be for one of these reasons:

1. God's time for us to spend is not yet. Perhaps God is opening a door that requires no expense, a door we are ignoring because we have our own ideas of how we should minister.
2. We should seek his face to know what he wants us to do about funds. Perhaps he has been showing us to take some action which we are resisting.

Someone has said, "Do what you can, with what you have, where you are." We would add, "Trust God to do his part."

God is more concerned with how we accept what he is doing in our lives - or how we accept what he is not doing - than what we are achieving! He can get "stones" to do whatever it is we think we are so good at doing. But God wants worshipers. He wants givers with cheerful hearts. He wants lovers. He wants servants who are totally dedicated to him first, and not to their work first. Servants are willing to obey, even to stand in a corner and wait for his signal.

Money is never a requirement for fruitfulness. If it were, Jesus would never have given the purse to a thief! Jesus showed us how important money is in the kingdom. He gave the purse to Judas. He sent Peter to a humble fish for a gold coin, so he and Peter could pay their taxes.

But we must be faithful with money, as with everything else. There is no justification for misusing funds. God is not teaching us to leave funds in the hands of thieves.

Illustration
14   **Should we build a new building, or divide into two groups?**

Build		Divide	
Advantages	**Disadvantages**	**Advantages**	**Disadvantages**
We will have our own place to worship.	Everyone will have to give a lot of money.	More of the elders will have the opportunity to minister.	We don't have anyone who seems ready to lead the new meeting.
We can keep the music ministry intact.	Maintenance will be expensive.	Usually, when groups divide, they both grow.	Fewer people could mean less interaction, less excitement.
We can decorate the way we like it.	The family whose house we now use will not have the blessing.	Another home would have the blessing of having the meetings.	Few would be willing to belong to the new group.
We can hold meetings anytime.	The lost will not come to a church building as readily as they come to someone's home.	We could continue to give as much or more to missions, and to the poor.	
We will have space for children's ministry		The new meeting would be in a neighborhood which is now receiving no ministry, so the lost there would have an opportunity to hear the gospel.	
We will have space for storing things.			
We won't have to carry chairs and equipment to our meeting place.			
We will be investing in our own property.			

How to Make an Important Decision

If you have sought the Lord about an important decision and cannot discern what he wants you to do, try this.

Create a form like the one in Illustration 14. At the top, write a brief form of the question you are asking the Lord. Draw three vertical lines as shown. Label the columns to suit your question.

With your spouse, and perhaps your children who are mature enough if this is a family decision, or with your team if this is a ministry decision, read James 1:5-8. Pray together. Ask the Lord for wisdom. Then decide together what are the advantages and disadvantages of each of the two decisions you might make. Use each suggestion offered by your spouse or family, or your helpers.

If there are more than two possible decisions to choose from, try to eliminate some so that you are left with only two. If it helps, use similar forms to eliminate some choices, comparing two at a time.

Now, pray again. Discuss what you believe the Lord has shown you. If you are still in doubt, try this.

For each advantage and disadvantage, assign a numeric value form 1 to 10. Try to pick a number that represents the opinion of the group as a whole. For advantages, assign plus values. For disadvantages, the values will be minus (negative) values.

Add the values for each of the four columns. For example, looking at Illustration 14 again, after adding the six values you have assigned to the advantages of BUILDING a new building, let's say the total is plus twenty-one (+21). Let's say the total for the disadvantages is a minus twenty-four (-24). The advantages of DIVIDING the two groups add up to +31, and the disadvantages to -17.

Now, combine the total value you arrived at for the choice "BUILD." This value is 21 - 24 which equals -3 (minus 3).

Finally, combine the total value for "DIVIDE." That total is 31 - 17 which equals +14.

The +14 for "DIVIDE" is higher than the -3 for "BUILD." This seems to show that the decision should be to DIVIDE.

There is one last step. The above process is a mental process. It might be valid. God does intend that we use the intellect he has given us. But we want to rely on the Lord. We want to use our own understanding, but we do not want to rely on it.

Therefore we suggest going once again to the Lord in prayer to ask him to confirm that he does approve our dividing the congregation, rather than building a new building.

James 1:5-8 shows us we can trust God to give us wisdom, if we are courageous enough to act on what he shows us.

How Valuable are all These Administrative Ideas?

Some of these ideas are of no use to you now. Consider them again when your ministry has grown. Try these ideas even if you're not sure they will help you. You might change them to adapt them to your needs. Do not reject ideas that might help, without trying them.

Administrative ideas are not a substitute for seeking the Lord, obeying him, being his servant, being a servant to those we lead, or walking close to the Shepherd.

Administrative ideas are not essential to ministry. They are not an end in themselves. Do not make these methods the center of your life or ministry.

God will bless our efforts to be more effective. He will curse anything we put in place of him, making it an idol.

Chapter 10
Questions

1. Your financial records must show…

   A. how much money your ministry has received each month and each year
   B. the date when the money was received and where the money came from.
   C. for each expenditure, how much money was spent, for what purpose, and the date.
   D. the circumstances surrounding each transaction, and why each expenditure was necessary.

2. About borrowing money, select the response that is contrary to the advice of the author of this book.

   A. Borrow, but look for the lowest interest rate.
   B. God is able to supply your needs
   C. Assume you do not yet need what you do not yet have money to pay for.
   D. Wait until you have the funds before beginning a work that costs money you do not yet have.

3. Concerning saving money…

   A. Jesus does not want us to have our treasure in earthly things but in heavenly things.
   B. God commands us to care for our families.
   C. A sincere Christian is one who has no money.
   D. We need to consult God about saving money.

4. You need a budget if…

   A. you think you cannot afford to tithe.
   B. you are not saving as much as God wants you to save.

C. you sometimes do not have money on hand for things that are necessary.

D. one or more of the above statements is true about you.

5. If we believe God has called us for missionary work but we have no money, which one of these is most likely a wrong conclusion for us to draw?

A. God has not called us for missionary service.

B. God's time for us to spend is not yet.

C. We should seek his face to know what he wants us to do about funds.

D. We should trust God to do his part.

6. God is more concerned with how we accept what he is doing in our lives - or how we accept what he is not doing – than:

A. whether we love him.

B. intimacy with us.

C. what we are achieving.

D. whether we worship the Father.

7. Jesus gave the purse to Judas. This shows us…

A. Jesus did not know Judas was dishonest with money.

B. money is not the most important thing.

C. Judas was trustworthy.

D. money is useless in ministry.

Chapter 11

Solving Problems God's Way

Two Kinds of Managers: Project Managers and Procedure Managers

Project managers have a keen sense of what goes into getting ready for a project, getting the project into motion, and finishing the project. They enjoy the challenge of solving a new problem.

Procedure managers have the perseverance required to see that workers under their charge follow procedures. A procedure is a set of chores that result in the achievement of a goal. Usually the set of chores must be repeated again and again. Often each worker will perform only one or two steps in the procedure.

Procedure managers ensure the quality of a product or service by overseeing a staff who must be kept faithful to a procedure or procedures.

Such a procedure was probably set up by someone whose special skill is managing a project. His project was: to establish a procedure for producing a product or providing a service.

In smaller organizations, the same manager is often called upon to do both jobs. He must manage both projects and procedures.

When delegating responsibilities to helpers, keep in mind these two types of management: project management and procedure management. Most helpers will be better at one than the other. Your managers will be more successful if you assign them what they are best at doing.

You, the missionary-leader, will probably be more of a project manager than a procedure manager at heart. God is calling you to go to an unreached people group and establish his kingdom among individuals who are now unbelievers. This is a very wonderful project. You cannot do it. But God will do it through you! Jesus said, "I will build my Church..."

You can do, and do well, whatever God calls you to do in partnership with him.

You will find yourself eventually establishing procedures so that certain routine aspects of your ministry will run smoothly. As God blesses you with helpers, or as you seek out and hire helpers, you will appoint managers to oversee the procedures you will put into place.

Be ready to change details of a procedure, or to throw out the entire procedure and establish a new one, when you see it is necessary.

Even if you are ministering totally alone, submitted to a person or a group of people who are far away, you will face problems. That is not bad. It will force you to your knees, to the One who can solve every problem. He will show you his love, his wisdom and his power. Be sure to thank him.

Often he will comfort you and let you use what he has already given you to solve the problem. Use the Solution Plan.

The essence of the Solution Plan is quite simple. You might need to adapt the steps somewhat to suit the circumstances of your specific problem.

Use this plan if something is going wrong and you need a solution. You need to change a faulty procedure. It's foolish to continue doing things the same way, expecting a different result. What is being done wrong? How should it be changed?

Keep in mind, it is not usually necessary, or even important, to blame someone for what is going wrong. As the leader, accept at least some responsibility yourself when something goes wrong, but without making blame sound like a major issue.

Many of the heart-attitudes you will need in using the Solution Plan are discussed in chapter 7 on managing God's people.

The Steps of the Solution Plan

1. **Pray.** If you do not have helpers yet, go through these steps with the Lord alone. Otherwise, call on your key helpers. Read James

1:5-8. Ask God for the wisdom you need. Then believe he is giving it to you.

God might give you a solution that seems totally illogical to you. Obey God. Let him show you what he wants to show you through simple, uncomplicated obedience. Of course, anytime you sense a "leading of the Lord" that requires you to violate some Bible principle of righteousness, you know it is not from him. Ask him whom you should call upon for help.

If God does not give you specific directions to solve your problem, he is telling you to use the wonderful intellect he has given you. He will give you the wisdom you asked for as you proceed.

Steps 2 through 5, below, show how you might use that intellect. Give God the glory. He gave you a team, and he gave all of you sound minds with which to deal with problems. From him you have the fruit of the Spirit, which grows as you cooperate with him. The fruit helps you maintain your love, joy and peace while you solve problems. Thank him in advance.

2. **Analyze the problem** by asking yourselves three questions, and write the answers.
   - First, what is good about the procedure I must change? You don't want to give up what is working well.
   - Second, what is not good?
   - Third, what should be the result of this procedure? In other words, what does success look like? What do I want to see happening?

If you cannot answer these three questions, you need more time to analyze the problem. You don't really have an understandable problem until you can answer these three questions. Instead, you have only a complaint.

Have an analytical attitude toward the problem. With effort you can discover why the procedure is not working well enough. With logic you can "get to the bottom" of this problem. Remember, God is helping you.

3. **Devise a logical plan** that, if well carried out, will solve this problem. Perhaps you will need to use the Control Form discussed at the beginning of chapter 5.

   Sometimes the Pareto Principle applies to the situation. This is the 80%-20% principle discussed in chapter 4. Should someone with higher skills have fewer unskilled chores to do, so he can spend more time on highly productive tasks? Can some trivial tasks be eliminated?

4. Put your plan into operation, always watching to see that this does solve the problem. If not, start again with step one.

5. If, after doing your best, with your helpers, to analyze the situation in writing, you still can not see what is wrong, or, having seen what is wrong, if you cannot plan the solution, ask the Lord to help you decide whom you should call upon for help. Get someone who knows as much or more than you do about this kind of situation. Together, all of you will probably come up with an effective plan.

Four Principles of Godly Management for Solving Problems

These are the principles on which the Solution Plan, above, is built. They will help explain the plan. By looking at these principles we will see that the important one is following Jesus in the temple of our own hearts. He will lead us his way.

Problem Solving Principle #1: Pray

Without a keen sense of who God is, who we are, and what our commission is, we find ourselves working on the natural plane, motivated by human motives, and frustrated because things go wrong. God will allow them to go wrong because he has a higher purpose than our earthly purpose. He wants us working with him to promote eternal values, not temporal ones.

Here is a simple but wonderful message the Lord spoke to my heart.
"My son, it is my joy to draw you to myself. You are my inheritance, my rich treasure. Come often to me. Let me lift you to heavenly heights."

Even as I write these words, that message is written, only a foot away from my eyes. When I turn my heart to the Lord, he uses these words to bathe me in his presence. You need a reminder, too. Either a verse or two of scripture, or words that are totally scriptural, words you believe the Lord spoke to your own heart. Something that will help you stop what you're doing and totally give your heart and mind once again to him.

Principle #1 then, is "Pray." Connected to him is the only way to face any problem. It is the way of peace, of joy, of love. Jesus is our life!

Ask your team to look to the Lord. You need wisdom. Take time to read together James 1:5-8. Sing a worship song. Enjoy the Lord for a few moments. Then go on.

Problem Solving Principle #2: Analyze the Situation

Make a list of all the steps you should take to analyze the problem. "Analyze" means to separate into parts, to see how each part is related to the other parts and to the whole thing.

When you analyze a problem, then, you separate the problem into its parts. You ask questions of those who are involved with the problem so you will come to know the importance of each part of the problem, and how each part is related to the other parts, and to the problem as a whole.

In examining all this, you will probably think of a good solution. But don't make any decisions until you have taken every step to uncover what you don't know. Added information will throw more light on the problem.

Keep in mind, you will only get one view of the problem from each person you question. Usually, each will believe the cause of the problem is something another person did. You must hear from all involved before making a judgment about how to change things so the problem will no longer exist.

Decide beforehand how you will interview the helpers involved. Some might help more if you interview them each by himself or herself. For some helpers, meeting with two or more at a time will be more productive because each will say things that will spark ideas and reactions in the others.

Those you question will think you want to assign blame. Usually no one person is responsible for the problem. Perhaps all of you are responsible in different ways. Instead of looking for someone to blame, it is better to find a solution, with everyone's help, so all can feel they have contributed.

Problem Solving Principle #3: Draw up a Plan That Will Change the Situation for the Better

You have learned how to draw up a "Solution Plan." Use those steps to change the way things were, to the way you and your team want them to be.

Remember to get help from the team. They are closer to the problem than you are. Their ideas will be more practical. Also, they will be more committed to make the plan work if it is their own plan.

Problem Solving Principle #4: Be in Control of What is Happening as Your Helpers put into Action the Plan that Might Solve the Problem

Inexperienced managers tend to lose contact with the situation, once everyone involved knows what he or she must do to resolve the problem. To avoid losing contact, you should put into the plan, dates when you want either a written report on progress, or a meeting in which the team will report. In this way you can keep in touch.

Be sure that, as a result of the report system, you have a record of what has been done, what has not been done, and who will do what, and when.

Further reports should then be arranged if necessary. At no time, even after everything is running smoothly, should you lose contact with any aspect of your ministry.

Ordinarily, keep in touch through the managers who are responsible for the helpers involved in the problem. Be sure to show confidence in the managers, but ask them detailed questions about how things are being resolved.

If there are no such managers, then you must supervise your helpers adequately, without attempting to "watch over" every decision they make.

Problem Solving Principle #5: Deal with your Helpers and Delegate Responsibilities in a Godly Way

A basic principle of management is to delegate, delegate, delegate. This is not to release you so you do not have to do anything. It is to release you so you can do the essential things well, without being hounded by details someone else can do for you.

Delegate to persons whose hearts are right, who can best do the jobs.

Trust these managers with responsibilities that might be a bit more than you feel safe about.

Keep in close touch with these managers through reporting.

Do not try to supervise their every move. This will discourage them and prevent you from achieving your own goals.

Delegate to benefit your helpers, to build them into experienced leaders.

You will see godly attitudes about how to deal with your helpers in Philippians 2:1-11.

If you become convinced that you have chosen the wrong helper for a certain responsibility, do one of these things:

1. Take that responsibility away from him or her, and give him some other responsibility. Or...
2. Give that helper an assistant who can handle his less demanding tasks under his supervision. This will enable that helper to be successful. Later his assistant might be unneeded. Or...
3. Give some of that helper's tasks to another manager or another helper.

Be willing to dismiss from service a helper who exhibits laziness, a wrong spirit, or a bad attitude. But take time to teach such a one. If he is willing to change, do not give up on him easily. There's more on this in chapter 7.

Your own attitude is under scrutiny. Both believers and unbelievers are watching. Pray that they may see Jesus in you.

Problem Solving Principle #6: Do Not Procrastinate

"Procrastination" is putting off until later what should be done now.

9 Ways to Defeat Procrastination

1. **Pray** for wisdom to understand, and determination to change.
2. **Review your priorities** so you can see how important or unimportant is the task you're postponing. If unimportant, should you delegate it? Should the task be dropped?
3. **Examine these causes** of procrastination.
   a) Fear of failure. "If I try to do this task, I might fail!" Renounce this fear. If you fail, you can get help. Realize that your value is in the fact that you are a child of God. He gave his Son to die for you! You are a worshiper of the one true and living God!
   b) Indecision. "I'm not sure this needs to be done!" See #2 above.
   c) Lack of information. "I need to know more about this task before I can do a good job on it." The remedy for this is to take action and learn what you need to learn. Or delegate the gathering of information to a helper.
   d) Lack of tools. Bring the needed tools together in one place before you begin the task.
   e) Poor work environment. If you have a disorderly work area, put things where they should be stored. A well-organized area will motivate you to work well.
4. **Do the worst first**. Develop the habit of attacking first the task you like least. Do this each day for six weeks. This is one of the best ways to overcome procrastination.
5. **The "salami method."** In the Western world there is a large sausage called "salami." It tastes good, but no one could eat an entire salami at one meal!

   If you have a task you dislike, a task that will take many hours or days, do not try to do the whole job during the next few hours or days. Instead, do it for half-an-hour each day until it is done. Or, work on it only in the mornings, or only in the afternoons. Trying to do it all at once will mean you must postpone other important tasks. It means doing a dull job over too long a period of time.

It often happens that, while using the "salami method," we realize how good it is to be getting this job done, and we work longer at it than we planned each day.

6. **What are the benefits** of doing this task? Write these down. It will motivate you to get the task done.
7. **Plan when you will do the task**. If urgent tasks prevent you from doing the distasteful task now, put this task on your calendar or your calendar chart. When the time comes, be faithful to do that task.
8. **Reward yourself!** Schedule a task you enjoy for the time immediately after that distasteful task is finished.
9. **Be creative about #4, above.** Doing the worst job first (#4 above) for a long enough time will probably break you of all procrastination. But you may not have enough distasteful tasks to do. Then, try this. Plan as your first task each day for a month, a brief distasteful task that may not be totally necessary. For examples:
   - Clean out correspondence files if some of the items in those files are too old to be useful.
   - Sweep the floor of your work area.
   - Wash some piece of equipment, even if it's not very dirty.

Do you know of something you're procrastinating about? *Anyone, then, who knows the good he ought to do and doesn't do it, sins* (Jas. 4:17). Procrastination is sin when the reason for delay is not serious enough.

If you recognize your procrastination as sin, be encouraged. The truth is setting you free.

If we confess our sins, he is faithful and just and will forgive us our sins and purify us from all unrighteousness (1 Jn. 1:9).
Confess procrastination to the Lord as sin right now. Receive your forgiveness. Take whatever steps the Lord shows you, or has shown you, to overcome procrastination.

A Final Note About Solving Problems

In general, problems require an intellectual process to find the solution. God does not normally do our work for us. He created us in his image. In limited ways, we are like God. He puts us to work. He honors us by involving us in his enterprise, the salvation of mankind. He helps us when we ask for his help.

But there are times when our problem has another purpose. God is at work within our hearts while he is at work winning the world. Often we need to seek after the Lord for a solution to the problem, rather than asking him to help us solve the problem. Here are two true stories that show God at work within us, while we are working for his kingdom.

1. One pastor was frustrated because his church was not growing. He prayed. God directed him to go door-to-door in the neighborhood to invite people to come visit his church.

    The pastor obeyed. He discovered joy in this. He found himself praying with people whom he would never have met if he had disobeyed God.

    Within a few weeks, new people began to come to worship on Sunday mornings. Strangely, he recognized none of them. Not one of the newcomers was someone he had visited!

2. Years ago I worked for a mission organization as a publications manager. Part of my family's support was to come from people who received my newsletter, telling of my work.

    Our income dwindled. I prayed. God said, "Trust me. Do as I urged you to do months ago."

    I obeyed. I began to send out a newsletter again, although I had little to write about. I included a short teaching and enjoyed ministering through writing.
    We received a large donation. We were overjoyed. We thanked God. But the donation was sent to us before the donor could possibly have received our newsletter!

186

In both these cases, God was looking for trust, with obedience. In each case, God's idea was supremely practical, yet God showed his power to rescue us without our help!

Perhaps you have marked things in this section on administration, ideas you want to revisit and plunge into, changing a less productive lifestyle for a more productive one. Talk to the Lord about applying what you have read. Talk to him now!

Don't procrastinate. Put a note on a calendar for implementation during a specific day or week, so your ideas won't become lost in a marshland of good intentions.

Chapter 11
Questions

1. Project managers…

    A. like to find ways of doing things that have never been done before.
    B. don't feel content when a problem arises.
    C. would rather quit than delve into some mess that causes a routine to fail.
    D. consider their superiors unreasonable when they ask them to solve a problem.

2. Which of these statements is least likely to apply? Procedure managers…

    A. find satisfaction in enforcing decisions made by others.
    B. want to have good results from their efforts.
    C. oversee workers to assure that they follow the proper routines to achieve good results.
    D. cannot tolerate initiative shown by their workers.

3. The Solution Plan. Which one of these steps involves three questions:

    A. Start out by asking God for help.
    B. Analyze the problem.
    C. Devise a plan that will solve the problem.
    D. Carefully observe how well the plan works.

4. The three questions. Which one does not belong?

    A. Who caused the procedure to fail?
    B. What is good about the way things are working?
    C   What is not good?
    D. What has to happen for us to be satisfied?

5. When you analyze a problem...

   A. you separate the problem into its parts.
   B. you ask questions of those who are involved with the problem.
   C. you let the team know you are totally dissatisfied with their handling of things..
   D. you get to know the importance of each part of the procedure or problem.

6. What God especially wants for us is...

   A. that we keep busy with things we feel we should do.
   B. that we work with him to promote eternal values.
   C. that we terminate relationships that are not productive.
   D. that we overcome every shortcoming in our character.

7. You, the missionary, need to keep in close contact with what is happening in your ministry...

   A. until the solution to the problem has been carefully implemented.
   B. until you and your helpers can see that the solution is working well.
   C. until many weeks of successful operation of the solution have passed.
   D. always.

8. The Pareto Principle...

   A. says we spend only 20% of our time on tasks that are most effective.
   B. cannot help us devise a plan to solve a problem.
   C. might come into play as we devise a plan to solve a problem.
   D. suggests we should consider whether we spend enough time on highly effective tasks.

9. You learned six principles for solving a problem. Which of the following is not among the first three principles?

A. Pray.
B. Gather your team together.
C. Analyze the situation.
D. Draw up a plan that will change the situation for the better.

10. Which of these is not among problem solving principles #4 through #6?

A. Be in control of what is happening as your helpers put into action the plan that might solve the problem
B. Interact with your helpers and delegate responsibilities in a godly way.
C. Interact with your helpers and delegate responsibilities in a logical way.
D. Do not procrastinate.

Section 3

Cultural Understanding is Vital for You

You will be able to give your adoptive
people the gospel message after you have
learned their language and their culture.
Then you will understand them, and they
will understand you, and trust you.

Chapter 12

Know Their Culture So You Can "Open Their Eyes"

Will You be Satisfied on the Mission Field?

We cannot prepare you for everything that might happen on the mission field, but we can deal with some things that often happen.

To begin with, you need to realize that any spiritual problems you are having now will not go away when you leave your own people and go to minister to a people different from your own. Deal with spiritual problems now while you're in training for missionary service.

For example, if you're experiencing conflict where you are, learn here and now how to deal with conflict. Resolve this conflict, using what is written in this book in chapter 9.

Is there any discontent in your marriage? Deal with this important problem now. Putting it off will not help. Listen to your spouse willingly, that you might understand. Speak to your spouse with love.

What we discussed in chapter 9 concerning conflict resolution might help you in your marriage if there is any kind of problem. However, there is a basic difference. Conflict resolution is one thing when it concerns helpers on your staff, and quite another when it concerns your spouse. Jesus tells us in his Word, that we are to love our spouse as Jesus loved the Church and gave himself (Eph. 5:25). We must be willing to lay down everything for our spouse. It is my conviction that God would have me interrupt ministry to others so that I can resolve any serious problem that exists between my wife and me.

Work with your counselor on any spiritual problem you have.

Happiness is Not the Same as Joy

Being satisfied on the mission field is not the same as being happy.

Happiness is something we all like, but can not always have. We can and will, however, always have joy if we are saved and have the assurance of our salvation. God intends that we have great confidence in him, and joy.

Happiness, on the other hand, comes and goes. Happiness is a feeling. It is a result of circumstances in our lives.

Joy is a fruit of the Holy Spirit. It was given to us in seed form when we received him, and it grows as we spend time with the Lord and as we read and study his Word.

You will experience some unhappiness on the mission field, or anywhere else. You will always have joy. To experience the joy, to feel the joy, you may need to reflect on a verse of scripture, or turn your mind and heart toward the Lord.

No one should venture onto the mission field if he cannot do what David did. *David found strength in the Lord his God* (1 Sam. 30:6).

Your satisfaction must be in the Lord, not in your success in ministry. Success produces happiness. The Holy Spirit has already produced joy within you. Now it's up to you to cooperate with him so that the joy will grow.

To find "strength in the Lord" you must look for it. Look in his Word. Look to him. Live in an awareness of his presence. Worship him often. *He will lift you up* (Jas. 4:10)

You have made known to me the path of life; you will fill me with joy in your presence, with eternal pleasures at your right hand (Ps. 16:11)

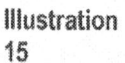
Illustration
15

Culture Shock

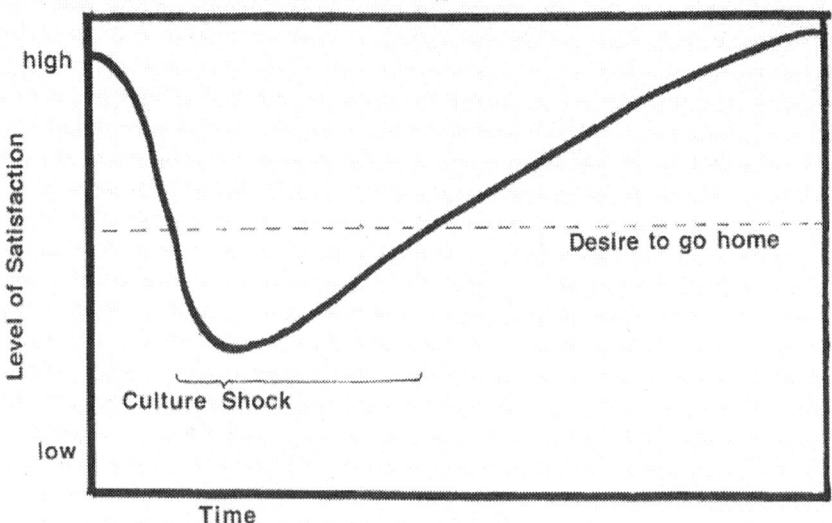

Based on Paul Hiebert's illustration, *Anthropological Insights for Missionaries,* p. 65.
Used with permission.

You Can Avoid "Culture Shock"

"Culture shock" is the feeling missionaries have when they think they cannot achieve their goals among the people God has sent them to evangelize.

Illustration 15 shows you that when a missionary first arrives among the people God has sent him to, he is usually very satisfied. He is happy. Everything is new and exciting. He finds the people friendly. He learns a few words in their language. He feels successful.

The level of satisfaction in the illustration is shown by the curved line.

The line starts out at the left side of the illustration near the top. Satisfaction is high at the beginning. Soon the line plunges down toward the bottom, showing the level of satisfaction is low. The missionary is not happy, not satisfied.

197

He has discovered that learning a new language requires great patience with himself and with the persons helping him. He has seen that these people have customs and ways of thinking that he cannot understand. He makes mistakes, causing them to laugh. Perhaps he has even become ill, and does not know how to get medical help.

Notice the horizontal line of dashes across the middle of the illustration. While the satisfaction line is above this dash line, the missionary wants to stay among this "foreign" people. But when the satisfaction line goes down below the dash line, the missionary wants to go back to his home.

Culture shock is illustrated by that portion of the satisfaction line that appears down below the dash line. The missionary at this stage wants to go home. He sees himself as a failure.

If You Experience "Culture Shock" You Can Recover

Don't take your situation too seriously. Most missionaries experience some degree of culture shock. Encourage yourself in the Lord. Keep up your sense of humor.

The way you handle culture shock will affect your ministry for many years.

From the beginning you will make some friends within the culture. You can share some of these feelings with these friends. They will help you, at least by listening.

Remember your identity is found in God. As you experience intimacy with God in worship, you will see things in true perspective, God's perspective.

Worship Prevents Culture Shock

Whether you experience culture shock at all, depends in part on you. You will not experience culture shock to such a degree that you want to go home if your relationship with the Lord is vibrant, if you are enjoying the presence of the Lord every day in genuine worship.

Do a Bible study about worship. Review parts of this book where we refer to worship. Ask a teacher or counselor to recommend a book on this subject. If you are to be a fully anointed missionary you need to be a worshiper.

You benefit by genuine worship. However, "self" is not a worthy motive for worshiping God. It is doubtful whether anyone who tries to worship God primarily for his own benefit can really worship. His glory, his pleasure, should be our purpose. But the wonderful fact is, when we worship him we sense our own worth. Perhaps this is because we intuitively realize in worship that he has created us for himself, and that we are most fully human, most totally alive, most wonderfully sane, when we are worshiping him.

Feelings of success or failure about our work fade into insignificance as we worship. We "see" him more clearly, we appreciate his greatness more fully, we surrender to him more wholeheartedly and adore him more completely when we worship him in spirit and in truth.

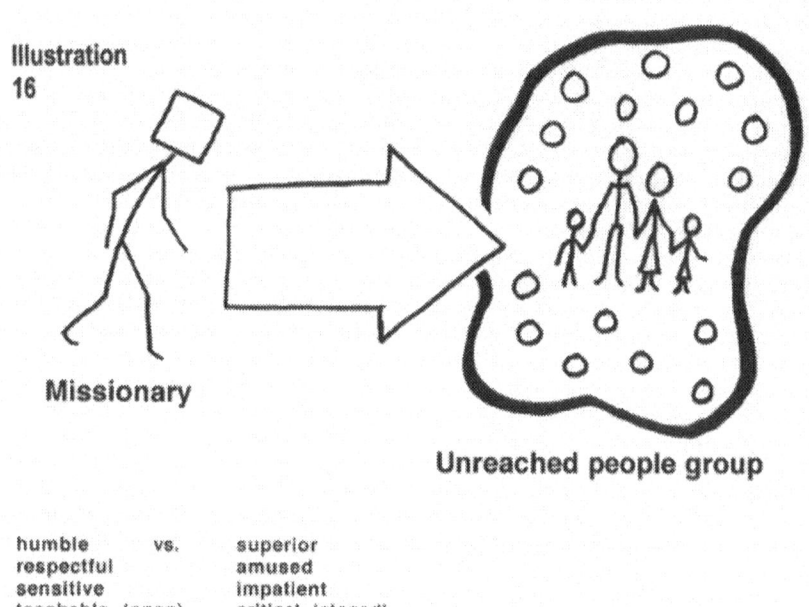

Illustration
16

Missionary

Unreached people group

humble   vs.   superior
respectful   amused
sensitive   impatient
teachable (open)   critical (closed)

Your Attitude Toward the People is Crucial to Your Success

Illustration 16 shows scriptural attitudes, and their destructive opposites.

Philippians 2:1-18 is our source on this subject. Read these verses. Compare them with the scriptural attitudes described below. Ask the Lord to mold you more and more into his likeness.

Humble. Jesus was God. Yet he did nothing to make secure his position among men. Instead, he suffered every insult and pain that we might understand his love more, and be freer in our own self-giving.

Give yourself away. Give yourself first of all to the Lord, and secondly to those to whom he sends you. Your position is secure in heaven. You can safely reach out to help others.

"Superior" is the opposite of "humble." God loves all equally. We are not superior. Acting as if we were superior is the sin of pride. We judge others as inferior. We expect special treatment. We choose our words carefully in order to promote ourselves in the eyes of others.

We are guilty of this offense when we give a testimony of how great God is, telling of how he healed our friend, but we choose words that clearly show it was because we, and not someone else, prayed.

There is a difference between letting Jesus, the light within us, shine before men that they might see our good deeds and praise our Father in heaven, on the one hand, and shining a light on ourselves to reflect what we want people to see so that they will praise us, on the other hand.

We are with a group of people who don't know us. We find an opportunity of saying something to the group. As we say it, we imply we are great ones involved in ministry. We say nothing untrue, but our words are selected to produce an effect, to give an impression, to promote ourselves in the minds of others.

If we give in to these self-promoting devices, we have a problem with pride, similar to the pride the Pharisees showed as they sounded trumpets to call attention to their good works (Mt. 6:2,5,16). On the field we will have a superior attitude toward people of the other culture. It will show!

Travel does not change our character.

Respectful. An important key to working or even just associating with other individuals is "respect." One minister has a whole teaching on marriage, based on spouses practicing respect for each other. If you will honor another as worthy of your esteem, he or she will feel safe and confident about you. Respect is the basis for a solid friendship that can deepen.

"Amused" is the word describing the opposite of "respectful" in our illustration. If you laugh at the culture of persons you want to befriend, they will not be drawn to you. They will feel they cannot trust you with the innermost facets of their culture. This will hinder you from learning their culture.

Sensitive. Always consider the feelings of others in the way you speak or act. The fruit of the Holy Spirit includes kindness and gentleness. Let these grow in your spirit as you cooperate with God in the way you deal with others.

"Impatient" is the opposite of "sensitive." Impatience prompts us to give in to anger when things do not proceed as we want. Impatience and anger are devastating hindrances to evangelizing. They also hinder the work of God within us!

Teachable. This means "open, ready to listen to others and willing to learn from them. It does not include willingness to adopt doctrine or customs that are unscriptural.

"Critical" or "closed" is the opposite of "teachable." A missionary is wise who withholds judgment of another's culture until he understands its details. We can all learn a great deal from each other, and even from each other's culture.

The fact is, every culture has much that is good, and too much that is evil. If we enter a foreign culture knowing we will find good things, we will appreciate the good, and probably do well in that culture. If we expect to find evil, or if we focus on the evil we discover, we will find ourselves judging as evil, and criticizing, things we don't yet understand, and perhaps even things that are neither allowed nor condemned by scripture.

The prophet Daniel did well in the Babylonian culture because he had an *excellent spirit* (Dan. 5:12; 6:3 KJV). He was a man of *understanding* (NIV). You will do well to bring with you this spiritual "equipment," a humble, respectful, sensitive and teachable spirit.

As you develop these scriptural characteristics in your heart, your mind and your speech, you cause yourself to appear less "square-headed" in Illustration 16, and more "round-headed" like the people God is calling you to lead into the kingdom. That is, you become more acceptable to them, even more like them, or at least more prepared to know them, love them, and help them to see and value the truth you bring.

What is "Culture"?

Illustration 17 shows culture as a sphere, or ball, set upon a holder or base. This ball has a center and three layers covering the center.

Behavior is the outer layer. Behavior is "what people do," their customs. As a missionary, the first things you observe in your adoptive culture will be part of this layer. In other words, you will notice things people do. In some cultures people eat rice more than any other food. In other cultures they eat meat... in others, maize... in others, fish. These practices are part of a people's behavior.

Values is the second layer of the "ball" we call culture. The "values" of a people group tell you "what is best" in the minds of that people group.

In some cultures a person values highly the approval of the chief before marrying, or selling land. In other cultures, a person is considered to be a rule unto himself. He can do anything he wishes unless it would be unjust to someone else.

In some cultures a person is important if he earns much money. In other cultures he is important if he has many children.

In some cultures a person is most important if he gives away much to those who are needy. In other cultures he is important if he has many possessions stored up for himself and his family.

> What values are reflected in your answers to these questions?
> •Who are the heroes in your culture?
> •Is a show of anger a good way to convince people in your culture?
> •Is a particular food regarded as especially valuable?

202

Illustration

17

What Is Culture?

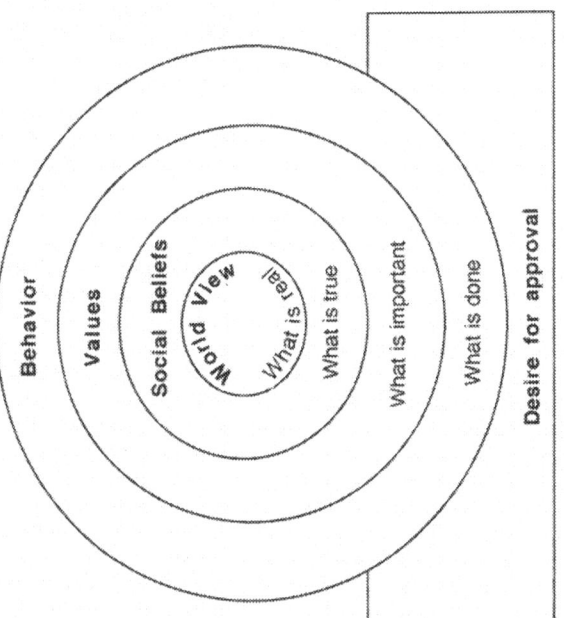

Illustration is based on Lloyd E. Kwast's in his article, "Understanding Culture," in Winter, Ralph, et al., editors, *Perspectives on the World Christian Movement, a Reader*, page 363. Pasadena, CA. William Carey Library, 1981.

Social beliefs is the third layer. These tell us "what is true" in the minds of the people of the particular culture. These beliefs include spiritual beliefs, and non-spiritual beliefs.

In some cultures, people believe they are controlled by nature. This means they cannot make plans, because the future is decided by the forces of nature. They cannot change conditions. In other cultures, people believe they can solve such problems, and believe they will control more and more of nature as they learn more and more about science.

In some cultures people believe that if a piece of food falls to the floor, it is dirty and must not be eaten. In other cultures it is still clean unless it is visibly dirty.

In some cultures a man must have no more than one wife, and a woman no more than one husband. In other cultures multiple wives are permissible. In some cultures multiple husbands are permissible.

In some cultures, parents are considered wise. In other cultures parents are considered to be unwise concerning the practical things of modern life. In some cultures, a man is considered more important than a woman. In other cultures, the mother is the ruler of the home.

> What social beliefs does your culture embrace regarding the following?
> - The importance of the nuclear family which means mother, father and children.
> - The importance of the extended family which includes other relatives.
> - Respect for the authority of political leaders.

World View is at the core or center of any culture. A people's world view shows us "what is real" to the people of that particular culture.

In some cultures microbes and germs are real. Other cultures do not acknowledge their existence. Demons are real to many cultures. Western cultures tend to deny their existence. In the west, UFOs are thought to be real by many. To others UFOs are merely the deceptions of demons.

Each of these four layers or elements of culture affects especially the elements that are shown in the illustration to be farther away from the core. In other words, influence is directed from world view toward behavior.

Therefore, world view affects all the other elements. Behavior is affected by all the other elements.

Because God is real to you, your beliefs, your values, and your behavior, are different from the beliefs, values, and behavior of those who do not consider God to be real. Because you have certain social beliefs, your values and behavior are affected by those beliefs. Your values affect your behavior.

Notice in Illustration 17 there is a bottom, a base or foundation. All cultures have the same base. The base of every culture is the human desire to be accepted or approved by other persons within the culture.

This is a good thing. God has built into man a desire to be approved. This is a powerful force that causes even unregenerate man to do "good" and avoid "evil." Unfortunately, the "good" is what society considers good. The "evil" is what society considers evil. In a culture where the world view does not have the concept, "absolute truth," the people of the culture come to a general agreement regarding what is good and what is evil. They are right about some things and wrong about others, and what they decide is "good" today might be labeled "evil" later..

From the time you were saved you saw absolute truth as a reality because you held as absolutely true all that the Bible teaches as true. This has given you a wonderful foundation for your world view. Your world view differs from that of non-believers within your culture. Therefore your culture differs from the general culture of your people, unless the majority of your people are saved.

This does not mean everything in your culture is ungodly. You can identify what is ungodly by comparing aspects of your culture with the Word of God.

That basal desire for approval, the base of all culture, the desire to conform, prevents many crimes from being committed. People fear losing the approval of their fellow man. If they are despised, they are in danger.

Jesus sent Paul of Tarsus to ethnic groups that did not have the good news, *to open their eyes* (Ac 26:18). He will now send you for the same purpose. You must open the eyes of a people group which does not have a knowledge of the true God, "turn them from darkness to light and from the power of Satan to God, so that they may receive forgiveness of sins and a place among those who are sanctified by faith in" Jesus.

You will be an instrument in the hands of God to change part of their world view, and some of their social beliefs, values and behavior. We deal with this later. It is important that you understand all you can about culture, not so that **you** can change their culture, but so that you can help them understand how God wants them to change it. They will always be the experts, not you.

Once born again, they will be able to *see* the kingdom of God (Jn. 3:3) and therefore able to see what is wrong in their culture. Your task will be to counsel them so that they do not change things God does not require them to change.

You might have to help them substitute something for what they do need to change, so that the society does not collapse. For example, a three-legged stool cannot stand if you cut off one of the legs. You must substitute some other leg for a defective leg, or the stool will collapse.

"The Axe Culture" Story is an Example

A missionary went and lived with a primitive people. He brought a few axe heads and gave them away as gifts to members of the culture who helped him build his house. He even gave one to a teen-age boy. He gave another to a woman.

In their culture, the chief had to be consulted about any major decision, but the missionary did not know this. He acted without consulting the chief.

Those who received the axe heads were astounded at their good fortune. Now they no longer had to go to the chief to borrow the chief's stone axe. The stone axe was never as sharp as these steel axes!

However, the stone axe was much more than an axe. No one in the village was permitted to make his own stone axe because the chief's axe was a symbol of his key position in the society. If you wanted to use the chief's axe, you must respectfully ask the chief. He would ask you why you wanted to borrow the axe. He would give permission for that one use. Then you were required to return it immediately to the chief.

Now that others had axes, sharp, steel axes, no one went to the chief to borrow his axe. The fact that even a boy owned a steel axe made the chief's axe seem obsolete and ridiculous.

Soon no one went to the chief for any sort of permission. Each one lost respect for the chief, and just did what he thought was right without consulting him or anyone else.

The missionary had changed the culture so radically, it could no longer serve to protect the people from disunity, chaos or violence.

What should the missionary have done? He should have consulted the chief before giving unusual gifts, or doing anything unfamiliar in that culture.

Another Example

In another culture, after some were born again, people began to neglect cleanliness! They were no longer in fear of the evil spirits who used to hide in dust and refuse, so they needed another reason to keep themselves and their property clean.

The missionary had to help the chief devise ways of encouraging the people to keep their homes and the village clean and tidy.

Problems like these help us to value each culture, even though we observe certain things we know are not in accord with the absolute truths of scripture. God will use his Word and the dedicated hearts of his children within the culture to change those things.

Chapter 12
Questions

1. About joy…

    A. David found strength, which is the joy of the Lord, in God himself.
    B. Every believer needs to find his satisfaction in the Lord, not in "success."
    C. Joy and happiness are the same thing.
    D. God will fill us with joy in his presence.

2. Concerning culture shock:

    A. "Culture shock" is the feeling missionaries have when they think they cannot achieve their goals.
    B. Missionaries usually start off happy and excited about being missionaries.
    C. All missionaries eventually become so discouraged they want to go home.
    D. Missionaries make mistakes about the culture they are adopting, causing the people to laugh.

3. If we feel we are failures, the feeling often fades into insignificance…

    A. as we talk to a friend.
    B. as we read the Bible.
    C. as we fellowship with believers.
    D. as we worship the Lord.

4. Scriptural attitudes and their destructive opposites. The missionary should be:

    A. humble rather than having a superior attitude.
    B. sensitive, rather than amused.
    C. teachable, rather than close minded.

D. self-confident rather than dependent.

5. The scriptural attitude omitted in question 4, above, is an important key to working or even just associating with other individuals. One minister has a whole teaching on marriage, based on spouses practicing it toward each other. This attitude is...

A. friendliness.
B. a sense of humor.
C. an attitude of respect.
D. a willingness to compromise.

6. The scriptural attitude "Teachable" involves a willingness to:

A. honor those of another culture.
B. learn from others.
C. confess our shortcomings..
D. refrain from preaching before others are ready to receive the Word.

7. The values held by the people of any culture tell you what those people regard as:

A. best, or more important, or most important.
B. of highest monetary value.
C. especially beneficial for physical health.
D. of highest importance for emotional well-being.

8. World view:

A. is the second "layer" of every culture.
B. shows us "what is real" to the people of that particular culture.
C. "Demons do not exist." This is an expression of the world view of some "advanced" cultures.
D. "UFOs are genuine vehicles carrying intelligent creatures from outer space." This is an expression of the world view of some western cultures or subcultures.

Chapter 13

Appreciate Their Culture

Is Their Culture Good or Evil?

All cultures have both good and evil aspects. This includes your culture and mine. We pray that the evil things will change. In general, most of any particular culture is either good or indifferent (neither good nor evil). God only wants to change the evil parts of the culture.

As far as the believers are concerned, in their own hearts and lives, their culture gradually changes. As they learn the Word, they turn from evil things they come to realize are embedded in their culture.

So we are looking at two different groups of people within the same culture, the saved and the unsaved.

Let us say the people whose culture we are discussing, are 90% unsaved. This means the society in general is unsaved. Though many will be influenced by the good they see in the believers, the general culture will not change until a much greater percent of the people are saved.

Missionaries do well to avoid trying to change the culture of the newly saved. Foreigners will not do as well at changing the culture, because their understanding of the culture is faulty. Believers born within the culture will do well, counseled by the missionary who has adopted their culture as his own, and who knows that culture well.

Remember, the experts on their culture are the people born within that culture. You, the missionary, are the expert on the Word of God. Teach them the Word. God's Spirit dwells in them. They will tell you when their culture is opposed to your teaching. They will want to change to God's ways.

With your help, they will decide what should be changed, and what that change should be. You will help them because you know the Word, and you know things they do not know about culture in general. Ask them if a change they are advocating in their own culture could affect other aspects of their culture. Explain the danger. You can help them adopt good practices that will not have undesirable effects on the culture as a whole.

How Many Cultures Must the Missionary Study?

The missionary must study three cultures: his own culture, the Hebrew culture reflected in the Bible, and the culture of the people God is sending him to evangelize.

You will do well to study your own culture, so you can understand what sorts of questions to ask them about their culture.

Know the culture of the Bible. Then you will see more clearly what are the basic principles God wants you to teach to your new people, and what are only cultural traditions of the Hebrew people. The Hebrews ate in a certain way. They also cooked, traveled, earned their living, and cared for the bodies of their dead in certain ways. These are cultural things. You, the missionary, must take from the Bible the basic principles God wants you to teach your people. He does not want you to take, along with those principles, cultural aspects that might have been good for the Hebrews. The ways of your new people are better for your new people, unless they embody evil ideas or practices.

Of course, besides your own culture and the culture reflected in the Bible, you must learn the culture of the people God is sending you to evangelize. Then you can help believers change evil aspects, as explained above.

Answering Certain Questions Will Help You Understand Your Own Culture

In your culture, which of the two values paired below is more important? In answering, do not consider how Christians think of them, but how the unsaved people think. Perhaps you can estimate how much higher or lower one value is compared to the other by drawing a bar-chart. Let the height of each bar show your estimate of it's value.

> Time or personal relationships?
> Education, or getting a job right now?

A high salary, or education?
Consulting parents about an important decision, or being independent?
Material possessions, or spiritual riches and wisdom?

In your culture, which of these two is the worse evil?
Fermented spirits (alcoholic drinks) or drugs?
Being unfaithful to one's spouse, or stealing?
Losing one's temper, or lying?

In your culture, certain people are admired more than others. Draw up a list of the five most admired occupations, or kinds of people. Then number them, placing the numeral-one beside the most admired.

When you arrive among the people God is sending you to evangelize, and when you get to know some of them well, you might ask them similar questions to learn about their culture, and let them know about yours. We discuss this more in the section on strategy.

Should You Learn Their Language?

Missionaries having no training tend to think they should avoid the chore of learning the language because it takes so long. Some feel their supporters expect them to plant a church within a year, so there is not time to learn a language. Some try using an interpreter because they have seen other missionaries doing that. However:

1. If you are penetrating an unreached people group it will be very difficult or impossible to find someone who understands biblical truth on a deep enough level to translate what you need to say.
2. Besides, you would never form close friends within the people group if you could speak to them only through another person.

You might plan to learn only the "lingua franca," the business language used by many people groups in the country where you will serve. But here again, you are placing an obstacle between yourself and the people. They will only appreciate you as a close friend if you speak the language they use among themselves.

The fact that you have learned their birth language, called their "heart language," shows you are deeply interested in them and their culture. You are clearly not there to gather information and photos, or to gain something for yourself while using them in some way.

Remember, you are not trying to make a few disciples. You are going to be used by the Lord to begin a people movement. If you do your work as Paul and other recent exemplars did, ninety percent of the people will want Jesus in their hearts and lives!

We will see how, with the Holy Spirit that has happened.

Chapter 13
Questions

1. The missionary needs to know much about three cultures:

    A. the culture of the Hebrew people
    B. the missionary's own culture
    C. the culture of the people group to whom God is sending him
    D. the culture of his co-workers on the mission field.

2. About learning the language of the people group:

    A. using an interpreter will be effective enough.
    B. the missionary needs to learn the heart language of the people group.
    C. learning the trade language is adequate for evangelizing.
    D. learning a dialect the people understand well will be sufficient.

Chapter 14

Here's How You Can Learn Their Language

There are Two Basic Methods for Learning a Language

You can learn a language from a college language course, if they offer the language you need. You can also learn a language from people who have spoken it from birth.

This second one is a more strategic way, for two reasons. 1) You get to know people of your new culture group this way. 2) You learn the language as it is spoken by the very people you want to evangelize.

Learning at a college or university will result in your speaking a very proper, learned form of the language. This is fine if you will be evangelizing learned people. It is a hindrance, however, if you will be evangelizing people who have little or no formal education. They will recognize your speech as different from theirs, and have difficulty regarding you as a close friend.

There is an excellent book listed in the bibliography for guiding you in the task of learning a language from speakers of that language. The book is, "Language Acquisition Made Practical," by the Brewsters. The title is often abbreviated, "LAMP."

We can give you here some idea of what the process is like. The book itself will give you much more, including pitfalls to avoid so you won't become discouraged. The book includes how to learn the new culture in a systematic and efficient way.

Here are some of the principles involved in learning the language from the people themselves. If you cannot find anyone who knows your language and who learned the local language from early childhood, you cannot use this method. You can and must learn their language anyway, but it will take longer.

1. **Find two persons who will help you.** If there is only one such person available, be satisfied with his help, at least for the earlier months of your learning. Remember, your helpers must understand your language. Both of them should be of your gender, so you avoid misunderstanding, scandalous rumor, and yes, temptation! They should speak their own language clearly. They should each be willing and able to give you one-and-a-half hours five or six mornings per week.

   Ask each to help you "just for this week." Then you're free to ask others next week, if you find you've chosen the wrong helpers.

   When you know you have good helpers, you might choose to pay them. In fact, to get help you might need to offer money from the start. Don't pay over the expected or appropriate amount. It would cause problems.

   The day before you meet with helper number-one, write, in three or four sentences, what you want to learn to say tomorrow in his or her language. Attempt more sentences later, if you are able.

   Write on every fourth line of your notebook page, skipping three lines beneath each line you write on. You will keep this record of sentences, so write on large paper. An 8 1/2 by 11 inch notebook or loose-leaf binder will do nicely.

   For your first day, the following sentences are recommended for you to learn.

   "Hello! I'm learning [write the name of the language here]. This is all I can say. Good bye."

2. **What to do during the mornings.**
   a) Show your number-one helper the sentences, in your language, you want to learn today. Ask your helper if he understands each sentence. For example, "Hello" is a greeting used for anyone, at any time of day or night. Ask him to write, below your writing, how these sentences are written in his language.
   b) Be sure your helper understands he is to write the way the people speak. He is not to give you a word-for-word translation.

c) Next, have him read what he has written. Invite him to change anything he's not satisfied with.

d) Beneath what he wrote, you write phonetically (according to the sounds) using letters and accent-marks, how each word sounds to you. Have him repeat one word at a time so you are satisfied you have written the sounds well.

e) Now have him read the first sentence he wrote. Ask him to speak at almost the same rate of speed he would use with his neighbor. Try to repeat his sounds exactly.

As soon as possible, look away from the written words and depend on his voice alone. Have him repeat the word you cannot say well. For long sentences, begin with the last phrase or word, and master one phrase at a time, adding each new one to the ones you have already learned until you get to the beginning of the sentence.

In "LAMP" the Brewsters give you several drills, or ways of practicing with your helper, that systematically attack each sentence so that you learn better. Basically, you need to have your helper help you by saying the word or phrase before you say it, or after, or both, until you are able to say the sentence perfectly. Then keep reciting, but from memory, without help except to correct you.

f) After about 90 minutes, your helper will be tired. Do not overwork him or he won't want to come back tomorrow. Your number-two helper should arrive now and help you further.

g) Before number-one leaves, ask "two" if he agrees with "one's" translation. Explain that two heads are better than one. If they can't agree, don't change what "one" has written.

h) Now have "two" continue to help you the way "one" has been helping, until you can speak these sentences almost as clearly and as fast as he does when speaking at his natural speed.

It is possible to use a tape-recorder instead of the helper we call "two." This would mean asking "one" to speak into the recorder before he leaves, reading all the sentences, then repeating parts leaving a short pause each time so you can later practice, during those short pauses, saying what he spoke.

i) Pronunciation is a major concern. Learn to pronounce the sounds of your new language exactly the way your helpers do. There are perhaps thirty sounds you will have to learn. Notice how your tongue, lips and teeth work to produce these sounds.

Make pronunciation your top priority during the first few months. Otherwise you will settle for your own faulty sounds. Your friends will learn to understand your "dialect," and never bother to correct you.

3. **What to do in the afternoons.**
   a) After lunch you will work without your helpers. Place thirty-five beans or small stones in an empty pocket. Bring also a pocket-size notebook and a pen or pencil, or small cards.
   b) Go out of your dwelling place and walk
   c) Find someone who isn't too busy. With a big smile, recite what you have learned, speaking directly to this person. Try to say it in a natural way, showing natural inflection and perhaps some enthusiasm.

You may be fearful at first. But do not let fear hinder you from learning the language you will one day be ministering in! You will find that most people you speak to are delighted that you want to learn their language. They might respond, "Oh! You speak very well! How long have you been studying my language?" This shows you are doing well! Of course you won't know what they are saying, but you will know they expect you can respond because what you said was spoken so clearly the listener thought you must know his language well! You can smile and repeat, "This is all I can say! Good-bye!" Don't forget to smile all during this experience. Your smile says as much as, or more than, your limited speech!

   d) Take one bean or pebble from your pocket and place it into another pocket.
   e) After speaking to a person, you might realize you need to be able to say certain things to make your experience more complete or more interesting. Jot down these ideas, and any other ideas, in your pocket-size notebook or on a card.
   f) Repeat "c" and "d" until you have no more beans in that first pocket.

g) Go back to your dwelling and evaluate your learning day.

4. **To evaluate, you need many small cards or pieces of paper.**
   So far, for equipment we have mentioned...
   a) the notebook in which you and your "one" have written your learning sentences in three ways: in your language, in his language, and your attempt at writing what he said in phonetic symbols (letters and accent-marks) so you could later repeat those sounds if you have forgotten how they sound.
   b) We also mentioned that a tape-recorder is optional.
   c) a pocket notebook for making hasty notes during your afternoon experiences using your new language. You can be more relaxed if you have that notebook in your pocket so you have nothing in your hands to hinder you from shaking hands or hugging, or whatever is culturally appropriate.
   d) 3 inch by 5 inch (about 8 by 13 centimeters) cards called "index cards," which you can buy at a stationery store. You can use pieces of paper instead of cards. They should all be the same size.
   Use each card or piece of paper for only one item.

5. **How to evaluate your learning day.**
   a) Begin by writing the sentences you think you will want to learn tomorrow. Use the ideas you wrote in your pocket notebook. Revise these sentences as you do the evaluation. Later you will write them in your large notebook.
   b) On cards (described above) write things that went well today. Write one idea or thing on each card. These are ideas you want to continue using the way you did today.
   c) In the same way, write things that went wrong. On one card write both what went wrong, and any comments about how you should have done it, or whatever will be helpful to keep in mind about that one item.
   d) Use one card for each word you still need to practice pronouncing. Soon you will be able to receive help from people you speak to in the afternoons. You will use that pocket notebook to write notes for yourself as people offer help. Jot down ideas you want to think more about later. During your evaluation time, rewrite these helps on cards.

e) If you need to keep something in mind about how you relate to "one" or "two," write that on a card. You might want to write something about their families, or snacks they like.

f) Examine whether your attitude toward your helpers and the people you met today is Christlike. Confess any failures to the Lord, and ask his help so you will improve tomorrow. Be especially alert about this. It can affect your future deeply.

g) Later you will write grammar rules you discover, and words that are difficult to spell. Even the names of persons you meet often in the afternoons, such as shop keepers, or persons waiting for a bus, with a note or two about each person.

h) Keep all your cards nicely organized in a box, with tabs plainly visible, marking the categories for your notes. This makes it easier for you to find the one you need later.

i) Review these cards every day during your evaluation time. Throw away any cards you know so well that you don't need to review them any more.

j) Finally, revise what you wrote in "a" above. Write this in your notebook as you did yesterday. Leave those three blank lines below each line you write on, so you and your "number-one" can write on those lines tomorrow.

Self-discipline is How You Learn a Language

It's not easy to learn a language. Give yourself time. You will not likely win anyone to the Lord until you have made some friends. While they're finding out who you are, what sort of person you are, you can be busy learning their language.

As you learned earlier, there are two basic methods for learning a language. One is to take courses at a university. Many languages are not taught in any school or university. The dialect taught in such classrooms is formal, spoken by the elite.

The other is to learn from the people who have spoken the language from birth, the LAMP method taught by the Brewsters, and outlined briefly here. You will readily bond with the people as you learn from them.

For some, it takes more self-discipline to learn from the people. You must be convinced that it's the better way. Your determination and your wits, plus the powerful help of the Holy Spirit, will give you a wonderful victory. If you think you don't have the self-discipline needed for this method, then take counsel. Perhaps someone who knows you well will help you decide whether to try it.

If you're not confident about this method, you might be able to combine the university learning-track with the LAMP method. A university counselor, the dean of the language department, or the professor who will teach you, might help you combine the two methods. The classroom structure will help your discipline. But you will learn an elite form of the language. This is fine if you will minister to the educationally elite of the people group.

We strongly recommend you obtain a copy of LAMP. See details in the bibliography. It will help you with both language and culture.

Chapter 14
Questions

1. For learning their language…

    A. Have your helper(s) help you in the mornings.
    B. Speak to 35 persons each afternoon, using what you have learned.
    C. Prepare the evening before, the sentences you want to learn the next morning.
    D. It's more important to just sit and enjoy the new sights and sounds than to get very serious about learning the language.

2. Some of the things to write on cards when you evaluate your learning day are these:

    A. things that went wrong during the afternoon
    B. a new word someone taught you during the afternoon
    C. a list of words you have trouble with
    D. names of persons you met for the first time

Chapter 15

Communication Is More than Words

Their Culture Will Affect Your Message in Three Ways

1. **You must speak your message in their language.** Their language is perhaps the most significant element of their culture. Jesus spoke a heavenly message, but he spoke it in Aramaic, the local language of the people. God the Son joined the human race and spoke a local, human language.

   Illustration 18 shows that a word in your birth language often cannot be translated perfectly by a word in their birth language. The ellipse to the left represents the meaning of the word in your language. The ellipse to the right represents the closest matching word in their language. The shaded area in the middle represents that part of the meaning of both words that is the same.

   But in using their word, you are adding some meaning that you do not intend. This is represented by the unshaded area (A) to the right. You are also losing some of the meaning of your word. This is represented by the unshaded area (B) to the left.

   Most words in your birth language have no perfectly matching words in their birth language. Keep this in mind as you learn their language. Pay attention to the differences. When teaching biblical principles, you will often need a sentence or more to translate a single word from the Bible, to communicate the exact meaning.

   We are told there are people groups who have no word that adequately translates our English word, "God." They have words for "powerful spiritual beings," but none of these words means, "The eternal, all-powerful, all-knowing One who is everywhere and who created all things."

Linguists must sometimes carry over into the target language, a word from the origin language. Occasionally they make up a new word for the target language. Carefully chosen people of the host or adoptive culture can help with such decisions.

**Illustration
18**

A word in one language does not match perfectly a word in another language.

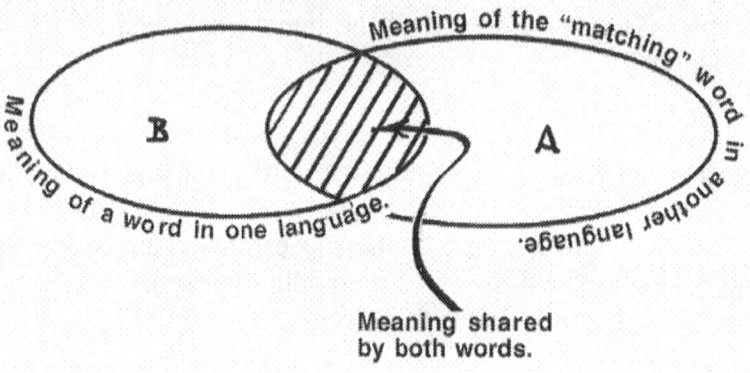

Illustration is based on Paul Hiebert's in *Anthropological Insights for Missionaries,* p. 157.

2. **You must "wrap" or "package" the message in ways that are familiar to them.**

A missionary began baptizing his first converts at the river. One of the old men said, "No! You cannot do this!"

The missionary asked, "Why?"

The old man said, "You, being a man, must not touch our wives!"

The missionary wisely called the elders of the group together for a conference. After discussion, the missionary asked, "Can we baptize the women this way? I will baptize all the men first. Then each husband will baptize his own wife. Will this be acceptable?"

Of course the men were both satisfied and affirmed. Not only were their traditions being honored, but they themselves, new Christians, were allowed to minister!

In the same fashion, we must not impose upon them our cultural ideas of what a church building should look like, or what Christian music should sound like, which musical instruments are suitable, how believers should worship, how to do a communion service, or even how a preacher should preach.

Every culture has forms and norms that are neither good nor evil. Let the new believers, as you teach them what the Word of God says, decide how things should be done. New believers have the Holy Spirit. He is responsible to draw the believers closer to Jesus, and to warn them about the pitfalls.

The missionary must teach biblical principles. If he sees the elders making a decision that will cause trouble, he should give his opinion. He should ask questions of the elders to ascertain that their decision is a scriptural one. He should also ask questions that will reveal whether their decision will affect the culture in any harmful way. Beyond This, he does well to leave decisions to those who know the culture best. As time goes by, and as the elders learn to listen to God, and to the missionary, Jesus will build his Church through them.

3. **The people must develop a moral code and an expression of Christian beliefs, that are totally scriptural, but are expressed in ways that fit their history and culture.**

Again, the new believers, being persons born and raised in that culture, and being old enough to have experienced much, will be better at making these decisions than you, the missionary. But they will need your help because you know the Bible so much better than they.

Unbelievers who are willing to listen to the gospel, will see it as their own "good news" if explained in terms of their own history and culture. The gospel will not only spread more rapidly this way, it will also penetrate the heart more radically. Even neighboring tribes will accept it more readily because it will have the right ring to it for them, even though their languages and cultures might vary from the tribe of first penetration.

The time will come when your disciples will realize they are called to the Great Commission just as you were! You will need to make them sensitive to cultural difference, so they, like you, will know how to give the gospel to a people whose culture differs from their own.

Three Things we Communicate When we Interact with People

1. **We communicate knowledge.** Words are used to give information. We choose our words carefully so we do not give incorrect statements to our listeners. If we are not sure of the accuracy of our statements we admit this, so our hearers will realize they cannot treat our statements as certain.

2. **We communicate feelings.** We often include in our communication, our opinions and our emotional responses. We might be telling someone what time it is. "It's 7:15." We are communicating knowledge. But the way we say these words can carry a message. Our heightened tone of voice, and our emphasis on the words "seven" and "fifteen," can tell our listener we are concerned that we are going to be late for the meeting. This is a paramessage. A "paramessage" is communication that goes along with the words we speak, and is communicated by the way we are standing or gesturing, or by our tone of voice, by the words we emphasize, by the expression on our faces, or even by our eyes.

   It is even possible for a person to say to another, "I'm just fine!" But by his manner, the tone of his voice, his emphasis on the words "I'm" and "fine," he is clearly communicating that he is very disturbed.

3. **We communicate judgments.** By these same outward manifestations mentioned above, we can, whatever the words we might be pronouncing, be indicating we are very unhappy about a person, a place, or a thing.

   For example, take the sentence, "I will not be giving you advice in the future." These words will be spoken very lovingly by a father to his

230

mature son if the son has proved he no longer needs his father's advice. His father might add, "You are indeed making excellent decisions, and I will be asking you for advice now."

However, the same first sentence (underlined) spoken in an angry tone will carry a paramessage of condemnation, of judgment.

More About Paramessages

Paramessages communicate feelings and judgments such as agreement, disagreement, respect, disrespect, trust, distrust, love, hate, anger, concern, boredom.

The sender of a paramessage is often not aware that he is sending this message.

We can send a message without words! If we avoid spending time with someone, we are telling that person how we feel and how we evaluate his or her company or friendship. Many loved ones have been deeply hurt by their spouses because of unspoken messages that had, or seemed to have, painfully clear meanings.

When the spoken message and the paramessage contradict each other, three things happen:

1. The receiver almost always believes the paramessage, not the spoken message.
2. The receiver distrusts the sender.
3. The receiver remembers the paramessage longer than the spoken message.

Examples of actions that carry paramessages are: smiling; frowning; bringing a chair for someone else; putting your arm around your spouse; pounding your fist on a table; giving someone special a gift; shaking hands with someone while looking around the room to see who else is there!

Try to be aware of your habits, your automatic gestures and tones of voice. Change the ones that need correction. It will help you in your ministry.

Gestures are Risky!

A gesture is a motion you make with your hand, head, or eyes, that is understood by people of your culture to have a specific meaning.

Some gestures have distinctly different meanings in different cultures. For example, patting a child on the head is a gesture of affection in some cultures. It is totally unacceptable in other cultures. Some hand gestures can be innocent greetings or grave insults, depending on the local culture!

The signal for "Come!" in one culture looks like the signal for "Go away!" in another culture. Giving your newborn the name of the chief in some cultures would be a high compliment. In others it is considered stealing.

In some cultures if you photograph a woman she believes she will never have another child.

Even within your own culture, some actions and some words are acceptable only when you are among one age group, but not another. Some actions depend on gender, or social position, or location, or other circumstances.

Don't use a gesture unless they use it. Don't use it until you know for certain exactly how to do the gesture, and precisely what it means. Don't perform any act, however innocent looking, until you have asked someone you trust in that culture whether it is acceptable, and whether it has a meaning you do not intend.

In some tribes, if a man says to a woman, "Would you like to come and cultivate in my garden?" he is asking her to marry him!

You will make many mistakes that will cause people of your adoptive culture to laugh. Laugh with them! Let them help you correct your mistakes. But avoid making mistakes that offend them. Most will overlook your mistakes, knowing you are just beginning to learn their ways. Very few will excuse your ignorance if they think you have been among them long enough to know better, or if they think you don't care.

Communication has Two Aspects

You have not communicated if you were not understood. Perhaps you have done everything right, by your own evaluation. But if your listeners have missed your meaning, communication has not happened.

Blame yourself when they fail to understand. Realize it is you who have failed. Otherwise you are not likely to improve. You can always find fault and blame someone else, but that will only frustrate you and your purpose. Your purpose is an eternal one. Aim carefully so you will hit the center of the target.

As you Communicate...

1. **Find out whether they have understood.** Get them to react. Ask them questions. "Does this seem correct to you?" "What do you think of this?"

   Invite them to do something with the material you have just presented. If some love to act, let them dramatize what you have taught.

   Usually you can find out how well they understood, by asking them, "Do you understand?" But you must know that they do understand before you go on to more material. If their culture demands that they tell you only what they think will make you feel successful, you will need to get more reliable evidence.

   Whatever you do, do it in a humble spirit, with friendly tones. You are their friend, not their disciplinarian. Lead them into truth. Don't drive them like cattle.

2. **Take the blame for their lack of understanding.** And do this sincerely. If you secretly harbor the conviction that you are doing a great job but that they are dense or not attentive, they will discern that, and the result will not be good for them or you.

3. **If you seem unsuccessful at communicating, do something different.** One definition of insanity is, "Doing the same thing over and over, each time expecting a different result."

Speak more slowly. Use only words they know well. Use simpler sentences. Repeat important ideas. Give examples. Use chalkboard illustrations. Stop and ask questions.

People who don't know you well, may hesitate to attempt to answer your questions. Don't give up. Explain that you realize these are difficult questions.

4. **If you discern they are becoming hostile or uncooperative, build trust and respect** both in yourself and in them. This might mean dropping your immediate plans and getting to know them better before going on.

If you are too goal oriented, you must guard against preferring what you see as productivity over bonding with the people. Especially in the earlier months, and even years, of your ministry among them, relationships are crucial.

God looks at our hearts. He sees our relationships with each other as more important than "our goals."

5. **Avoid distracting them.** Work on your accent. Avoid little habits such as rubbing your nose, adjusting your spectacles, walking continually back and forth. Don't wear "strange" clothing that differs from theirs. Ask your assistant if you are doing anything that disturbs them.

In one situation, the missionaries did not share their food, electrical devices, guns, among a people for whom sharing was a principle sign of friendship, kindness and acceptance. This sent a negative paramessage to the people.

Two lady missionaries taught Bible concepts to a people group. They used excellent visual aids which they made themselves. They came to each session well prepared. This took much time. They persevered for twenty years.

But no men attended their sessions. They never asked why! Eventually missionaries found out that in that culture, women are not permitted to stand as they teach men.

Bond especially well with one or a few people you will come to trust. Ask them for help so you can avoid these cultural pitfalls.

6. **Practice what you preach.** Do not have what they consider luxuries while you teach them to be content with a simple lifestyle.

7. **Learn from them.** Be teachable. They have much they can teach you. Learn to listen well. Communication is two ways!

Some Statistics about Communication

We remember	after 3 hours	after 3 days
what we hear	70%	10%
what we see	72%	20%
what we see and hear	86%	65%

Obviously, visual aids will help greatly as you teach. George Patterson[5] had an artist create posters which George used in Honduras for teaching Bible stories and principles to pastors who could not read. He gave copies to his "Timothies" as needed so they could use his techniques.

Within **the same culture,** expect 70% of your message to be understood. Within **a foreign culture**, expect 50% of your message to be understood.

These estimates are averages. You can do better - much better - if you take extra care. Follow the suggestions given above.

God Will Use You

Whether you are educated or uneducated, whether you communicate brilliantly or not, God will use the man or woman who worships him, whose heart and mind are set on him, who walks humbly before God, who desires that the Lamb receive the reward of his sacrifice and that people be saved from eternal loss.

---

[5] Patterson was a Southern Baptist missionary who planted 50 strong, reproducing churches in 13 years. See the bibliography. Some of his strategy appears in the last section of this book.

Get whatever education and training God directs you to acquire. Do all that God shows you, to make your ministry more effective. But realize that the only eternal good that will come, will be the result of the grace and power of God.

God will use you for his glory and for the salvation of an unreached people or peoples. And you will be filled with his joy in the process.

The Gospel Changes the Culture

New believers learn truth from the Word of God, and begin to change. This affects their culture, especially if the believers grow to outnumber the unbelievers.

But the gospel also affects the people economically. Men and women of faith become responsible toward each other and toward their children. Even their neighbors benefit. Believers no longer spend their time and resources in drunkenness and disregard for the concerns of others. They care.

The result is, people are lifted out of conditions of degradation and are lifted to a state of self-respect, productivity and provision. Missiologists call this process, "redemption and lift."

Missionaries whose call is to evangelize, often agonize over the miserable conditions of those they work among. They know the greatest need of the people is that they be saved for eternity, but they desire to help them economically.

Such missionaries need to be sensitive to the Lord who might be showing them some way of benefiting the people materially, even before they accept him. But they should also understand that the most important way to help the people is to lead them into the kingdom. Then they will experience "redemption and lift."

When they do, the lift will be a permanent lift. It will not be a temporary rescue from squalor of the people's own making, resulting from their negligence. It will come from the presence and power of God, an inner motivation that will cause them to value righteousness. The gospel changes people's hearts, causing them to care for their families and for each other.

Therefore, if anyone is in Christ, he is a new creation; the old has gone, the new has come! All this is from God... (2 Cor. 5:17)

When missionaries discover sickness and build a hospital, they run the risk of never getting around to evangelizing effectively. In these cases, sickness become their main focus and the gospel never gets preached successfully.

With the Holy Spirit the people will be mightily blessed and will reach out to other people groups so that they also will receive the blessing spoken of by God to Abraham. *All peoples on earth will be blessed through you* (Gen. 12:3).

Chapter 15
Questions

1. The culture of your new people group will affect your message in three ways:

   A. You must speak your message in their language, the most significant element in their culture.
   B. The people will demand you accept their evil practices.
   C. You must "wrap" or "package" the message in ways that are culturally familiar to them, and therefore acceptable.
   D. The people must develop a moral code and an expression of Christian beliefs that are totally scriptural, but are expressed in ways that fit their history and culture.

2. When the spoken message and the paramessage contradict each other, three things happen:

   A. The receiver almost always believes the paramessage, not the spoken message
   B. The receiver distrusts the sender.
   C. The receiver believes the spoken message and distrusts what he thought the sender was revealing by his behavior.
   D. The receiver remembers the paramessage longer than the spoken message.

3. As you communicate…

   A. Find out if they have understood. Get them to react to what you have taught. Ask questions.
   B. Take the blame for their lack of understanding..
   C. If you seem unsuccessful at communicating, keep repeating until they understand.
   D. If you discern they are becoming hostile or uncooperative, take time to build trust and respect both in yourself and in them.

4. The gospel and the culture.

   A. When many people accept Jesus, the culture changes.
   B. The economy changes as believers begin to care more for loved ones.
   E. Missiologists call this change, "redemption and lift."
   F. When missionaries discover sickness and build a hospital, they run the risk of spending too much time evangelizing.

Section 4

Mission Strategy
That Will Make You a "Paul"

Chapter 16

Bonding, an Essential Foundation for Evangelization

What is "Bonding"?

Bonding is the process by which a missionary, and some members of the people group to whom God has sent him, become genuine friends, as close as brothers and sisters.

We could demonstrate bonding with two sheets of paper and some glue. Spread glue on one sheet. Press the other sheet onto the glued sheet and leave them to dry. The two sheets of paper become bonded. If you pull them apart you damage both beyond repair. Each is so severely torn, neither will ever be the same!

Can people bond so closely? David and Jonathan seem to have achieved a closeness that deeply affected David long after Jonathan's death, to the benefit of Mephibosheth.

Dare we hope to bond so closely?

Look at Jesus and the eleven. Judas allowed something else to become uppermost in his life. But the others loved the Lord so much they were unwilling to leave him even when his teaching was difficult for others to accept. Peter knew he could never depart from Jesus. "Lord, to whom shall we go? You have the words of eternal life!"

These words surely represented the convictions of the other disciples also. We can only imagine what the resurrection meant to them! Studying the words and actions of the disciples who stayed in Jerusalem, and the ones on the road to Emmaus, gives us some idea of the bewilderment and discouragement they suffered. Then they heard of the resurrection and felt tentative joy mixed with unbelief. Better yet was the quiet but explosive presence of the resurrected Lord himself in the upper room, and then elsewhere.

For three years they had bonded with Jesus and with each other before the crucifixion, and for forty days after the resurrection! We need that same bonding experience with our adoptive people. That genuine sharing of life itself with others will position us so we can properly deliver God's message to them.

You, the future missionary, will be a precious "taste" of Jesus for those to whom the Lord directs you.

Why Bond?

1. **The greatest influence toward Jesus an unbeliever will experience will be Jesus himself, seen in you.**

   The unbeliever can easily discard a tract. Many do. The unbeliever can change the channel on his TV. The unbeliever will soon forget the Jesus film. The busy unbeliever might postpone reading a Bible. It's such a big book!

   Having a genuine friend is a very different situation. Even an unbeliever will listen to his friend. The unbeliever's friend knows his hopes and fears, his strengths and his faults. His friend has been with him in difficulties, even when he was in the wrong. His friend risked their friendship and honestly, with love, told him the truth when he needed to hear it.

   Less than 10 percent of Muslims in Islamic countries have ever met a committed Christian. They only know us from the films and TV programs they believe come from a Christian country. They are horrified by much of what they see and hear!

   The greatest influence toward Jesus a Muslim will experience will be Jesus himself, when the Muslim sees him in you!

2. **If you choose to remain aloof from the people, they will conclude you do not love them.**

   Being aloof is the alternative to bonding. Time is the greatest thing we can give anyone. Marriages fail because spouses do not have time for each other. Children go astray because their parents did not spend time with them, not only counseling them, but simply enjoying them!

God works more through human relationships than we realize. James wrote, if you control your tongue, you're mature. You do not control your tongue apart from other people. Relationship is a school of growth which the Holy Spirit uses. And he uses relationships between believers and non-believers to multiply believers.

3. **By bonding, you become a "belonger" within the people group you will evangelize.**

Especially at the beginning, members of the group will be curious about you, and will want to spend time with you. If you feel the same about them, some of them will teach you their birth-language and their culture. You will learn their ways, and adopt all that is not sinful. Eventually, they will no longer think of you as a foreigner, but as one of them. You will think of yourself as a member of their ethnic group.

The parallel between this process and what Jesus did in joining the human race, is obvious. His impact upon us has grown and grown over the past 2000 years. His way, bonding, is our best route to evangelism.

Illustration 19 Shows Illustration 15 with Added Features

Notice the addition of the word "Bonding" in Illustration 19. The satisfaction level takes a turn for the better and bonding begins to happen. You are not likely to have at the same time both bonding and deep dissatisfaction, because bonding is the chief cause of satisfaction, and failure to bond is the chief cause of dissatisfaction.

In other words, in order to be fulfilled working with a people not your own you will almost certainly need to have good friends within that people.

As soon as anyone recognizes he is in the process of developing a friendship, his dissatisfaction begins to evaporate remarkably. This will be especially true for you, as a missionary, for you will realize you are making great progress toward leading this people group to the Lord! Bonding is that important.

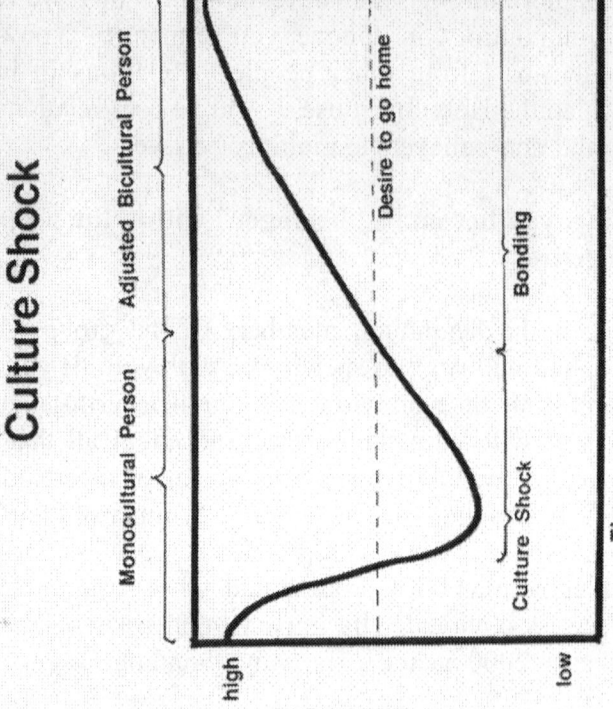

Culture Shock

Based on Paul Hiebert's illustration, *Anthropological Insights for Missionaries*, p.65. Used with permission.

Illustration
19

Notice also the terms "Monocultural Person" and "Adjusted Bicultural Person." You will be a person of one culture at the beginning of your experience among the unreached people. Their culture will be foreign to you until you learn enough about it, and adopt enough of it, so you no longer want to quit and return to your old, or birth culture.

You now are a person of two cultures, each of which you esteem and love. At times you catch yourself in patterns of your old culture, but you also adhere to much of the new. You are especially "new culture" while you are among people of that culture, and think of your friends back home with tender memories. You are especially "birth culture" while you are on furlough, and soon begin to count the days before your return to your new home and the good friends you have there.

Remember this: That deep dip in the satisfaction line, labeled "culture shock," need never happen. We considered this in chapter 12.

How Can You Bond with the People?

1. Intercede for the people group God has chosen for you to reach.

God will soften their hearts toward you. He will also soften your heart toward them. Pray for them with earnest desire that they might be saved. Jesus said, "Whatsoever things you desire..."

2. Live without possessions that mark you as foreign.

Don't take with you luxuries they do not have. When you arrive in their country, adopt their style of dress. Eat what they eat.

Your purpose is to be accepted as one of them. This will take time. Eventually you will reach such a degree of closeness with a few of them, that you and one of them will find yourselves sharing deeply personal matters. Then you will see what are his heartfelt needs, and he will come naturally to see what is your spiritual solution to your inner hunger.

You will experience this same sharing process with some others. This level of friendship is the bridge over which the life of Jesus can flow from heart to heart.

3. **When you first arrive among them, mingle immediately with some of them.**

Do not seek out members of your own culture, if any are in evidence.

You will need help when you arrive. Ask for help from members of the group God is sending you to evangelize. Someone might help you find a place to stay. Someone of your gender might have a bed you can sleep on. This will help you bond with that person.

Getting help from them, and not your own people, from the beginning, is important for bonding. If you postpone bonding, you will develop habits of avoiding the local people. It will be more difficult to change later.

Bond from the beginning while you are an object of great curiosity to them. This dulls with time.
Bond from the beginning while your hesitation, or even fear, has not had time to develop in your mind as a formidable enemy. Once you overcome this hesitation by stepping out in faith, you are free to make friends and can enjoy your new neighbors.

Most of us have had the experience of moving into a new neighborhood. Until you go next door and borrow a can opener, or to meet your neighbors, you wonder if they are nice people. After you take that first step your view of them is almost always very favorable.

4. **Live with a family for two months.**

Extend this to several months if they truly want you to stay. You can then learn how they live, and you will have many opportunities to use your new language.

Observe how they cook, set the table, treat the dog, greet visitors, entertain guests. The family will help you find language helpers which we describe in chapter 14.

Become a servant to them. Some will take advantage of you and you will have to make adjustments. After you form some solid friendships you will have someone you can ask for advice. They will help you deal with people who want so much from you that you have no time to work

5. **Use the means of transportation they use.**

In a bus, you will have the opportunity of meeting people and using your new language. If you ride a motorcycle or drive a car you will meet no one, and you will be branding yourself a rich person unless most of your neighbors have this equipment.

6. **Learn their language from them, the people you will be ministering to, rather than from professional teachers.**

Teachers will want to direct your learning, and will probably teach you a very formal dialect.

You are not likely to bond with professional teachers. They tend to treat you as clients rather than friends.

7. **Accept or choose a new name, one that is suitable for a member of their ethnic group.**

They may assign you a name they feel good about. Your acceptance will further the bonding process. If they don't suggest a name you might ask them for one you might adopt.

8. **Become adopted into the people group, or become a citizen of the country, or both, if you feel the Lord is leading in that.**

Some adoption ceremonies have demonic or immoral elements. Explain to your closest friend that you must avoid these elements because your God does not permit you to engage in them. Perhaps the ceremony can be modified to omit the evil parts. If not, decline politely, but continue to be enthusiastic about the culture in general.

9. **Ask the Lord if you should seek part-time employment.**

"Part-time" and not "full-time" because you want to earn only what you need. Your main occupation is "learner." You might not need money at all if your church back home is supporting you.

Even so, would it be more acceptable to your adoptive people if you worked alongside them in some way? If you don't work you can learn the language more quickly, but how will your people view this?

Be sure you are not accepting help from them which they are required by their culture to offer, but which you are expected to refuse! Perhaps you can work for your food and lodging by teaching reading or some other skill or craft to one of more members of the family. Refrain from asking for food or lodging on the promise that you will learn the language and then tell them most interesting and inspiring stories. Your ministry should be totally a gift to them, not payment. Promising anything for the future can sound like deception. Avoid even the appearance of evil.

Paul the apostle supported himself by making tents. Many missionaries do the same. They are called "tentmakers," whether they actually make tents or sell fish or teach a language.

You might take counsel from the elders of the family on the question of how to support yourself as you learn their language and their culture. In any event, remember what Jesus said about doing more than is required of us. We should "go the extra mile." We should give also our tunics. We should not demand pay-back. These are attitudes of heart Jesus is teaching. They are examples of what kingdom dwellers do for others, because of their love for God and neighbor.

With Whom Should You Bond?

Bond with the influential men among the people group. The strategy we are detailing here is a strategy for beginning a people movement. We are not aiming at founding a church, but at planting strong churches that will multiply within an entire unreached people group. The most effective way of leading an entire people group to the Lord is to start with those in authority, or those of greatest influence. Their influence will affect those of least influence. Influence helps! Like a river, influence does not readily flow upstream.

If you have no choice but to work among people of least influence, accept that. Jesus worked among the less educated, the fishermen. Some claim these fishermen were owners of successful businesses. This may be true, but they were not people of influence. As Galileans, they were looked down upon.

Avoid bonding with members of the other gender, except while their spouses are present, and then know first how the culture views what you will be doing. If you are a single woman, read carefully the story of Joanne Shetler in the next chapter. She bonded with influential men in her translation work, and with women in her social life.

It is not so easy for a single woman to lead a people movement, except among a people where women are regarded as leaders of their families. There are some! As a single woman, your challenge will be to target influential people without violating their rules of conduct. If God sends you, he will guide you as you lean on him.

Unless God leads otherwise, avoid bonding with persons who are viewed as renegades, or outlaws, or rebels. Leading these to the Lord first, will cause prideful, law-abiding people to reject your message.
In almost every culture, men will not follow the women or children. Pride again? But both women and children will follow the men. Less influential families will follow more influential families. This is especially true in tribal societies, but it is universal.

Bonding with influential people can help you begin a people movement. If it is not possible to get close enough to people of influence, try to avoid people who are regarded as least influential, unless God directs you to them.

You won't do things perfectly. Don't fret. Doing things perfectly is God's role. Trust him. He is faithful. He looks at your heart.

Bonding is a Natural Process at "Beginnings"

We have stressed that bonding happens best as you **begin** your life among the people God has sent you to evangelize. This phenomenon has been observed in nature.

Konrad Laurenz, a Nobel Prize winning naturalist, has photos of himself walking through the forest, and even swimming in a pond, always followed by three ducklings whose hatching he had observed. Because

251

they saw him immediately after emerging from their shells, and not their mother duck, they assumed he was their parent.

Similar studies have been done involving other animals. They and their adoptive "mothers" all experienced a close bonding if they were aware of each other at birth. This bond endured even after short periods of separation.

Must You Accept Everything in Their Culture?

One missionary in Africa was approached by an old man, and told that he did not eat what the people ate. The missionary objected! He had adopted their diet, he believed.

The old man said, "Come to my hut tonight."

The missionary came. He found the old man sitting outside his hut, waiting for him. The missionary sat beside the old man. The man's wife emerged from their hut with two covered pots and placed them beside the old man. He uncovered one, and took from it a handful of maize mush which he skillfully shaped into a ball.

The missionary expected this. He had learned to relish this simple food, the staple of many African tribes.

Then the old man uncovered the second pot. He placed the ball of mush into the pot and pressed it gently into the contents. Then he withdrew the ball. To the horror of the missionary, the ball of mush was now covered in furry caterpillars, struggling to free themselves from the sticky maize!

Of course the old man deftly popped the ball, alive with squirming caterpillars, into his mouth. His countenance reported the taste as good. The missionary knew what he must do. He did it, closing his eyes and trying to think of something pleasant as he bit into the unthinkable combination.

To his surprise, a delicious flavor burst across his palate!

This would be one of the more debatable rewards of missionary life. Agree or disagree, you do generally need to eat what the people eat if you are to bond with them.

However, be sensitive to their attitudes. In some situations they will not expect you to follow all they do, and will enjoy your hesitations, your amusing reactions and responses, such as, "I'm sure it is delicious, but for now I will just take your word for it. Let me get more used to your ways before I join you in this one."

If a custom is sinful, you can explain that your God does not allow you to indulge. Most people groups will accept this explanation. They will not want you to disobey your God. Some will fear his wrath might fall upon them.

You can never totally give up your own culture. Illustration 20 shows you become more and more their culture, and less and less your birth culture. You will never actually lose your own culture completely. You will never become 100% their culture and 0% your birth culture.

This is not something to be regretted. It is a fact of life.

A missionary to a primitive tribe we'll call "Sandu," befriended and converted one member we'll call "Tungo." He taught the missionary his language and culture.

They were together on a long journey in Sanduland. At sundown they went into an inn and the missionary asked, in excellent dialect, for a room. The Sandu innkeeper responded, "Yes, we have a room for you, foreigner."

The missionary was shocked. He turned to Tungo. "How did that man know I am not a Sandu? Tungo, you have taught me your language and your customs. I even wear the clothing that clearly mark me as a Sandu. How did he know?"

Tungo thought for a moment and said, "My friend, I cannot understand it." Then came a moment of inspiration for Tungo. His face lit up as he added, "Ah! But I do know! It's the way you walk!"

Illustration
20

You never become 100% your adoptive culture.
You never lose 100% of your birth culture.

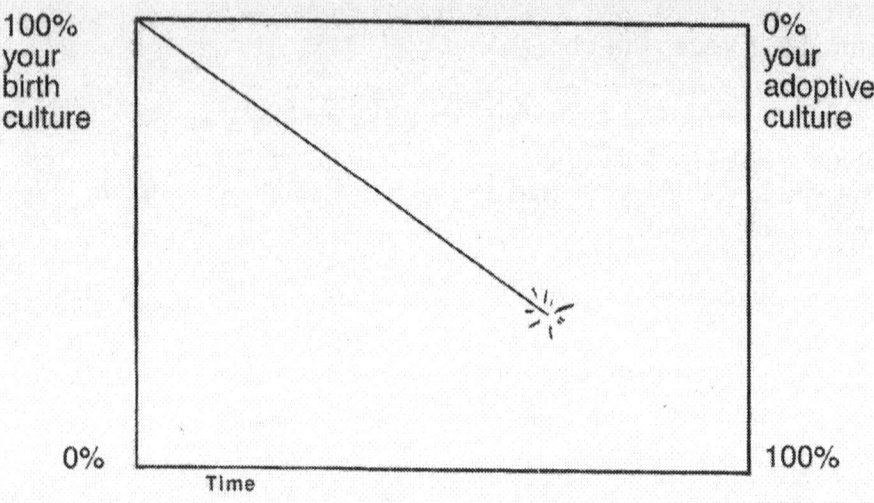

Tungo then simulated the very erect posture of the missionary and his determined step, walking across their hotel room. "We Sandu do not walk like this! We walk like this!" he explained as he demonstrated, this time slouching his shoulders a bit and letting his arms hang loosely.

The missionary was delighted with this new revelation. "Tungo, show me that again."

After much coaching and correction by Tungo the two retired for the night, confident that the problem was solved.

The next day they rose early and got out on the road. Many hours later, at sundown, they still had many miles to walk. They entered an inn and the missionary asked for a room.

"Certainly!" came the courteous reply. "We have a room for you, foreigner."

Shaken visibly, and hardly able to speak, the missionary whispered, "Tungo, this is amazing! How could he possibly know?"

Discouraged, the two trudged off to their room, Tungo meditating on what could be the answer. As they closed the door of the room it struck him like a bolt of lightning! "My dear friend!" he said, looking into the missionary's eyes, "I know the answer to your question!"

"Please tell me!" pleaded the missionary.
"It is your mother!" Tungo revealed in an awed tone. "She is not a Sandu!"

Chapter 16
Questions

1. The missionary, and some members of the people group to whom God has sent him, become genuine friends, as close as brothers and sisters. This process is called:

   A. bonding.
   B. building relationships.
   C. executing the plan.
   D. providing a basis.

2. Why establish genuine close relationships with members of your adoptive people group?

   A. The greatest influence toward Jesus an unbeliever will experience will be Jesus himself, seen in you.
   B. You then become a "belonger" within the people group you will evangelize.
   C. They will help you if you have a personal need.
   D. If you choose to remain aloof from the people, they will conclude you do not love them

3. How many cultures will you have?

   A. You will always be a monocultural person.
   B. You need to become an adjusted bicultural person.
   C. You can become totally of the culture you have adopted.
   D. A missionary must disassociate forever from friends of his birth culture.

Chapter 17

Strategies Differ, but Principles Are Consistent

A Sound Strategy will Embrace Many Sound Principles

So far in this book we have looked at many mission principles. To the extent that they are reliable, you need to know them and adhere to them, no matter what strategy you adopt or adapt.

We will examine in detail one strategy that incorporates nearly every missionary principle. We will briefly examine other strategies.

What Will be Your Strategy?

When you begin ministering on the field, you will have evaluated the situation you are facing, and you will have decided the general framework of the strategy you hope to use. Your strategy might be a combination of elements from several strategies.

Factors that will influence your decisions about strategy will include these:
- The openness to the gospel among the people.
- The degree to which you have been able to bond with them.
- Advice you have been given by your close friends within the culture.
- The availability of resources.
- Your need or your choice to do secular work, either to support yourself or to give yourself the same economic status they have.
- The heartfelt needs they are experiencing.
- Cultural elements the Lord will show you that can be used to help explain the gospel to persons of that culture.
- Your own personal abilities and limitations.

Can a Woman Missionary Lead a People Group to the Lord?

Yes!

In most people groups, a woman must minister under constraints which men do not face. Perhaps some Muslim groups would present limitations which make it inadvisable for a woman to attempt to plant churches among them. But the short answer is, "Yes!"

Joanne Shetler Brought the Gospel to the Balangao

It is not the preferred way of evangelizing for Wycliffe, but they did send two women to the Balangao of the Philippines. They were to translate the Bible, and to teach the Balangao to read and write.

Soon, one of the women returned to her country to marry, leaving Joanne to work alone.

In the process of bonding, learning the language, and then translating, Shetler learned how enslaved the people were to demons. Her translation helpers included one elder man, the most respected in the village. He and others were so amazed with the Word of God they accepted the Lord without her preaching to them!

Joanne then became the Bible teacher for the new believers. Her victories over evil spirits convinced many. The church grew naturally, through the witnessing of new believers.

God gave Joanne wisdom as she needed it. On one occasion, at a leaders meeting, the leading elder and the group discussed a social problem and then made a decision that was unscriptural.

Shetler did not panic. She knew it was not culturally acceptable for a woman to contradict an elder. She simply said to him, "Oh! Now what will we do? The Bible says..." and she quoted a verse or two showing a change of decision was in order.

The leader immediately opened the floor for discussion on the topic, "How can we obey God in our way of dealing with our problem?" A scriptural solution was found and accepted.

Joanne Shetler faced difficult times during her many years with the Balangao. When she first arrived, for example, she was unaware of the power of demons. But by the time the Bible was finally translated, a strong church with a vigorous missionary outreach to other tribes, was firmly in place.

The Holy Spirit used the Word of God with life-giving power, to give new life to the Balangao. He used a single, dedicated woman to make it all happen!

Be sure to read Joanne's book.[6]

---

[6] *And the Word Came with Power,* subtitled, *How God Met and Changed a People Forever.* See the bibliography.

Chapter 17
Questions

1. Joanne Shetler practiced sound principles of mission strategy among the Balangao.

    A. She demonstrated her superiority in spiritual matters.
    B. She bonded while learning their language.
    C. She sought the help of the respected elder of the village.
    D. When the new believers made an unscriptural decision she showed them what the Bible says, and allowed them to solve the problem in a scriptural way.

Chapter 18

The Strategy of the "Eight Effective Roles"[7] of the Missionary

What is a "Role"?

In Illustration 21 you see the eight roles of the missionary. "Role" is described in the dictionary as, "a part taken or assumed by anyone."

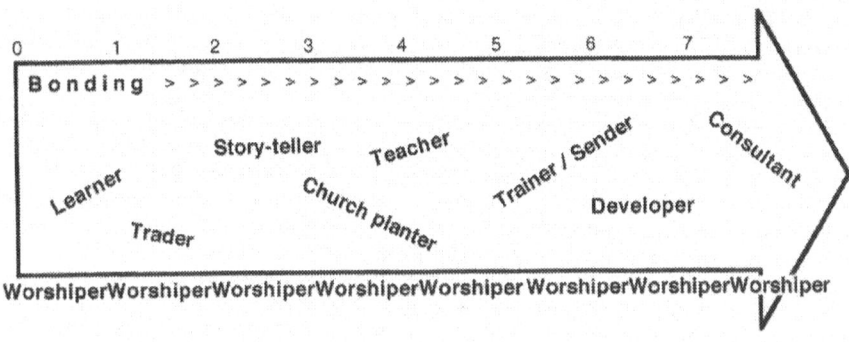

Illustration 21   The Eight Roles of the Missionary

Each of the roles we describe here is a part assumed by the missionary who is in the process of giving the gospel to an unreached ethnic group.

For example, role #1 is "learner." "Learner" is a "role" you will adopt. Your essential calling from God is not to be a "learner." Your calling is to

---

[7] The first three "roles" are based on Don Larsen's, "The Viable Missionary: Learner, Trader, Story Teller," *Missiology: An International Review.* Arthur F. Glasser, ed., April 1978. Reprinted in *Perspectives on the World Christian Movement,* 1981, pp.444-451.

be a missionary. However, if you follow this strategy, you will adopt that role, "learner," as the principal part you will assume in the first stages of your ministry among your adoptive people. "Learner" will be the first task at which you will labor.

Unfortunately, "role" is also the word actors use to describe the part they play in a drama. Do not confuse this "role" with your "role." You will not be playing a part in a drama, but assuming an authentic task, an identity that is real.

In the same way, "bonding" is the making of genuine friendships, which some call "integrity friendships," not imitation, or pretended friendships.

Bonding is the Continual Goal of the Missionary

Look again at Illustration 21. The numerals just above the arrow-shaped frame indicate the passage of time. They are not years. How long each role will require depends on circumstances. The roles start at the left and flow toward the right, but the timing will vary from people group to people group. The ability and training of the missionary are also factors.

The word "bonding" appears to the left, above the roles. While bonding is not one of the roles, it is the fundamental ingredient in any strategy. It continues throughout the life of the missionary. The small arrowhead to the right of the word "bonding" emphasizes this.

The roles, on the other hand, are adopted one by one as the missionary begins and continues in his career. Roles overlap far more than can be shown in the illustration. Some roles are temporary.

We Have Benefited by the Mistakes of Those Who Have Gone Before Us

Let's go back fifty years. You are visiting some part of Africa. You see a white missionary. You ask four local non-believers, "Who is that foreign looking man?"

The answers might be like these:

- "He is a wealthy businessman who is here investigating how he might increase his wealth in this place. His possessions are beyond anything we have ever seen. Many large steel drums containing the most exotic luxuries were brought on seven ox carts a few weeks after his arrival. One of his servants is my cousin's wife."
- "He is a teacher from a far-away country. His customs are strange. His teachings seem as foreign as himself, and totally unneeded here. No one seems to know much about him."
- "He is a prophet and speaks for a foreign god who wants to come and rule over us. He lives with his foreign wife behind a very high, thick wall with sharp glass spikes projecting from its top. His iron gate is always locked. He has two big, foreign dogs whose teeth are very sharp and whose bark is angry. We all hope he feeds them well, but they seem always hungry for our flesh!"
- "He is a judge. He tells us we are very evil people. He wants us to offer sacrifices to his god. He knows nothing about the spirits we fear and obey. No one can teach him much, but he is trying to learn our language."

In those times, the missionary's strategy often resembled that of the soldier living behind the protection of his fort. He would venture out to do battle in daylight. The gate would be carefully locked behind him. He would risk his life on the mission field, then return to the safety of his fort before sundown.

This is a harsh view of men and women who did in fact risk their lives in untried circumstances. Personal safety was always in question. Their spouses and children were in real danger, daily. Presently, the danger is diminished.

We honor those brave hearts. Their strategy seems more reasonable when we consider the conditions. Many died at the hands of local people who did not understand their mission. Perhaps more died from diseases.

Role #1: Learner

Missionaries of the more recent past have given us the benefit of their experience and wisdom. We now know it is unwise to go to an unreached people group appearing to be rich, or speaking as a judge, a teacher, or even a man with superior spiritual knowledge. We need to be learners, admitting to the locals that their language and their culture are valuable to us. This is the truth! We tell them we need their help, because we do!

If you adopt this role you will satisfy the people. Some of them want to feel important to you. They are! They want to be useful. They can be!

It will also satisfy you. You will be able to relax and be what you are, a student.

"Learner" is a non-status role that clearly fits with our divine model, who came *as one who serves* (Lk. 22:26, 27).

"Learner" parallels "servant" nicely. Neither a servant nor a learner holds a high position demanding respect. Neither tends to intimidate. Neither makes important decisions, except perhaps for himself.

Jesus is our model! He not only became one of us, he joined us as an infant, depending totally on mankind for every human need, just as any infant must.

We do not join our new people as infants. But we must have the same heart and mind Jesus had. *If anyone wants to be first, he must be the very last, and the servant of all* (Mk. 9:35).

Philippians 2:1-18 shows us the humble character of Jesus. We saw this in detail in chapter 9, and in chapter 12.

As a missionary, you will cause the people to see Jesus in you by adopting a humble position. The role of learner helps you prepare the hearts of the people to receive the gospel.

"Learner" also seems the most effective beginning role for the missionary for it is crucial that he learn everything about his adoptive people before evangelizing.

What Will be the Result of the Missionary's Role as Learner?

As we have said earlier, as Learner, the missionary learns the language and the culture. This is his task for as long as it takes him. He must learn the language well enough to explain spiritual concepts such as God, salvation, redemption, justification.

If you hope to bond with people, you must speak their language well. You must be able to express and to understand the deepest emotions of the human heart. Friends talk about such things. A friend takes time to listen when his friend has a problem. Even more difficult for many, a friend is willing to admit he has a problem, and to ask his friend for advice.

Greg Livingstone[8] lived in a Muslim city, in an apartment building managed by an older Muslim with whom Greg had bonded to some degree. The man invited Greg to his apartment upstairs. He wanted to talk to him. Greg went immediately. The man poured Greg a cup of tea and soon got to the subject on his mind.

"Never," the man emphasized, "never divorce your wife and marry your mistress."

Greg was astonished with this advice because nothing in his previous words to the manager could have prompted these words of wisdom. Greg wanted to honor this man's age. This is most important in Islamic cultures. He did not want to say anything that might lessen the bond between them. "Thank you!" he said, "I will follow this advice."

Such an answer leaves the door open for the bonded friend to speak about whatever personal problem brought about such a statement. Greg might have said, "But I would never divorce my wife. And I would never have an intimate relationship with a prostitute."

But at that stage of their friendship, this would only have been received as a claim to superior spirituality. It might have ended the openness the manager was showing toward his foreign friend.

As you study the language, you will want to begin evangelizing. You can't. You don't know the language well enough to explain spiritual truths clearly. It is normal to take much time to learn a new language. It is normal to feel discouraged after the newness of your efforts wears off.

---

[8] *Planting Churches in Muslim Cities,* by Greg Livingstone, p. 129.

Your relationship with God will be your greatest source of encouragement. Review chapter 12 which tells about overcoming culture shock. See chapter 14 to review how to learn a language.

Learning some language skills will result in your taking on your next missionary role.

Role #2: Trader

The word "trader" means "one who exchanges goods or services for something of value."

The missionary role, "Trader," means that the missionary exchanges (trades) cultural information with a member of the people group whose culture he is studying.

If you, as a completely foreign person, were to ask a stranger of another culture questions about his values, you would not likely get much information. Many would tell you only things that might cause you to admire their customs, and avoid totally anything that might shock you, or that you might not easily understand.

But at this stage of your learning, you are by no means completely foreign. You know the language well enough to discuss culture in their own language. You are initiating the subject with a friend or friends with whom you have done some genuine bonding.

Further, you are beginning this discussion by sharing with them details about your own culture. This interests them because you are their friend, a friend who is interested enough in them to have spent many months studying their language.

Show your friends photos that picture the marriage ceremony, and other events, from your birth culture. This is a good way to start. Photos from your own wedding, or photos cut from a magazine will make your trading much more natural and interesting.

Your language helper can prepare you for these discussions. Choose a text each day that will contain sentences you will need. Ask yourself, "What will I say as I show my friends this photo?"

What questions will you ask to encourage your friends to tell you more and more about their own traditions? Have your language helper prepare you to ask these questions.

The book, "Language Acquisition Made Practical," by the Brewsters,[9] is an excellent source of help in learning a language from native speakers of the language. It includes much that will help you see what questions to ask them about their culture.

In Their Culture There is a Key!

Keep this in mind as you learn. You want to know what is in their culture that God will use as a key to open their hearts to the gospel.[10] *He has also set eternity in the hearts of men* (Ecc. 3:11).

In the culture you are studying there is something planted by the Lord. Some custom, belief, or hope about the future, will be the link you will use to connect the gospel to the needs of the people. This tradition will act as a key to open their hearts.

For example, the Damal people of Irian Jaya have handed down, from generation to generation, the belief that a "golden age" was coming. Then there would be no war, and very few illnesses.

When a missionary came and explained the kingdom of God, an elder stood up and with emotion said to his friends, "Recently I buried my father, who taught me about the golden age. He did not live to see it. Neither did his father or his grandfather. This man is telling us of the golden age. Let us not miss it ourselves!"

The gospel was well received within that tribe because God used an unbeliever to connect their tradition with the gospel message. Usually the missionary is the one to see the connection, or to find the key.

---

[9] See the bibliography.
[10] Don Richardson in his *Eternity in Their Hearts* has these examples of people groups whose legends contain culture keys for evangelism.

The Karen people of Myanmar expected for generations that a teacher of truth would come to them carrying a black object under his arm. God sent to them a missionary carrying his black Bible under his arm!

Jesus also fulfilled what should have been the expectations of the people. The Hebrews knew the prophecies about the Messiah. Jesus fulfilled those prophecies, though not in the way the people anticipated!

The result of your adopting the role of "Trader" will be: you will learn more about the culture of the people God is sending you to evangelize. The people will also learn more about you!

The Maasai Culture Contained the Key

Among the Maasai of East Africa there lived a missionary named Malcolm Hunter. Malcolm and his family had been laboring for some years. It was time to return to their British homeland for a furlough. But God directed Malcolm to bring food to a certain Maasai village. With his vehicle loaded with food, he and a Maasai believer we'll call "Ikji" drove off.

"Ikji," said Malcolm, "if there is any ministry to be done today, you be the one to minister. I am so weary. And my heart and mind are already in my homeland, on leave." Ikji agreed.

Before arriving at their destination they stopped at a bank where Malcolm was to exchange British pounds for local currency. The Maasai bank teller, hearing why they had come, did something that puzzled Malcolm. He placed his hand under the iron bars, through the opening where money and documents are to be passed. His fingers were spread apart, stretching toward Malcolm.

Malcolm quickly asked Ikji, "What do I do?"

"The same!" came the whispered reply.

Malcolm complied, extending his finger tips to touch those of the teller. The teller then received the British money and counted out the equivalent in local currency. Malcolm pocketed his money and the two travelers left the bank.

Malcolm immediately asked, "Ikji, what was the purpose of that little ceremony?"

Ikji explained, "It is an old Maasai tradition. When you touch fingers you are agreeing together, giving your word that you will deal honestly with each other in this transaction. But in ages past, the fingers were cut, and the blood of each man was mingled with the blood of the other in a most solemn covenant of lifelong brotherhood."

Malcolm was impressed!

He had heard about this Maasai covenant. When a strong chief invited a lesser chief to accept his protection, under a covenant, the lesser had two options. He could accept the protection and rule of the more powerful chief, or he and his people would be overtaken by the stronger, with much bloodshed.

The two arrived at the Maasai village. They began distributing the food, standing in the bed of the pickup and explaining to the smiling Maasai that this food is from "the Biggest of the Big," the Maasai name for God.

A Maasai chief saw all this from outside his nearby hut. He was curious about this foreigner. He walked up to the pickup and shouted, "White stranger, when you have finished here, be my guest," gesturing toward his hut.

Malcolm knew this would mean drinking milk mixed with the blood of a cow from a gourd that had been hollowed out and purified with the urine of cattle herded by this semi-nomadic tribe.

With a smile he graciously accepted the invitation from the kind chief, reflecting on his weary mind distracted by preparations for furlough.

Once inside he noticed the smooth surfaces of the hut, smeared with now dried cow dung mixed with mud. He partook of the chief's anticipated hospitality. Immediately came an electrifying question. "White stranger from a distant land, what message do you bring?"

Malcolm's felt a powerful anointing. With a vigorous voice, in vibrant tones, Malcolm heard himself say, "Chief, I bring you a message from the Biggest of the Big. This day he commands you to touch fingers with him.

If you will accept his covenant, he will make you a member of his own tribe, and extend to you the same loving protection which he provides his people. You will receive his very life in your spirit, and you will live forever with him in triumph when you pass from this earthly life."

The chief was stunned. He fully understood fully this good news. He was gripped to his innermost depths.

As for Malcolm, he too was stunned. The door to this division of the Maasai tribe was now fully opened. After his furlough, Malcolm would return to a waiting chief and his people, totally willing to receive teaching from the book containing the words of the Biggest of the Big.

"Touching fingers," an ancient tribal tradition, was the key to showing the chief and his people that they needed to surrender themselves to their Creator. Malcolm did not find this key without learning the language and the culture of the Maasai people.

Role #3: Story Teller

You are ready to begin your formal ministry when you have learned their language well enough to explain biblical concepts, and when you know their culture well enough to pinpoint at least one of their major heart-felt needs.

Without adequate language you would more than likely be badly misunderstood as you tried to teach spiritual truths. Without knowing their needs, you would likely be offering them something they could not relate to. But if you see the culture key they themselves have been holding for generations, and if you have the language ability to show them how Jesus is the fulfillment of what they long for, then you will see wonderful fruit.

Then you become for them a "Story Teller." Your stories are the best ever heard anywhere on earth. They come from the heart of God and are found in his Word.

Every ethnic group loves stories. From toddlers to gray-haired grandfathers and grandmothers, every person loves stories. In primitive societies, stories are a principal teaching tool. In sophisticated groups, stories are greatly appreciated.

Peoples are divided into literate societies and oral societies. Both love stories. Literate societies learn from the written word. Oral societies learn from the spoken word.

Literate societies keep written records of the past. Oral societies keep memory records of the past, in the form of stories, dramas, poems, proverbs, songs, chants, and riddles.

Wherever God sends you, the people have been reading or listening to stories and singing songs that are meaningful to them. They have heard these over and over from their early years. When you are ready to begin, you will offer to tell them a story they have never heard.

By this time, they know you well. They have been won over by your energy and accomplishment in learning their language. You have adopted so much of their culture they realize you genuinely love and respect them. Now, when you offer to tell them a story they will be attentive for two reasons. First, you are their friend. Second, they are ready for a new story!

Begin with stories from the Old Testament. Many peoples do not understand the nature of God at all. Everyone needs to understand better! The story of Adam and Eve will help. Be patient if your story seems too much like one they have learned from childhood. When you get to the story of Jesus, you will know how to present him in a way that is most meaningful to people of this particular culture.

Perhaps not on the first occasion when you introduce him, but eventually, hearing more and more about Jesus, some will accept him as their Savior and Lord.

The result of your role as Story Teller will be a small group of believers, a tiny church!

Role #4: Church Planter

This small group of believers is your first little church. Further church planting will be done mainly by your disciples. We will deal with this subject in the next chapter.

For now we emphasize, your goal in this strategy is not to hold evangelistic rallies, though these are good. Your goal is to begin a people movement. To do this you need to bond with the people while you become a learner, a trader, a story teller, and a church planter of at least one church.

Elder Men First!

In almost every society, women and children will follow the elder men in any major decisions they decide are right. It seldom happens the other way. Elder men seldom go along with decisions made by the women or the children.

When you tell your Bible stories about Jesus, you might make a special effort to direct much of your story to the eyes, ears and hearts of these respected men of the village.

When the time comes for you to invite your listeners to accept Jesus as Savior and Lord, let God show you whether you should meet separately with the men, and perhaps with the elder men. Your invitation to enter God's kingdom is something the decision-makers of the tribe would normally decide for the others. Of course, one can enter the kingdom on the basis of what his or her tribal leaders have decided, but you need their approval of the gospel message to preach it freely and openly. Usually, everything has to be out in the open for all to see if you are to begin a people movement to Jesus. When you know they approve, and especially if the leaders themselves have believed, you can ask them if they approve your inviting the people to accept the Lord. You might even ask the believers among them to give testimonies.

You could suggest that they go to their homes and invite their wives and children to accept Jesus, leading in a prayer, those who want that.

This deference to their leadership will have its effect. They will see that you do not do things in chaos, without due process. You honor their customs. You respect their ways. You rely on their counsel, their wisdom. This will help you bond and establish trust among them.

In these paragraphs we have been referring to evangelizing a tribal people. Evangelizing a people group having no tribal pattern of rulership would have different boundaries and guidelines within which you must function. Learning the culture will show you how to proceed... always with prayerful dependence on the Holy Spirit.

What is a "People Movement"?

A "people movement" is what happens when new believers tell relatives and friends about Jesus, leading many to the Lord. These in turn spread the faith to others who also pass it on. Quite rapidly, the entire people group hears the gospel and a vast majority of the members of the group become Christians.

Future missionary, you can begin a people movement. Go to an unreached people. Become one of them. Learn their language and their culture. Follow their cultural norms. Obey biblical principles of church planting. God will use you to begin a people movement.

In a people movement, the usual barriers to success have been avoided. The usual barriers are called "culture barriers." Illustration 2 in chapter 1 shows a people group. Each individual is shown with a round head to illustrate that they all have the same culture. The "barrier" tends to keep out persons and ideas from other cultures. These are seen as foreign and undesirable, even untrustworthy.

In a people movement, the gospel is presented in a way that is culturally meaningful. The gospel itself is presented, but the old cultural packaging is left behind. The new packaging is now the wrapping of the culture in which the gospel is being introduced. The persons of the unreached people group then see that the gospel satisfies their deep spiritual needs, and that it is not foreign. It belongs within their own culture.

The gospel can only be presented in this way with the Lord's wisdom and by his grace and power. You, the missionary, will cooperate with God by knowing well the culture in which you will present the gospel.

Role #5: Teacher

Now that you have a tiny flock of believers, you are responsible to teach them from the Word. Begin with the "Nine Basic Commands of the New Testament."[11]

1. Repent and believe. The new believers have already done this, but they need deeper teaching about salvation. Teach this one first.
2. Water baptism. Teach about this, and baptize those who are willing.
3. Be filled with the Holy Spirit. Lead them into this experience.
4. Pray. With each command, teach and then lead them into obeying the Lord. Love is our motive for obeying.
5. Give. Do not neglect this command. If you do, the people will be deprived of part of the Christian walk, and much of the joy.
6. Love.
7. The Lord's Supper.
8. Witness. You might teach this one second. New believers are most enthusiastic about leading neighbors to the Lord as soon as they are saved. Some will even go to nearby villages. Show them how to help others accept Jesus. Lead them. This command is about sharing their faith with people of their own culture.
9. Go make disciples of all nations. This command is about sharing their faith with people whose culture is different from their own. Invite them to pray for people groups yet unreached. Invite them to send missionaries. Challenge them to be missionaries.

You can find more commands in the New Testament, but it seems better to stay with these nine at the beginning.

Teach your new believers to obey through love, not fear. If they obey because they fear hell, they will be trying to earn their salvation, which is a denial of grace. They should understand well, from your first lessons (#1 above) that they cannot earn salvation. It is totally a gift from God,

---

[11] Patterson has seven of these commands. We have added #3 and #9. Patterson advocates founding churches on the solid foundation of obeying Jesus through love (avoiding legalism). See his, *Obedience-Oriented Education.*

earned by Jesus alone. They can only receive it by faith, total trust, which is also a gift.

Teach them that once they have accepted salvation as a gift, they will be changed. They will want to obey God who has given them what they could not earn, eternal life! They will love the Lord and desire to please him. Show them these truths in the Word.

The point is, avoid legalism. Many unsaved people are striving to be good enough to face God after death, to be found righteous because of their good works. No one can be that good. No one can be saved by his own goodness, or good works. All fall short!

When we're saved, we receive a wonderful gift: relationship with God, "eternal life." We become members of his family. We cannot deserve this gift. Jesus earned it for us on the cross.

You cannot have a strong church unless the "believers" believe, that is, trust in Jesus completely, and have the assurance that they are saved. If they think they are working for their salvation, that they are becoming worthy of heaven through the good they do, they are not trusting in Jesus alone, but in themselves (Eph. 2:8, 9). Without faith, total trust, it is impossible to please God.

Unless they accept the gift as a gift, earned by Jesus alone, they are not believers at all! If they are not believers, you do not have a church.

If these basic truths are understood and accepted, you will have a body of joyful Christians who want to "turn the world upside down, bringing other peoples to Jesus, that they too might worship him." True believers know they have received as a gift the "pearl of great price." They want to please God who has mercifully given such a valuable gift. In their grateful hearts and conduct, they grow more and more into the image of Jesus.

Though you understand this, you would benefit as I did by reading, and rereading, *Grace Works,* by Dudley Hall. I had been saved for decades when I discovered this book. Only in reading it did I realize I had missed much of the truth Hall lays out in very readable form.

Seekers who are trying to earn heaven are placing their confidence on themselves. Their lives center on good works. Most of their energies are spent trying to avoid sin. They sin, and have no Savior to forgive them. They are not trusting in relationship with God. They have only enmity with God.

Once these seekers surrender completely to God's mercy, trusting in the work of Jesus on the cross to save them, they will change. They will see their conduct improving. The good works done by saved persons merit rewards in heaven, but good works cannot earn heaven itself.

Their good works are important indicators that they are saved. *Faith without works is dead* (Jas. 2:26).

Your church will grow and multiply. We examine this further when we look at church planting.

When the nine basic commands have been taught, other Bible principles should be taught. The commands need reviewing occasionally as new believers join the church, and to keep the elder believers refreshed on basic truths.

Role #6: Trainer / Sender

When some of your people show they can minister on their own without regular teaching from you, it is time to begin training some to be missionaries to other people groups that have not yet received the gospel.

Some new believers might immediately go to other people groups and lead individuals to the Lord. If they do, take care to nurture these new missionaries on a regular basis. Guard against the possibility that they will not understand the difference between the power of God and the power of the enemy. Set up a training program for them so they can receive consistent teaching from you for years. Otherwise you might find they are mixing sound doctrine with traditional practices that are not of God!

All believers need to be involved in reaching other people groups who have not yet heard the good news. All will pray. Prayer is the most powerful thing anyone can do, but prayer is not a substitute for sending a missionary. Praying and supporting a missionary are not a substitute for going yourself, if God is sending you!

Role #7: Developer

By now, many years have passed since you began your work among this your adoptive people. As the missionary-founder of a group of churches, you realize three things.

    a) One day, you will no longer lead this movement.
    b) The transfer of authority will be smoother if you are able to oversee it and guide it.
    c) Perhaps, when this transfer is complete, God will move you to repeat this same long process of evangelization in another place.

Realizing all this, you can begin now to ask God to show you whom he has chosen to replace you. When you are confident you know the answer, begin to develop that person, giving him more and more responsibilities. If God confirms that this is the man, you will tell him so. Eventually you will "hand over the keys," publicly giving your successor full authority over the work.

Role #8: Consultant

When your replacement is totally in command, you still need to be available for advice. "Consultant" is best demonstrated by drama. Picture the only actor in this drama standing with his arms folded, looking into space, humming softly.

What is he doing? Nothing? No! He's waiting. Waiting for his replacement to come to him with a problem.

As consultant you will pray! When your replacement asks your advice, he might say, "What shall I do in this situation?"

This question you cannot answer. Only your replacement himself can answer that question. He is the decision maker. But you can tell him what you would do if you were in charge. The decision however is his, not yours, because he has the responsibility for the results.

You would do well to discuss with him all the options, and to encourage him to write them down. Ask him what he sees as the advantages and disadvantages of each option. In chapter 10, we discuss how to write these down, and how to evaluate each, as part of a method for making an important decision.

All your discussions with him are confidential. This is important! Do not give in to the temptation to trumpet that your replacement cannot manage without you. This might gratify your ego, but resist the abominable sin of pride. You need to be to him as Barnabas was to Paul before Paul's ministry expanded.

At some point, the Lord will release you from your role as consultant. Illustration 21 is arrow-shaped to show that the career of the missionary continues beyond the illustration. He might send you to another area, among people of this same culture, to work in the same way. You would then already know their language and culture.

But how would you bond with the people? Bonding and servanthood would require new ideas. You cannot bond through learning their language because you already know their language. God would show you how to take a humble role, a servant kind of role so you could form genuine friendships!

Or, God might send you to a totally unreached people among whom no ministry is happening. You would then begin as a learner, as you did years before for your first unreached people.

Can a Missionary Give His Work into the Hands of Another?

He can. Surely he will, if God directs him.

The decision to do this is not easy. If the missionary has been wonderfully successful, he will naturally want to stay and continue in a leading role. In some circumstances, God might want this.

Most founders cannot bring themselves to give over any responsibility with authority to another. The typical founder of a small ministry cannot delegate substantial decision-making responsibilities. He explains that his subordinates have proven to be incapable. All fail when given a chance to lead, he thinks.

This attitude causes the founder's most capable helpers to seek opportunities for leadership roles elsewhere. In this way, the founder of a small ministry continues to lead a small ministry, and of course it becomes true: he does not have anyone he can promote into a leadership role. Each maturing helper leaves too soon.

Founders and other leaders who cannot delegate, notice that when they give a helper a chance to lead, he makes mistakes. Mistakes are part of the learning process. If the leader would give proper training and wise increments of responsibility over a reasonable length of time, many trainees would prove themselves capable.

The leader expects too perfect a performance too early in the process. He forgets how gradually he himself learned to lead.

The leader also confuses mistakes with creativity. The helper is creative. He is taking a risk, trying to find a better way of doing something. He deserves to be congratulated for taking initiative, unless the risk is clearly foolish.

The advantage of the founder delegating successfully is this: he will soon be able to turn over leadership totally to his replacement. The founder can then take his wonderful experience and begin a new people movement among another totally unreached people! Does that not exceed in importance the mistakes that will occur while his future replacement is learning to lead?

Mistakes made while the founder is in control, should be fairly safe, if proper safeguards are part of the procedures.

Why is "Worshiper" Mentioned Below the Giant Arrow in Illustration 21, Rather than Within the Arrow?

An illustration showing the roles of the missionary seems incomplete without mentioning worship. Worship must be part of the missionary's life. However, it is not just a phase of his work, as each of the eight roles is. Rather, it is his lifestyle as a believer.

It seems safe to say, if the missionary is not a worshiper, he will lack much in his efforts to give his newly adopted people a true belief in the one true God. God births many fruitful works in our minds and hearts as we worship him in spirit and in truth. No strategy is going to be good enough unless it is born of God. More important, God works his wonders in our hearts as we stand in awe, amazed at his greatness. He prepares us to minister in his name.

When you are disappointed with your results, push all else away and focus on the Lord. Worship him. God will surprise you with his creativity, his marvelous solutions, his details that will produce success.

Have a notepad ready.

Even more important, he will lift you up as you "see" the splendor and majesty of him who commissions you, who anoints you for his glory and for your deep, abiding satisfaction, not so much in your work as in him.

You must be a worshiper. The missionary as worshiper is bonding with God! Jesus put it this way: "Abide in me."

Don't "worship," if it can be called that, mainly as a means of getting God to do something for you. Let's worship God for who he is, not for what we want.

Even now, as you study strategy, keep giving your heart to the Lord in worship. Forget what you think you need. Give him glory. You were created for this! Then, let him do what he wills.

I believe we come into our best position when we worship God. This position makes a way so that God can work in a more fruitful way through us! Worship will condition your heart so you can receive what God is doing, submitting to him even when his ways are so far above yours that you cannot understand them.

At some stage of your spiritual growth you found yourself in genuine worship for the first time. You wished it would never end. You wondered if you could ever repeat it. Can you worship with this freedom and intensity anytime you choose?

You can! God must play the key role in worship. But he is always ready to do his part.

You can worship right now. Using a scripture, or using your own words to say what God wants to hear from you, give God first place in your heart. As you do, if you are concentrating on him, and on giving to him, you will experience an "anointing," or "unction."

The Lord suddenly seems present. The words you've spoken, suddenly, like wine exploding from a tired old wineskin, gush out in full meaning and aroma. I believe this is a spiritual experience. God is communing with your spirit most effectively at that instant. I believe we will commune with God this way in heaven. Without words, God will infuse us with the information or the message he wants to communicate to us.
Together with that gush of understanding, there is an emotional response that comes from deep within. These two experiences, understanding and sensing or feeling come so fast, one after the other, that they seem to be one experience.

You will eventually no longer complain that you cannot pray for more than five minutes. You will no longer say, "After I have spoken to God for five minutes, I'm stuck!"

If you haven't broken through this barrier into this two-fold experience yet, you can. In chapter 3, we give you seventeen things you can do in your prayer time. Start with some of these. You might try them all, over a period of time.

The most important one, and the most rewarding one, is worship. Be sure to take time every day to worship. Only in worship can you sense the importance of who you are in Christ. This realization produces in you a wonderful understanding of the greatness of God and who he is, compared with the relative "unimportance" of what you do in your ministry.

What we do is very important. God however is so much bigger that our ministry looks small by comparison. God is infinite. Our ministry is finite. Worship is eternal. Mission is temporal.

God is after you, more and more of you! Your service is not his goal. Your whole being is. God does not need your service. You need to serve God to be full of his joy, to be whole. You need to reach out to others and God intends that. Through you he will bring others into his kingdom where they too can glorify him and be fulfilled themselves in that process.

God has you, but he wants all of you, in every way. That's who you are. You are his person. He gets more and more of you during worship. The more fully you are his, the more freely you can worship.

A "Whole Person" is One Who is Centered on God

It is said that unmarried persons must first learn to be satisfied to live single. Then they are ready for marriage because they are "whole persons."

If as single persons a man and a woman cannot find their joy in God, each is looking to something or someone else for satisfaction. Usually each is seeking a spouse as the solution to the problem of singleness. If they marry, the marriage will have problems because each is so needy.

Each will depend upon the spouse for happiness. There are two things wrong with this kind of dependence.

1) Neither spouse can carry the heavy responsibility for making the other happy.
2) Neither should give anyone the power to make him or her miserable. Each of us should look to God for our fulfillment. These two will love each other, with one condition: that happiness is the result. God loves much better than that! God loves unconditionally!

Their conditional love will not satisfy these two spouses. They each need what the other cannot give, unconditional love. God alone loves each of us unconditionally.

If, on the other hand, each spouse is content in Jesus, then each has the security needed to risk reaching out to the other in love. They have no fear of rejection because they have the ultimate acceptance. Each knows from experience in worship, that his or her acceptance, significance and fulfillment are in God.

This Basic Principle Applies to Ministry Also

If we must be in ministry to be content, there is something lacking in our worship. In worship, we minister to the Lord, and he to us. Once we are fully satisfied in him, we have that "wholeness" only God can give. Then we are free to take on ministry and we will see results and be satisfied.

But if we jump into ministry to satisfy ourselves, to "get happy," we will have problems. The ministry is then mainly a means for us to get what we need or want. We will promote self.

Ministry works much better, for us and for others, if it pours out of a heart content to worship. Self will always be there to some degree until we've gone to be with him. God looks for pure hearts who are centered on him (2 Chr 16:9).

Chapter 18
Questions

1. Roles of the missionary include these:

   A. learner
   B. trader
   C. bonding
   D. story teller

2. Results of the missionary being a learner include these:

   A. He learns their language and their culture.
   B. He bonds with the people.
   C. He can immediately begin to evangelize them.
   D. They will accept him as a friend and begin to trust him.

3. Roles of the missionary also include these:

   A. church planter
   B. teacher
   C. evangelizer
   D. trainer of missionaries / sender of missionaries.

4. Select a statement that is **not** correct.
   A "people movement" is what happens when:

   A. new believers tell relatives and friends about Jesus, leading many to the Lord.
   B. quite rapidly, the entire people group hears the gospel and a vast majority of the members of the group become Christians.
   C. the missionary trusts new believers to evangelize.
   D. the missionary uses great caution, allowing only Bible school graduates to minister.

5. In his role of teacher, the missionary:

    A. begins with the nine basic commands of the New Testament.
    B. teaches the new believers to obey through love, not fear of hell.
    C. encourages them to be good enough to face God after death, to be found righteous because of their good works.
    D. exhorts them to obey God who has given them what they could not earn, eternal life!

6. Select one set of statements, A or B or C or D, whichever one has an underlined expression that **disagrees** with what you studied in this chapter.

    A. When you are disappointed with your mission results, push all else away and focus on the Lord. <u>Worship him</u>. God will surprise you with his creativity, his marvelous solutions, his details that will produce success.
    B. God will lift you up as you "see" the splendor and majesty of him who commissions you, who anoints you for <u>his glory</u> and for your deep, abiding satisfaction, not so much in your work as in him
    C. We come into our best position when we <u>praise</u> God. This position makes a way so that God can work in a more fruitful way through us!
    D. God is communing with our spirit <u>most effectively</u> at that instant while we are worshiping him in spirit and in truth.

Chapter 19

Teach Your Timothies to Multiply Churches

The Importance of Role #5: Teacher

"Teacher" is your most vital role as a church-planting missionary using the strategy we describe in this book. If you don't want to teach, this might seem disappointing. Wait until you know more, before you judge whether you can teach, or want to teach.

Perhaps you would rather think of yourself as a preacher, not a teacher. A preacher proclaims God's truth and exhorts people to accept and obey.

By using the term "teacher" we emphasize the learning process. If people learn what God says, they will be motivated to obey. The basis of their obedience will be the truth they have accepted intellectually, and their love for a Savior who gave his life so he could give them freely the eternal life they could never earn.

Anyone who teaches God's Word will be proclaiming his truth, and will find himself exhorting, encouraging his hearers to obey God. Preaching is important, but for solid beginnings among an unreached people group, we place the emphasis on truth, and on teaching and learning, and on obeying through love.

If you are called to plant churches among an unreached people group, you will want those churches to multiply rapidly and yet be strong. Therefore, teach the Word of God to a few leaders. These churches will be fed through the teaching you will give the leaders. They will pass the teaching on to faithful men who will be able to teach others (2 Tim. 2:2). This is a vital element to the strategy we are describing.

Here is another: Everything you as teacher do in your missionary work is to be imitated by your disciples who are leaders. This makes for solid teaching and equipping of the saints. Your Timothies will imitate your fidelity in teaching Bible principles to those they have led to the Lord. This education system requires simple reproduction by each Timothy of the teaching he himself has just received from his Paul. The result will be rapid multiplication of strong churches.

Paul Trusts Timothy to Minister

As you learned in chapter 3, you the missionary will become a teacher after you have made some converts. You will gather these new believers together as often as seems right. You will begin by teaching them the nine basic commands of the New Testament, listed in chapter 3.

As you teach about a command, you will lead your little flock into obeying Jesus through love. Show them how to obey that command.

When the new believers learn about witnessing, teach them how to share their faith with their relatives and friends. Go with them to demonstrate, but have each of them present part of the gospel message. Do only as much as you think they need. Let them do the rest. In witnessing to the next person, let them do everything. You observe and evaluate, so you can advise them privately later. Adapt this pattern as needed, but don't do for them what they can do themselves. Otherwise they will think they cannot succeed without you.

Then send them out on their own. Some will win people to the Lord. These who are successful as witnesses are your new leaders, your "Timothies." You are like Paul to them. You teach them in private sessions.

Once your Timothies have their own converts out witnessing, your Timothies will have their own Timothies. From that point onward, your Timothies will be like Paul to their own Timothies.

A Timothy is any believer who has successfully witnessed, that is, has led some to the Lord, and is willing to teach them what his Paul teaches him. For this purpose, Timothy receives private instruction in the Word from the believer who led him to the Lord, his Paul. Every Timothy teaches his converts the Word of God, including lessons on witnessing. In this way, every Timothy becomes a Paul to his own successful witnesses who become his Timothies.

Every successful witness becomes, not only the evangelizer of a group of relatives and friends, but also their teacher if he is willing to teach them. If he prefers not to teach, he should bring his converts to a meeting led by the one who led him to the Lord, or to any meeting where they will learn to love and obey Jesus.

This pattern of reproduction produces an "education chain," with the same instruction being handed down from Paul to Timothy, down to the most recently successful Timothy. There will be as many education chains as you yourself started, each emanating from a successful witness whom you yourself trained, and whom you are continuing to teach from the Word.

All down the education chains, new converts are trusted to minister to the persons they have led to the Lord. Each successful witness learns from his "Paul." He then turns to his own "Timothy" and, like Paul, teaches him. This pattern has three advantages:

1. **Trusting the new believer to minister is scriptural.** In 2 Timothy 2:2 Paul wrote to his own disciple: *And the things you have heard me say in the presence of many witnesses entrust to reliable men who will also be qualified to teach others.*

   This is one of the reasons why Paul and his company were able to turn *the world upside down* (Ac 17:6 KJV). Paul favored placing ministry responsibility into the hands of new believers.

2. **New believers are best qualified to lead their relatives and friends to the Lord.** They are best qualified because the persons being evangelized are persons who totally trust the bearer of the message. The new believer, ministering within his own birth culture, can best pinpoint reasons why his relatives and friends need the Lord. New believers are often more excited about their salvation, and more energetic to obey the Lord in witnessing, than mature disciples!

3. **A new believer can witness immediately and begin a church in a short time.** This we will now explain using Illustration 22.

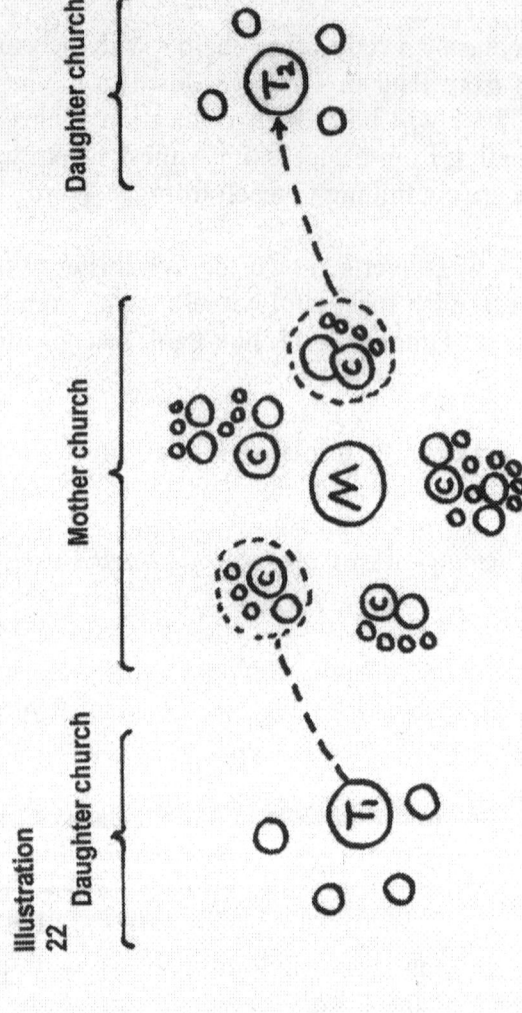

Illustration
22

Daughter church

Mother church

Daughter church

The churches will multiply

as Timothies (T_1, T_2, etc.) lead people to Jesus and begin meeting with them on a regular basis.

The missionary (M) will have a successful leader take his place as teacher of the mother church, so he can concentrate on teaching his own Timothies, and on helping Pauls and Timothies down the education chains.

The "Paul / Timothy Method" of Multiplying Churches

You, the future missionary, will be "Paul" to those new believers who have successfully led others to the Lord. These successful witnesses are your "Timothies." You will have a special teacher-student relationship with them. You will meet with them every two weeks to teach them, so they can meet with their new little flocks often and teach them those same truths, at least twice each week.

Each Paul has two major teaching responsibilities.
1. He teaches his little flock of converts twice or more each week.
2. He teaches each of his Timothies, one at a time, every week or two, on a regular basis, just as his Paul is teaching him. Why one at a time? Each Timothy has different problems in his church, and needs Paul's undivided attention as Paul helps him solve specific problems.

Illustration 22 shows **you** as the "M" (missionary) inside a circle. Your converts, older, respected men, are each shown as a "c" inside a circle.

What about your converts who either have no converts themselves, or do not want to teach them? These will continue to be members of your flock. If they lead anyone to the Lord, they will invite these new believers to come with them to your church meetings. Your flock will consist of these, and their wives and children. Other circles represent wives and children.

Your Timothies will not attend your church meetings. They will be leading their own church meetings. In Illustration 22, this is shown. That illustration shows two of your converts have become Timothies. They are represented by circles T_1 and T_2.

Illustration 22 shows three tiny churches. For the two churches planted by your Timothies we show only the original converts. But wives, children, friends and relatives will also be part of these new flocks.

Now look at Illustration 23. Large circles are for leaders who have succeeded in leading others to the Lord. They teach their own little flocks of converts. Small circles represent converts.

You, the missionary, are represented by the circle labeled "M." Two of your converts in the illustration successfully witnessed to four persons each, represented by more small circles. These two successful witnesses leave the mother church to teach their own tiny churches what you teach.

Every successful witness teaches his flock the nine basic commands of the New Testament. This is what he is learning from his Paul, the person who led him to the Lord. Love is the motive for obeying Jesus.

When these commands are well taught, Paul and Timothy learn and teach other lessons from the Bible. They occasionally review the basic commands.

Notice in Illustration 23, four dash circles each containing a smaller circle and the letter "c" (convert). Each of these converts has successfully witnessed to a group of unbelievers, leading them to the Lord. Therefore T_1 and T_2 each have a Timothy. The two education chains have become longer.

You will probably have more than two education chains because more than two of your own converts will probably be successful witnesses.

Patterson Planted 50 Strong Churches in 13 Years

George Patterson, as missionary to Honduras, is the one who devised this method of church planting. He calls it, "Multiplying churches through obedience-oriented education."

George has written two excellent works. "Obedience-Oriented Education" is a booklet. He later wrote, "Church Planting through Obedience Oriented Teaching" published by the William Carey Library, Pasadena, California. George's writing is clear and practical.

Patterson has a track record of success. There is much material in his writings that we have not covered here.

Patterson says each Paul and each Timothy can be compared to a link in a chain.

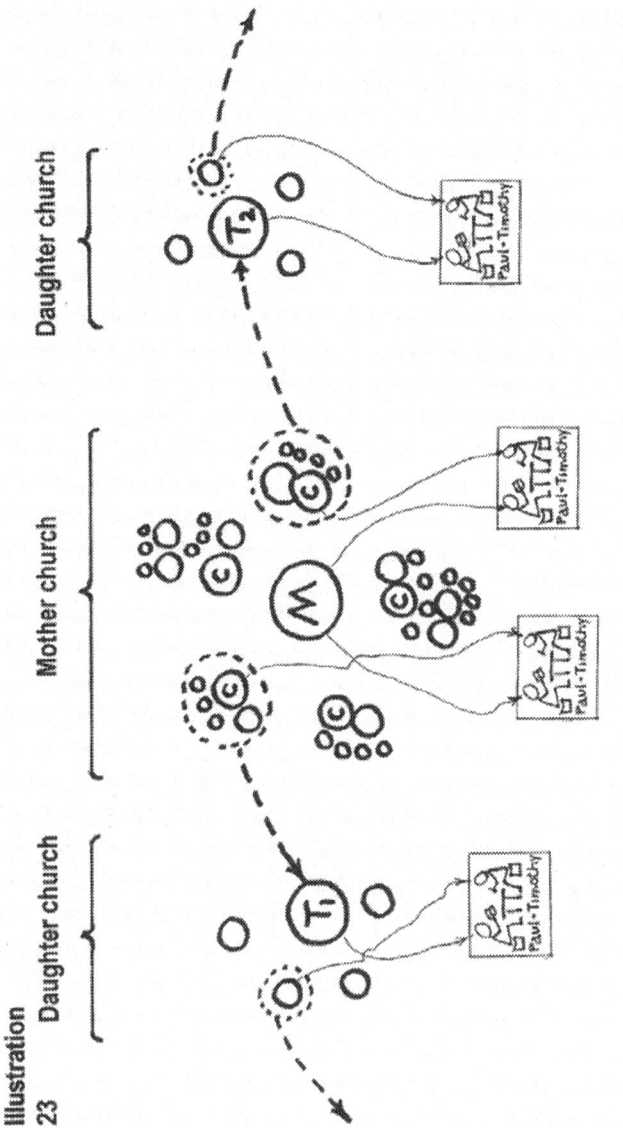

Illustration
23

Daughter church

Mother church

Daughter church

The teaching is the lifeline of the system of churches.

Each successful witness can become* a "Timothy." His Paul is the
person who witnessed to him.

Each Timothy becomes "Paul" to his own "Timothies."

Teaching is handed on down the education chains from each Paul to
each of his "Timothies."

*If a successful witness chooses not to be a
leader (Timothy) he should of course continue to
attend church, and should bring his converts to a
church near them.

"A chain is only as strong as its weakest link." This applies to the education chain. As a missionary, one of your major challenges will be to find any weak link, any Paul who is not doing a responsible job of teaching his Timothies, and encourage him, help him do better.

Never replace him with yourself. You will be fully occupied with teaching your own Timothies, and with overseeing the education chain and solving problems.

You will need to replace yourself as pastor of the church you established, the mother church, the first church planted in this system of churches. Merge this church with another that is close by. You will have too many things to do as principal teacher of the entire system, and as chief problem solver.

Patterson's book has directions regarding teaching materials, mainly booklets which he has written on each of the commands and on other Bible themes. He wrote these as he saw the need, and sold them below cost to his Timothies as they had need. He does not favor giving materials away. Some receivers will regard as unimportant, anything that is free. They will take better care of materials they have paid for, even though the price was low.

Patterson has suggestions about forms that will help each Paul keep aware of what his Timothies have taught, and of how faithfully the members of the churches are obeying. Reports of what happened during each Paul-Timothy teaching session are also kept. Copies of reports are sent back up the education chain to you, so you can spot problems.

The Four Rectangles in Illustration 23...

... show Paul teaching Timothy. This is to emphasize the vital ingredient in this strategy, namely the teaching each Paul gives to his Timothies. If that teaching is not life-giving, the system will die. If that teaching is not consistent, if Paul or Timothy fails to participate, the system has a weak link and will need your help.

This is a most successful way to plant a system of churches among an unreached people, if you, the missionary, will be faithful to the Lord and to his people. Don't miss a teaching session. Be prepared when you come to each session. Be punctual.

Chapter 19
Questions

1. Select one set of statements, A or B or C or D, whichever one has an underlined expression that **disagrees** with what you studied in this chapter.

   A. "Church planter" is your most vital role as a church-planting missionary using the strategy we describe in this book.
   B. Teach the Word of God to a few leaders. The churches will be fed through the teaching you will give the leaders. They will pass the teaching on to faithful men who will be able to teach others (2 Tim. 2:2).
   C. Everything you as teacher do in your missionary work is to be imitated by your disciples who are leaders.
   D. When the new believers learn about witnessing, teach them how to share their faith with their relatives and friends. Go with them to demonstrate, but have each of them present part of the gospel message

2. Select one set of statements, A or B or C or D, whichever one has an underlined expression that **disagrees** with what you studied in this chapter.

   A. the vital ingredient in this strategy is the teaching each Paul gives to his Timothies.
   B. If that teaching is not life-giving, the system will die.
   C. If that teaching is not consistent, if Paul or Timothy fails to participate, the system has a weak link and will need your help
   D. Don't miss a fellowship session. Be punctual.

Chapter 20

Plant Indigenous Churches

What is a Pastor?

Patterson does not call his leaders of flocks "pastors." He reserves that term for veteran leaders who have faithfully taken his training, and are continuing in ministry. He calls his future pastors "workers." He is concerned about giving any leader the impression that he has now arrived, or that he no longer needs to study the Bible.

Patterson is not satisfied with TEE, or Theological Education by Extension. He calls his training that is handed down from Paul to Timothy, "TEEE which is an abbreviation for "Theological Education and Evangelism by Extension. This draws attention to the fact that there is an immediate use for the training. Each Timothy, after receiving teaching from his Paul, will that very week teach his converts that very material. This causes Timothy to be highly motivated to come to his learning session, and to learn well.

Workers are Successful if Their People are Obeying Jesus

Patterson's workers earn certificates by meeting objective requirements. The sign of success for his trainees is that their churches are obeying Jesus.

This criterion is very different from Bible school requirements, or even TEE requirements. Both give written tests, and perhaps oral examinations, to determine whether the student has mastered the material. A better test would be whether the student is successful in his ministry!

With TEE, candidates do not know whether they are gifted as evangelists or as teachers until they have received training. With TEEE they begin one-on-one training because they have experienced success in ministry. Then they keep ministering as they learn. Their work demonstrates, to the students themselves and to all that they are leaders.

Are the Churches Indigenous?

If you adopt the Patterson strategy, your leaders will not leave their homeland for training. You might make an exception for the leader you eventually develop to replace you. Sending prospective pastors to another country or another culture can be less productive than training them where they live. There are two reasons.

> a) Most pastors who study far from their homeland are taught how to minister in that culture, rather than their own. Their training is less relevant.
> b) Many pastors who go to a more materialistic or "advanced" culture do not want to return to a simpler lifestyle, so they remain in the foreign country where they may be less needed.

There is something else that obviously makes a system of churches indigenous. It is the fact that the leaders are indigenous. They were born of parents who belong to the culture. You are the exception to this, but you have learned their language well, and you have adopted their culture. Also, most of your leading is done through nationals.

You have "contextualized" the gospel. That is, you have taught from the Bible in terms that are culturally appropriate. This is a major factor in making the churches indigenous.

Use Only Means of Evangelizing and Training That are Indigenous

Do not use a moving-picture projector, or videos, or tape recordings, unless your workers have access to these devices. Otherwise they will tell you they cannot minister because they do not have the equipment. This will be a sincere explanation. You will have trained them by your example. They can only do what they see you do. If they cannot afford the equipment you use, what good is your training?

If you use another strategy, you might use electronic equipment, speak to thousands at a time, and perhaps lead many to the Lord. However, electronics can multiply you electronically. Multiplying yourself through flesh and blood takes advantage of the passion and commitment of other disciples. It gives receivers of the gospel the chance to meet a genuine believer, rather than being ministered to mainly by your image on a TV screen.

Many who are lost have no access to TV receivers.

We should use everything the Lord provides to accomplish his work. Every strategy has potential. Follow what God is saying to your heart. In a later chapter we explain how mass media can help **start** a movement that will multiply churches.

If you are sent to lead a people movement, every decision you make must be made with that goal in mind. You must reproduce yourself in others, as Jesus did. That is, you must train others so that they can do what they have seen you do. Some will do better than you because of their perfect identity with the culture.

Using on a regular basis equipment they cannot use will give you a foreign look, and will discourage them from leading. Using electronics regularly might multiply your personal effectiveness in making disciples, but it will militate against your reproducing yourself in others. It will cripple your efforts to lead a people movement.

If you train others to be effective leaders who use the Word and their knowledge of their own culture, you can lead an entire people group to the Lord. Of course, some individuals within the group will choose not to believe.

This will be far more effective than your preaching to huge crowds, leading helpers who know they cannot imitate you. Such helpers often feel called only to take minor roles, helping you establish a mega-church with a foreign-born and foreign-trained pastor from another continent.

Foreign trimmings give rise to distrust among unbelievers.

What Makes These Churches Grow?

1. **The missionary trusts new believers.** In training leaders, nothing succeeds as dramatically as trust. A missionary who will trust new believers to minister will plant strong, growing churches.

   There is a youth minister whom I will call Mike. He loves preaching and teaching the Word of God to teenagers. Years ago he realized he had two teens who themselves loved the Word and loved teaching it!

He decided to give them a chance to teach a few younger teens as an experiment.

They were ecstatic! They prepared well, and taught well. They understood the needs of their students.

Mike asked the youth group "elders" if others would like to try. Several responded. He met with them and the original two, and discussed what to teach and how, and what to be careful about. Almost all were successful.

Mike restyled his own ministry. From that point, Mike entrusted teens to teach much of the material. He prepared them well, on a regular basis. Mike did some preaching at every meeting, but poured his heart into the older teens who were willing to minister. He was actually sharing his ministry with them.

This is strikingly similar to what Jesus did with the twelve.

Mike's youth group increased in size. They confronted problems Mike was insecure about. He was willing to try their new ideas.

They got into drama. They held outreach nights, inviting unsaved teens. These meetings featured simple sport competitions, music by their own combo, worship, drama, and Mike's preaching. Then all regular attenders were trained to witness to their peers. They were encouraged to mix with the "outsiders" during outreach nights and look for opportunities to lead someone to the Lord.

This gave every member of the youth group an opportunity to minister. The group grew even more! The teens dropped the expression, "youth group" and called themselves a "youth ministry."

Trusting the believer to minister, and equipping him to do well, is an exciting and explosive ingredient in church planting.

2. **The natural process helps churches to grow.** An infant develops naturally, if his parents give him nourishment, fresh air, lots of love with correction, good times with the family, and exercise.

Your churches will grow naturally if you give them good teaching from the Word of God, lead them into the fullness of the Holy Spirit, give them love with correction, fellowship, and encouragement to obey the Lord.

3. **Your consistent teaching from the Word causes the churches to grow.** If there is one ingredient that is more important than the others, it is the Word. His Word does not return void. His Word is sharper than any two-edged sword. His Word is a light to the path of every believer. Without his Word, people will perish in their affliction (Ps. 119:92). Believers find their delight in the Word (Ps. 119:47, 77, 92, 143).

If, on the other hand you begin to be inconsistent with your teaching of your trainees, they will grow weak and cold, and begin to dislike the struggle of trying to minister without being prepared.

Eventually some will be able to feed themselves from the Word. Do not take this as a sign that you can now discontinue teaching. They will still need seminars and retreats.

4. **Purity of heart among leaders promotes church growth.** No one can cleanse himself from selfish motives. God is the one who purifies us.

May God himself sanctify you through an through. May your whole spirit, soul and body be kept blameless at the coming of our Lord Jesus Christ. The one who calls you is faithful and he will do it (1 Th. 5:23).

We will be perfect when Jesus comes for us. On the way to becoming blameless we will see much that is imperfect in ourselves. But let us strive to cooperate with God. Our Father is a giver. Let us imitate him. Let us give to God and to others.

Lack of selfish motives is possibly the most striking character trait we see in spiritual men and women that attracts us. It also attracts the blessing of God on our hearts and our work.

You, the missionary, must live, teach and preach this openness and giving attitude of heart. It helps if you confess you are learning it yourself. If you know in your heart you are submitted to God in this area, you will be free to preach it.

Be careful. Self-promotion is one of the easiest sins to fall into. Our cleverness tells us we can promote self and hide it so that others will think we are giving glory to God. Some will be fooled.

God wants purity of heart. Without it, we run but become weary. We need the peace and joy that comes with doing the right thing for the right reason!

5. **Dependence upon God, not man, brings God's blessing on our work.** As a missionary, you might be receiving financial help from your birth-people-group who sent you. This is not likely to be a threat to your dependence upon God. Thank God every day for his provision, acknowledging it is from him.

Resist the temptation to pay your workers who have successfully led their relatives and friends to the Lord, and who are teaching what they have been taught by their Pauls. These helpers need to be congratulated because they are giving of themselves to teach others. They have not given up their jobs to enter the ministry. They are able to give time to the Lord's work without being paid to minister.

Otherwise, you will draw people to yourself who are looking for additional income, or people who have no employment. It will be difficult to know who is a disciple and who is a hireling.

Before you send missionaries, decide whether the churches will support missionaries, and with how much. Should the support be forever, or until when?

Be aware that, under some circumstances, money corrupts the work of God. In one case, a missionary who was using this strategy lost half of his pastors when another missionary came along and offered them money to join his association! About a year later, almost all of these workers returned to the missionary who trained them. They recognized a difference.

By seeking funds from the West, many ministries in less developed countries have been birthed and grown. But some have been crippled.

Even now, the church in some parts of the world looks to the West for funding. The local believers just look out for themselves. They have been taught to receive, but not to give. Perhaps as much as one-third of their walk with God is crippled. A believer who cannot give to God, is a believer who cannot trust God with his material things. But without faith it is impossible to please God!

Strong churches are not built of weak members.

Dependency is a pitfall in planting churches in another culture. Many churches have been planted cross-culturally in such a way that they are dependent for finances or for leadership or both, upon the mission agencies or the missionaries that planted them.

This dependency is avoidable. It is brought on by well meaning mission agencies and missionaries. Some who mean well are motivated unknowingly by a desire to feel needed. In some cases they make themselves permanently needed. This is not healthy for the new churches. It is not healthy for the agencies or missionaries.

Dependent churches are lacking the strength that comes from depending primarily on the Lord, and secondarily on the local leaders. The mission agency representatives are missing the maturing experience of being servants or partners with those local church leaders. Instead they maintain positions of grand importance, unwilling or unable to let the local leaders make decisions for themselves.

Once the dependency is established it is difficult or impossible to eliminate it.

You may see a system of dependent churches and admire how efficiently they operate. What you don't see, usually, is a people movement happening. You seldom see believers in such churches giving of their resources to send missionaries to another people group. That concept is not easily communicated to people who are, in their own eyes, not involved, not needed. Everything happens to them or around them. They know only how to sit back and let those givers from distant lands joyfully plant seed all around them.

Such believers miss out on the Great Commission because they feel disconnected from the vibrant life of the full-message Church of Jesus.

One cause of dependency is the natural tendency of many missionaries to take charge. They appreciate being servants, but are trained as decision-makers. Usually their supporters back home expect them to be in charge of something important.

We can all agree, no missionary should avoid responsibility because he is not willing to take on difficult tasks! But often, a missionary should refuse to accept responsibility for an aspect of ministry that can be led by a national. In such a case, the missionary can accept a role of assistant, or advisor to that national.

This is a very involved problem that needs more space, and more expert analysis.

You can avoid making your churches dependent. Don't establish dependency among your new believers by attempting to do all the ministry yourself. If you go to an unreached people and start a church, don't pastor that church and be content stay there forever. If you do, you will always be needed in that church. The word "missionary" means apostle. A missionary should plant many churches. He should trust new believers to plant churches

If you back up all you do with foreign money so the people never have to give, your foreign money will always be needed. If you follow the strategy recommended in this book, you will avoid dependency from the beginning.

From the beginning you will use no expensive equipment your leaders cannot obtain to do the Lord's work. This demonstrates that the ministry is spiritual, and is not dependent on costly devices.

From the beginning you will trust new believers with the responsibility of witnessing, and then discipling their new converts.

From the beginning you will teach your "Timothies" the basic commands of the New Testament, commissioning them to teach their new converts.

From the beginning you will exhort your Timothies to give their time, abilities and spiritual gifts to the task of teaching and equipping others.

From the beginning your Timothies will work in their spare time for the Lord, without pay. They will continue to support their families through secular jobs until their church is able to support them, or they will always work their secular jobs. We share more on this when we discuss house churches.

From the beginning you will form a council consisting of successful Timothies, your workers, who are leading tiny but growing congregations. You will take their advice seriously. You might even decide many matters by a majority vote. This will show your Timothies this is their ministry.

When the time is right, you will give special training to the local leader who will eventually replace you as the chief decision-maker and chief teacher for the association of churches. This is the ultimate statement of your confidence in the people God has chosen as his own, and whom you have trained under his inspiration.

In all of this, local believers are being trained to depend on God and on their ability to seek him for themselves without direction from outside.

We will see that building buildings is not necessary. The early Church met in homes. If buildings are to be built, the local people will build what they can afford, in the style that, in their culture, is meaningful. Worship patterns and preaching styles should be decided by the local leadership.

Illustrations of Bible principles will naturally come from their own cultural background.

In this scenario, dependency has no chance to take hold.

In obedience-oriented church planting, churches are taught to give. From the beginning, the emphasis is on giving and doing, not on receiving and being acted upon.

Instead of being a field for some other people group to do mission, these churches are places of worship and submission to Jesus, from which mission soon springs as an outgrowth of worship. They then become a base for cross-cultural outreach to neighboring people groups.

It is conceivable, and perhaps even axiomatic, that the poorest congregation of believers in the most primitive village in the least developed country on earth will give more glory to God and be more effective in outreach with no dependency on outside help, than the most internationally endowed flock anywhere on the planet! The crucial factors in such effectiveness we have discussed in this book. Perhaps at the top of the list should be this one element: a pastor who has been trained in Bible principles including the primacy of worship, the sufficiency of God's grace and importance of giving, obeying Jesus through love.

That training can come from outside, but from a missionary who has become an "insider." The training must be administered without building dependency on outside help!

6. **God does wonders!** The supernatural will **naturally** play a role in making the churches grow both in number and in maturity. Let God do what he wills, without attempting to force him to move.

On the other hand, if you believe he is leading, move like David and take on whatever Goliath comes along. Be spiritually prepared for a "power encounter." That is, be ready for God to create or permit a situation in which you call upon God to show himself powerful against the enemy.

God responds to faith. He is bound to the greatest good. He therefore promotes his own glory. He did that when Elijah moved against the priests of Baal, and he will do it when you trust him to honor his Word, to bring glory to his name

Members of an unreached people group need to see Jesus. They will see him in you, and eventually in other believers. They need this.

Chapter 20
Questions

1. Select one set of statements, A or B or C or D, whichever one has an underlined expression that **disagrees** with what you studied in this chapter.

   A. Patterson's workers earn <u>a salary</u> by meeting objective requirements. The sign of success for his trainees is that their churches are obeying Jesus.

   B. With TEEE they begin one-on-one training because they have experienced <u>success</u> in ministry.

   C. Patterson's workers <u>keep ministering</u> as they learn.

   D. <u>Their work</u> demonstrates, to the students themselves and to all, that they are leaders.

2. Select one set of statements, A or B or C or D, whichever one has an expression that **disagrees** with what you studied in this chapter.

   A. Use sophisticated equipment. You can reach more people.

   B. Multiplying yourself through flesh and blood gives receivers of the gospel the chance to meet a genuine believer, rather than being ministered to mainly by your image on a TV screen.

   C. Many who are lost have no access to TV receivers.

   D. We should use everything the Lord provides to accomplish his work. Every strategy has potential. But do not use equipment your Timothies cannot use when you are modeling how they should minister.

3. Select one set of statements, A or B or C or D, whichever one has an underlined expression that **disagrees** with what you studied in this chapter.

   A. Resist the temptation to <u>pay your workers</u> who have successfully led their relatives and friends to the Lord, and who are teaching what they have been taught by their Pauls.

B. Otherwise, you will draw people to yourself who are looking for additional income, or people who have no employment. It will be difficult to know who is a disciple and who is a hireling

C. In every circumstance, money corrupts the work of God.

D. Many churches have been planted cross-culturally in such a way that they are dependent for finances or for leadership or both, upon the mission agencies or the missionaries that planted them

Chapter 21

Yes, You Can Plant Strong Churches
that Will Multiply

You Can Do It if You Use the Strategy Taught in this Book

With a good knowledge of the Bible, you can plant strong Churches that will multiply:

1. if you can learn a language and adopt a culture.
2. if you can bond with a few people of the new culture.
3. if you can tell Bible stories.
4. if you can teach the Bible on a consistent schedule.
5. if you can trust new believers to minister.
6. if you can keep things organized.

Is Any One of These Beyond Your Ability?

Perhaps you cannot, at this time, succeed at number 4 (above). Perhaps you need to learn more about the Bible.

If so, attend a good Bible school. If possible, choose one with an emphasis on mission to people groups that are unreached with the gospel.

Many Christians do not answer their missionary call because they think it cannot be coming from God. They give reasons like these:

1. "I am not like the apostle Paul. He was special."
2. "I am not holy enough yet."
3. "I don't have the money."
4. "I want to be a missionary for the wrong reason. I don't like my job."

The first three of these are not valid. Paul was very much like you. You will never be holy enough. God will supply your needs, though he may require you to get a job on the field.

But number four does deserve some attention. Some would-be missionaries think it will be an adventure. It will be, when you first arrive on your mission field! If seeking adventure is your primary motive, you should not go, at least not now. This motive will keep you on the field only until the novelty wears off.

Some want to better their station in life. They dislike their jobs, or they think people will respect them if they become missionaries. If one of these is your primary motive, don't go now.

The fact is, many who go to the mission field find that their lives are an adventure! This fact should not cause anyone to stay home. It might be an unimportant secondary motive.

The fact is, for many believers, becoming a missionary does give them more respect from other Christians. This fact should not cause anyone to stay home.

The fact is, the life of the missionary would be, for many believers, a much more challenging and exciting life than the one they are living now. This fact should not cause anyone to stay home.

We all have one or more less important motives in doing the good things we do. If we allowed this fact to turn us away from doing good, we would do very little good, if any.

The enemy uses this to try to get us to stay. He will remind us of these lesser motives as if they were our primary motives.

Our primary motive must be to glorify God through the worship which a people group yet unevangelized will eventually bring to the throne.

A wonderful secondary motive would be to benefit eternally the individuals within such a people group, individuals who have not had an opportunity to accept Jesus as their personal Lord and Savior.

That would even be a fine primary motive, running alongside the motive of the glory of God.

Seek Counsel Before Making Any Big Decision

Your pastor, or someone who is close to the Lord and who knows you well, can help you sort out what God is saying to you.

If you know God wants you to go to a Bible school, ask him to lead you to the right one. He can do this in many ways. He might do this through your counselor.

In the next chapter we focus on cell churches and house churches. Currently, some of the most dynamic strides in world evangelization are happening where churches that meet in homes are flourishing.

Patterson's Strategy Does not Include the Full "House Church" Concept

In the next chapter we add certain aspects of the "house church" concept to our church planting principles. This will add a remarkable ingredient that will make your churches multiply even more rapidly.

Chapter 21
Questions

1. Select one set of statements, A or B or C or D, whichever one has an underlined expression that **disagrees** with what you studied in this chapter.

    A. Believers <u>should not avoid</u> missionary service because their secondary motives are imperfect.
    B. We all have one or more less important motives in doing the good things we do. If we allowed this fact to turn us away from <u>doing good</u>, we would do very little good, if any.
    C. Our primary motive must be to <u>glorify God through the worship</u> which a people group yet unevangelized will eventually participate in.
    D. <u>An unworthy motive</u> would be to benefit eternally the individuals within an unreached people group, giving them an opportunity to accept Jesus as their personal Lord and Savior.

Chapter 22

Church Planting Movements[12]

The Patterson Church Concept

In chapters three to six of this section on mission strategy we have been looking at the strategy of the "Eight Effective Roles" of the missionary. These roles include "Story Teller," and "Church Planter." As you function in these two roles you will tell stories from the Bible, leading up to the story of Jesus. In telling about Jesus, you will lead some of your listeners to the Lord. These then become your first church. You will meet with them to teach them more Bible, beginning with the basic commands of the New Testament.

You learned that, as you teach, your disciples will obey the Lord by witnessing to their relatives and friends. Some will believe. Each of your disciples who succeed at evangelizing will then become your "Timothy." George Patterson calls this "Obedience-Oriented Church Planting." This title emphasizes discipleship, obeying Jesus because we love him and want to follow him.

You recall, this Timothy or "worker" will meet frequently with his new converts, teaching them just as you have been teaching him. (That "him" will become "him or her" if you believe women are called to evangelize and teach.) In this way, you will soon have daughter churches. By reproducing this process, your Timothies will plant granddaughter churches when their own disciples witness and lead people to Jesus.

Here in this chapter we look at a different concept which you may want to add to your description of the tiny, new churches your disciples will plant under your instruction. There are three ways in which cell or house

---

[12] Information in this chapter is based on material published at www.missionfrontiers.org under three titles: "Church Planting Movements," "Ten Universal Elements in Church Planting Movements," and "Church Planting Movements, A Story from the Field." These were written by David Garrison and published in Mission Frontiers Bulletin beginning in the April 2000 issue. The information originated from the Baptist denomination.

churches differ from the churches planted according to the "Effective Roles" strategy.

1. A new cell or house church is planted by a group of believers who leave their church and meet together at a new location. One of them becomes the leader. In the "Effective Roles" strategy one successful witness from the church leads some of his relatives and friends to the Lord and begins to meet with them as their teacher. He becomes a Timothy to his former teacher, his "Paul," who continues to teach him, now in private teaching sessions.
2. When each cell or house church numbers 15 to 30 persons, it splits to form two smaller churches. In the "Effective Roles" strategy we have been studying, only Timothy and his family parted from the mother-church to form the daughter church.
3. In these cell or house churches, there is no plan for any church to grow beyond 30 members. There is no plan for the worker to quit his regular paying job to become a pastor fully supported by his flock. In the "Effective Roles" strategy a successful evangelist will convert some, and as he teaches those, other seekers will join his flock. When his church becomes large enough, he will leave his secular employment and become a fulltime pastor, supported by his flock. His church might become very big. There is no plan to split into two churches. Some of his flock will witness successfully and form small churches, causing the multiplication we learned about.

Let's now look more in depth at these cell churches or house churches which divide into two tiny churches as part of their process of multiplication.

Cell or House Churches

These are the tiny churches that meet in private homes. Their rapid reproduction makes possible what is being called a "Church Planting Movement."

What is a Church Planting Movement?

A CPM is a rapid multiplication of indigenous (not "foreign") churches that plant other churches within a given people group.

When you finish studying this chapter you will be able to decide which concept you will prefer for leading a CPM. You might be able to use both concepts. You might prefer to let your new believers decide whether they want to launch out and evangelize their friends, and then meet with them and become your Timothies. This will be following the "Effective Roles" strategy. Then, when your remaining mother-church members are 15 to 30 in number, you can have them split into two groups. This will be following the cell or house church strategy.

If you do this, be sure to give the leadership of the remaining mother-church to someone who will replace you as their leader. You will have too much to do, as overseer of the entire movement, as you will see in this chapter.

You will be used by the Lord to initiate, to spearhead, to guide, to enable, under the Holy Spirit, such a monumental movement as could only happen through someone like you, and many anointed and divinely motivated believers. These your helpers will need what you bring to the movement, and you will need what they bring.

The rapid multiplication of churches will keep you so busy with priority responsibilities such as leadership mentoring; you will be in earnest prayer often. Your teaching will be the vital "food" supply God will use to nourish "Pauls" down the education chains.

Further, things will happen that will demand your attention down each exploding education chain. Only God could empower you to keep up with the demands that will eventually be made on your time. As you discover you are spending too much time on less important tasks, you will appoint others who will demonstrate an ability and a willingness to share these responsibilities with you. In other words, careful delegation is the remedy.

Much of your time will be spent training others to take over these less important responsibilities for which you no longer have time.

You will be tempted to neglect worship. You might find yourself spending less time in private worship. You might also notice you are sometimes "too busy" to be present for entire public meetings, and that you come late for the worship part.

Worship, however, is most vital for success in any ministry. In worship, God will give you creative ideas that will make it possible for you to carry on with joy, and success.

You will find yourself creating new positions that give responsibility to capable helpers you will appoint to serve under you. In other words, you will delegate wisely. God will show you how to do this, and much more, as you worship him with confidence and gladness.

The Strategy of Cell Churches or House Churches

Cell and house churches are multiplying with amazing speed in many parts of the world. This multiplication is happening so quickly and spreading throughout a people group so rapidly the branches are being referred to as Church Planting Movements.

Read these brief testimonies.

A missionary strategist in Ethiopia...
...spent 30 years planting four churches. His people then started 65 cell churches in only nine months.

Southeast Asia
In 1993 there were 85 believers in 3 churches for 7 million people. In 1997 there were 55,000 believers in 550 churches.

North Africa
An Arab Muslim preacher complained that more than 10,000 Muslims in the mountains had become Christians.

One City in China
From 1993 to 1997, over 20,000 people accepted Jesus in more than 500 new churches.

Latin America

Under persecution from the government from 1990 to 1998, two Baptist unions grew from 235 churches to more than 3,200.

Central Asia

In 1996, one strategy coordinator found his efforts resulted in 15,000 baptisms that year! Previously there were only 200 believers.

Western Europe

In 1998 one missionary started 15 cell churches and went home for a six-month assignment. He returned to find 30 verified churches but believes the actual number could be 60 to 90.

Church Planting Movements are happening in many parts of the world.

Overview of a Church Planting Movement

Briefly, this is what happens.

A missionary comes to an unreached people group he believes God is calling him to evangelize. He comes equipped with a great sense of dependence on God. He knows he cannot do anything in the spiritual realm without the anointing of the Holy Spirit.

He is a man of prayer, by which he sustains this fortifying conviction about his utter dependence on the Lord. He is a man of worship. He realizes that if he accomplished nothing more in his lifetime than honest, aggressive worship of the one true and living God, he would have lived purposefully, and would have glorified God wonderfully. He understands his identity is based on who he is in Jesus, and on what he has from Jesus.[13]

Operating out of this unshakable position of deep and abiding strength, he goes about his mission with confidence, not in himself but in the One who has sent him. He easily avoids the panic experienced by the salesman on commission, who must sell so his family can survive. Such a salesman often fails simply because he is too tense to relax and enjoy the people and

---

[13] Jesus tells of our identity, who we are and what we have in him, in John chapter 17.

the work. God intends that those who work under his commission enjoy people, and enjoy their work.

The missionary, then, is fortified by his relationship with God. He is nourished by a keen awareness of his dependence upon God. He is strengthened with worship. He comes with something else also. He is equipped with two fundamental tools unsuccessful church planters lack.

1. He is totally convinced that he can, he should, and he will as God blesses, plant churches among this people.
2. He knows new believers can minister the Word of God if he teaches them well.

He knows he will soon have such ministers helping him. He is convinced he must trust them with leadership roles.

What does he do?

He plans some sort of mass communication of the gospel to a wide audience of persons of this people group he has been sent to. This might be by a series of radio programs aimed at people who are interested in spiritual things. He motivates them with some teaching about Jesus. He has them assemble at some public arena or hall where they will learn more.

In that arena meeting he gives them enough of the gospel that they hunger for more. He directs them to small group Bible studies in which they can receive more information and ask questions. He would probably have them understand they will learn at these small group meetings how simple it is to receive from God himself, the gift of eternal life promised in the Bible.

The radio series plus mass meeting will result in the formation of a number of participative Bible study groups for unbelievers who are seeking truth.

Where will the leaders for these first-generation Bible studies come from?

Usually, within the unreached people group, there have already been a very small number of Christians meeting regularly in a very few churches. Our missionary church planter will, with God's direction, find these committed believers who know the Bible well enough to lead those Bible studies after receiving specific directions from the missionary.

During a short series of these Bible study meetings, attendees will learn enough of the gospel to accept Jesus as Savior and Lord. Now the Bible studies have become small cell churches or house churches. A house church is a small group of believers meeting regularly in a house.

If these churches meeting in houses are tied together by some sort of hierarchical structure, they are called cell churches. A cell is part of a living thing. If they are independent of each other, even with some affiliation together, they are called house churches.

Under the direction of the missionary these cells become evangelistic. This we saw in our study of the Patterson obedience-oriented churches as they learned to obey Jesus by witnessing to their relatives and friends.

New believers are quick to witness to their loved ones and even their acquaintances. In church planting movements, multiplication comes through division. The cells quickly expand to fifteen members and split into two groups. Some missionaries feel fifteen members is not enough for a split. They make this number no larger however than thirty members. They then are divided into two cells. These two groups of seven or more members are now ready to expand further and eventually split again, and again.

A few of them will grow into large churches with no plan to multiply. Under a gifted leader they will become less active in this CPM though their leader will continue to receive private, personal teaching from you, the missionary, or one of the "Pauls" down the education chain. This church is not a threat or danger to the movement. It will minister to many who are drawn to its doors. We discuss your role in this situation further in the last chapter.

Obedience to Jesus' directions in the Word is an important characteristic of these cell or house churches.

The leaders are unpaid. They give of themselves freely, as they themselves have freely received. There is no plan for them to be supported by the churches they lead.

327

Evangelism within the people group, as we have seen, is an important part of the life of the churches. Cross-cultural evangelism is also encouraged. This brings the gospel to neighboring, or even distant, people groups where the entire process can be replicated by a new missionary who has himself risen to leadership through this CPM.

How Can Such Growth Happen so Quickly?

Here are ten characteristics of the work that produce a church planting movement (CPM):

1. **Prayer.** The missionary who plans to start such a movement makes prayer the primary or fundamental first ingredient in that plan. Also, because prayer is vital in his own personal relationship with God it becomes vital in the churches he plants and in the lives of the leaders he trains.

2. **Mass media proclaiming of the gospel.** The missionary planning this CPM finds ways of letting everyone know it's happening, and telling how the gospel will change their lives. Testimonies are an important part of this proclamation. Mass meetings and radio messages can help greatly. Where persecution forces the churches underground, CPMs are not flourishing.

3. **The missionary makes church planting the important goal from the beginning.** Churches begin small, but every member participates in bringing outsiders to the meetings. Every member participates in the multiplication process, either by going to a new location with half of the church members and starting over, or by remaining behind with the other half of the members and starting over from the old location. Every member focuses on growth, both by prayer and by action. **Cell churches** are linked by one prominent leader or by a leadership structure. This helps keep the doctrine the same in all the linked churches. **House churches** are usually not linked. This helps them survive and even thrive under persecution. Both types can appear within the same movement.

4. **All accept the Bible as the authority on what is right.** Most CPMs have the Bible in the birth language of the people, if not in written form, at least for oral communication..

5. **The missionary who plans the strategy and brings the gospel does not plant many churches himself.** He does plant some, to

328

model how it is done. This is how he gets local believers into leadership.

6. **Lay leadership is vitally important**. If the missionary continued to plant churches it would cause locals to leave it to him to do it all. This would eliminate rapid multiplication of churches. Churches must plant the churches through ordinary members if you are to have a church planting movement. Remember, a CPM is a rapid multiplication of indigenous (not "foreign") churches that plant other churches within a given people group. The leaders continue to support their families through their occupations, while holding leadership roles in the churches.

7. **Unusual situations do occur, but do not enhance multiplication.**
   a) Some leaders do eventually receive salaries, but the rapid growth comes mainly through unpaid lay leaders with no seminary training. Many new believers can learn from their teacher-leader and relay this teaching to those they have led to the Lord. Thus the CPM has a great store of leaders. This is vital, for many leaders are needed immediately if the CPM is to continue its rapid growth
   b) Church buildings do appear in Church Planting Movements. However, they are the exceptions. Most churches will split before reaching 30 members. Otherwise the movement would be slowed down.

8. **Churches plant churches**. This will happen if the members believe it is natural for them to plant a church, and if they believe they can do it without help from outside their little congregation.

9. **Fast reproduction**. This is always present in a CPM. If the speed slows down, the CPM has lost vitality. The speed demonstrates the importance of believing in Jesus, who is being accepted by so many so fast. When the speed is evident it is because there are no hindrances, and the laity are really aware that they can plant churches.

10. **Healthy churches**. In every CPM the churches were doing these five essential things: 1) worship 2) neighbor evangelism and evangelism in another unreached people group 3) education and discipleship 4) ministry 5) fellowship. Healthy churches do these five things. The unreached people group being evangelized is often a group that has long resisted foreign missionaries.

Here's a true story telling what happened in a certain region of China in the early 1990s.

1. **The Baptists sent a missionary to China.** For one year he studied the language and culture, and learned there were 7 million people in 5 different people groups in that region, some in cities and some outside in rural areas.
2. **The missionary tried to start church a few times and failed each time.** He discovered three house churches with elderly Christian members.
3. **He got help from some Christians across Asia.**
4. **He formed teams of these and some local Christians.** They planted six new churches in one year. Next year, they planted 17 more! After three years they had a total of 195 churches among all five people groups.
5. **The missionary left the local believers to carry on there, and he went elsewhere to work.**
6. **With the local people doing the planting, during one year the total climbed to 55,000 Christians in 550 churches!** This means the membership for each church averaged 100 persons. Some churches must have dropped the idea of splitting after 15 or 30 members. Big churches do not multiply quickly. They do not contribute much to the movement's rapid growth in total number of churches planted, but they do not ruin the movement because there are not many of them.

Factors that Helped this Church Planting Movement in China

1. **The missionary prayed much even before he went to the mission field.** The early believers also adopted this attitude of prayer.
2. **The missionary was faithful to train his helpers well.** Every leader understood the CPM principles and was faithful to them.
3. **The missionary used video, radio, or mass meetings to contact those interested in spiritual things.** You might be able to inform the population of your offer to help them spiritually through some other less expensive method. You might be able to buy space in a local newspaper. You might be able to have believers distribute leaflets. If you want to plant many churches early in the process, it's important to sow lots of seed in a short time. Then you can arrange to meet in small groups with those interested. This factor can be too expensive for some missionaries. The question then becomes, Can I sow seed quickly without expense.

If You Have no Funds for Mass Media...

Many new missionaries think they cannot evangelize, cannot plant churches, cannot bring the gospel to an unreached people group, because they do not have funding.

The only thing you would not be able to do is this one aspect, the mass sowing of seed aspect, factor #3, above. You could use the CPM structure in all its other aspects.

Use the roles of the missionary studied earlier in this book. Take the time to bond, to learn the language and the culture of your adoptive people group, and start small. In other words, follow the "Effective Roles" strategy. But let your churches be house churches, or cell churches with a strong central organization. Emphasize commitment to quick multiplication. Train the churches to multiply either by the "witness who becomes a Timothy" method or by the "dividing church" method. You might adopt both methods, allowing your leaders to choose.

You will take years longer to get started if you cannot use radio or television or a big notice in a newspaper, or wide distribution of leaflets, but you will succeed in planting strong churches that will multiply.

The Structure of a Church Planting Movement can be learned using two acronyms: POUCH and MAWL.

> P. **Participative Bible studies and worship**. This is where seekers are gathered in small groups to discuss the Bible and hear the gospel message.
> O. **Obedience to Jesus.** This could be done through teaching and practicing the basic commands of the New Testament, as we learned in chapter 18 of this section.
> U. **Unpaid leaders** who support their families through their regular employment.
> C. **Cell churches or house churches** that split and multiply once they have acquired a certain number of believers, either fifteen, or at most 30.
> H. **House churches** are cell churches except that their affiliation is not for governing but exists for mutual benefit and ministerial fellowship and some level of accountability.

This completes the acronym, POUCH. Now we spell out the acronym MAWL.

> **M. Model.** The missionary models church planting so his leaders, who are new believers, will see how to witness to their relatives and friends and gather them into a participative Bible study, and conduct their studies as participative meetings. Discussion is a helpful ingredient.
>
> **A. Assist** the newly planted church to reproduce a daughter church.
>
> **W. Watch** to see that three generations of churches are reproducing successfully.
>
> **L. Leave** in order to make the movement truly indigenous, when believers are faithfully applying the POUCH and the MAWL principles. This means that some believers are going to other regions and starting CPMs there, and some are doing this among other unreached people groups.

Make Disciples, not Just Believers

There are (1) people who say they are Christians but are not. They say they are Christians, but only because they know they are not atheists or Muslims or Hindus or Buddhists, and their parents used to take them to church.

There are (2) Christians who believe Jesus died for their sins and are trusting him to save them from hell, and he is.

There are (3) Christians who know they are saved and who are disciples of Jesus. That is, Jesus is their teacher on the important issues of life and faith. These Christians are living in the fullness of faith to the best of their understanding. They worship Jesus. They abide in him. They obey him because they love him. They speak to him and they discern his voice.
Christians are not perfect. Both types, (2) and (3), sin. They confess to the Lord and he is faithful to cleanse them from all unrighteousness (1 John 1:9). But the disciples (3) are generally more satisfied in their warm and vibrant relationship with Jesus. The other believers find themselves failing more, and discouraged more about life's upsets.

Perhaps nondisciples are unsure in their faith. Paul mentions, "Your good works produced by faith." Our faith produces our works. Some who believe but are not walking closely with Jesus are not sure they believe everything Jesus said. They perhaps believe Jesus believed it all, but they are confused about Jesus being their life! They find themselves following other goals with more enthusiasm. Twisted faith, or confused faith, would produce its own works.

Nondisciples who have the basic faith needed to receive the gift of eternal life will find the gates of heaven open to them when they die. However, they will face extra uncertainty and unnecessary misery here. The Spirit of God does actually indwell them! But the disciples have a different walk. They know God is in them from experience as well as from the Word. Life's upsets are not going to shake such believers, or at least, not as much.

Leaders often scold their disciples for their works, preaching much against sin, rather than emphasizing belief. Focusing on Jesus, being amazed at his gift of everlasting life, is more effective than focusing on the avoidance of sin. However, believers need to know right from wrong, and the destructive nature of sin.

What we truly believe influences our behavior quite completely! If we are to obey Matthew 28:18-20, making disciples, we are certainly going to lead believers into a firm faith in Jesus and his Word. As we teach his Word, faith will grow and works will follow.[14]

In the Next Chapter...

We assume, in this book, you will make your own decisions regarding how you will minister. If that is not the case, and if your supervisors will decide how you will work, you will nevertheless benefit by knowing the principles involved in mission. These are best studied as parts of a viable strategy for planting churches, a whole scenario, detailed as much as is

---

[14] Dallas Willard, in his masterful book, "The Divine Conspiracy," has clearly defined the lack of discipleship in the Christian Church, and motivates us wonderfully to lead people into following Jesus wholeheartedly. Every future missionary should read this book. It is required reading for this course.

reasonable so you can understand. We believe we have given you that in this final section.

Chapter 23 will give you a glimpse of some other strategies. There are as many strategies as there are missionaries! Every missionary who studies someone else's strategy and decides to use it, uses his own adaptation of it.

If you are free to choose, decide which strategy is best for you. Then adapt it as you go. That is, change details of it so that it fits better into the situation you face.

We suggest you recognize some principles for missionary service as foundational, and adopt them as your own. Let God show you. Ask him to give you your basic plan. Write it down. Few of us receive plans from the Lord in perfect form. When you get to your mission field, make changes prayerfully as you proceed. As you learn among the people, you will see what to do. Seek the Lord. The Holy Spirit will lead you.

Pray much!

Chapter 22
Questions

1. In the "Effective Roles" strategy one successful witness from the church leads some of his relatives and friends to the Lord and begins to meet with them as their teacher. A new cell or house church is planted…

    A. in the same way.
    B. by the missionary himself.
    C. by a group of believers who leave their church and meet together at a new location.
    D. whenever a member wants to break from the group and start one.

2. Which statement is false?

    A. When each cell or house church numbers 15 to 30 persons, it divides.
    B. In cell or house churches, there is no plan for any church to grow beyond 30 members
    C. Among cell churches, most pastors will eventually have very large congregations.
    D. With house churches there is no plan for the worker to quit his regular paying job to become a pastor fully supported by his flock.

3. On your mission field, or even now, you can decide which multiplication concept you will use for leading a CPM, the "effective roles" strategy or the house church strategy.

    A. You might combine them by sending out missionaries to plant churches in unreached people groups, or evangelists to plant churches among their own people.
    B. You might combine these strategies by letting your new believers decide whether they want to launch out and evangelize their friends, and then meet with them and become your Timothies. Then, when your remaining mother-church members are 15 to 30 in number, you can have them split into two groups.

C. You might send out only Bible school graduates to plant churches that will grow under their teaching.

D. You might combine strategies by calling in elders from other people groups and have them plant house churches that will never split for any reason, and form a strong association to keep the teaching strictly uniform and biblical.

4. You, the missionary founder of a group of churches, will find yourself so consumed with top priorities you will save time wisely by:

A. spending less time in worship, both private and public.

B. neglecting to meet with your Timothies for private Bible teaching.

C. delegating less important tasks to others.

D. working longer hours than ever.

5. Successful missionaries who begin church planting movements have these advantages. Select the one that is not true.

A. Their relationship with God fortifies them.

B. Worship strengthens them.

C. They are convinced they will plant churches among the people group God has sent them to evangelize.

D. They are brimming with confidence in themselves.

6. One thing more…

A. They trust only in themselves to minister to the people.

B. They know new believers can minister if they are well taught.

C. They are willing to give up worship time if they are too busy.

D. They know the Bible better than those who fail to plant churches.

7. These are steps most successful CPM founders take:

A. They make a series of radio messages giving some information about the gospel.

B. On the radio they announce a mass meeting in which more teaching will be given about Jesus.
C. During the mass meeting they announce how seekers can find out where small group meetings will be held for Bible discussions.
D. Money or food is offered to those who come to these small group meetings.

8. These small group meetings…

A. will be abandoned after a few weeks of Bible discussion.
B. will be combined to become a church led by a pastor from a foreign people group.
C. will become cell churches or house churches.
D. will elect officers and meet on a regular basis.

Healthy churches.   In every CPM the churches were doing these five essential things: 1) worship 2) neighbor evangelism and evangelism in another unreached people group 3) education and discipleship 4) ministry 5) fellowship.   Healthy churches do these five things.   The unreached people group being evangelized is often a group that has long resisted foreign missionaries.

9. Every successful CPM has churches doing these five things:

A. worship
B. neighbor evangelism and evangelism in another unreached people group
C. education and discipleship
D. all the above three, plus ministry, and one other thing found in number 10, below.

10. The fifth thing all successful CPM churches do is:

A fellowship.
B. establish social clubs based on occupation or hobby.
C. arrange athletics for the youth.
D. schedule field trips for seniors.

Chapter 23

Other Strategies

Basic Principles of Strategy

In the previous seven chapters we have recommended and detailed a strategy for the most difficult task a missionary can undertake, the delivering of the gospel to a people group that has not heard the good news.

In this chapter we briefly describe other strategies. Throughout the earlier chapters we discussed several basic principles that apply to every strategy. We will not repeat basic principles here, but the reader will realize that these strategies incorporate many of the basics.

Some of these strategies seem too simple and too effective too quickly to be believable. But if you consider the circumstances in which they have yielded great fruit, you will realize that either the environment was friendly to the gospel, or God sovereignly moved hearts and minds, or the strategy involved some cultural element that made it immediately attractive to the people.

Unless God gives you a remarkable strategy for your specific situation, you will do well to follow the strategy we have detailed, until God changes your direction.

Gospel Recordings

Gospel Recordings (GR) is a mission organization whose goal is to supply every unreached people with a tape-recorded message that explains the gospel in their own language.

Here are some of their strategies for using these recordings.

1. **A GR representative meets with local church leaders.** They form a committee to evangelize through recorded messages. GR gives one

leader, who is willing and able, a bicycle. He visits villages and families and plays the cassettes. He answers questions. When some accept the Lord he gets them started as a new church.

In one unreached African tribe almost every village had a respected elder who was blind, and would sing about the tribe's history, and sing traditional stories, every night.

A missionary gave to each of these blind elders a Gospel Recording and a player. The elder would play the recording and then put the message or the story into song. Some had more than one recorded message, so they did this with a series of recordings.

Soon every village had a church!

2. **Cassettes that went ahead of the missionaries, preparing the way.** In Burkina Faso GR cassettes were sent to an unreached tribe in their own dialect. A missionary couple were soon to follow and begin a ministry. The couple never arrived.

Fifteen years later another couple did arrive. They found that the people knew the gospel and the stories they had memorized from the cassettes. The messages were still "alive," though the cassettes were worn out, and useless!

The people were glad the missionaries came to start churches.

3. **Cassettes and a loud speaker.** A missionary to a certain tribe in Central America had to return to North America after years of fruitless efforts to evangelize. He discovered that many members of that same tribe had emigrated to the USA, and were living in an orange orchard nearby. He took a GR cassette in their language, and drove through the orchard playing the message in their language over a loud speaker.

Hundreds of these tribesmen came running after the loudspeaker to find out where the voice speaking their birth language was coming from. The missionary stopped and explained he would hold a meeting and tell them more that evening. Now there are many churches among this people group.

340

4. **GR cassettes are played for people waiting** at a clinic or hospital.

5. **GR cassettes combined with the Jesus film.** Sometimes the Jesus film in language "A" is shown to a mixed group. Some who understand "A" and some who understand only language "B." Before, during or after the film, one or more cassettes are played in one area of the open field, or the building, for speakers of "B" so that they will understand what the film is about.

School-based Church Planting

In an area where the Christian population is less than 1% but Christians can function fairly openly, this strategy is proving successful.

Missionaries from a nearby people group go to the targeted people group and offer to open an elementary school for their children. If they get a favorable response they open a class or classes at the beginning level and add a grade each year.

Their primary objective is to create opportunities to speak to the parents:

a) to form genuine **friendships** with the parents.
b) to **explain** to the parents why they are teaching their children, witnessing to them about the Lord.
c) to **pray for the sick**, knowing God will provide his own witness to his power and his love, healing the afflicted.
d) to **initiate regular meetings** with the parents during which the children might perform. Either the children or the teachers (missionaries) might tell, or act out, Bible stories.

Soon they open a Bible study, meeting regularly. This eventually becomes a house church whose aims include planting more churches among that people group, using new believers to do the witnessing and even the teaching. Believers are gradually added to the church and then discipled.

One of the problems with this strategy is the fact that the teachers in these schools have no training to teach. However, the parents appreciate greatly the fact that their children are learning to read, write and do basic math.

They also learn about the Bible, how to sing action songs about the Lord, and how to have Jesus as their best friend.

The parents notice an improvement in the behavior of their children. This becomes a powerful witness to the wonderful influence of Jesus in those young lives, causing the adults themselves to desire to know the Lord of heaven and earth.

Children at Prayer!

Children are not ready to go to the mission field yet, but some have an effective strategy for evangelizing unreached peoples.

In 1985, the Director of Gospel Recordings spoke to a Sunday school class of 13-, 14-, and 15-year-olds at the Park Street Congregational Church, a mission-minded church in Boston, USA. He told them about the Kreen-Akore, a tribe living in the Amazon jungles of Brazil. There are only about 85 of these tribes people left. No missionaries are allowed in that area, and they have no scripture.

The children were interested. They collected copies of National Geographic Magazines containing pictures of the Kreen-Akore. They prayed.

A year later the Director of GR was in Brazil having lunch with a missionary who served in a hospital in Brasilia, the capital city. She told the Director she worked with the Kayapo, who bragged about their practice of crushing the skulls of an enemy tribe called the Kreen-Akore.

She continued, "Last year the chief of the Kreen-Akore brought his daughter to the hospital in Brasilia. She was very sick. The chief said, 'If my daughter dies, I will kill ten white people here in this hospital.' The staff became nervous.

"The girl was in a coma," said the missionary. "She had meningitis! She couldn't last more than two days."

"A staff member went to check on the girl. To everyone's amazement, she was completely well!"

You can guess the message this chief brought back to his people!

The GR Director asked the missionary, "When did this miracle happen?"

"Last April," she replied.

The Director was impressed. April was when that Sunday school class of 13-, 14- and 15-year-old children began to pray! He wrote to the class telling them of the miraculous way God answered their prayer.

They were ecstatic! They cheered... and they prayed! The job isn't finished.

In heaven one day, these children expect Jesus will show them their Kreen-Akore brothers and sisters.

The Messiah Dance[15]

God can give you a totally unexpected strategy in a flash of inspiration! He did just that for Steve, some years ago.

The wedding celebration had already begun. Muslim dance professionals, called girots, were performing their tribal dances, some honoring ancestors, others depicting historical legends.

This was to be a wedding with a difference. The entire wedding party, though Muslim, were looking forward to seeing the *Jesus* film.

Missionary Steve* and his handful of new-Christian friends, his "A-Team," were to bring the film. As they approached the village, already enrapt in the joyful festivities, the children ran to meet them. They were the first to hear the disappointing news.

"No film!" the children reported sadly as they ran back to the grownups.

---

[15] Based on "Unveiled at Last," by Bob Sjogren. YWAM Publishing, 1992. Pp. 23-26. "Steve" is not the missionary's name.

Steve and the "A-Team" greeted their hosts. "Our equipment was damaged in a storm. We're so sorry but we cannot show the *Jesus* film." The people were disappointed. Silently they sat to enjoy the customary and predictable traditional dances.

Steve and his team sat on the grass, adding themselves to the large circular audience admiring the dancers.

Time passed. Steve's eyes were on the dancers but his mind was on something else. He turned to his team. "Could I do a dance illustrating the crucifixion?"

Steve respected his team's opinions on cultural things . After all, this was their culture, not his. "No!" was the consensus. The team were probably thinking of how those dances were often used to honor evil spirits.

The missionary seldom went against culture-related decisions of his advisors.

Suddenly, at a quiet moment between traditional dances, Steve rose up and took center stage in the celebration circle. He had no special costume. He was not a dancer! His only prop was a stick, the dried, thick branch of a tree he had been using to push aside the foliage as he and his "A-Team" trudged through miles of dense brush.

His tall, slender figure, his light skin and sun-bleached hair brought all eyes his way. He stood there, the stick upon his shoulder, his eyes cast down.

Then, slowly, when a hushed silence fell upon the gathering, he placed one foot forward. As if the weight of his stick were overwhelming, he struggled on, trudging slowly around the center of the "stage."

The drums began to punctuate his ponderous moves, adding solemnity and drama.

He fell. With great effort he rose again and continued slowly, footstep after "painful" footstep, under his "heavy" load.

He stopped. He froze there for some moments. Finally, with the attention of all riveted upon his every pained facial expression, he straightened his back, looked up to the sky, and placing the stick behind his neck, wrapped one arm over one end of the stick, then the other arm over the other end. With his body thus forming a cross, he turned to face each direction so that all could see.

Soon he let the stick fall to the ground as he himself fell, limp. He lay there. Slowly he began covering his torso with dust, using only his right hand. Then, even that action stopped.

Now there was absolute silence among the crowd, and no movement whatever by Steve. Every eye was trained steadfastly on his seeming lifeless body.

Finally he stirred. He sat up. He got up on his feet. He smiled broadly. He stretched his hands toward heaven, smiling as he seemed to focus on something or someone above.

He danced! He began with hand-claps and slow but mirthful strides. The drums began to echo his joyful rhythm! Louder and louder, faster and faster they affirmed the glory of the moment.

Soon Steve was dancing with all his might!

The girots ran over to Steve's friends. "What does this dance mean?" They asked. "He died, didn't he? Did he then come back to life? Please explain! We do not understand!"

Shouts of rejoicing from the gathering prevented any explanations from Steve's "A-Team."

Steve finished his dance, soaked in perspiration, and rejoined his team. He was glad to sit, exhausted from the extravagant gyrations of his African-style dance and from the stress of the long journey. Gasping for breath, he carefully answered all the questions of the tribal dance professionals.

They were moved by the depth of meaning Steve expressed. The dance had meaning beyond anything their traditional dances contained. Eternal life, earned for man, by the only Son of Creator God! This took over their imaginations and captivated their hearts. They practiced the dance several times, imitating Steve.

Needless to say, Steve was delighted with their interest in his impromptu efforts to communicate what was so vital to their lives, here and hereafter! Then, to Steve's amazement and to everyone's delight, the girots did the dance for the crowd, while the head girot gave the explanation. His words were so true to the scripture that Steve offered no corrections whatever.

Since that eventful day, these Muslims have been going about, from one wedding to the next, doing this "Messiah Dance," with careful explanation of how Jesus paid the price for our sin! He died that we might live.

They know they are doing something that is not just entertaining. Something that breathes life into their gatherings, even beyond their own comprehension.

Is it possible the girots, in preaching this message, have committed their lives to the Savior? Are those in attendance saved in the process of realizing their sins are paid in full? Do some of them actually trust in the sacrifice of Jesus enacted in this culturally meaningful way? Are they recipients of God's unmerited favor, seen in this wonderful story?

Perhaps by this time someone can answer these questions.

If Steve attempted to repeat this dance, hoping to evangelize at local events, he might evoke suspicion as a foreigner, and perhaps all sorts of opposition. The fact that the girots themselves are doing the "Messiah Dance" makes it totally acceptable! After all, they are Muslims, the professional teachers of tribal history through dance.

At the very least, the girots are preparing hearts for the full gospel story! They are softening hearts to listen to the missionaries. They are preparing the way for the Messiah himself!

You realize, this is not a complete strategy. The follow-up will have to be far more complex and challenging than the Messiah Dance itself! Yet it is an example of how God can work through us.

Principles of church planting can be enhanced by many different sub-strategies. If we know the basic principles we will be prepared for whatever God will do through us.

A Team Strategy for People Groups in Cities Unfriendly to the Gospel

Even in a big city, the missionary does well to target, not the city, but one ethnic group in the city.

Greg Livingstone has founded "Frontiers," the largest mission agency that uses a team strategy aimed at planting churches in Muslim cities.[16]

Most missionaries to the Muslim world do not attempt to plant churches. The need for secrecy leads them to try to convert one Muslim at a time. Converts then have no Christian community to join when they are excommunicated by their families and friends. Frontiers, however, aims at planting churches.

We outline here the Frontiers pattern.

There are six to twelve missionaries on each team, all sent to the same city with two assignments:

> 1. Each must befriend Muslims with the aim of leading them to the Lord. Livingstone favors the three roles we discussed in chapter 18 of this section: Learner, Trader, Story-Teller.
> 2. Each has one or more part-time tasks to perform to achieve the secular objectives of the team.

Each team member has a task that fits his gifting.

One of the members is an executive leader. He does advance work to get the team to the target city. He then gets the team established in the secular work they will be doing. Frontiers has a number of ways of gaining legal entrance for the team.

Another member has a pastoral position. He looks after the spiritual well-being of the group. He becomes the executive and pastoral leader of the team once the team is functioning well, and the executive who set up the team's secular purpose withdraws.

---

[16] *Planting Churches in Muslim Cities,* by Greg Livingstone.

Several members of the team will have an evangelistic call on their lives. They will help the others lead to the Lord Muslims they have befriended. Disciplers on the team will teach new converts.

There might be an elderly couple on the team who will care for children of the missionaries when they meet at night.

Some members are administrators. They help manage the affairs of the secular project in which the team is engaged as their non-spiritual purpose for being in the country.

For best results, the team needs a pastor who can lead well. It needs encouragement from the supervising agency. It needs a resource base which can send a replacement if a member cannot continue.

Eventually the missionaries have made a number of Muslim friends, and have told them about Jesus. The Muslims have shown an interest. Now each of the missionaries will say to each of his Muslim friends, "Would you like to meet with my Christian friends and with Muslims like yourself who want to know more about Jesus?"

Those interested meet together regularly for fellowship and teaching. This part of the work is done openly. Prospects are drawn by the person of Jesus, by his role of Savior and his offer of forgiveness and eternal life. They are drawn by the realization of God's unconditional love for them, revealed in the Bible. They are also drawn by the harmony, the understanding, and the loving relationships they perceive among the missionaries.

What about the danger of being arrested for evangelizing? One or more of the missionaries should expect to befriend an influential person, or join a society that is Muslim but tolerant. If trouble comes, friends might prevent the team from being expelled.

The Christian Mosque Strategy

Here is an example of contextualizing the gospel. This idea might be used as part of the team approach for cities, referred to above.

In a certain Muslim city there is a mosque for Muslim converts. Islamic patterns are followed. Shoes are left outside. Before worshiping, believers begin by a ritual washing of hands, feet and head. They kneel on mats. They pray aloud together, bowing their heads to the floor repeatedly and in unison. They chant in Arabic. They worship on Friday, not Sunday. They pray five times a day. They participate in the Ramadan fast.

All this happens in any mosque, but these worshipers trust only in the saving work of Isa on the cross for their eternal salvation. "Isa" is the name for Jesus used by Muslims and found in their holy book, the Koran.

When visitors come, they realize they can accept Isa without leaving their culture totally. They see they would be joining an existing community of former Muslims.

"Pub churches"

In the British Isles a group of Christian musicians approached the proprietor of the local "pub" or "public house" and made this offer. "We'll give you one hour of traditional music every Sunday if you'll let us preach for ten minutes."

The proprietor agreed to try it out with his customers to see if they would like this. They did. Thus began a church among a group of people who might never have entered a formal church.

The ministry time was clearly too short to meet people's needs. Undoubtedly the leaders have resolved that.

The pubs of Europe differ in atmosphere from the saloons or bars of North America. Besides drinking, pub attendees might eat, they always meet friends, and usually enjoy hours of singing together.

Miracle Teams

In Mindanao there is a team of disciples who target an unreached tribe, live among them, and learn their language in six months. God works miracles causing many to accept Jesus, and a people movement begins.

The difference in this strategy is the occurrence of impressive signs and wonders that seem to make it less necessary for the team to spend so much time before evangelizing. However, for the church to be strong, there must be teaching, which must be done in appropriate, cultural ways.

Networking

This is not so much a strategy as a relatively new idea missionaries and mission organizations can adopt and adapt for greater efficiency. Networking is what happens when two or more agencies or missionaries share resources or cooperate together to achieve a goal that is important to all.

The union is informal. It is temporary. There can be some agreement in writing, but this is not necessary. It will only work if all parties are givers.

Networking is a wonderful sign to the unbeliever. They see two persons or groups having differing points of view, but able to work together for the glory of God and for the salvation of the lost!

The Public Giving of a Bible

In Latin America, the father of a family will gather his relatives and friends together to enjoy refreshments, and then make a speech in which he announces a big decision he or one of his offspring has made.

Some missionaries have successfully used this tradition. They suggest to the newly saved father that he hold such a meeting to announce his new life in Jesus and tell how God has changed his life.

If he agrees, the missionary attends the meeting and publicly presents this father with a new Bible. The missionary follows this up by explaining to the group the scriptural basis for what this father has experienced. In a society where the gospel is not foreign, the missionary even invites people then and there to accept the Lord.

Then, if some have believed, the missionary will ask the fathers of families among the new believers if they would like to have a Bible presentation in their homes.

A Strategy for Nomads

Story telling is useful in changing the world view of nomads so they can understand somewhat the nature of the true God. Many nomads consider all spirits to be neither morally good nor bad. Therefore, spirits are fair game for those humans who are clever enough to manipulate the spirits into giving them what they want.

For these nomads, interfacing with evil spirits is part of life. There is no real distinction between spiritual beings and humans.

Through the stories of the Bible, nomads can come to see that God is absolutely faithful and good, and that the devil and his demons are totally evil and will never really benefit anyone.

The stories of the Bible will appeal to the nomad. He sees himself reflected in the nomadic life to which God called Abram, and in the wanderings in the desert of the children of Israel. He will be impressed by how God led the Hebrew people, who literally walked before God with their flocks and herds.

As with other ethnic groups, nomads must see and know Christians before they can even listen to the gospel. A one-hour presentation from a stranger will not make sense to them. It will take many years for Christians to live their lives out among a nomadic group so that they know and trust them. The nomads must see they can be Christians and still be nomads.

Living among nomads, even among a group that is sedentary during much of the year, is tiring and often boring. Perhaps God will show you how to help the group satisfy a need. You might do research and learn of a better kind of seed which will help semi-nomads grow more nutritious or disease-resistant crops.

God will provide circumstances for you to demonstrate his love working through you. Use these opportunities. Do not hide the fact that you follow Jesus. Let God show the nomads the difference that makes in a life.

Above all, be patient. It could be that God will use your life and the lives of others just to penetrate the darkness, preparing nomadic hearts to receive his piercing light when others continue what you have started, and spent a lifetime to build. Let God determine what the results of your work will be. But you must follow him.

Jesus said the same to Peter. Jesus hinted at the kind of death Peter would die. Then he said to him plainly, *"Follow me"* (Jn. 21:19).

Peter saw John following them and said to Jesus, *"Lord, what about him?"*

Jesus said to Peter, as he says now to each of us, *"If I want him to remain... what is that to you? You must follow me"* (v. 20-22).

One missionary spent many years among a group of nomads. He befriended their religious leaders and discussed Jesus with them, even reading scripture to them. He also succeeded in helping them improve their living conditions, which they appreciated.

After many years and only one convert to Jesus the missionary obtained the permission of the chief to hold sessions during which he would explain the gospel. The sessions grew to include about forty nomads. Then the local religious leader interrogated the people who attended, and found they believed the missionary. Why? Because the missionary lived the life he was preaching about.

The religious leader was angry and shut down the meetings.[17]

That missionary says his nomad friends are looking for a power that will sustain them through all of life's problems. He says they are watching him to see how he handles the upsets in life. They want to know more about what God will do for them here and now, and are less interested in what he will do for them after they die.

---

[17] Sourcing this brief summary could compromise security for the missionaries on the field.

Many of us would call on God to work miracles among them, proving himself the powerful one who can supply all their needs if they will follow him.

This missionary apparently does not agree. He says we must not mindlessly emphasize too much the work of the Holy Spirit. The Spirit works most often, he says, through our perseverance.

He admits now that he is spending too much time helping these people overcome physical and material problems, and not enough in dealing with their need for faith in Jesus. This missionary considers giving physical and material help must be linked together more tightly with words of witness.

There are probably more than 100 million nomads in the world. There may be as many as 200 million. Some nomads are hunters-gatherers, many keep herds, some provide services such as entertainment or repairing pots and pans, and most depend to some degree on crops they raise.

Because of their mobility, they are difficult to evangelize. Because of their Muslim belief their world view is a barrier to the gospel.

Be aware of your nomadic neighbors. They are watching you to see how Christians live. God might call you to a nomadic people. He might give you the opportunity to tell others about nomads.

He will surely remind you to pray for them.

A Strategy for These Unusual Times

This is for you, wherever you dwell, if you see an unreached people group gathering near you, emigrating from its homeland. This is a strategy for bringing the gospel to such a people group. In some parts of the world many people groups are gathering to escape war, famine or flooding.

This strategy is not a substitute for the Great Commission. It is a way of obeying the Great Commission for those whom the Lord so directs.

Jesus sent his disciples to the uttermost parts of the earth, to where the unreached people groups have their homelands. He did not specifically send them to the thousands of visitors in Jerusalem for the major feasts. But here and now we see, not visitors to our own land, but immigrants. We see them here by the thousands and even the tens of thousands, from many of the unreached people groups.

We know why they are here. As a nation, we have not gone to them, so God is sending them to us.

There can be no question about it, by going to these neighbors we are going to the unreached peoples. This is now a viable Great Commission strategy. It could also be, for you, a way of getting your feet wet in cross-cultural ministry, a part of your preparation course for ministering in those uttermost parts of the earth.

What are the main ingredients in a ministry to the unreached peoples who live among us?[18]

Friendship. Immigrants often face questions that are new to them. Newly arrived immigrants especially have many questions, many concerns. Often they have been writing to relatives in their adoptive nation, and have come to live next door to them. They will share their concerns with them. If no relatives are nearby, they might talk to those who have come before them of the same ethnicity, if they feel free to speak to strangers within their people group. For many, that is not culturally acceptable.

If they are totally alone, or feel alone, they will welcome you're interest in helping them, once they get to know you.

You can usually get to know them by asking them about their children if they have any. This is especially easy if you also have children.

You will find these immigrants in parks and in malls. Often the older men will gather there. Perhaps their wives are shopping while the men sit on benches, chatting in their birth language, or playing chess. You might approach them with a greeting and express an interest in them. If they are playing a strange game, perhaps they will include you if they see you want to learn. Ask them if they find your country all they thought it would be.

---

[18] See *Global Prayer Digest* for July, 2001, pp. 4, 37-39.

Experiment. Some questions will be counterproductive. Try to find out what you can do to help them adjust to this country, or to cope with its complexity.

Gender is important in this. Don't attempt to befriend members of the opposite sex unless their spouses are present. Most cultures have strict rules about this. If it were not so, you would still have to protect your own soul from carnal involvement.

Servanthood. If you are qualified to do a good job at it, you might help them improve their use of your language, or with getting rid of their accents. If you have some other self-improvement scheme that has helped you, it might also help them. Offer to teach them, but be careful not to imply you are superior to them.

For example, there are memory skills that can be very helpful for remembering peoples names, or other facts. These skills challenge the memory and develop it for many profitable uses.

Some libraries have sections of books in foreign languages. Find out if there language is represented. Take them to the library and show them how helpful the librarians are.

If your new friends are in financial distress, find a barber at your church, or at any church, who would be willing to cut their hair once a month. See if there is free bus service for the needy. Investigate whether your new friends are entitled to food stamps or bureaucratic help such as free training for job placement.

As you get into their hearts and heads you will find out what their greatest needs are. Investigate how you can help with those needs.

Some people are naturally investigative. If you are not, seek the help of your spouse or of a friend, or anyone who has that enthusiasm and skill to solve problems.

In dealing with friendship, we are not suggesting you deceive anyone into thinking you want to help him and his family. You must love them and sincerely desire to help them. God has already told you so in his Word.

This is not to be a pretence or a game. You are seeking to build genuine friendships. Be willing to invest yourself in this venture of helping someone, or a few, in ways that are meaningful to them. If they never show any interest in Jesus, even after a long time of friendly relationship, remain their friend. God will do something, and you may never know in this life what that something is. Trust God. Follow Jesus. Leave the results to the Holy Spirit of God who is able to do more than we can imagine even to ask!

Genuine friends share with each other the concerns that touch them most deeply. Your genuine friends will listen to you when you tell them what Jesus means to you. Take time to establish friendship and trust before you tell them. God will open a door. Pray for that.

Pray for these whom you hope to help, even before you meet them. Prayer is the most powerful thing you can do for them! Be totally open with the Lord about what you hope to achieve in this ministry. If you're on track, then it was all his idea in the first place. He wants you to succeed. If you're off track, if he intends that you follow a different path, he will nudge you in another direction, probably through your desires. He is able to direct you. Express your confidence in him. Take time to listen to what he wants to tell you. Write down what you believe he is saying.

Don't make big radical changes in your life without giving God time to confirm what you believe you heard from him.

Fellowship. Eventually you will find yourself either leading or facilitating a gathering of your new friends, or some of them. Make this meeting and subsequent meetings casual in tone but focused in purpose. They should be friendly and even fun, but they should not waste people's time.

The purpose of these gatherings might be to help them learn English, or to fill out their tax forms. At some point, God will prompt you to share some aspect of your relationship with Jesus.

I visited the adoptive parents of a ten-year-old boy I was teaching in public school. They were having serious problems trying to get this boy to learn, and so was I. After hearing all they had done to try to help him, I said, "You have certainly done everything you could possibly do for Paul."

Suddenly the Holy Spirit gave me a very clear urging and I heard myself say, "Well, not everything. There is something else you can do, and I will tell you what that is before I leave." Then I went on with other things I had prepared to say to them.

Later they sensed I was getting ready to leave and one of them said, "You told us you had one other idea we might try."

"Yes," I replied. "When my wife and I have any problem with our boys we turn to the Lord and pray."

I went on to explain how we had established a relationship with God long ago, and what a change that had made in our lives, and in our boys' lives. As a public school teacher, I had some hesitation in bringing the name of Jesus into our conversation, but I knew it was right.

They both prayed the sinners prayer with me. The mother was in tears. The father seemed sincere.

They had a deeply felt need, the well-being of their son. In a two-hour visit we bonded over that common interest. Without intending it, I succeeded in having them ask me to share something I valued. They were therefore prepared to listen to anything I would recommend.

I had no idea I would be giving my testimony before that moment when God nudged me. In your case, you will be looking for that nudge from God, and even praying for the opportunity. As you serve them in one way or another, keep your focus on just that, serving them. What you do for them, you are doing for Jesus. Be ready for that nudge of the Holy Spirit, but don't jump ahead of him. It could take a long time to establish that necessary bond.

It will be wonderful if they themselves ask you for a gathering focused around answering their questions about who Jesus is, or about what the Bible says about heaven. If it doesn't happen that way, you might find an opportunity to suggest that those subjects be discussed in the next meeting, if you have already shared enough about the Lord to build their interest.

Be open to all they want to say about God, Jesus or the Bible. Listen. Your top priority at the beginning, is to listen. It doesn't change much over time. In this way you will learn what they think, what is important to them. You are touching on their values and their world view. This is vital information for you. Better still, this is vital understanding for you to absorb. Listen well.

Listening proves something most important to them. It proves you value their ideas. It demonstrates, as nothing else can, that you respect them and even that you love them!

If your friends have never heard of Jesus, you have to decide whether to start telling them stories from the Bible about creation first, or about Jesus first. The Spirit will show you, probably through your friends, by what they say perhaps.

Remember what you learned about stories. Everyone loves them!

Evangelism. Eventually you will lead some or all of these friends to the Lord. If you have no format for doing this, you can rely on the Holy Spirit. Salvation is his work. But you can find a wonderful gospel presentation in James Kennedy's book, "Evangelism Explosion."[19]

Your purpose is not just their salvation, but also that they be formed into the image of Jesus more completely. This small group is now a church. You are their pastor, though you probably won't use that term. Your aim is to teach them those basic commands of the New Testament, and then to teach more from the Word. Your aim is to lead them into deeper knowledge of Jesus, into intimacy with him in worship, and into obedience to him.

Mission. This book gives you ways of succeeding in spreading the gospel throughout the entire people group. Your unreached people is located in at least two parts of the world. Eventually you, through the churches you establish, will train and send missionaries to their homeland, and perhaps other places where "your" people dwell.

If you have learned well from what we have presented in this simple volume, this people is truly your people. You have adopted them and they you.

---

[19] See the bibliography. Pages 16, and 24-44 are most vital. The rest is analysis and excellent training.

Back to Joanne Shetler

This successful missionary to the Balangao on the island of Luzon told this story at one of the Urbana Conferences. Joanne was undoubtedly overwhelmed one day among the Balangao. She was listening to words that must have made her spirit "tingle."

She had given years of her life to learning their language. She now knew a great deal of their culture. The people loved her. A few of the elders were helping her translate God's Word into Balangao.

The chief elder of the village said these words to her. "This is very wonderful material! If the people could hear this they would believe it."

Those words coming from the most respected man in the village must have sounded heavenly to Joanne.

Immediately she asked the question the Spirit must have put into her heart, a question that challenged that tribal leader. She said, "What will we do to make sure they hear?"

The man left. Soon he came back to her door with dozens of Balangao. "Here we are," he said. "Teach us."

We can only imagine how thrilled Joanne felt when she heard these unforgettable words. Can you imagine how excited you will be if someday, something like that happens to you?

Perhaps it already has! Perhaps God himself is showing you an unreached people group who have gathered in your town, city or countryside and is saying to you, "Here they are. Teach them."

Chapter 23
Questions

1. Which strategy was conceived as a result of damage done to a missionary's equipment, preventing him from using his normal method of introducing Jesus?

    A. The Messiah Dance
    E. Gospel Recordings
    F. Presenting a Bible as a gift
    G. A team strategy for people groups in cities unfriendly to the gospel.

2. Which strategy was introduced using sentences like those italicized here: *Most missionaries to this part of the world's population do not attempt to plant churches. The need for secrecy leads them to try to convert one person at a time. Converts then have no Christian community to join when they are excommunicated by their families and friends.*

    A The Messiah Dance
    B. Gospel Recordings
    C. Presenting a Bible as a gift.
    D. A team strategy for people groups in cities unfriendly to the gospel.

Chapter 24

The Master's Plan Is Your Only Choice

Jesus Chose a Few Good Men[20]

Through the power of the Holy Spirit, John the Baptist created a spiritual awakening among the people of Israel. He wonderfully prepared the way for Jesus.

In the dynamic flow of that awakening, Jesus could have established a political party. By majoring on public speaking, by playing upon the political needs of the people, by exploiting their hunger for righteousness in government, and by multiplying more loaves and fishes, he would have become a most popular king.

Instead of promoting himself, however, Jesus concentrated his efforts on twelve men, twelve who were willing to learn from him. He chose men whom he would train as leaders, not for a popular revolt, but for bringing the people into a genuine relationship with almighty God!

He wanted his work to continue for as long as it would take to reach every nation, every ethnic group, long after his death. He wanted every people on earth to be taught the significance of his crucifixion. He knew they would need keen teachers who would lift the people above foolish human effort to earn salvation, to a spiritual conviction where they could trust him, relying on his sacrifice on the cross to pay the total price for their salvation. He longed for them to turn from sin, to receive the gift of eternal life, and to be received into close fellowship with himself. They were to become his rich treasure, his inheritance.

Jesus knew the people would need strong, upright leaders to follow. These leaders would be disciples who knew him intimately. He wanted the people to be able to experience leaders who thought, spoke and lived like Jesus himself.

---

[20] Much of this chapter is based on *The Master Plan of Evangelism,* by Robert C. Coleman.

For this reason, Jesus chose to train the twelve. This was his top priority. He spoke on many occasions to the crowds. It touched his heart that they were like sheep without a shepherd. He wept over them. He healed many. He held their children. He told them what the kingdom of heaven was like.

Jesus' first priority for the people was their redemption. His second priority was the training of twelve men who would carry out his plan of winning mankind for the kingdom. He concentrated his unlimited abilities, his unprecedented qualifications, on leadership training.

He appointed twelve... that they might be with him... (Mk. 3:14). He wanted them to be like himself. He also wanted their friendship. He was human. He cherished their company.

Why are These Things Written in the Bible?

We know that what we see in the Word of God is written for our emulation. In your ministry, imitate Jesus the trainer of leaders. Like the master, bond with the people God sends you to evangelize. Form close friendships. Train those who will lead.

Jesus was interested, not only in satisfying his own need for fellowship, but also in benefiting his disciples. He wanted to help them grow in the fruit of the Spirit, that they might enjoy a mature and secure relationship with him and with the Father.

We know these things, not so much from any one verse of scripture, but from the four gospels as a whole. We see these truths most of all in the Book of John, chapters 13 through 17... especially chapter 17 where Jesus prays for his disciples.

Throughout the Bible, God's delight with men, his desire to benefit each of us, his nurturing Spirit, are clearly manifest.

There is a portrayal of the Son of God on videotape, called "Matthew." It is every word the Gospel of Matthew. In that portrayal, the actor who plays the role of Jesus has, with the help of the director of the video, captured something of the character and personality of Jesus that we have not previously seen in such works. Even in the eyes of this "Jesus" our thoughts are directed toward the warm friendship between the real Jesus and his disciples. In that smile we seem to behold the delight of Jesus in his twelve intimate friends.

Of course these details are the interpretation of the makers of the videos. But if you view this four-cassette video, it might help you better understand the real Jesus! Seeing this portrayal of his joy with his twelve companions, you can imagine his joy in being with you! It will help you understand how to befriend the people to whom God will send you.

After Jesus ascended into heaven, the Sanhedrin recognized the effect of Jesus personal influence on his disciples. The Sanhedrin listened to the bold and wise words of Peter. They knew Peter and John were unschooled. They were astonished, and *took note that these men had been with Jesus* (Ac 4:13).

Minister in the Spirit of Jesus

As you learn the language of your newly adopted people group, you will bond with members of that group. Eventually you will share the gospel, bring their respected leaders to Jesus, and form a mother church from these new converts and their families.

Some of these new church members will soon lead others to the Lord, following your instruction about witnessing. These successful witnesses will become your Timothies.

What Will be Your Attitude Toward "Timothy"?

Will you see him as a potential instrument of your success as a church planter? If he turns against you, will you regard him as an obstacle to your success, or will you see him as a man who needs your help?

What if one of your developing pastors discovers he is genuinely anointed by God? He finds he loves to preach the truth in such a dynamic way his church explodes in rapid growth. In a few months he decides to meet in a rented facility.

What if he wants to cut himself off from your leadership and be independent?

Will you regard his as a rebel and tell your followers to keep away from him? In that case he will indeed be beyond any help you can give him. If he begins to draw people to himself, to teach what promotes his ego, to build himself a bank account, to fall into sexual sin and cause many to devalue the gospel... it will all be his fault, of course. But is he really any worse than the rest of us? You will always wonder if you made the decision to disown him because it suited you.

On the other hand, what would Jesus do? Jesus *appeared to Peter, and then to the Twelve* (1Cor. 15:5). Peter, who denied having anything to do with the Lord three times, was the first Jesus visited with after his resurrection from the dead!

Everything that comes to mind in the scriptures tells me I would be following the Holy Spirit if I blessed this Timothy, from the very first sign of his choosing to go his own way. I would not wait to see if he will come to me. Jesus came to seek and to save.

Tell him you will be helping him learn more about the Word, if he would welcome that. Tell him you are impressed by his gifting, but you hope he will not stop studying the Word. Give him a study book he can use on his own if he refuses to meet with you. Remember he is still a growing Christian.

He might be plagued with prideful ambition. Be patient with him. You are his servant, as Jesus was to the apostles. Offer to go over the lessons in that study book with him. Make it clear that you are concerned for him. You want him to succeed. The sheep he leads need a good under-shepherd who will follow close after the Good Shepherd.

Don't expect anything in return. One day he might thank you. Be content to win the battle over your own pride in the situation, and to follow Jesus yourself.

This Timothy might help you teach something to your other Timothies! If he is able to grow a big church, using his own submission to Jesus as a way of drawing disciples to the Lord, perhaps he can help communicate this ability to others!

There are obvious dangers in this. Decide only after serious prayer, and consultation with those you trust.

All this might be a much bigger challenge if the occasion arises, than it appears to you now as you read. You will benefit greatly by meditating on Romans 12:5-21. These verses contain many gems such as:

Love must be sincere... Honor one another above yourselves... Share with God's people who are in need... Bless those who persecute you; bless and do not curse... Do not repay anyone evil for evil... If it is possible, as far as it depends on you, live at peace with everyone. Do not take revenge, my friends... If your enemy is hungry, feed him... Do not be overcome by evil, but overcome evil with good.

Draw your Timothies to yourself "that they might be with" you, not for your glory, but for the glory of Jesus and for the benefit of those you draw. Earnestly desire to enrich them with good teaching. Become involved with the personal problems of each. Show them how to lean on *the everlasting arms* of the Lord (Dt. 33:27).

God created these friends that they might worship himself, for his glory and for their deepest delight. Nurture them.

Jesus often prayed alone. Otherwise the twelve were continually with him. He did spend time with the crowds, but then Jesus would take the twelve aside and teach them further.

They listened to him. They absorbed his teaching. They asked him questions.

On one occasion, after speaking a parable to the crowd, Jesus said to the twelve, *The knowledge of the secrets of the kingdom of God has been given to you, but to others I speak in parables, so that, ... "though hearing, they may not understand."* Then he explained the parable to the twelve.

Training leaders was a high priority in the Lord's ministry. As his three years with them drew near the end he spent even more time sharing more intimately with them, giving more insight to them about his relationship with his Father.

After his death and resurrection he continued to teach the twelve. When he departed this earth he left the twelve standing, looking up at a cloud that had just received him out of their sight.

Two angels appeared to the twelve and comforted them, encouraging them to get on with the work, explaining that Jesus would return just as they saw him going up to heaven.

There is a poignant story some preachers tell relating to that moment of Jesus' ascension into heaven. It seems when Jesus entered that cloud he found he was not alone. There were three angels in the cloud, waiting to greet him.

"Oh, Jesus!" one of them exclaimed, "How beautiful! Your redemption was so overwhelming! We are in awe of your wisdom and your love for people!"

Another angel broke into this acclamation asking with a frown, "But Lord, how will you spread the good news of salvation to the entire world? What is your plan to let the other peoples of earth know that their sins are forgiven if they will just trust you to save them?"

Jesus replied, "Didn't you see the twelve men I chose? I poured myself into them for three years. They will go to the ends of earth for me!"

The three angels were aghast. When they recovered, the third angel asked in a disappointed tone of voice, "Then you have decided to entrust with humankind the awesome responsibility of seeing to it that the entire planet hears the gospel? Jesus, in case that plan should fail, please tell us, what is your backup plan?"

Jesus looked intently into the three angelic faces and said with just the faintest trace of a confident smile on his glorious face, "I have no backup plan. You will see. Those who love me will go to the ends of the earth for me."

The story is fictional of course, but this much is true: There is no other plan. We are "it." The Church, the Body of Christ, will do the work. Many of us might leave it to the others, but we, the Church will do the work, anointed and carried along by the Holy Spirit.

God depends not on our cleverness, but on our willingness. He trusts us, not because we never fail him, but because we rely upon him. He is sending us, not because we are educated, but because we know him. He calls us, not because we are brilliant, but because we love him.

Three Principle Ways to Communicate[21]

1. **Monologue** is the familiar way for a preacher or teacher to exhort or to give instruction. A monologue is a long speech spoken by one person. Using monologue, you can communicate much material to many people in a short time.
2. **Dialogue** is conversation. Using conversation, you can communicate information and let your listener enter into the process of his own learning. He can ask questions. He can put your teaching into his own words to see whether he has understood you. He can agree or disagree with you. He can give you illustrations of your teaching from his own life experience.

   In dialogue it will take you longer to cover the material, but your student will long remember what you have taught him.

   In dialogue, your student will get to know you well! And you him! You can easily become good friends this way.

   Jesus used monologue in speaking with the crowds. He used dialogue in teaching the twelve. But there is another far more impactful method than either of these.
3. **Life involvement** is sharing your life with your students beyond formal instruction sessions, through extensive contact. This is the principle method Jesus used with his twelve.

   In John 1:14 we learn that the Word of God, God's message to us, became flesh! Jesus is the Father's incarnate message to us! When God wanted to tell us how to establish a relationship with him, he joined us. He became one of us. He surrounded himself habitually with twelve men and taught them.

---

[21] Charles Kraft, *Communicating the Gospel God's Way,* pp. 44, 45.

He ate with them regularly. He slept with them. He laughed with them. They observed him continually. They learned from him even when he was not explaining anything!

In life involvement you can teach the most precious values in a way that will have the most lasting results. What you teach with words might be well taught and well learned. But what you teach by example will never be forgotten. This teaching will be internalized. It will affect your disciple's life deeply. It readily becomes part of his character and even his personality.

You can teach facts using monologue and dialogue. With life involvement you teach life, and a lifestyle.

Translators of Mark 16:15 record Jesus saying, "Go into all the world and preach the gospel..."

Greek scholars tell us this verse could have been rendered, "Go into all the world and communicate the gospel..."

"Communicate" can mean several things. "Preach" is only one of them. We learned in chapter 15, that we send paramessages while we speak and even when we are silent. These messages are conveyed by "body-language," by the way we spend our time and our money, by the way we live.

What About You? What Will You Do?

Ask Jesus to what extent you can imitate him in his life involvement with his leaders.

If you are married, you must spend significant time with your wife. Otherwise you cannot love her as Jesus loved the Church and gave himself for her. If you have children you must minister generously to them. Your wife and children must know they are your highest priority after God himself. We discussed this in chapter 4.

If your marriage is in disorder you will live on sinking sand. Jesus is the Rock... not part of Jesus, not biblical principles you prefer, but the whole counsel of God.

If God places you in a very public ministry, where you become well known, you will face serious temptations toward pride, toward acquiring unnecessary wealth, and toward sexual immorality. Be submitted to other leaders who will be bold enough and loving enough to tell you if you take one step in the wrong direction.

Even if your place of service will be out of public view, you will need the same safeguards. In any case, your personal prayer life and your awareness of the presence of God will be vital. Being accountable to another leader or leaders will help you greatly.

If as you read these words you realize your marriage has a problem, ask the Holy Spirit for wisdom and courage. Take action to change radically, not your spouse's heart but your own. God will help you. As you take the first step toward unconditional love of your spouse, with no thought of turning back, you will experience the joy again.

1 Thessalonians chapter 1 is God's encouragement for you, the future missionary. You will need his encouragement. He has not called you to a task you can do alone. You will need him every moment. Let him bless you richly from his wonderful Word.

Someday you might say to your own disciples something like what Paul wrote to the Thessalonians. You might say...

"I am so grateful to God for what he has done in you. I pray for you always, because the good works you are doing are so beautiful, produced by your faith in Jesus. You obey God, you do the work of the ministry, because you love him. You keep on doing the will of God because of the hope, the certain knowledge of what will happen when you go to be with Jesus forever.

"I remember when I first began telling you my stories, which you listened to with such interest, stories about Creator God, and about his Son Jesus. We were bonded together, you and I, in such rich friendship! You listened to me so intently as I told you with great conviction how Jesus changed my life.

"I lived among you for your sake, so you would have what I myself had, eternal life. You wanted it, knowing me well. You even imitated me. I had to keep reminding you to focus on Jesus. He is our perfect model.

"The Holy Spirit gave you such joy as you heard the message and followed the Lord, you did not seem to mind the suffering caused by those who did not yet understand.

"You became a model for all the villages, and now even for the surrounding tribes!"

Consider what it will be like in heaven if the Lord does not return as soon as we expect. Over the years, persons from your adopted people group will come to their eternal reward. They will worship God in spirit and truth, with joy unspeakable. They will find you and thank you for bringing to their ancestors the wonderful news of the kingdom. In that kingdom they will live forever and ever because of what Jesus did and also because of what you did!

In his presence you and they will experience fullness of joy, and eternal pleasures at the right hand of the Father (Ps. 16:11)!

And now, *We... pray for you, that our God may count you worthy of his calling, and that by his power he may fulfill every good purpose of yours and every act prompted by your faith. We pray this so that the name of our Lord Jesus may be glorified in you, and you in him, according to the grace of our God and the Lord Jesus Christ* (2 Th. 1:11, 12).

Chapter 24
Questions

1. Jesus' highest priority concerning the people was:

    A. preaching to the crowds
    B. conveying ideas through parables
    C. redemption for mankind
    D. training leaders

2. Jesus' second priority concerning the people was:

    A. training their future leaders
    B. teaching about the kingdom of heaven
    C. convincing the people they needed to have righteousness beyond that of the Pharisees.
    D. demonstrating his power to prove who he was

3. One method of communication with those seeking more of Jesus can be described in these terms: *sharing your life with them. This goes beyond formal instruction sessions. It involves extensive contact. This is the principle method Jesus used with his twelve.* In our textbook, this method of communication, named by Robert Coleman, is called:

    A. meaningful fellowship
    B. intensive monolog
    C. dialog
    D. life involvement

End of Chapter Answers

Section 1

Chapter 1 –

1. D, 2. C, 3. D, 4. B, 5. C, 6. A, 7. A, 8. A, 9. C, 10. C, 11. A, 12. D, 13. C

Chapter 2 –

1. A, 2. B, 3. B, 4. D, 5. D, 6. C, 7. B, 8. D, 9. C, 10. C

Section 2

Chapter 3 –

1. D, 2. A

Chapter 4 –

1. C, 2. B, 3. D, 4. B, 5. D, 6. B

Chapter 5 –

1. A, 2. C, 3. D

Chapter 6 –

1. B, 2. D, 3. C, 4. C, 5. B, 6. D, 7. C, 8. A, 9. D, 10. C, 11. A, 12. A, 13. B, 14. D

Chapter 7 –

1. D, 2. D, 3. D, 4. C, 5. D, 6. A, 7. B, 8. D, 9. D, 10. C

Chapter 8 –

1. D, 2. A, 3. C, 4. B, 5. D, 6. A, 7. C, 8. D

Chapter 9 –

1. A, 2. D, 3. C, 4. B, 5. B, 6. C, 7. D, 8. C, 9. A, 10. C, 11. D, 12. B, 13. C, 14. B, 15. A, 16. C, 17. D

Chapter 10 –

1. D, 2. A, 3. C, 4. D, 5. A, 6. C, 7. B

Chapter 11 –

1.A, 2. D, 3. B, 4. A, 5. C, 6. B, 7. D, 8. B, 9. B, 10. C

Section 3

Chapter 12 –

1. C, 2. C, 3. D, 4. D, 5. C, 6. B, 7. A, 8. A

Chapter 13 –

1. D, 2. B

Chapter 14 –

1. D, 2. C

Chapter 15 –

1. B, 2. C, 3. C, 4. D

Section 4

Chapter 16 –

1. A, 2. C, 3. B

Chapter 17 –

1. A

Chapter 18 –

1. C, 2. C, 3. C, 4. D, 5. C, 6. C

Chapter 19 –

1. A, 2. D

Chapter 20 –

1. A, 2. A, 3. C

Chapter 21 –

1. D

Chapter 22 –

1. C, 2. C, 3. B, 4. C, 5. D, 6. B, 7. D, 8. C, 9. D, 10. A

Chapter 23 –

1. A, 2. D

Chapter 24 –

1. C, 2. A, 3. D

Bibliography

I am deeply grateful to the following authors and their works. I have synthesized their ideas with my own. I have tried to simplify the language, both for readers unfamiliar with missiological terms and for readers of English as a second language.

Brewster, E. Thomas, and Elizabeth S. Brewster. *Language Acquisition Made Practical, A Comprehensive "How-To" Book for Learning Any Language.* Colorado Springs, CO: Lingua House, 1976.

---. *Bonding and the Missionary Task..* Dallas, TX: Academic Publications, 1982.

---. *Community Is My Language Classroom.* Pasadena, CA: Lingua House Ministries, 1986.

Coleman, Robert C. *The Master Plan of Evangelism..* Old Tappan, NJ: Fleming H. Revell Co, 1964.

Dayton, Edward R. and Ted W. Engstrom. *Strategy for Living.* Glendale, CA: G/L Publications, 1976.

Douglass, Stephen B. *Managing Yourself.* San Bernardino, CA: Campus Crusade for Christ, 1978.

Hall, Dudley. *Grace Works.* Ann Arbor, MI: Servant Publications, 1992.

Heflin, Ruth Ward. *Glory.* Hagerstown, MD: The McDougal Publishing Company, 1990.

Hiebert, Paul G. *Anthropological Insights for Missionaries.* Grand Rapids, MI: Baker Book House, 1987.

---. *Case Studies in Missions.* Grand Rapids, MI: Baker Book House, 1987.

Kennedy, D. James *Evangelism Explosion.* Wheaton, IL: Tyndale House, 1977.

Kraft, Charles H. *Communicating the Gospel God's Way.* Pasadena, CA: William Carey Library, 1986 (fifth printing).

Larson, Donald N. "The Viable Missionary: Learner, Trader, Story Teller." Reprinted in *Perspectives on the World Christian Movement, A Reader.* Pasadena, CA: William Carey Library, 1981.

Livingstone, Greg, *Planting Churches in Muslim Cities.* Grand Rapids, MI: Baker Book House, 1993.

Mahoney, Ralph. *The Making of a Leader.* Burbank, CA: World Missionary Assistance Plan, 1985.

McGavran, Donald. *The Bridges of God.* New York, NY: Friendship Press, 1955.

Olson, Bruce. *Bruchko.* Lake Mary, FL: Creation House, 1995.

Parshall, Phil. *The Cross and the Crescent..* Wheaton, IL: Tyndale House Publishers, Inc., 1989.

Parshall, Phil. *Bridges to Islam..* Grand Rapids, MI: Baker Book House, 1983.

Patterson, George. *Obedience-Oriented Education.* Alta Loma, CA: Community Baptist Church, 1978.

+---. *Church Planting through Obedience Oriented Teaching.* Pasadena. CA: William Carey Library, 1981.

Piper, John. *Let the Nations Be Glad..* Grand Rapids, MI: Baker Book House, 1993.

Richardson, Don. *Eternity in Their Hearts.* Ventura, CA: Regal Books, a division of G/L Publications, 1981

---. *Peace Child.* Ventura, CA: Regal Books, a division of G/L Publications, 1974.

Shetler, Joanne. *And the Word Came with Power.* Portland, OR: Multnomah Press, 1992.

Sjogren, Bob. *Unveiled at Last.* Seattle, WA: YWAM Publishing, 1992.

Smith, Oswald J. *The Challenge of Missions.* Toronto, Canada: The Peoples Church, 1959.

Willard, Dallas. *The Divine Conspiracy. Rediscovering our hidden life in God.* San Francisco, CA: Harper San Francisco, 1998.

Winter, Ralph, et al., editors. *Perspectives on the World Christian Movement, a Reader.* Pasadena, CA William Carey Library, 1981

Note:

Readers are encouraged to subscribe to: *Global Prayer Digest.,* edited by Keith Carey. This is a guide for daily prayer for the unreached peoples. Published monthly by the U.S. Center for World Mission, 1605 Elizabeth St., Pasadena, CA 91104.